CW01431412

What it Was

BOOK 1 IN THE OFF ICE SERIES

GRAYCE RIAN

What It Was is a work of fiction, created without use of AI technology. Any names, characters, businesses, places, and events are products of the author's imagination, and used in a fictitious manner. Any resemblance to actual events, places or persons, living or dead, is entirely coincidental or fictional.

Copyright © 2024 by Grayce Rian

All rights reserved.

No part of this book may be reproduced in any form—by any electronic or mechanical means, including information storage and retrieval systems—without written permission from the author, except for the use of brief quotations in a book review.

Book Cover Design by Madison Lee of Love Lee Creative

Editing and Proofreading by Caitlin Lengerich LLC

Dedication

To those who have loved, lost, and persevered.
This one's for you.
Keep fighting the darkness.
One day, you'll find your sunshine.

Content Warning

This book contains mature themes and potentially triggering content, including (potential spoilers): on-page descriptions of loss, grief, depression, death of a sibling, substance abuse, premature birth, and off-page death of a parent. Despite being a romance novel with a happily ever after, readers should be aware of these themes.

CONTENTS

Playlist

Cruel Summer – Taylor Swift
Baby Blue – Surfaces
Nonsense – Sabrina Carpenter
Speechless – Dan + Shay
I'm Only Me When I'm With You –Taylor Swift
You Are My Sunshine – Music Travel Love
golden hour – JVKE
You Belong With Me (Taylor's Version) –Taylor Swift
Kiss Me – Sixpence None The Richer
I Wanna Dance With Somebody (Who Loves Me) – Morgan Harper-Jones
Favorite T-Shirt – Acoustic Version – Jake Scott
Fearless (Taylor's Version) – Taylor Swift
Falling Like The Stars – James Arthur
Always Been You – Jessie Murph
Fall Into Me – Forest Blakk
What Was I Made For? – Billie Eilish
Unsteady – X Ambassadors
Love Is Gone - Acoustic – SLANDER, Dylan Matthew
Ghost – Justin Bieber
Skip This Part – Alexandra Kay
Half a Man – Dean Lewis
Falling – Harry Styles
broken – Jonah Kagen
Breathe (feat. Colbie Caillat) (Taylor's Version) – Taylor Swift

if you only knew – Alexander Stewart
I Would've – Jessie Murph
Stayed A Summer – Erin Kinsey
Killing Me To Love You – Vancouver Sleep Clinic
Growin' Up Raising You – Gabby Barrett
No Caller ID – Megan Moroney
Try Losing One – Tyler Braden
Never Get Over You – Stephen Dawes, Dylan Conrique
Isn't She Lovely (Acoustic) – Callum J Wright
Sun to Me – Zach Bryan
My Home (Acoustic) – Myles Smith
Still Into You – Paramore
Bigger Than The Whole Sky – Taylor Swift
This Love (Taylor's Version) – Taylor Swift
Married Young – Jake Scott
Can't Help Falling in Love – Haley Reinhart
In Case You Didn't Know – Brett Young

Prologue

GRIFFIN

I stand in shock as I stare into the icy-blue eyes that have haunted me for the past two years. Her face has paled into a ghostly shade of white, and she looks like she's about to faint at the sight of me.

"Mama! Look! Mama!"

The fact that I can hear anything over the ringing in my ears is a miracle. This has to be a sick joke, because the scene playing out in front of me isn't real life—it can't be.

I try to gather myself, but I can't. I'm stunned, frozen at the sight of Kenna, *my Kenna*, shrugging away from the guy with his arm draped over her shoulders.

And Kenna's twin brother, Carson, is holding the blonde baby girl who just called her "Mama."

Kenna goes to grab the baby girl from Carson and wraps the little girl into her arms, nuzzling her neck—breathing her in.

"Hi, baby," she coos to the girl.

I watch as the little girl pulls back and grabs Kenna's cheeks, placing a big, sloppy kiss on her face before giggling.

How is this happening? I knew it was over. We hadn't spoken since that night in Boston, the night that changed everything.

But now it's *really* over . . . for good. Kenna has moved on. She created a life with someone else. They started a family.

A family you'll never be a part of.

My stomach sinks at the thought, my throat clogging with the realization.

Kenna turns her back to me, leaning in to whisper something to her brother.

The next moment happens as if in slow motion. The little girl peeks up at me over Kenna's shoulder and the moment her dark, coffee-colored eyes meet mine, *I know*, beyond a shadow of a doubt, that's my daughter.

PART 1

Before

Two Years Prior . . .

1

McKenna

MAY

The packed bleachers are a sight I'm familiar with, seeing as I'm the captain of our three-time, championship-winning volleyball team. However, tonight, the gym has a stage with a podium, a large projector screen, and seats currently occupied by our principal, teachers, and other faculty members.

My leg shakes, exposing my nerves, as I await my turn to stand and make my way toward the makeshift stage. I must not have realized how much I was shaking because I jump as my twin brother Carson's hand smacks down on my right knee.

"Chill out, Mack. You're going to freak out Wilson even more than he already is," Carson says as he reaches his left arm behind me to smack Jackson Wilson in the back of the head.

"Why did I think today would be a good day to wear heels for the first time?"

Carson doesn't try to hide his chuckles. "I've got no clue, seeing as you're the clumsiest girl I've ever met whenever you're off the court."

"I'm seriously freaking out right now, Carse. Where's the reassurance I'll do fine?"

Carson rolls his eyes and attempts to appease me. "Mack, I'm going to strut across that stage, grab my diploma, and scream for you on the other side, just like I did while waiting for you to hurry up and come into the world."

"You're only older by two minutes; it's not like you had to wait long." I sigh. "I wish Principal Lennon would've let us walk across together like we asked."

"Mack Attack and Carse Man—the dynamic duo—it would've been epic," he announces, waving his hand through the air.

"Katie Turner," the speaker announces my best friend's name. Carse and I go crazy, screaming and cheering as she crosses the stage to get her diploma. The only people to out-shout us are her dad and older brother, Griffin.

My eyes move away from Katie and glance up in the top left section where Katie's dad and Griffin sit beside my parents. How has Griffin gotten even more irresistible since I saw him two summers ago?

He pushes back his dark hair—it looks like he's cut it since the hockey season—and he's clean-shaven, making his sharp jawline look delectable.

I'm so distracted by this swoon-worthy man I don't realize it's our row's turn to line up beside the stage. Carson grabs my hand as we walk toward the stage, squeezing it as we climb the steps.

"Carson Wilder."

I can't contain my volume as I cheer and pump my fists as Carse grabs his diploma. Turning around, Carson waits for me on the other side of the stage with a smile that takes up almost his entire face.

"McKenna Wilder."

I force myself to put one unsteady foot before the other as I cross the stage toward Principal Lennon. I shake her hand, close the distance between me and Carson, and wrap him in the tightest hug.

"We fucking did it! We're done with this place and moving onto the next stage, and together, no less." Carson beams.

I don't say a word, and instead, soak up this moment with my twin. We've been through everything in life together—he's my forever best friend, and we've been each other's biggest fans. I can't contain my excitement for this final summer before we go to college together this fall.

Abbott University, the largest college in our home state of Minnesota, has always been our first choice. Luckily, I'll play volleyball there, while he lives out his dream of playing hockey.

Carson and I grew up at the hockey rink. Breathing the cold air as I cheered him on never got old. I even played on his mite and squirt teams when we were younger.

As we got older and the boys outgrew me, Mom and Dad thought it was time for me to move to the girls' team. I stuck with hockey until middle school, when I fell in love with volleyball.

Standing at six feet tall, I often tower over most of the guys in my class. I first shot up in sixth grade, before I started playing club volleyball. It's taken a lot of training and time in the gym, but I'm no longer the spindly, awkwardly tall girl I was back then.

Carson and I share many of the same traits. We are both tall, share the same light blue eyes, have wavy blonde hair, and look like we should live on the West Coast instead of in the Midwest.

Carson also had his growth spurt early on. He's now six-foot-two and spent extra time in the weight room to fill out this year.

He was the leading scorer in the state for the past two seasons. His new team is lucky to have him, but he doesn't let it get to his head or affect his drive. If anything, it pushes him each day to be the best.

Principal Lennon congratulates our graduating class, and cheers erupt as we throw our caps in the air alongside our classmates.

After we get our caps, I grab Carson's arm and drag him to find Katie. I run up to her once I spot her and capture her in the tightest squeeze.

"We did it, Katie!" I say.

"Damn straight, babe!" Katie agrees as she laughs into my embrace.

As soon as we let go of each other, Katie is wrapped up in a bear hug by her older brother, Griffin. He swings her around and tells her, "I'm so proud of you, Katie Cat. Graduating with honors—now there's no doubt you're the smartest."

"As if that was ever up for debate, Griff," she teases.

"All jokes aside, I am so proud of you, little sis," he says as he steps aside so his dad can wrap Katie up in a big hug.

Griffin turns around and does an elaborate handshake with Carson.

"Carse, my man. Congrats on the state championship and winning Mr. Hockey. Abbott is lucky to have you. But you're going to get your ass kicked when it comes time to face-off with us."

"We'll just have to wait and see, G. Good to see you, buddy."

"I think we're gonna give you a run for your money in more than one sport this year," Katie teases further.

"If you come to my hockey game in anything but Elite red, I'm disowning you," Griffin retorts.

"I'll be an Abbott Bobcat, too, come August, Griff. You can't possibly make me choose between you and school spirit," Katie whines.

"Have all the school spirit you want, aside from the games we play versus each other. Come on, Katie Cat, I need a fan in the crowd. Kenna will wear Carson's jersey—I need someone supporting me."

He glances at me as he says my name. Heat instantly warms my cheeks as his chocolate-brown eyes connect with mine for the first time in two years. Griff is the same height as Carson, so I have to lift my chin slightly to look at him. My stomach dips as the butterflies take flight.

"Oh, yes, I'm sure you're lacking in fans—what with all the puck bunnies you have wearing your number on their shirts, cheeks, and probably underwear," Katie says as she rolls her eyes. "But alright, I promise I'll always be your number-one fan whenever I'm at one of your games," she adds.

My parents interrupt the debate by making us pose for what feels like a thousand photos. Katie and I put Carse in the middle, kissing his cheeks while holding up our diplomas.

Next, my parents group the four "lakeshore kids" together. My mom requests we recreate a pose we've been doing since we were younger—Carson gives me a piggyback ride, and Griff picks up Katie the same way.

Then Katie, Carse, and I say goodbye to our families and head to the cafeteria to grab our stuff.

As we're walking out of the gymnasium, I look over my shoulder to catch one last glimpse of the boy who was my first crush. Only he's no longer a cute boy I'm crushing on, but a gorgeous man I'm lusting after.

I quickly look forward and tell myself to get it together. Griffin Turner has a girlfriend and is my best friend's older brother. Nothing good can come from my infatuation with him.

***

I open the double doors leading to my balcony that overlooks our lakefront property. It's the perfect size for a patio bench and side table and the sunset view is the ideal backdrop while I read or study.

Guests will be arriving soon for our graduation party. Carson and I convinced Mom and Dad to let us have a joint grad party with Katie.

Katie and I have been best friends since she moved in next door when we were five. We've gone through everything together—she's the sister I never had. From the first day of school, first slumber party, first crushes, first heartbreaks, and first periods—we've experienced it all, side-by-side.

As close as I am with Carson, there's just so much a girl can't confide in her brother. That's where Katie comes in. Thankfully, she's literally just a few steps away.

Speaking of—footsteps pad down the hallway and I turn as Katie opens my bedroom door. She waltzes in like she owns the place because, let's face it, she spends half her time here, and we spend the other half in her room.

Her light brown hair is curled into loose waves that fall just above her shoulders. She's opted to wear her contacts instead of her wire-framed glasses, which I love. Her creamy skin looks dewy, her makeup flawless.

"Hey girl, are you ready for the world's most epic grad party to start?" she asks as she looks up from her phone.

"Yes, I just need to finish getting dressed."

"Have you finally decided what you're going to wear?"

"I've narrowed it down to the two on my bed."

She walks over to my bed and declares, "The red set is obviously my choice. You know I've always been a fan of you in red. It does amazing things for your skin tone. The white dress is cute, but that's not what we're going for."

"Oh, and what is it we're going for? This is a family function, Katie!"

"I know, I know. But all of our friends will be here, too. And all the boys, including Drew."

"Ugh, don't remind me," I whine.

"Looking hot is the best form of revenge."

"I don't need revenge, Katie. It's been months, and he didn't even wait until I broke up with him before he had another girl beneath him. Can we skip to August so I can avoid him for the rest of the summer?"

"Forget him, Mack. Tonight is the kickoff to the best summer yet. It's our first real chance at having a hot girl summer. We've finally filled out, and these curves need the attention of a real man." Katie squeezes her boobs for emphasis.

"Dear *god*, Katie." I snort.

"What? We're already dedicating almost our entire summer to our workout regimen. Can you blame me if I don't want this summer to be all work and no play? I *will* be playing with more than just volleyballs." She cups her palms in front of her and acts like fondling balls.

Christ.

I roll my eyes and reply, "Alright, I'm with you there. I don't want this last summer before the craziness of college to fly by without making the best memories."

"Plus, it's not like you'll be hooking up with anyone this summer now that my brother is back and single," she adds casually while looking at her nails.

"Wait, what? He and Emily broke up?" I nearly screech out the question. Griffin, goes to college on the East Coast. He received a full ride to Emery University in Boston and is the first-line center on their hockey team.

Griffin met Emily during move-in week, and she's had her claws sunk in him for the past two years. I never met her personally, but Katie despised her, and that was enough for me. It had nothing to do with the fact that I'd been pining over him for years.

According to Katie, Emily was territorial, controlling, manipulative, and jealous. Not exactly the best traits for someone dating the face of one of the best college hockey teams in the nation.

As I wrap my head around Griff being single, Katie continues, "Yeah, I guess he broke up with her a few months ago. Thank god. Since the draft last summer, she had been crazier and more possessive. If that's even possible."

Griffin was drafted last summer to the Colorado Summits. He opted to finish his college career before he signed his contract with them.

But I'm sure when the time comes for him to play in the National Hockey League, the fans will go even crazier for him.

"I know this probably comes off as biased, but I never did like Emily," I admit sheepishly.

As cliché as I feel for crushing on the boy next door, I've never kept secrets from Katie. My crush on her brother is old news to her.

"Mack, I've always known you had a major crush on G. You haven't exactly been subtle with your heart eyes," she teases.

I chuck a throw pillow from my bed at her. "Stop it!" I say as I cover my face to hide my embarrassment.

"It's adorable how much you're blushing right now. I mean, don't let me stop you from finally going after him. I would absolutely die from excitement if you officially became my sister by marriage!"

"Pump the brakes, princess! Just because I've had a slight crush on your brother does not mean I will do anything about it. And marriage? Are you high?"

"Mhmm, slight my ass." She rubs her hands together and says, "Oh, this hot girl summer will be good. I can't wait to see what G will do once he sees how the guys follow you around like little puppy dogs waiting for you to give them an ounce of attention."

I flip my hair over my shoulder to feign indifference. "I'm not sure how the guys that chase after me this summer have anything to do with your brother."

"Mack, I say this with love. You're delusional if you think your crush is one-sided."

I guess I'm delusional then because my crush has always been unrequited.

But if seeing other guys hit on me is what it will take to finally get Griffin Turner to see me as more than just his little sister's best friend, then let the hot girl summer commence!

2

Griffin

JUNE

I took my time showering and changing into my board shorts after Carson and I did our morning lifting and cardio sessions.

Living next door to a former teammate and now a fellow D1 hockey player has had its perks over the years. One is that I've always had someone to train with. Carson may be two years younger than me, but he's a hell of a hockey player and never stops striving to be the best.

He's eighteen now, so I was surprised to hear at his graduation party that he's waiting another year to enter the NHL draft. I hope we play on the Summits together someday. We've always had a great connection on the ice—it just clicks when we play together.

I cross our yard and punch in the code to open the side gate to get into the Wilder's backyard. My favorite pup ever, Kenna's dog, Ranger, greets me by jumping up on his hind legs and licking my chin. "How's my Goodest Boy doing today? Huh, buddy?" I ask, petting behind his ears, just the way he likes.

"She's here, isn't she? Am I screwed?" I ask Ranger. His response is a bigger tail wag.

Turning the corner of the house, I stop in my tracks when I see her. McKenna Wilder.

I'm so fucked this summer.

McKenna has grown up over the past two years, and it shows. I know it's not just that enticing hot pink bikini, or this summer heat getting to me. Ever since I saw her at her graduation, Kenna has had my full attention.

It felt like torture trying to play it cool at their graduation party. Guys were hanging off her every word, totally entranced by her. And who could blame them?

Let me preface this by saying, I'm not the kind of guy who gets jealous because of a girl. I've always told myself that I'd get over my feelings for Kenna—that they were fleeting; they needed to be. She's my little sister's best friend, and she's two years younger than me. The four of us have always been close—me, Katie, Kenna, and Carson.

But seeing her in that red outfit at her graduation party, with her honey-blonde hair curled in waves down to her waist, I was feral each time a guy approached her, touched her arm, or made her laugh.

Looking at her now, perched back on her elbows, with her hair pulled up into a messy bun, leaving her slender neck exposed, soaking in the sun . . . I'm a goner.

See ya.

Bye.

And that body. *Oh my god, that body.*

The bikini she's wearing doesn't leave much to the imagination, which I appreciate. Kenna's breasts weren't there the last time I saw her. At least, they've changed significantly from what I recall. They're probably the perfect handful—not too much to handle for someone with bigger hands like me.

Her slender stomach is lean and highlights her toned abs, which she has undoubtedly worked hard for. As an athlete, I can respect how much time she puts in at the gym.

Kenna's once lanky legs are now tanned and toned to perfection, making her athletic figure even more appealing. *What I wouldn't give to have those legs wrapped around my waist, anchoring herself to me. Get a grip, man.* This girl . . . I'm twenty—I shouldn't let her get under my skin like some hormonal teenager. I've got too much to focus on.

"There he is. Griff, my man! Come and play water volleyball with us. We'll play 2v2—us versus the girls," Carson says when he notices me.

"Alright. Let's take these ladies down a few notches," I challenge as I rub my hands together.

Kenna snorts. Turning her head toward me, she taunts, "Yeah? Let's see if you can handle the duo that'll be owning the beach, pool, and court this summer."

"I have no doubt Griff and I will be doing just that," Carson replies.

"Katie, let's show our brothers what it's like to have their asses handed to them by their sisters," Kenna says.

"Correction, *baby* sisters," I emphasize in a condescending tone and wink at her.

Kenna scoffs, rises to her feet, and struts over to me. *Don't look at the way her tits bounce as she walks—eyes up, fucker.*

We're nearly chest-to-chest when she says, "I'm not a baby anymore, Griff. I'd say it's about time you realize that." Her voice is lower, sultrier.

Well, shit. My eyes deceive me and trail down Kenna's bronzed frame. She crosses her arms over her chest, making her perky breasts even more noticeable. And trust me . . . I notice.

Two can play this game, baby doll. I raise both my hands up as if to show I'm surrendering. But instead of letting them fall, I bring them to the back of my neck and slowly lift my shirt over my head.

I throw my shirt onto the lounge chair next to us, exposing the body I've worked my ass off for. Yeah, I might be making a show of it as I lightly scratch my bare chest.

It's Kenna's piercing aquamarine eyes that deceive her now as they rake down my traps, deltoids, and muscular chest.

She continues her survey over each rivet of my washboard abs. Her breath hitches when her gaze gets to the growing bulge in my shorts.

Kenna's eyebrows raise almost to her honey-blonde hairline as her eyes meet mine again. Giving her my most debonair smirk, I shrug. "What can I say? The thought of smacking your ass in volleyball really gets me going."

"God, you're insufferable." Her lips curl up like she's disgusted, but her eyes are still heavy with lust. She's just as fucked as I am.

Check. Mate.

***

"Twenty-four all," Katie says as she serves the ball over the net. It has a wicked float that's too much for Carson to handle. She gets an ace.

"Fuck! My bad, G. I've got the next one," Carson assures me as he throws the ball back to Katie.

"You better, big bro. It's match point after all. Wouldn't want to get manhandled by your sis," Kenna mocks.

"You're right. I'd never want to get manhandled by you, but I wouldn't mind if Katie handled me."

"Carse, what the fuck? That's my little sister." I smack him over the back of the head.

"I'm obviously trying to mess with them, G. You know, trying to get in their heads so we can win this." He scoffs at me like I'm an idiot.

"Oh yeah, the thought of handling your tiny package really has me out of sorts." Katie snickers as she turns toward Kenna, and they high-five.

They laugh together for a few more seconds before Katie goes back to serve again. This one comes over the net, and Carson's serve-receive is spot-on.

Instead of setting him up like the girls are expecting I smash the ball off his pass. It spins down over the net, right at Kenna. Before she can put her arms out to react, the ball makes contact with her chest, hard.

Carson and I shout as we do our special handshake. I turn back around toward Kenna. "Want me to nuzzle that spot for you? Looks like that hit left a stinger."

"Eyes up, asshole," Kenna says as she glares at me—her competitiveness is such a turn-on. She throws Carson the ball but keeps her glare glued to me.

"Come on, that hit was a beauty. Don't even act like it wasn't. Did you see me take that on two?"

"I've done better and been hit by worse." Kenna continues, "Besides, we both know your ego can't handle any more inflation. I won't give you the satisfaction."

"Oh trust me, you could satisfy me just fine."

Carson throws the ball at the back of my head and says, "Get your mind out of the gutter and head back in the game. It's tied up, twenty-five all."

He throws the ball up and jumps from the water as he serves the ball toward Katie. It's a solid strategy, trying to throw them off their game. Katie is a setter, so when she has to receive the ball it means she either has to hit it, or get a good enough pass up to let Kenna hit it on the second touch like I did.

Katie's pass is perfect, clearly unfazed by Carson's serve. Kenna positions herself, biting her lip in concentration as she jumps out of the water for the hit.

I'm so distracted by her sinister mouth and her wet tits bouncing out of the water that I forget I'm supposed to block her hit. She makes solid contact and gets the kill to take the lead.

Jumping up and down to celebrate, her tits are taunting me. Thank god the water is hiding what's going on below deck.

"Fuck if that's fair." I throw my hand up at her chest.

"What, did the girls distract you?" She feigns innocence, batting her lashes. She knows she's affecting me. "I thought I was just Carson's baby sister."

Carson grimaces. "Jesus Mack, put a T-shirt on or something. I think one of them almost popped out. That's the last thing I need to see."

She catches the ball Carse throws to her and heads back to serve. "Twenty-six to twenty-five, match point."

Kenna effortlessly tosses the ball up, makes contact, and the ball lurches over the net. Right at me. It has some sinister spin on it, the ball moves side to side before I can react. I barely get a hand on it as I shank it out of the pool. She aces me, and it's game over.

Kenna and Katie jump up and down as they wrap their arms around each other. Carse and I line up at the net to shake their hands. We've been raised to be good sports.

The girls shake our hands, and I hold on to McKenna's while I ask, "Are you going to Jackson's tonight?"

"Of course we are," she replies.

I watch as Katie and Carson get out of the pool before lowering my voice. "Tell me you're planning on changing first," I say before I realize the words are coming out of my mouth. *Way to sound like a total douche, asshole.*

18

Kenna looks genuinely thrown by my statement. She grips my hand a little tighter and replies, "Of course, I plan on changing. I plan on stripping down, taking a scalding-hot shower, and getting ready."

My brows shoot up. Her answer not only surprises me but leads me to visualize Kenna in the shower. Hot. Soapy. Wet. *Christ.*

I've been half-hard since I set eyes on her an hour ago. I'm also going to need a long shower so I can work her out of my system before tonight.

Kenna interrupts my daydreaming when she says, "Not that it's any of your business what I wear. I'm not your sister, and you're not my keeper."

"Trust me, baby girl, no need to remind me that you're not my sister," I reply with a wink.

"Good. Because I'm not sure whatever's going on in your shorts right now would be very brotherly of you," she mocks as she lets go of my hand and gets out of the pool seemingly unfazed by our conversation.

I watch her walk up the steps of the pool—jealous of the way the water trails down her perfect body—salivating at the way her hips sway as she walks over to her towel.

Who is this girl? Kenna and I have always been able to banter back and forth, but this feels different.

And what in the actual fuck is happening to me? None of my teammates would believe what just went down.

Typically, when girls throw themselves at me, I politely turn them down. At least for the past two years I've been in Boston I did, because I'd been in a relationship off and on.

My ex-girlfriend, Emily, was always so insecure about the attention I received. That's how I knew we were short-term. She couldn't handle the fact that girls threw themselves at me. She didn't trust that I'd be faithful to her. Which I always was.

I honestly didn't have the time to juggle multiple girls, especially when Emily tried to consume all my free time, and more, to compensate for her lack of confidence.

When you're one of the top college hockey players in the nation, it's almost impossible to fly under the radar. Whenever we had an away game, and I was tagged on social media in pictures from fans, Emily would lose it.

She'd spend the entire night blowing up my phone with texts and calls. It got to the point where I just couldn't take the fighting and insecurity anymore.

My teammates were all surprised I stayed with her as long as I did. None of them understood why I had a girlfriend to begin with, and not one of them liked her.

What they didn't realize was that when I had a girlfriend some of the girls on campus left me alone. Especially once they saw what Emily did to girls who would approach me at parties we were at together.

It may sound crass when I say it like that, but I did have feelings for Emily. She was different when it was just the two of us. I knew she could tell I wasn't all in, but she stayed with me anyway. Maybe it was for the status that being with me brought her—I'm not sure.

Since I broke up with her, the girls have been relentless on campus. There are even TikTok and Instagram accounts dedicated to my hockey flow.

I snap myself out of the mental rabbit hole I've just gone down and get dried off.

"Hey man, I'm going to head home to shower and get ready. Want to order pizza when I get back, and then we can take an Uber to Jax's?" I ask Carse on my way through the house.

"Yeah, sounds good to me. Think three larges will be enough this time?"

"I don't know if Katie and Kenna will be okay with splitting a large. But they're sure as shit not touching any of mine."

"You're right, four it is. Cold pizza as a late-night snack doesn't sound bad if there are leftovers."

"Damn straight. Later, C."

I head across the yard to my house and take a long shower, letting thoughts of Kenna in that pink bikini consume me.

3

Griffin

JUNE

Carson and I arrive at Jackson's sometime after nine and the party is in full swing. The girls were taking their sweet ass time, so they said they'd get their own Uber and meet us here.

"Turner, what's up, man?" Jax yells from the kitchen island when he spots us.

I shake his hand and bring him in for a one-arm hug. "Not much, Jax. Just putting Carson through the grind, trying to bring him up to speed," I taunt and look over his shoulder at Carse. He knows I'm just giving him shit.

"What about you? Something has to be keeping you busy if we haven't seen you at the rink or the gym yet."

"Yeah, yeah, I hear ya. Not something, someone." Jackson wraps his arms around the waist of a girl with raven hair and kisses the top of her head.

"This is Tae. Tae this is Griffin Turner, and you've met Carson, right?"

"Yeah, you introduced me to him after one of your games this spring," Tae says.

"Nice to see you again," Carson says as he grabs a cup and fills it up with a rum and soda mix.

"Babe, Turner used to play on our high school team with us. Now he's big time at Emery before he heads to Colorado," Jax explains as he nuzzles into her. I've never seen Jax with anyone for longer than a one-night stand, so this is weird.

I think Tae murmurs a response, but I'm completely distracted by the girl who just entered.

Kenna is wearing the shortest pair of black cutoff shorts with a black crochet crop top that leaves very little to the imagination. She looks good enough to eat.

I clench my fists and I'm immediately on edge thinking about all the other guys here who will be fawning all over her.

"Yo, Carse." I smack his chest. "You alright with your sister wearing that?" I nod my head toward Kenna.

Carson nearly chokes on his drink and then shakes his head at me. "You gotta compose yourself, G. Subtlety has not been your strength when it comes to Mack today." He rolls his eyes as he adds, "And for the record, I don't give a shit what she wears. Especially when Katie and the rest of the girls here are wearing just as little."

That makes me spin my head to do a double-take. Lo and behold, Carson is right. Katie is also wearing cut-off shorts and a crop top. Though I'm not filled with anger and jealousy when I think of the guys here looking at her.

Jealousy? Come on, G. Get your shit together.

I grab a cup and pour myself a rum and soda too as the girls try to make their way over to us. They're stopped by several of their friends on their way to the kitchen.

"Kitty, we're partners for beer pong," Carson shouts to Katie as she approaches us. Kitty is an innocent nickname from when we were younger. I've always called her Katie Cat and Carse, being Carse, decided to call her Kitty from then on.

Although, I haven't heard him use the nickname in a while, he must already be feeling it. We took a few pregame shots while we ate our pizzas.

"Okay, but Kenna and I were just about to join a game of Never Have I Ever. So put our names on the list, but let's wait for a few rounds," Katie replies to Carse.

"For sure. G, are you in for a game?" Carson asks me.

"I'm game," I say as we head outside through the back of the house. Once we're outside, we join a few others who are gathered around a fire. I take a seat on one of the Adirondack chairs that surround the fire pit.

Carson sits in the chair next to me and Katie and Kenna sit on the arms of each of our chairs. Kenna chooses to sit on my chair.

She's close enough that her scent wraps around me. Her signature citrusy perfume is mixed with the faint smell of her sunscreen from earlier in the day.

That makes me smile to myself. She's not like most of the other girls here. She didn't fuss over getting ready—she doesn't need to.

Kenna has always been effortlessly beautiful. With her wavy, honey-blonde hair coming to just above the waist of her shorts and sun-kissed skin, she looks more like a Cali-girl than the Midwestern goddess she is.

I'm tempted to reach my hand up and run my fingers through her hair. Massage my fingers on her scalp. Wrap her long locks around my fist and—*fuck*.

I try to subtly adjust myself to hide my semi and shove those thoughts from my head before I sit here with a raging hard-on.

"Alright ladies and gentlemen, let's get this game started. Everyone has a full drink?" Jackson asks.

24

We all hold our drinks up as he says, "Good. I'll go first. Never have I ever given a lap dance."

I just about shit myself when both Katie and Kenna take a sip from their drinks. *The fuck?*

Katie looks over and shrugs when she catches me glaring at her. She just shrugs! We will most certainly be circling back to that tomorrow.

"This won't be any fun if you're just going to judge your sister all night," Kenna says as she swats my chest, breaking my glare off with Katie.

"I'm not judging anyone. Can't a guy contemplate how the hell his baby sister grew up so fast?"

"One, she's not a baby, I thought we established that earlier. Two, she didn't say *who* she gave the lap dance to."

I raise one of my eyebrows at that. Then both fly to my forehead as she says, "It was me. We went clubbing, and all the girls we were with were rubbing up on guys, crawling in their laps, and we thought it'd be funny to give each other lap dances so the guys would stop hitting on us."

I chuckle. "And how'd that go for you?"

"It backfired immensely. Who knew guys loved girl-on-girl action so much?"

"Everyone. Literally everyone," I deadpan. "Though seeing you grind on my sister would have definitely deterred me."

A flash of hurt crosses over Kenna's face before she quickly masks it with a roll of her eyes.

"My turn. Never have I ever kissed more than one person in twenty-four hours," says Katie.

Well, thank fuck for that I think as I take a sip of my drink.

I know. I'm a hypocrite.

"What's your record?" Kenna asks.

"Record for what, darling? You'll have to be more specific. I hold a lot of them," I retort.

She rolls her eyes again and I want to spank the defiance out of her.

Woah, where did that come from?

"Number of people you've kissed in twenty-four hours?"

"Mmm, not sure. Five or six?"

Her eyes go wide as she says, "Glad to see Boston's keeping it classy."

She's got such a smart mouth on her. The back and forth with her draws me in and leaves me wanting more.

"Easy there, Mack Attack. I'll have you know it was freshman year of high school during a game of Spin the Bottle. It's like there was a magnet stopping the bottle on me at every girl's turn."

"Oh," she says as she bites the corner of her plump bottom lip. She's wearing a sheer gloss that makes me want to lean in and finally find out what she tastes like.

"Oh? Come on, you can do better than that, babe."

Kenna takes that as a challenge and turns herself more toward me. She looks down at me as she says, "I hear you're single for the summer. I'm sure kissing five or six girls in one night will become just another summer night for you soon enough."

I move my hand to her thigh that's resting on the chair and draw slow circles with my thumb. God, I want to inch my way up higher.

"I've got my eyes set on something this summer, that's for sure," I say as I stare into her cerulean eyes.

Her breath hitches and her cheeks flush just enough for me to see in the dim firelight.

"Never have I ever dated someone older than me," Carson says.

Both Kenna and I take a drink. Arching a brow at her I ask, "Who did you date that's older than you?"

"Drew. He's in the grade between us."

"Drew Hutton? You can't be serious?"

"Unfortunately, yes. He was terrible. In every way." Her shoulders shake as she shivers at the thought.

There's more to unpack there. I want to know so much about her. I want to get to know this adult version of Kenna. She's a far cry from the girl who used to spend every other weekend at our house growing up.

"Never have I ever cheated on someone," Tae says. No one drinks. Nice.

"Never have I ever been cheated on," says a girl I haven't met. Kenna and another kid I don't recognize bring their cups to their lips.

Who the fuck would cheat on Kenna? If it was Drew, I'll kick his ass.

"Never have I ever had sex with a dude," Carson says.

Kenna takes a sip and something turns in my gut. Jealousy rips its way through me. Not because she's not a virgin, but knowing that someone else got to touch her. Taste her. Fuck her.

"Never have I ever wanted to get back with an ex," Kenna says as she looks at me.

I don't even flinch toward my cup. Was that directed at me? Does she honestly think I'd want to get back together with Emily? Maybe she's testing the waters to see where I'm at.

I meet her stare and smirk at her, just enough to make my signature dimples come out.

"Never have I ever been in love," I say, and only Tae and Jax drink.

Interesting, so she didn't love Drew. At least there's that.

Kenna's eyes are still stuck on me. She's looking at me as if I'm a puzzle she's trying to piece together. Maybe that's a good thing—she's always loved puzzles. She used to do the crossword in the Sunday paper growing up when she stayed over. My dad would sit at the breakfast table reading the sports section, leaving the crossword and a pencil in the spot she'd sit in.

"Kitty, I just got the text that we're up next for beer pong," Carson says to Katie, and that seems to break whatever trance Kenna and I were in.

"Do you want a refill?" I ask Kenna, still mindlessly rubbing circles on her thigh.

Kenna clears her throat. "Yeah, I could use another."

We top off our drinks and I ask, "Do you want to go back out to the fire and keep playing?"

Kenna nods, and I can't help but feel mesmerized as I stare into her gorgeous aqua eyes. I want to get lost in them.

I follow her lead through the packed house back outside. Taking her hand in mine, sparks shoot up my arm from the touch. I see the slightest blush on her cheeks at my gesture.

Once we get back outside, we notice the game is over, and everyone else must've gone in to get refills and watch the beer pong match.

"Do you want to go back in?" I ask.

"Maybe we could play a little game of our own?" she asks.

I'd like to play a lot of games with you.

"Yeah. This time, let's play two truths, one lie," I suggest as I take a seat back in my chair by the fire.

"Isn't it supposed to be two lies, one truth?"

"Not sure, honestly. But this way, I'll get to catch up with you more," I say as I smirk.

She smiles back at me. "Griffin Owen Turner, if I didn't know better, I'd say you're trying to charm my pants off with those dimples."

"I'm guessing it'd take more than these hideous indents in my cheeks to make that happen."

"Hideous? Blasphemy! You know I've been a sucker for your dimples since we were kids. They're my kryptonite."

I do know that. Any time Carson and I would do something to upset Kenna and Katie, I'd break out the dimples, and she'd convince Katie that all should be forgiven. But hearing her say it makes me smile like the Cheshire Cat, only enhancing the dimples more.

Kenna bites at her bottom lip again, and my thoughts spiral.

I need to know what she tastes like. What would she do if I leaned in right now and kissed her? Would she pull away? Would she lean into it?

Stop being such a bitch, Turner, and kiss her already.

Kenna's voice breaks through my thoughts. "My favorite snack is an apple with peanut butter. My first pet was Ranger. My biggest fear is never taking chances."

"What kind of chances do you want to take, Kenna?" I ask as I pull her into my lap.

"What?" she responds with a breathlessness. "How did you know that wasn't a lie?"

"Easy. You used to come home every day after school or practice and cut up an apple with peanut butter for as long as I've known you. And your first pet was Bits the Bunny, who passed away when you were eleven. That was before your mom and dad got Ranger to help you deal with the loss of Bits."

Kenna's breath hitches as she stares into my eyes. "I want to take as many chances as I can. What's a life without risk? Without risks, there are no rewards, right? That's my biggest fear—if I don't take any chances, I'll have a boring, unfulfilled life."

I keep my eyes locked with hers. "You know, I've always been one to live just enough on the edge, like each day is my last. But I'm never reckless. I can't be. Katie and my dad would kill me. We've been through enough after losing my mom."

Pushing my hand slightly higher on her thigh, my thumb continues to make circles. Kenna places her hand on top of mine and gives it a gentle squeeze.

I look down at her hand on mine. "Guess it's my turn." I swallow the lump that forms in my throat whenever I think of Mom.

"I can't afford any distractions this year. It has to be my best season yet." I hold up one finger. "I cried like a baby when I got back to my hotel room on draft night." I hold up a second. "I've never wanted any of my sister's friends," I finish, holding up a third finger.

The slightest frown appears on Kenna's face.

"Which is the lie, Kenna?"

"Well, I know every season matters for you guys. But this season, I'm guessing you could get pulled up with the stats you pulled last year. So that's a truth." She hesitates before she says, "I've only seen you cry once and that was the day your mom passed."

"So you think that's my lie?"

Kenna looks at me and shrugs. "Sure. I mean, I know you've always said Colorado was your first choice. So I'm sure you were ecstatic, but I can't see you crying on the best night of your life."

I brush my hand up the side of her thigh and wrap it around her waist.

"Wrong. The emotions of my dream coming true and my mom not being there to see it were too much. I cried so hard Katie thought I was hurt when she came into the room. She said it had to be that or that Emily trapped me with a baby." I snort. "Thank fuck that didn't happen."

"So . . ." Kenna pauses.

I rub my palm up and down her lower back and move my head closer to her.

"Yeah, so . . ."

Her breath hitches again as I grab the side of her face to pull her in.

I press my forehead to hers as I say, "It was my lie, Kenna. I've wanted to kiss you for-fucking-ever, but I didn't know how you'd react." I take a deep breath.

Am I really going to do this?

Before I can second guess myself, I take the plunge and rasp, "Can I kiss you?"

The words barely leave my lips before Kenna softly presses hers to mine. A bolt of energy passes through me with just one touch.

Is this really happening?

I kiss Kenna intently, exploring her pillowy soft lips, bringing her plush bottom lip forward and biting into it.

I groan at the first delicious taste of her. She tastes better than I could've dreamed, like vanilla and mint wrapped together.

Passing my tongue over her lips, she opens for me. In an instant, the kiss deepens, turning desperate.

Her touch is intoxicating. She's a high I never want to come down from.

I'm completely gone for this girl after only one kiss and fuck if it doesn't feel right.

4

McKenna

JUNE

A curl of heat erupts in my stomach as Griffin grips my waist and pulls me down so I'm straddling his lap.

His fingers curl into the hem of my shirt as he kisses across my cheek, leaving trails of kisses along my jawline.

Is this really happening? If this is a dream, I think I'll die of disappointment upon waking. Griffin's lips are back on mine. A gasp leaves my lips, opening them. In a second, Griff's tongue tangles with mine again, and I moan.

I. *Moan.*

I've never moaned from being kissed. But, my god, he tastes delicious. Griffin. Fricken. Turner.

I bring my hands to the back of his neck and run my fingers through his dark hair. We get lost in a clashing of tongues, teeth, and lips before Griff pulls away. I let out a whimper at the loss of his mouth on mine.

He traces his thumb over my bottom lip before he asks, "Can I take you out?"

Still somewhat dazed, it takes me a few seconds to register what he just asked me.

"Kenna?"

"Wh-What?" I ask as I open my eyes to stare into his chocolate-brown eyes, which are currently so dark they look black as coal.

"I asked if I could take you out. I know Katie won't care, and I doubt Carse would either."

I take a good look at Griffin to make sure he's serious. A look of nervousness crosses his face.

"L-like a date?" How can one question have me stumbling over my words? A question I've wished most of my life to hear.

His lips turn up into a devastating smirk that makes his dimples pop.

"Yes, Kenna, a date. I'd say it's about three years overdue at this point. Let me take you out. Are you free tomorrow?"

I take a deep breath and pull myself together. I tap my chin in a teasing way before I reply, "Depends. Where would we go?"

Griffin's smirk grows into a panty-melting smile as he says, "There's my girl. That mouth of yours."

He grabs my chin again and pulls me in for a kiss. My mind is still trying to process the fact that Griffin Turner—the boy I've crushed on for as long as I can remember—referred to me as *his* girl. If I'm not dreaming, I have to be delirious, intoxicated, *something*.

I let myself get lost in the feel of his lips on mine, in the feel of his hands gripping my waist, and the feel of his growing bulge pressing against the perfect spot between my legs.

Griff grinds his hips up into mine, and we both moan together. This is what euphoria feels like. This feeling is what turns people into addicts.

I'm high just off the fact that I can make him react this way. That he's turned on by me. I just hope the high I'm chasing can last. That it doesn't leave me free-falling.

The noise of a throat clearing has us slowly pulling away from each other. I glance up over Griff's head and see Katie and Carson standing there with their arms crossed, mouths in straight lines.

They lose their stern looks a moment later as smirks slowly spread over their faces.

"I'll take that hundred bucks now, Carsy," Katie sing-songs, holding her hand out to him.

"It was a bet I was willing to lose for the greater good," Carson retorts.

"I'm just glad we came out here when we did. No way do I want to see where that was likely heading," Katie says as she shivers dramatically.

Griffin rolls his eyes at them, then turns to me and winks.

Good god. I need to climb off his lap before my panties melt off, and Katie and Carse get exactly the show they weren't looking for.

I go to stand, but Griff quickly grips the back of my thighs. From that one touch, heat pools to the base of my stomach.

"Don't go. We can still stay out here. I'll put a few more logs on the fire, and we can talk some more. I want to hear all your truths, Kenna."

How has he always had the ability to say the right things? The smirk reappears on his face as I lower myself back down.

"Alright, but our lips will only be talking. Got it?"

He lifts his hands up in surrender, and I pout at the loss of heat from his hands.

"So what's it going to be? Talking or pouting," he teases as he lifts me off him and adds two more logs to the fire.

"Hey!" I smack his chest. "Just because we're talking doesn't mean you have to keep your hands to yourself."

Griffin turns me around so my back is pressed to his chest and wraps his arms tightly around my waist. He breathes me in as he kisses my temple, then down my jawline, moving a trail until he's at the base of my neck.

Every touch comes so naturally. To anyone else, it'd look as if we'd been together for a while when in reality, tonight is the first time we've crossed this line.

"Watch yourself, Kenna," he whispers in my ear. "If you take a chance on me, I won't stop until you're mine," he says as he pulls me down with him onto the chair again.

With his large hands wrapped around me, we sit and talk for hours until the fire is nothing but dulled embers.

I can't think of anything in this world I'd want more than to be Griffin Turner's girl.

The next morning I take one last glance in the mirror, put on my favorite chapstick, and walk out of my room.

Pausing at the top landing, I listen to Griff and Carson discussing their dry land practice for tomorrow.

"Are you cool if Mack and Katie join us? They said they don't need to get on the court until ten."

"Yeah, that's cool. Though Katie's a bear in the morning," Griff replies. He sounds like he's right at the bottom of the steps.

I start down the stairs and pause in the middle to grip the railing. Griff's broad back is to me. He's dressed in a light blue, button-down, short-sleeved shirt that molds to his arms, with white shorts and white sneakers.

He turns around, and our eyes lock. A slow smile takes over his handsome face. Those damn dimples pop, and heat rushes up my neck and warms my face. Butterflies take flight in my stomach as he rubs his hand over his jaw.

"McKenna, you're stunning."

My blush deepens as I make my way to the bottom of the stairs. I inhale sharply when Griffin wraps his arms around my waist and pulls me in for a kiss.

He tastes like mint and something entirely *him*. I don't think I'll ever get over the feeling of his lips on mine. I'm lost in the most delicious haze as he pulls away far too soon.

"Don't get me wrong, I'm team McKiffin, or maybe it should be Grenna." Carson shakes his head, then continues, "But it will take some getting used to seeing the two of you making out."

Griffin chuckles. "That was hardly making out, Carse. Nothing but an innocent hello kiss. Though, I wouldn't recommend sticking around for the goodnight kiss."

"Gross, G. Have her home at a decent time, yeah?"

"You got it, man. I'll see you tomorrow morning," Griffin replies.

Griffin places his hand on the small of my back as he guides me out to his red Jeep Wrangler. I've always loved his Jeep, though I've never been in the front seat and alone with him.

He opens the door for me and I smile back at him. "Guess chivalry isn't dead after all. There's still hope for mankind."

"I'm always a gentleman, though, admittedly, you make it hard on me looking as gorgeous as you do."

He shuts my door and walks around to his side. Once we're buckled, he pulls out of my driveway. His right hand makes its way to my thigh, and butterflies erupt in my stomach. I love his need to touch me.

"So, where are we headed?" I ask as I turn to look at him. His one hand is gripping the top of the steering wheel. God, he looks so good it hurts. His shirt melds to his upper body, with the top few buttons undone, giving just a peek of his chest. I can appreciate each and every ridge of his muscular body. My type is, and has always been, Griffin Turner. All the time he puts in at the gym and rink has done wonders for his body.

"I picked you up early because we've got a little bit of a road trip ahead of us. Don't worry, I didn't come empty-handed," he says as he hands me an iced caramel macchiato.

"Oh my gosh, I could kiss you right now!" I say as I take a sip, and my eyes roll back with how good it tastes.

"I take it your coffee order is still the same?" He laughs and then points to the backseat. "I also got us some snacks, the typical road trip essentials."

"And what would those be?"

"Oh, you know, sunflower seeds, jerky, chips, and Twizzlers."

"Stop. Are they the pull-and-peel kind?"

"Is there any other kind?"

"Well, there are, but none that matter," I reply and smile sheepishly at him. "So, where is this road trip leading us?"

"Have you ever been to Stillwater?"

"Yeah, when we were little, we went there a few times as a family. But I haven't been there in years." I smile as I think of all of the memories Carson and I had growing up. Katie even went with us once.

"It's a cool spot for sure. We used to go there all the time as a family before Mom died," he says as he stares out the dashboard at the road ahead.

"Yeah, that's what Katie said when she went with us one time. Doesn't your uncle live there?"

"Yeah, my mom's brother, Adam, lives there. It's actually where they grew up. He's the only one who still lives there, though. He's got a great house that overlooks the river. I'd never leave that place if I were him."

"Maybe we could stop and see him if he's there," I blurt without thinking about it. "I mean, if you don't mind seeing him when I'm with you."

Griffin turns his head to look me in the eyes and smiles at me. "We can see if he's around. I'm sure he'd love that." His hand squeezes my thigh, and I think it's meant to reassure me that I shouldn't be embarrassed.

The drive to Stillwater isn't really much of a road trip. It takes us about forty-five minutes with traffic, but not a minute goes by in silence. Griffin made a playlist for the drive. I can tell he made it with me in mind whenever a Paramore or Taylor Swift song comes on. His dimples were on full display when I sang "I'm Only Me When I'm With You" and I may have fallen just a little when he started scream-singing along with me.

Little did he know her albums were played on repeat many times throughout high school. It was like Taylor made a soundtrack to my life. And yes, it killed me any time I looked out my window and saw Griffin taking off with some girl.

Once the song ends, Griff turns down the volume and looks over at me.

"Do you ever wonder what it would've been like if we had dated in high school?"

I look over at him with wide eyes. It's like he was reading my thoughts. "I mean, you never would've gone for me when we were both in high school." I laugh, trying to brush off his question.

"You can't possibly say that after what I told you last night. I've had my eyes on you for years, Kenna."

"Oh, yeah? Since when? When was the first time you looked at me as anything other than your little sister's awkward best friend?"

"First day of school my junior year. I was about to walk out to drive Katie and me to school when she let me know you and Carse were going to ride with us. I remember being annoyed that we'd probably have to wait, and I wanted to make sure Katie had plenty of time on her first day of high school to find her classes." He pauses and takes a deep breath, grabbing my hand in his.

"You were outside waiting by my Jeep, and I stood still and stared when I caught sight of you." He smiles over at me again quickly before looking back to the road. "You had your hair down, and you were wearing a jean skirt and a blue shirt that made your eyes pop. Suddenly, you weren't just Katie's best friend anymore, but the girl next door that starred in all of my dreams."

I'm stunned silent for a moment by his recollection of that day. Of course, I remember it. I was filled with anxious nerves when Katie said Griffin would drive us all to school. I spent hours looking through my closet the night before, trying to find the perfect outfit to make him finally see me.

I look over at him. "But you completely ignored me the whole ride there. Actually, you ignored me for most of that year, if I'm being honest."

"I had to. I didn't think I was good for you then. I wanted you to have all the experiences high school had to offer without my influence or interference. That's why I asked if you ever wondered what it would've been like. Because the what-ifs have taken over my mind since I saw you on your graduation day."

"I mean, you were my first crush, Griff. I've thought about what it would've been like a million times. But then I tell myself how much harder it would've been when you went off to college." I squeeze his hand as I continue, "There's no telling what would've happened, but I have a pretty good feeling we wouldn't have made the long-distance thing work. I was only a junior in high school, and you were the hot, freshman standout for all of D1 hockey."

"Are you saying you thought I was hot, Wilder?"

"Ugh, don't call me that. It makes me feel like you're talking to my brother!"

He throws his head back, laughing, and pulls me into him as we sit at the red light. The light press of his lips to mine is too quick, leaving me anxious for the chance to kiss him properly.

"Is babe better? Darling? Honey? Angel face? I'm guessing 'baby' is off the table since you didn't like me referring to you as Carson's baby sister." He fires off the nicknames at me at rapid speed.

I roll my eyes at his nonsense.

"I've got it! Sunshine. It's perfect." He beams over at me, his smile is brilliance personified.

"What made you land on that one?"

"We've been through a lot together, even when I tried to keep you at a distance. When my mom was going through chemo, some days were really rough. You'd come over to help distract Katie, but just your presence brought positivity and rays of light into the darkest corners of my mind."

Butterflies erupt throughout my entire body. I love it. Griffin gives me a quick peck and then winks at me as he turns his attention back to the road.

"We're almost there, Sunshine," Griff says, squeezing my thigh as he exits the highway.

Well, shit. This man is giving me all the feels, and far too quickly.

5

Griffin

JUNE

It's already eleven by the time we take the exit for Stillwater. I decided to take Kenna to lunch at Tilly's, a little malt shop my mom used to love. I haven't been there in years, but their burgers and shakes have always been my favorite.

I find a parking spot and turn off the engine. "Wait here," I say to Kenna before I hop out and round the hood to open her door for her.

"Wow, you're really taking the chivalry thing seriously," she teases me as I help her out of the Jeep.

"I'm trying to hook you, Sunshine. I've got to pull out all the tricks. Ever been to Tilly's?"

"No, but Katie told me about it the last time we were here. The line was down the block, so we ended up going somewhere else."

"They've got the best burgers and shakes around, so that's not surprising."

I grab Kenna's hand as we walk toward the restaurant, loving the way her hand fits in mine. We stop on the curb, waiting for the walk signal, and turn to take her in. She's so effortlessly stunning in her jean shorts and white tank top, and her blonde hair flows down her back in loose waves that I can't get enough of.

Kenna looks over at me, catching me ogling her. She quirks her brow and asks, "Why are you looking at me like that?"

"Like what?" I feign innocence.

"Like, I don't know"—she waves her hand up and down—"like that."

"I'm just trying to figure out how I managed to get you to go out with me. You're so clearly out of my league, Kenna."

The words barely leave my lips before Kenna's cheeks darken with a deep blush.

"Now I know you must be starving. You're delirious, G."

"I'm not. I mean, starving, yes. Delirious, no." The light changes, and we cross the street.

"Do you want to eat inside or out on the patio?" I ask her as we approach the restaurant that sits on the corner of the block.

"I've never been inside, and I love that it's a retro diner. Can we eat inside?"

"Of course." I smile down at her as she claps her hands together in excitement. I love how expressive she is; she wears her feelings on her sleeve.

We walk inside and take a seat at one of the booths. I watch Kenna as she takes in all the old-fashioned paraphernalia that lines the walls.

"This place is great, I can see why you guys love it so much."

Just then the waitress walks up and asks if she can get us started with any drinks. I don't need to look at the menu, I get the same thing every time I'm here.

Kenna peeks up from her menu at me and says, "Can I take a guess at what you're going to order?"

"Sure, but there's no way you'll get it right."

"Challenge accepted." She looks up at the waitress with a huge grin and says, "He'll take an Oreo shake, please, and can we add peanut butter?"

"We?"

"Well, yeah. It looks like the shakes are meant to share."

"What little faith you have in me," I say as I grab my chest, feigning offense.

"Well, I didn't hear any arguments about what I ordered, so I assume I chose correctly."

I turn to look at the waitress and add, "And she will take a strawberry shake. Can we add peanut butter to that too, please?"

"Coming right up," the waitress says as she walks away.

A slow smile spreads over Kenna's face. "You remembered. I haven't had a strawberry peanut butter shake in forever."

I reach across the table and take her hand in mine, intertwining our fingers. I rub my thumb in circles along her wrist.

The waitress comes back with our shakes and I take my hand from hers. Kenna does the pouty frown again, and it's so cute the way she's unaware of her body's subconscious need for ours to touch.

Kenna puts her straw in her shake and moans when the shake hits her lips. Every noise she makes does me in.

I turn to the waitress and order our burgers and fries. Then I start on my own shake. When the Oreo and peanut butter hit my tongue, I let out a low groan. Looking up, I find Kenna slack-jawed and staring back at me.

"What? Did I get some on my chin?" I grab a napkin to wipe my face, but there's nothing there.

Kenna's still staring at me, and I can't help but laugh. "Did I break you, Sunshine?"

That seems to bring her out of her stupor.

"Har har," she deadpans. "You'll have to do far more than let out a guttural groan while sucking down a shake to break me."

43

"Noted," I respond as I wiggle my eyebrows up and down. "Just preparing you for the noises you'll hear when I sink my teeth into that bubble butt of yours."

Her cheeks stain the same color as her strawberry shake, and I can't help but bask in the contentment I feel whenever I'm with Kenna. It's so effortless. I can just be myself. I don't have the anxiety that comes with always needing to be on like I do when I'm on campus.

"Can I have a taste of yours?" she asks.

"You don't ever have to ask, Kenna," I say as I slide my shake toward her. I grab hers and slide it toward me, and we each take a sip of the others' shake.

"Mmmmm. You're right. The Oreo and peanut butter pair perfectly together."

"If you think the shakes are good, just wait until you taste the burger and fries."

She mumbles something to herself under her breath that sounds a lot like she can imagine a few things she'd like to taste. That gets me smirking at the way she's thinking.

Oh, Sunshine. The things I'm going to do to you. Just you wait.

We worked off our lunch as we walked along the river. Then I took Kenna to some of my mom and Katie's favorite shops that line the historic downtown shopping area. I guide her into one little store with my hand on the small of her back, and pride strikes my chest at getting the chance to be this way with her.

This store is filled with handcrafted jewelry, crystals, and other knick-knacks. I watch Kenna as she looks around the store, taking it all in. When I see a piece of jewelry catch her eye, I know I can't leave this store without getting it for her. The turquoise ring is oval and fits her finger perfectly.

"We'll take this one, please," I say to the woman working the register. She looks up with kind eyes and smiles when she sees what I've pointed to.

"Oh, what? No. I was just trying it on," Kenna starts, but I don't let her finish.

"It looks perfect on you, Sunshine. The color kind of reminds me of your eyes when we're by the lake."

"You're too sweet, but really, I don't need it."

Ignoring her, I turn to the woman and pay for the ring.

"Afraid to put my ring on your finger, Kenna?" I tease as I pull her in and kiss her forehead. I can't say it doesn't fill me with satisfaction to see Kenna with my ring on her finger.

She flashes me her hand with the ring on her right pointer finger. "Wrong finger, wrong hand, Mr. Territorial."

Wrapping my arms around her waist and bringing her even closer I respond, "Oh, I'll be territorial if that's what you want, Sunshine. Isn't that what all of yours and Katie's favorite book boyfriends are?"

"Wait, how do you know what a book boyfriend is?"

"Katie's mood completely changes based on what kind of book she's reading. She's happiest when the book boyfriend is a caramel roll or something like that."

"Oh my gosh, it's a cinnamon roll. And you're right, she loves a good 'he falls first' trope," she gushes.

"What exactly is a trope?"

"It can be a storyline, theme, or character trait in the book. Most books have several tropes and micro-tropes in them."

"Okay, now I'm curious. What would ours be?"

"Well, obviously best friend's brother romance," she ticks off her fingers as she continues, "sports romance since we're both athletes, friends to lovers, and secret pining."

"I think you forgot one more," I say as I grab her hand and lead her out of the store.

"Oh, yeah, age gap," she says as she gives me a teasing hip check.

"Not at all what I was going to say. Shouldn't the age gap be more than two years?"

"You're right. Your sister loves to read books with a ten to fifteen-year age gap," she teases.

I heave out a long sigh. "I did not want to know that tidbit. I was going to suggest you add the boy next door to your tropes list."

"Oh, yes! I used to seek out young adult novels where the boy would fall for the girl next door, just hoping that one day you'd think of me that way," she says bashfully.

Tipping her chin up to look at me, I tell her, "One day is now, Kenna."

McKenna

We get back to my house just as darkness creeps over the sky. Today has been one of the most romantic days of my life. After we left the downtown area, we stopped at Griff's uncle Adam's house. He wasn't home, but Adam called Griff and told him to take me out for a boat ride before we headed back. So we packed up some sandwiches and snacks and had dinner on the river.

His uncle was absolutely insane for letting us take out his boat, which was really more like a small yacht.

Once we were anchored down, we ate a picnic-style dinner. Griff played music on the boat's speakers and asked me to dance with him. He said we needed to find "our song." He searched his playlists for a few moments before an acoustic version of "You Are My Sunshine" wafted through the speakers. His deep voice serenaded me as we danced on the bow of the boat.

He wrapped me in his arms and held me like he'd never let me go. I rested my head on the crook of his neck and kissed his collarbone as I soaked it all in. The way his warm body felt pressed against mine. The way his sun-soaked skin smelled of sunscreen and cedar—a lethal combination I didn't know I'd love so much. It was a surreal moment and one I know I'll never forget.

Now that we're back, I was expecting him to walk me to my house, but instead, he leads me to his backyard. Once he opens the gate, he flips a switch at the back of the house. I let out a small gasp as strings of Eddison lights illuminate the backyard. Taking in the space, I notice there's an outdoor projector screen and a bed of what looks like dozens of blankets and pillows in front of it.

"Griff, what is all of this?" I ask, bewildered.

"Katie helped me set this up before we left this morning. I thought we could extend the day just a little bit longer and watch a movie together. Or if you'd prefer to look at the stars, I can turn off the lights."

"No, this is perfect. I can't believe you did all this for me." I shake my head in amazement.

"I'd do anything to keep that smile on your face, Sunshine. Come on, let me show you what your snack options are," he says as he moves over to the makeshift bed. It looks like he took two air mattresses and put about all the blankets and pillows they could find around the house on top. Next to the bed, there's a basket of movie snacks.

"Alright, so I've got kettle corn because I know you like it sweet and salty." He wiggles his eyebrows at me. "Then I've got peanut butter M&Ms, chocolate-covered cookie dough bites, and sour gummy worms. Oh, and I've got Cherry Coke in the fridge. Give me a sec, I'll be right back," he says as he's about to jog over to the outdoor fridge. But I stop him when I throw my hands around him.

He lifts me up and splays his hands under my butt as I wrap my legs around his waist. I touch my nose and forehead to his.

"I seriously don't think you'll ever be able to top this day. No one has ever done anything like this for me. Thank you so much, G. I'll never forget this day for as long as I live. It's perfect. You're perfect."

"Just know, it's only going to get better from here, Sunshine. I'm not perfect by any means. But I want to be my best for you. I want to give you everything if you'll let me."

"Griffin Turner, are you trying to make me fall head over heels for you at record speed?"

He flashes those dimples that do me in and asks, "Is it working?"

Instead of answering him, I take his handsome face in my hands and press my lips to his, letting my kisses translate all the things that are far too early to declare.

He walks me backward until the back of my knees touch the mattress. Scooting back to the middle of the mattress, he climbs on top of me, kissing me again with an intensity that I match. I wrap my legs around his waist and pull his chest down until it meets mine. He rocks his hips into me, causing heat to flood my panties.

Griffin sits back on his heels and takes me in. It feels like he's undressed me with just his gaze. I let out a whimper as he slowly drags his finger from my bottom lip, down the column of my throat, between the valley of my breasts, along the middle of my stomach, and to the edge of my jean shorts.

My impatience with him must be written all over my face, because he asks, "Is my girl feeling needy?"

"Yes. Touch me, Griff. Please," I beg.

"I am touching you, love."

"More. I need more."

"Do you like it when I kiss you . . . here?" he asks as he kisses the pulse point on my neck.

"Yes," I moan in answer.

"What about here?" he asks as he licks the valley between my breasts, then lifts my tank as he trails open-mouth kisses down my stomach to the top of my shorts again.

"Please, don't stop," I gasp.

He shakes his head and places his arms on either side of my head, bracing his weight on his forearms as he hovers above me.

"There's plenty of time for that. But for now, we're going to live out one of my teenage fantasies."

"Oh yeah, and what's that?" I ask in a breathy voice.

"You're going to dry hump my cock until you come like the desperate girl I know you are."

Oh, god.

Griff rocks his hips into my center, making my pussy throb. The friction of his length through the fabric of my jean shorts has my clit pulsing within seconds.

He kisses me as he continues to grind into me. I'm breathless; my heart pounds like I've just completed an intense rally on the court. Griff kisses down my jaw, sucking and biting on my neck, making me moan louder now that his mouth isn't on mine.

I can tell he is big. Like gloriously big.

Our hips meet thrust for thrust over and over again, pushing me over the brink. His tongue drowns the moans and whimpers as I come the hardest I've ever come in my life. White light flashes behind my eyelids as I continue to ride out my orgasm. Griff kisses down my jaw, my neck, to behind my ear, then groans as he rocks into me one last time.

"Jesus, Kenna. You just made me come in my pants for the first time in my fucking life."

"If dry humping you made me come that hard," I pant, trying to catch my breath, "then I can't wait until you actually fill me up."

"You and me both, Sunshine," he says as he trails kisses along my cheeks and forehead.

"I'm going to change quickly. Want to wear a pair of my sweats and a shirt?" he asks.

"Yeah, that'd be great," I say, my voice sounding sleepy. I can't tell you the amount of times I've dreamed about wearing one of Griff's shirts.

"Alright, come here," he says as he helps me up off the mattress.

Griff picks me up and swings me over his shoulder, making me yelp at him that I'm too heavy.

He swats my butt. "I can bench press twice your weight, Kenna. Stop insulting me and enjoy the ride. I know I am." And he punctuates that with another swat before he smooths his hand over my cheek.

Griff takes me upstairs to his room and hands me some clothes to change into.

"I'm just going to get cleaned up quickly," he says, pointing over his shoulder to the bathroom.

"Alright." I giggle at the slight blush on his cheeks. I made Griffin Turner come in his pants. I made a teenage fantasy of his come true.

"Hey, Griff?"

"Yeah?"

"You said that was your teenage fantasy. Am I supposed to believe you've never dry-humped someone before?"

"That was never my teenage fantasy, Kenna. The fantasy was watching you come undone beneath me without me so much as using my hands, mouth, or having my cock buried inside you," he answers with a cocky smirk.

"Oh. So, coming in your pants wasn't the fantasy," I tease.

"No, that was more so what I would do when you were in the room next to me, sleeping over, as I ran through all of the dirty things I wanted to do to you."

I'm stunned speechless. I was sure that all those years I had lusted after the boy next door, my best friend's older brother, that my feelings were one-sided.

He kisses me softly, taking his time as he molds his tongue with mine. I feel everything from that one kiss. Slowly pulling away, he sighs with his eyes still closed, shaking his head to himself.

"What is it?" I ask.

Opening his eyes, he looks down at me. "I never thought it could be like this. I didn't think anything besides hockey could consume my thoughts. But here I am, with you still in my arms, thinking about the next date I'm taking you on, and all of the ways I want to watch you unravel."

My heart expands in my chest, making my next breaths shutter in and out of me.

I'm falling for the boy next door. But, then, I have been for years, so what does that tell you?

I've already fallen.

I just hope the place I land is as soft as the way his lips feel on mine.

6

Griffin

JUNE

Birds are chirping and the air smells like summer mixed with a familiar citrusy scent. Warmth consumes me and I open my eyes to find Kenna's blonde hair splayed across my chest.

The sun is starting to rise, lighting the backyard in a golden glow. We must've fallen asleep last night after the movie. We stayed up talking and kissing until we struggled to keep our eyes open.

I don't want to wake her when she looks so peaceful, but we're supposed to go to the gym with Katie and Carse this morning. I take a few more moments to bask in this moment.

"Good morning, beautiful," I rasp as I adjust her in my arms so I'm able to roll onto my side. I start laying kisses along her forehead, her jawline, her closed eyelids, and her nose, and just as I'm about to claim her mouth she shoots her hand up over her lips.

"No kissing until I've brushed my teeth," she mumbles under her hand.

I kiss the ring on her hand that covers her lips. When I move her hand away, she tries to shoot the other up, so I pin them above her head. I'm able to fit both of her wrists in one hand and use my other to tilt her chin up to kiss her sweet mouth.

"Sunshine, your dragon breath doesn't scare me. I don't think there's a thing you could do that would turn me off."

Then, I kiss her. She moans into my mouth as I open hers, and our tongues twirl. Kissing Kenna feels like the first breath after being underwater. It's all-consuming and invigorating.

Our kiss deepens, shooting desire down my spine. Bringing my hips down, I grind into Kenna, only the fabric of our sweatpants between us. I tell myself we should stop, that we've got places to be, but Jesus—Kenna is the drug I know I'm never going to be able to quit.

"Ahem." I hear a throat clearing from the back porch of my house.

Looking up, my eyes connect with my dad's as he stands outside the sliding glass doors, holding his mug of coffee.

"Hey, Dad," I start as I roll onto my side, removing my hand from Kenna's wrists.

"Good morning, Griff. And-ah, good morning to you, Mack," my dad says, sheepishly as if he's the one who was just caught with his hand in the proverbial cookie jar.

Kenna sits up with me but hides her face behind my shoulder as she mumbles, "Good morning, Mr. Turner."

"Mr. Turner? McKenna Marie, I've known you for the better part of your life. What's with the sudden formalities?"

"Sorry! Good morning, Jack," she says as she slowly peeks her head from behind her hiding spot, her lips grazing my shoulder as she does.

I look down at her and brush my lips across her hairline. Her face is practically as red as my away jersey.

"Well, I can't say I'm surprised this is finally happening. Though I can't wait to hear what Theo has to say about it," he says as his eyes glint with mischief. "He's going to put you through the wringer, Griff."

My eyes shoot up to meet my dad's. "Why would he do that? Teddy has always loved me like a second son."

"That was before he knew you were having sleepovers with his only daughter." He chuckles.

I look back down at Kenna. "Do you think he's right?"

"I mean, he's not wrong. I am, and always will be, his little girl."

"Good, let him give me the third degree. Some have said I'm as charming as they come."

Not letting my eyes leave Kenna's, I ask my dad, "Did you need anything, Dad? We're going to head to the gym with Carse and Katie in a bit."

"Nope. Just came out here to enjoy my morning coffee and thought I'd give you some shit since it took the two of you so long to figure out what your mom and I saw from the start."

My throat clogs with emotion, the way it does any time I think of my mom, and I struggle to get out a reply. Kenna's breath catches and her eyes glass over with unshed tears.

Dad continues so we don't have to. "She always loved you, Mack. I think it must have been the day you fell off the treehouse ladder, and Griff refused to let you out of his sight. That was it. That's when my Catherine said she knew the two of you were going to end up together. I told her it was just wishful thinking since she was so close with your mama. But she said it was a mother's intuition. I've seen glimpses of it over the years, but my son is a stubborn ass sometimes." He winks at Kenna as he takes a drink from his mug.

Well, that feels like he just dropped a couple of cinder blocks to my chest. I didn't know she felt that way. I mean, how could I? Mom passed before we ever got the chance to talk about girls and crushes. The weight of missing her comes and goes, but I find comfort in knowing she thought Kenna and I would be together someday.

"We've, ah, we've got to get going to the gym," Kenna mumbles as she quickly stands up. "I'm going to go get changed, and I'll meet you out front."

She begins to bolt away, but I wrap my arms around her waist and scoop her into my arms.

"Wait just a second." I bring my lips to her ear. "Don't run off without kissing me goodbye, Sunshine."

"It's not goodbye. We're literally going to be riding to the gym together in five minutes." She giggles as I tickle her neck with the scruff of my five o'clock shadow.

I kiss her neck once, twice, before she pulls out of my hold. I swat her ass as she spins to start toward her house. She winks at me over her shoulder, and I bite my lip to fight back a groan.

Backing up a few steps, I turn and jog up the back steps to my house.

"Don't start," I tell my dad as I walk through the sliding door when he gives me a knowing look.

"I didn't say a thing." He continues, "But have you thought this through? I don't want to see her get hurt if you're not ready for this. What's going to happen when you go back to Boston in a couple of months?"

Though we haven't discussed it yet, I know I can handle making Kenna a priority.

"I've thought a lot about this. For years, really. I wouldn't risk my friendship with Carse, or Kenna's with Katie if this wasn't something I wanted. I think we can make long-distance work. We're both athletes and will be busy, but thankfully, our off-seasons somewhat align. I'll make the effort to come home more, and I can see if she'd want to fly out to visit."

"I'm glad to hear it, Son. I think she's good for you. Just be sure the two of you are on the same page. Don't wait until the end of the summer to have the tough conversations," he adds. His concern is written all over his face—Kenna is like a second daughter to him.

I nod, then turn to head upstairs to get changed. I pull a clean pair of gym shorts out of my dresser that stands next to a row of three picture windows. I'm putting on deodorant and looking out the window when I spot movement in the house next door. Kenna's room is right across from mine, and growing up, I might have glimpsed out there a time or two . . . dozen.

Kenna's standing at her mirrored armoire, and it looks like she's touching her neck and shaking her head in disbelief—likely at the line of hickeys marking her neck and collarbone. A tightness fills my chest at the thought of my marks on her skin.

She turns and looks out her windows across from mine, catching me watching her. A leisurely smile spreads across her lips as she slowly raises the hem of *my* T-shirt she had on over her head. I bite my knuckles and groan at the sight of McKenna Wilder across the yard from me in nothing but a pair of pink panties. This is everything my teenage fantasies were made of.

All breath escapes my lungs as she slides her panties off and glides her hands up her toned stomach to grab and pinch her nipples. She bites down on her plush bottom lip as she gathers her hair into her hand and turns around to give me a glimpse of her delectable ass. I palm myself over my shorts, gripping my rock-hard length.

Jesus *fuck*. I want her so bad. I'm not sure I've ever been this hard in my life.

Kenna peeks over her shoulder at me, turning completely to face me once she realizes I'm joining her little tease fest. I drop my shorts and boxers then firmly stroke myself to the sight of her.

She turns fully again, giving me another eye full before reaching and pulling the curtains shut.

I pull my phone off the dresser and call Kenna. She picks up the phone, sounding breathless when she says, "We're going to be late."

"What is it you're trying to do to me, Sunshine? I can't go work out with your brother under these conditions."

"Then I guess you'll have to be as quick as you were last night while you take care of that situation," she teases.

"Shouldn't be hard to do with all of the spank bank material you just gave me. Do you know how many nights I'd stare across to your bedroom windows?"

"Good to know I wasn't the only one trying to catch a glimpse," she quips.

"Kenna, get moving, or we're gonna be late." I hear Carson holler in the background.

"I'll see you in five, G. Be sure to take good care of yourself until then."

I'd like her to put that smart mouth of hers to work doing something else.

I can officially say I've died and gone to heaven. Or maybe this is hell? I can't be sure because my brain is short-circuiting as I watch Kenna jump up and make contact with the hundredth ball.

She finishes one kill just to transition back to the ten-foot line and do it again, over and over.

My eyes trail down her body as she turns away. She's pure perfection. The way her delectable ass slightly jiggles in her spandex, to the way her sweat-slicked shoulders and arms glisten, is doing things to me. Things that I'd rather not feel while I'm right next to her brother.

I'm supposed to be putting up a block against her alongside Carson, but after jumping with a semi-hard dick for the past twenty minutes, I had to take a break.

Getting to see this side of Kenna, up close, feels like a privilege. Her passion and drive are such turn-ons.

"Alright, let's call it. I'm getting blisters from these new shoes," Katie says finally.

"One more, I need Griff to put up the double block with Carse so I can get this line shot down," Kenna says.

"Sorry, give me a minute, and I'll be right over," I say as I recite a list of Stanley Cup winners in my head.

When I've listed about the last dozen, I walk back up to the net, nodding to her that I'm ready.

"I'm not sure how you two are still standing right now, considering you slept outside last night," Katie teases us.

Kenna tries to hide her smile when I wink at her but fails miserably. She goes up for one last hit and smashes it down the line over our double block. Dammit, that's hot.

"Should we address the eggplant in the room?" Kenna asks sweetly.

"You mean elephant?" Katie corrects.

"No, I said what I said." She smirks looking down at my tented gym shorts.

"Dammit, Mack. He's my brother. Stop it before I gouge my eyes out."

"I believe elephant was the more accurate descriptor for my dick," I toss back.

Knowing we need to get out of here, and that I do, in fact, now have a raging boner, I grab my water bottle and gym bag.

"You guys go ahead, I'm going to shower here," Katie says.

Kenna looks her over. "Hot date today, right? What's his name again?"

"Blondie, you're breaking girl code. Just get my brother and get out of here, please."

"No need for hostility, Kitty," Carson says as he comes up behind her, squeezing her shoulders. "Gah! Make sure you don't miss the shower, yeah? Wouldn't want your date running off on you—" He's cut off when Katie turns and lightly sack-taps him. "What the fuck was that for, Katie?" Carse groans as he doubles over.

"Just remember the pain you're feeling the next time you want to tease me about something, Carsy-Baby," Katie purrs at him.

I step behind Kenna, wrapping my arms around her, her back nestled against my chest. "And on that note . . . let's get going, Sunshine," I whisper in her ear.

We walk out of the gym holding hands through the parking lot. This time, she beats me to her door while I'm tossing my gym bag in the back of the Jeep.

"Do you want to go home and shower, then grab a bite to eat?" I ask Kenna after I start the Jeep and am backing out of the parking lot.

Her breathing picks up when I reach over and begin rubbing circles along her inner thigh with my right hand. I've come to love doing this.

When we pull up to the stop sign, she turns to look at me. "I was thinking we could—uh, shower at your place."

Fuck. Yes.

That's exactly what I was hoping would happen.

My dad is working a shift at the hospital this afternoon, and Katie said she was meeting up with a guy she met at Jackson's. I know the house will be empty for a few hours, and I intend to utilize every single minute of alone time wrapped up in Kenna.

"Yeah, we can do that," I say, trying to keep an even tone. I don't want to press her on whether or not she meant we'd be showering together at my place, or if she just meant we'd both shower at my place, separately.

When we get to my house, I quickly round the hood of my Jeep to open Kenna's door.

"I'm perfectly capable of opening my own door, Griff."

I know that, but it doesn't mean I'm going to stop doing it. Instead of answering her, I bend down and wrap my arms around the back of her thighs, lifting her over my shoulder.

She swats at my back, struggling to tell me to put her down through her fits of laughter.

Only after I get us inside and up to my room, do I lower her down on the ground.

"Let me get you a towel and start the water for you," I say as I start to make my way to the bathroom.

"Griff, wait," she says as she grabs me around my waist. Turning in her arms so I can see her, I'm surprised to see Kenna somehow managed to take off her shirt, leaving her in only a sports bra and those damn spandex.

"I guess I wasn't clear enough on the drive back here. What I was trying to say was, I think we should conserve water . . ."

"Conserve water?" I ask, hoping I know where this is going. But I need to hear her say it.

"Yeah, you know . . . for the environment and all that," she says as her cheeks heat.

"So, how exactly would you like to conserve water?" I'm goading her at this point, completely failing to hide the smirk on my face.

Hiding her face in my chest, she mumbles, "Are you really going to make me say it?"

"Does my dirty girl need me to wash her off?" I ask as I lift her chin and meet her baby-blue eyes. Her eyelids fall, and lust takes over her gaze.

"Ohmygodthatwashot," she blurts out.

Biting back a laugh, I tell her, "Sunshine, I need you to tell me this is what you want."

"Yes, Griff. I want this—want you." I don't need to hear another word, I claim her lips in a searing kiss that makes me so hard my vision blurs when I finally step back and open my eyes.

"I need to see you, need to feel you on my skin," I implore as I strip my shirt off and start to do the same with my shorts and briefs.

Kenna stops me, covering my hands. "May I?" She takes over for me, looping her fingers into my waistband and dragging my shorts and boxers off of me.

I watch as she strips her sports bra and spandex off next, tossing them next to my clothes.

I look at her, and I'm momentarily speechless. "Fuck, Kenna. You're gorgeous."

She slowly steps up to me, her peaked nipples flush with my chest, making goosebumps erupt from the touch. Her hands make their way to my waist, and she trails kisses down my pecs and abs.

"Come here," I command as I lift her up, her legs wrapping around me as I walk us to my en-suite bathroom. I start the shower and make sure the temperature is good before I carry her inside.

I set her down, but neither of us breaks our embrace as the hot water rains down, drenching our skin.

We both reach for my body wash at the same time, "Let me clean you up, G," she breathes.

Handing her the bottle, she opens it and then pours it onto my chest, letting it drip down my pecs and stomach.

"Your body is a masterpiece, Griffin Turner," I watch her eyes follow the trail of body wash from between my pecs, down my carved abdomen, before landing on the base of my fully-hard cock.

She begins rubbing in the body wash, starting with my chest, shoulders, and arms. Her breath catches as she moves over each rivet of my abs. She bites her bottom lip, eyes connecting with mine, looking hesitant, before rubbing the soap along the base of my cock with a soft, unsure grip.

"Harder," I command, and she complies instantly, causing me to growl my approval.

I pull her into my arms under the rainfall shower head and passionately claim her mouth. Breaking the kiss, I tell her to turn around and begin massaging her shoulders with soap.

My hands explore her body, taking my time as I wash her back, and her toned stomach, then moving my hands up to cup her perfect breasts. She turns slightly, arching her arm around my neck to kiss me.

She breaks the kiss and glances over her shoulder at me, biting that damn bottom lip again, pure temptation.

"Are you going to tease me again? Because you were in this exact position—looking over your shoulder, biting your lip—this morning. It was absolute torture watching you from my bedroom, knowing I couldn't touch you for hours while we were at the gym."

Turning to face me, Kenna explains, "I wasn't teasing you. I was giving you a show. You know, for teenage Griff to live out his fantasies," she says in a teasing tone.

"Is that what that was? Well, if that's the case. Let's check off some more fantasies, shall we?"

"And what would those be, baby?" she practically purrs.

"On your knees, Sunshine," I say in a commanding tone.

Without a moment of hesitation, I watch as my dream girl lowers herself to kneel before me, resting her palms on her thighs.

"What next, Hotshot?" she taunts me with a wiggle of her brows.

The mouth on this girl. I've been dying to have Kenna in this very position—on her knees, ready to wrap her luscious lips around me.

"Fist my cock and suck me like the dirty girl you are."

Kenna stares up at me—never breaking eye contact with me as she fists my cock in one hand, then glides her tongue up along the base of my shaft, circling the tip before taking it deep into her hot, wet mouth.

My hips jerk, causing her to take me to the back of her throat. She doesn't gag, though.

I can't believe McKenna Wilder is sucking me off. She's causing my brain to short-circuit.

Kenna can't quite fit the length of me inside her mouth. She uses her hand to pump at the same time her mouth bobs up and down my cock.

Holy shit. This blowjob is . . . well, it's . . . fucking life-changing . . . mind-altering.

"Jesus, Kenna. Look at you, taking me so well," my hoarse voice barely lets out.

She moans at the praise and begins to touch herself, grinding on her hand that isn't gripping me.

I watch as Kenna pulls back, releasing the tip with a pop before she looks up at me and says, "I want you to let go, Griff. Don't you dare hold back on me."

How can I deny a request like that? I tangle my fingers through her hair and nudge her mouth open, not holding back when I drive my cock to the back of her throat and hold it there a few moments before pulling back.

"Is that all you've got?" she taunts.

I think I'm going to die from her smart mouth. I hinge her jaw back open with one hand and slap her tongue with my length a few times before I push back in. I fuck her mouth ruthlessly, just like she asked. I don't slow down even as she begins to gag.

"Yes. Fuck yes, just like that. I love to see you choking on my cock."

With only a few more punishing thrusts, I'm coming down her throat without warning. The force of my orgasm causes my vision to blur, and I have to catch myself on the tile as I pull out of her mouth. When my vision comes to, I watch Kenna stand up, my cum still dripping down her lips.

I nearly pass out at the sight of her dragging her fingers through the cum and rubbing it over her nipples, causing her to moan.

I pull her against my chest and kiss her with desperation. This girl—this fucking vixen. I break from her mouth, kissing down her chest and sucking her right nipple into my mouth, tasting myself on her. I'm completely untamed at the thought of marking her with my cum all over every inch of her body.

"Fuck, Kenna. I need to taste you," I plead as I nip at her chest, then lick a trail down the valley of her toned stomach. I place a kiss on her right hip bone, skimming my lips across to drop a kiss on the left one.

She grips her fingers in my hair and stops me from moving any lower. "Griff, I-I haven't done this before. Y-you don't—"

Taking in a deep breath along her slit, I look up at her. "I'm going to cut you off right there, Sunshine. I'm absolutely going to, if you'll let me. Because I can't wait to devour this pussy. I've wondered what you taste like for weeks now—hell, years if I'm being honest. So don't think for one second that I don't want to eat your sweet cunt."

"Holy. Fucking. Shit," she heaves, breathless from desire. Kenna gives me a small nod, giving me permission to pursue paradise.

Keeping eye contact with her, I lap my tongue through her folds up to her clit.

That first taste of her makes me come undone. Knowing I'm the first person to give her this experience, to make her come with my tongue, has my dick stirring again.

She tightens her grip on my hair, nearly pulling it out—pushing me on. Gripping her hips, I pin her against the shower wall and place her legs over my shoulders, suspending her.

I devour her like a starved man, not even bothering to come up for air. And when she tilts her hips, grinding herself on my face, I know I'd gladly suffocate in her pussy.

I fall into a state of euphoria at the noises she makes. Each one pulses through me, making my cock throb again with need.

"Oh, fuck! Right there," she moans, and I don't let up, pushing her to the brink. "G-baby—yes!" she nearly screams her release as she comes all over my face.

I lap up her orgasm, slowly bringing her down from her release, placing kisses on the inside of her thighs.

"You are fucking scrumptious, Sunshine."

"And you . . . are a fucking wizard with your tongue," she replies.

I chuckle at her response, rising to my full height to wrap her in my arms. As I come down from the sex-induced high, I find myself needing to ask her if she's okay. "I wasn't too rough with you, was I?"

"I told you not to hold back on me, G. And I meant it. That was perfect."

"Did I hear you scream 'G-baby' when you were coming?"

She's bashful again, trying to hide her blush in my chest. "That may or may not have been what I've referred to you as, behind your back, of course, since I was fourteen."

I angle her head up to meet my eyes. "Don't hide from me, Kenna. I want to know everything. All your truths, remember?"

"All my truths," she repeats as she links our hands together and kisses me deeply. So deeply, it's as if she's etched herself inside my soul.

7

McKenna

JULY

There's a loud knock on my door.

"Everyone decent in there?" Katie asks. "I've learned my lesson by now—I'm knocking, alright?"

It's got to be the actual ass crack of dawn, and Katie's not a morning person. "Why are you awake right now?" I shout to her.

"It's nearly ten o'clock! Griff, I know you're in there. You said we needed to get on the road by nine-thirty. You've boned long enough, let my poor best friend up for some air, and put my bags in the Jeep."

Right. So, *not* the ass crack of dawn. How did we sleep in so late? I guess that's what happens when you exchange orgasms—multiple orgasms, might I add—then stay up talking for hours, wrapped in each other's arms.

I shift in his arms, coming face to face with the most gorgeous, sleepy brown eyes. Placing my palm on his jaw, I say, "Good morning, baby. How did you sleep?"

"Morning, Sunshine. Apparently too good," he jokes as he wraps his arms around my naked torso, warming my skin with his embrace. He kisses me softly, and I let him. I guess I've gotten over my objections to morning breath kisses in the past month.

A month. That's how long it's been since I first felt Griff's lips grace mine. And what a month it's been. We're about to head up north to the cabin for the Fourth of July—the reason Katie said we needed to get up and get in the Jeep.

Every summer, for as long as I can remember, our families have gone up to our cabin on Mille Lacs Lake. I know . . . why would we have a cabin on a lake when we live on a lake? Well, the lake we live on is in the suburbs of the Twin Cities. Our cabin is in Bayview, which is a cute, unincorporated town north of the Twin Cities. It's quaint and the perfect place to reset and unwind. The "cabin," however, is a six-bedroom mansion that my parents inherited when we were young but recently remodeled. It's my favorite place to be, but we don't go nearly enough.

This will be our first Fourth of July up there with just us kids. Our parents are attending a charity gala my mom is coordinating for the hospital Griff's dad works at. They left last night to stay the weekend at the upscale hotel it's being held at.

"We should probably get ready to leave," I say as I move to straddle Griff.

He grips my waist and pulls me down as he grinds his morning wood into me. I can't seem to get enough of this man—even after a night full of orgasms. Although, we haven't taken it all the way yet. He's had no problem scoring hat tricks of orgasms with his mouth, hands, and a lot of dry humping. But I'm ready. I've been ready. There's nothing I want more than to feel him inside of me.

"Mmm—we probably should," he replies in a raspy voice before he pulls me down for a long, searching kiss. Tangling one hand in my hair, he runs his other hand down my spine, gripping my ass in a bruising hold.

"I mean, what's five more minutes?" I ask as I continue to grind and rotate my hips.

"McKenna," he growls, "we need to get going. There will be plenty of this all weekend." He punctuates his statement with one final thrust before he takes my hips and moves me off him.

"Promise?" I pout my lip at him.

He chuckles at my antics and then kisses me on the cheek. "Yes, Sunshine. I promise," he whispers in my ear, causing me to visibly shiver.

I watch as Griff gets up from my bed and pulls on his gym shorts, forgoing his shirt. "I'm going to head home to shower quickly and put mine and Katie's bags in the Jeep. I'll come back up to get yours once I'm done. Think you'll be ready to leave in fifteen?"

"I can work with that," I respond, getting up to give him a quick peck before I shower.

I'm happy to say I was downstairs and ready to leave, with my bag and snacks packed within fifteen minutes. We packed up the coolers last night and put those in the Jeep so we could roll out "bright and early."

"Thank god, you've finally escaped your sex dungeon!" Katie teases me.

"Fuck off, Katie. I don't want to hear that," Carson whines.

"Whatever. I'd just like to point out the fact that my best friend has been far too preoccupied with my brother this summer. The very summer we were supposed to use to have a hot girl summer before college . . ." she points out.

"Kitty, retract your claws. You've seen Kenna every damn day this summer," Carse says.

"I got Funyuns and Dr. Pepper . . . if you forgive me, I'll share my road trip snacks," I bribe my bestie.

"All is forgiven. Give me the DP," Katie says as she makes grabby hands at me.

I watch as Carson spits out the Gatorade he just took a pull from. "Jesus Christ, Kitty. Give a guy a warning before you demand the DP. Which DP would you like . . . double penetration, deep penetration, perhaps a little bit of both?" He prompts with a waggle of his brows.

"What the fuck did I just walk in on?" Griff questions as he wraps his arms around my waist from behind.

"Well, Katie was just asking for the DP. I believe she was referencing the Dr. Pepper I was bribing her with, but now I'm not quite sure," I say as I nuzzle into Griff's embrace.

"Missed you," he whispers in my ear, then places a chaste kiss on my neck.

I giggle in response, wrapping my arms over his, interlocking our fingers around my waist. "You just left my bed . . . I bet it's not even cold yet."

"Are you trying to tell me you didn't miss me?" he questions, grinding his erection into my butt.

I turn in his arms, locking my hands around his neck. "You're insufferable."

"I know, Sunshine. I can't help myself when it comes to you. But, I stand by my words . . . I missed you."

Giving him a quick kiss that he tries to deepen before I pull back, I ask, "Are you all set? I've just got to pack up a few more things."

"Yep, all set. I've already got the most important things in the Jeep—you know, Ranger's food and water bowls, treats, food, and toys."

"What a good Doggy Daddy you've become," Katie teases as she hip-checks Griff on her way outside.

"He's more like a brother than a Doggy Daddy," Carson scoffs when he passes by us.

"The two of you are ridiculous!" I shout at Katie and Carse, then turn my attention back to Griff. "Thank you for doing that. Are you sure you're okay with Ranger riding in the Jeep?"

"He's the best passenger pup. Of course, I'm sure."

"Aren't you worried about all the dog hair?"

"It's the perfect day to have the top off and let the wind blow through Ranger's hair."

"I know. But this is our first Fourth without any of our parents being up there, and Mrs. Anderson down the street said she would watch him. It's different when he's in the back of Carson's truck."

"He's coming, Kenna. It's not the Fourth without Ranger at the cabin."

Why do I love that he said that in a commanding tone? I also love that he knows how much Ranger means to me.

"Alright. Ranger Boy, let's go!" I holler down the hall to where he's lying on his dog bed. A few moments later, I spot Ranger's golden mane around the corner. I'm not biased when I say he's the most handsome Golden Retriever. He just got back from the groomer, so his coat is cut shorter to avoid matting, and he has an American flag handkerchief around his neck.

When he gets to my feet, I bend down and kiss his nose. "Who's my Goodest Boy, huh?" I coo at him as I rub behind his ears. He answers me with licks across my face.

"You are the best, aren't you, boy?" Griffin asks him as he scratches down his back. "Do you need me to grab anything else?" he asks as he meets my eyes.

God, he's so damn handsome. Scratch that; he's downright sexy when he's showering my dog with affection.

I tell Griff we should be all set then he grabs my hand and leads me outside as Ranger follows behind. Griff wanted me to sit up front, but

I told him we should let Carse sit up front, and I'd sit in the back with Ranger and Katie.

We're over halfway to the cabin when the entire car starts scream-singing the lyrics to "You Belong With Me (Taylor's Version)." Listening to Griff sing the lyrics, I can't help but think back to when I'd listen to the *Fearless* album in my room during my freshman year. I'd be sitting in my room, looking out the window, and Griff would be heading out in this very Jeep to pick up a girl for a date. My pining for this man started early, and this song was the anthem for my unrequited crush on the boy next door.

I'm snapped out of my daydream when Griff's gaze connects with mine in the rearview mirror. He winks, and warmth unfurls in my stomach.

The remainder of the car ride is filled with scream-singing more T-Swift, snacking, and stealing glances in the rearview. The drive to the cabin isn't too long—just under two hours—but it both flew by and drug on this time around. Time flies by when we're having fun together, but it drags on at a torturous pace when I want to be wrapped in Griff's arms.

We pull into the circle drive of the cabin, and my chest squeezes with nostalgia.

The cabin has a lodge aesthetic and is expansive from the front, with large stone and cedar beams that score to the second story. My favorite view, though, is from the lake, where the walkout basement is visible. At night, when the house is all lit up, it's magnificent.

Griff and Carse get out of the Jeep, and Ranger jumps out the driver's door, following behind them.

Katie unbuckles her seatbelt then leans over and gives me a hug. "Being here always puts me in the right headspace. Have I told you how much I love you lately? Coming here every summer with you and your family is the best tradition my parents ever started."

I squeeze her back, trying to channel my love for my best friend through our embrace. "I love you too, Katie. I know being here brings back so many memories—mostly good—but I know it makes you miss your mom. Let me know if you need to talk or a shoulder to lean on."

"I promise, if it gets to be too much, I'll come to you. Well, I will if my brother ever lets you disentangle yourself from him."

"Not likely—the entanglement is mutual," I say as we break from our embrace. "But you'll always come first, Katie. Please know that."

"I know, I know. Hoes before bros. Chicks before dicks, and all that." She giggles.

We get out and grab our bags. After a few trips back and forth, the four of us have the Jeep unpacked.

Once we're inside, Griff grabs my hand and pulls me close, wrapping his arms low around my hips. "Which room are we taking this week? Yours or one of the primary bedrooms?" His lips graze my ear, sending chills down my neck and arms.

"We can take the primary bedroom down here on the main level. Katie and Carson's rooms are both upstairs, so . . ."

"So . . . what? Being on a different level won't stop them from hearing you scream my name all night, Sunshine. You're smart, gorgeous, funny, athletic, witty, and all the things, but you're not quiet, my love. At least not when my fingers or mouth are between your legs."

Wiggling out of his embrace, I take the two steps down into the great room—one of my favorite rooms at the cabin. It has vaulted ceilings with exposed cedar beams, floor-to-ceiling windows that overlook the lake, and a two-story stone fireplace. The furniture is oversized to make the space feel cozy instead of cold and grandiose. Mom and Dad replaced the furniture when they remodeled the place four years ago. What used to be a dark, outdated house is now beautiful with warm tones and modern rustic finishes throughout.

I walk to the back wall of windows that overlook the lake and take in the scenery. The room Griff and I are staying in faces the same direction and has a floor-to-ceiling view as well. Griff comes up behind me, making my back melt into his front. I love when he wraps his arms around me like this. I've never felt more safe and secure than I do when I'm wrapped in his arms.

"I think we should get our bags unpacked. I'll get Ranger's food and water dishes set if you want to move his dog bed from your usual room into our room."

Griffin has been so considerate today. It makes me want to show him how appreciative I am of him.

"Thank you. Once you get his bowls set up, will you meet me in our room?"

"Mhmm," he murmurs in my ear, placing light kisses down my neck before he says, "why do I love hearing you say 'our room' so much? Watch out, I could get used to that, Sunshine."

Butterflies swarm out of their cage in my belly, causing me to literally gasp at his comment. I think he takes it as I'm shocked by his words because he chuckles as he steps away into the kitchen. But really, I'm trying to grasp the fact that my wildest dreams are coming true at this moment.

Griffin

I'm standing in the doorway of our bedroom, finishing a reply to the text my agent, Jared, sent me about possible Name, Image, Likeness, or NIL, deals he has in mind for me. He wants me to give him a call after the Fourth of July to go over this new policy the NCAA passed. I tell him I'll get back to him early next week. These deals could be huge for me and my teammates. There are several guys on the team who have to work full-time jobs over the summer to cover living expenses not covered by their scholarships.

The sound of a throat clearing has me looking up from my phone.

In front of me is the most bewitching sight I've ever seen. Kenna is standing in front of me in a revealing, lacy, red bodysuit.

"Holy fuck, Sunshine. You know I love you in red," I say as I close the door and flick the lock behind my back, not willing to take my eyes off her. "What's the special occasion?"

"No special occasion . . . I just wanted to show you how thankful I am for you. Do you like it?"

"Is that a serious question? I love it. I'm obsessed." I pounce on her, pulling her in for a desperate kiss. Dragging myself away from her lips, I step back and circle my fingers at her, signaling her to give me a full look. Kenna turns around slowly, giving me a luscious view of her thong-clad ass. Just above her left hip bone, I notice something stitched into the fabric of her lingerie.

"What is this?" I grasp her hips to stop her from turning.

"I may have stitched your number on here as a little surprise," she says in a shy voice. When I look up at her, her cheeks are flushed, and she smiles bashfully back at me. I look back down and see a small ninety-one stitched in black thread.

"Love, if you keep this up, I'm going to have a hard time going back to Boston in the fall."

Her face falls as the meaning of my words sinks in. Before I can try to reassure her that we'll be fine come the fall, there's a loud knock on the door.

"Stop whatever you're doing and get your asses out here. We're going for a boat ride in five," Carson hollers through the door.

I sigh before I give Kenna's ass a squeeze. "Unfortunately, for what I have planned for you, we're going to need a lot longer than five minutes. *This* is getting put back on later," I demand as I trail my fingers along the fabric covering her pussy.

"Mmm—you're soaked, Sunshine." I groan as I crash my mouth to hers. Right as I'm about to say fuck it to the boat ride, Katie pounds on the door.

"Hurry up, you two harlots!"

"Did she just . . ." I trail off, shaking my head at my sister's antics.

"She did. Come on, we both know she's not moving away from that door until we're both out there."

We change into our suits and head out for a day of wakeboarding and tubing with Carson and Katie before the others get here this evening.

After a late dinner, Kenna and I walk down the steps to the lake and sit beside each other on the dock. It's so peaceful down here, away from the party that's started up at the house. I've always liked being by the water when I'm stuck in my head.

"Every summer, can you just promise me one thing?" Kenna asks, looking over at me.

"Anything."

"Promise me we'll always come back here—to the water, to these moments—and make more memories together."

"I can't think of anything I'd rather do in the offseason. Seeing you in a bikini is always an easy yes," I reply playfully.

She smacks my chest lightheartedly. "I'm being serious! These are the moments I live for. The four of us at the cabin, out on the water, down by the beach, soaking up the sun. Every summer, no matter what happens. Can you promise me that?"

"I'll certainly try my best, Sunshine." I stare back at her, the fading sunlight casting a golden glow on her skin and hair. Next to the water, like this, her eyes take on an almost turquoise hue. She looks angelic.

There's something I've been putting off for the past month, trying to somewhat play it cool, but I need to finally ask her. The sun is setting across the lake, painting the sky in pastels of pink and orange. This is the perfect moment. I just need to man up and ask her.

I take Kenna's right hand in mine and rub circles over the ring on her finger as I look into her eyes and ask, "McKenna Marie." I pause to clear my throat. "Should we make this official?"

"Make what official?" she asks with an unsteady voice, causing my nerves to skyrocket. Shit, did I read this all wrong?

"You know . . . make *us* official. I'd be your boyfriend, and you'd be my girl." I'm proud to say my voice remains steadier than I feel.

"Does that mean you'd be willing to do the whole long-distance thing?" she questions.

"I thought that was obvious by now. But in case I haven't already done so, let me make myself clear. I know I'm asking a lot of you to be tied down in a long-distance relationship your freshman year. I get that this won't always be easy—not seeing you every day, not getting to kiss you, touch you, hold you—but I'd rather put our relationship to the test than have an easy, meaningless one with someone else.

"I'll fly back here to visit you, fly you out to visit me, FaceTime you every possible second I can, and shower you with my affection from afar. What do you say, Sunshine . . . will you take a shot with me?"

"I say . . . is that your way of asking if I'll be yours?" she asks in a teasing tone.

"Quit being a brat," I protest.

Kenna covers her giggles with her left hand and nods her head yes.

"I'm going to need to hear the words, Kenna."

"Yes, Griffin. Of course, I'm yours!"

I do a quick fist pump, then scoop her up in my lap. Our kiss ignites a fire in my chest, and the way I'm feeling is something I've only ever felt when I was drafted. It's exhilarating to know McKenna Wilder is finally mine. Nothing has ever felt so right.

8

McKenna

JULY

T he next morning, I woke up early to an empty bed. My head doesn't pound nearly as badly as I thought it would. We did a few too many shots to celebrate officially becoming a couple and to welcome everyone that came up.

Last night, a group of our friends joined us to stay a few nights. Jackson and his girlfriend Tae rode up together with Bennett, Jackson's older brother, and Griffin's former teammate. Katie and I also invited our fellow freshmen teammates, Alexa and Brooke, whom we'll be playing with this fall.

I roll over to get out of bed, stopping when I see a note on the bedside table that says, *Drink this and take these, xx-G.*

Briefly smiling to myself, I take the pain relievers and drink the water. I quickly go to the bathroom, brush my teeth, put my hair in a braid, and wash my face.

As soon as I open our bedroom door, I'm hit with the mouthwatering scent of bacon and coffee. I tiptoe down the hallway in search of Griff to avoid waking everyone up.

When I turn the corner, I'm not ready for the ridiculously sexy view before me. Griff stands shirtless in front of the gas range, flipping bacon. The dish towel thrown over his shoulder is doing nothing to hide his rippling back muscles, and he's clad in only a pair of low-slung athletic shorts that highlight his bubble butt.

I must actually groan out loud, because a second later, Griff turns, his face lighting up with that megawatt smile of his. He turns down the burners before pulling me in for a scant, tease of a kiss. "Good morning, *girlfriend.*"

With my arms still wrapped around his neck, I reply, "Good morning to you too, *boyfriend.* Although, leaving me to wake up in a cold bed on day one of our relationship might be the cause for our first fight."

"You weren't supposed to wake up for another fifteen minutes. I was going to wake you up with a kiss and breakfast in bed," he says as he kisses my forehead. "So turn around and get your fine ass back in bed so I can spoil my girlfriend on our first official morning as a couple."

Well, when he puts it like that . . .

"No need to twist my arm, I'll be in our bed if you need me."

"Good girl," he says as he smacks my retreating ass.

Griff and I eat breakfast in bed, only coming out after we've both thoroughly riled one another up. Not that we tried to tease each other . . . we were just interrupted . . . again.

Now, we're both in our swimsuits, grabbing Ranger's leash and supplies before joining the others. We've got a boathouse down by the water where we dock our two boats and four jet skis. When we get down there, they're all waiting for us on our pontoon to go to the beach across the lake.

Griffin gets Ranger on the boat, then gives me a hand as I hop on before helping push the boat off the dock. Carson is driving the boat, and with the nine of us plus Ranger, it's a bit snug. Griff pulls me into his lap, draping my legs across his and gripping the side of my hip to hold me snugly against him.

He looks so gorgeously relaxed right now, like there's nowhere else he'd rather be. Griff's got his Ray-Ban sunglasses on, his snapback is turned backward, and his longer hair is fanning out the back. I wrap one arm around his shoulders and play with the hair on his nape.

Leaning into his ear so he can hear me over the boat engine, I say, "You know, you're supposed to save the hockey flow for the season, right? I don't think you've cut your hair yet this summer."

"Do you like it better when it's longer or shorter?" he asks.

"I like having something to grip onto, but when you don't have a hat on right now, it's getting a little unruly."

"I'll have Katie cut it tomorrow," he replies instantly. "I didn't want to take the time away from you this past month to get it cut. Shit, that makes me sound super clingy, doesn't it?"

"That's alright, baby. I love it when you're clingy," I say before giving him a quick peck on the cheek.

We're pulled from our little bubble when we hear Bennett say, "Carse, I'm not going to drink much today. If you want, I can drive us back to the house."

"Yeah, go for it, man. Much appreciated," Carson replies.

"So, Carson, your best friend is dating your sister, and you're dating his sister. Did I get that right?" our teammate, Alexa, asks Carson.

"For the most part, except I'm not dating Katie. What made you think that?" Carson questions, raising his voice to be heard over the roar of the engine . . . I think.

Alexa's cheeks turn pink, which puzzles me. Alexa doesn't seem like the type to blush. From what I've gathered about her so far, she's more outgoing and blunt, whereas Brooke, our other teammate, is more shy and reserved.

"Oh, my bad. I was just getting couple-vibes from the two of you. Katie said she was casually seeing someone, I guess after last night, I just assumed it was you."

I'm trying to sort through my memories of last night to see what would make Alexa think my brother and best friend were an item when Katie chimes in. "Carson is the world's biggest flirt. After a full day at the beach, you'll think he's an item with a dozen different girls. He's all bark and no bite, though."

Carson flashes Alexa and Brooke his dazzling smile. "Don't you worry, ladies. I'm single. Feel free to spread the word across campus come August. I wouldn't want the girls in your dorm to think the world's biggest flirt is taken." He punctuates his sentence by winking at Katie.

I shake my head and laugh at Katie and Carson's banter. These two are constantly giving the other shit when it comes to everything, and that's how it's always been.

Carson slows the boat to a trolling speed as we approach the no-wake zone that surrounds the beach. The Bayview beach is filled with white sand, and my personal favorite: beach volleyball courts.

We find a spot to dock the boat by the waterfront bar and grill that's right next to the beach called The Watering Hole. It's a place we've frequented since we were kids since it's one of the few bars with docks on the lake.

Once we've found a spot on the beach and have our towels laid out, I take off my swim cover-up and then toss my bottle of sunscreen at Griff. "I'll rub yours if you rub mine."

He catches the bottle, then bites on his lower lip to try to stop a low groan from slipping out. It still slips out, and the noise makes my stomach clench in response. I walk up to Griff just as he squirts some sunscreen in his palm.

I turn around so he can rub the sunscreen over my shoulders. Just as he starts to massage it into my skin, he lowers his lips to my ears and asks, "Are you trying to make me hard in front of our friends and innocent beachgoers?"

In my most innocent voice, I respond, "I have no idea what you're referring to."

"Hmm," he tsks in my ear. "Why do I get the feeling you're lying to me?"

I back up a step, just enough to brush my ass against his growing erection. "Need me to take care of that for you? I was referring to rubbing your back with sunscreen, but now I think I need to rub something else . . . Walk with me to the showers?"

Before he can answer, and before I can let my fantasies play out any further, we're interrupted, yet again, by Jackson. "Alright, we've got four college volleyball players, four hockey players, and one future Grammy-award-winning artist. I say we play boys versus girls beach volleyball, and my girl Tae can be the referee."

I hear Carse swear under his breath before saying, "Yeah, G and I tried to take down Kenna and Katie many times already this summer. I can say with absolute certainty, if we play guys versus girls instead of splitting teams up, we're going to get our asses handed to us."

"Damn right, you would," Katie quickly agrees.

"Fine. We split up teams. Kenna and Carson, you two be team captains and split up the teams. Ladies first, Kenna." Jackson gestures toward me.

"I'll take Griff," I say.

"I see where I rank. What happened to hoes before bros?" Katie pouts.

"Awe, don't be jealous, sis. Green doesn't look good on you," Griff taunts her. "Didn't take long for Kenna to love me more than you."

83

Griff says it in a teasing tone. But the reality of his statement sinks in, making my stomach clench for a different reason. Do I love him? I'm definitely falling for him. Hell, I have been for years.

I'm quickly snapped out of my thought spiral when Carson calls for Katie to be his first teammate. Interesting.

"I'll take Alexa," I say. She played a lot of setter in club volleyball, though she likely will play defensive specialist this year. But with Katie on the other team, I need someone who can set the ball well.

Carson takes Brooke and Jackson, and I take Bennett to round out our team. Tae is a good sport and referees the game for us, stating she doesn't have an athletic bone in her body.

The match was neck and neck, with a few volleys that lasted long enough to earn us a crowd of spectators. The crowd cheers on our group of overly competitive college athletes as we go all out diving for plays and putting up double blocks. In the end, my team came out victorious, and I leaped into Griff's arms in celebration.

After that intense match, we're all sweating and needing a break. Griff tightens his hold on me, refusing to put me down, as he sprints toward the water. He flops to his back once the water reaches his waist and crashes us into the water. The cool rush feels amazing against my skin. This summer has been milder, so the water isn't too warm and still feels refreshing.

"Are you having fun, Sunshine?" Griff asks, his hands gripping my ass as I wrap my legs around him under the water.

"So much fun. But I can't wait to get you alone later."

"Mmm," he groans into my neck as he places kisses in the way I love, from my collarbone up to my jaw. "I think we should head back now. That game left me famished."

"I've got snacks in the coolers. What do you want? I've got cheese and summer sausage, chips—"

"Kenna, I can't exactly feast on what I'm craving at the beach," he cuts me off, punctuating his statement by grinding his erection into me.

My cheeks flush. "Oh, right. Well, I think we're going to have to put a pin in that for a little bit longer. Rain check?"

It's been a really great Fourth of July so far. We spent the day soaking up the sun, playing volleyball, football, and paddle boarding. Once we got back from the beach, we grilled out and started a fire.

The whole group is currently sitting around our firepit at the cabin, making smores, listening to Jackson play the guitar, and singing a duet with Tae. They've played a few covers, and they sound amazing together—their voices harmonize beautifully. They're currently singing "Kiss Me" by Sixpence None The Richer, and it's making me want to sneak away with Griff and do just that.

I've been very patiently waiting for an opportunity to arise, and I turn to ask him to sneak away when he says, "The fireworks are going to start soon, Sunshine."

"I don't want to watch them out here. There's a better spot where we can watch them."

"Do you have a secret spot you've been holding out on all these years?" he asks incredulously.

"No, I just don't want to watch them out here with everyone else. There's a really good view of the fireworks over the lake from our bedroom patio."

"Are you sure you don't want to watch them with everyone else out here?"

"Exactly, everyone will stay outside to watch them . . . meaning we can finally be alone for some uninterrupted time together."

"My girl is so damn smart," he says, grinning as his mouth covers mine.

The rest of the group is so entranced in the song, that they don't notice us sneak off toward the house.

Once we close the sliding glass door to the house, Griffin picks me up bridal style. He carries me with such ease—it makes me feel feminine in a way I'm not used to with other guys. I couldn't be. They couldn't make me feel small in their arms. But this man, this gorgeously chiseled man, makes me feel vulnerable in the best way.

Griff doesn't set me down until we're standing in front of our bed. He cups his hands around my jaw, pulling my bottom lip down with his thumb.

"God, I love your lips," he rasps before crashing his lips against mine in a searing kiss. My stomach flutters, and I can feel heat pooling between my legs.

We continue to kiss while Griff begins undressing me. He slides his fingers up under the hem of my swim coverup, pulling his lips from mine so he can slowly peel it over my head. He places open-mouth kisses along my collarbones as he tactfully unties each knot of my swimsuit until it pools at my feet. Griff's shirt and board shorts quickly join the pile of discarded clothes.

We fall onto the bed; he moves me up toward the headboard in a swift move that ends with his cock grinding against my bare pussy.

"Mmm—I'm going to worship." *Kiss.* "Every fucking inch." *Kiss.* "Of your scrumptious body." *Kiss.*

He drifts his lips across my chest, pulling my nipple into his mouth, making me moan. His eyes connect with mine, and his face lights up with that wicked smile of his. Those dimples should come with a warning label.

CAUTION: Guaranteed to melt your panties.

He places a single kiss on each of my ribs as he moves lower, causing chills to erupt across my body. When he groans, the sound ricochets in my stomach, sending tingles straight to my core.

A zap of pleasure hits me when his hand cups my bare pussy. It's sensory overload—his hands and lips all over me. I can't concentrate on what feels best before he lands on a new spot that feels even better.

Griff strokes my clit in just the right spot, causing my hips to jolt off the bed. I grind into his hand, my wetness coating his fingers. He takes two fingers and plunges them deep inside of me. His thumb continues to circle my sensitive bundle of nerves as his fingers hook inside of me, finding that devilishly deep spot that makes me soar above myself in an out-of-body experience. I could come just like this.

Just as that thought enters my mind, Griff slips his fingers out of me and hovers above me on all fours.

"Spread your legs wider for me, Sunshine. I want to see how turned on this sweet pussy is for me," he says as he moves down and shoulders his way between my legs, linking his arms around my thighs to keep me from moving. "Fuck, Kenna. Your pussy is glistening for me."

Griff licks me in one long stroke, his tongue flat, from my entrance to my clit.

My building orgasm comes roaring back, his tongue stroking my entrance before moving back to my clit. When he begins sucking my clit with fervor, my eyes roll to the back of my head, and I think I'll pass out from the intensity of the pleasure—of this moment.

A needy moan escapes my mouth just as Griff slams two fingers back inside me. The combination of his fingers hitting my G-spot and his tongue working magic on my clit sends me soaring into a climax I can only describe as other-worldly. My legs shake and spasm. For fuck's sake, I'm convulsing over his face and fingers.

"Oh, fuck. G—oh my god!" I scream into the pillow, trying to drown out the noise.

Griff continues to work me through my release, pressing light kisses along my thighs and hip bones as I come back down to earth.

Griffin

I kiss my way back up Kenna's body, worshiping each swell and valley with my lips and tongue. Tiny goosebumps appear as my mouth moves along her soft skin.

When my trail of kisses finally leads back to her mouth, I devour her, tangling my tongue against hers, giving her a taste of herself. I grind my hips into hers, loving how my cock glides against her wet pussy. Deepening the kiss, I continue to drive my hips into hers. This feels so good—too fucking good. My cock is so hard I could come just like this.

"I need you, Griff. Please don't make me wait any longer," she pleads. I'm desperate for her too, but for some reason, I'm a complete asshole and need her to beg before I bury myself inside her.

"Tell me exactly what you need, Kenna," I demand.

"I need you to fuck me," she says as she tugs on my hair. "I can't stand the thought of going another minute without knowing what it feels like to have you inside me."

Needing to be inside of her as much as she wants—needs—me, I leap from the bed to get a condom from my wallet.

Kenna's eyes widen. She bites her lip as I tear the condom wrapper open with my teeth.

I pause at the look on her face. "You look like you're hesitating, Kenna. We can wait if you're not ready."

"Don't you dare. I'm ready—I'm just trying to figure out how you're going to fit inside of me without splitting me in two. You're huge. I mean, I knew you were huge. It's just seeing it now, and knowing where it's going, you're . . . well, huge."

I'd be lying if I said hearing her say that didn't inflate my ego tenfold. "Trust me, Sunshine. We'll make it fit. You're so ready for my cock; you're making a mess of the sheets."

Heat flushes her cheeks, and I shake my head at her. "I didn't say that to embarrass you. It turns me on so fucking much—you're going to feel so good."

"Then stop talking and make me come again," she sasses.

My fucking Sunshine.

Settling between her knees, I run my length up and down her slit a few times, before slowly pushing inside her a few inches. I groan at the way her pussy clenches my cock.

"Griff," she whimpers. "So full."

"I'm not even all the way in yet, baby. Take a deep breath for me so I can slide home."

She inhales, and I do just that, slamming my hips flush against hers. Holding myself there so we can both adjust.

"Fucking *fuck*. You're so tight—" I grit out, trying not to finish from how fucking euphoric her pussy feels.

"Oh, god. Move. I need you to move, Griff."

I start to pump in and out of her. Quickly realizing I'm not going to last long. She's so fucking wet. So fucking tight.

Pulling out of her, I flip us over so she's straddling me. "Ride me, Kenna,"

She lifts herself up on her knees, lining my cock up before she sinks down. My eyes nearly roll to the back of my head. Nothing has ever felt this good. I look down at where Kenna's pussy is strangling my cock.

"You're such a good fucking girl. Look at your pussy taking me so well," I urge her, pointing her chin to look down at where my cock moves in and out of her.

She looks down, biting her lip to suppress her moans. I take her lip from between her teeth. "I want everyone in this house to hear you scream my name when you come."

I grip her hips and begin to frantically piston my hips up into her, using my thumb to rub her clit to get one more orgasm out of her.

"Yes—Griff. Don't stop, *ohmygod*—don't stop."

I'm definitely *not* going to stop.

"Come for me, McKenna," I command.

"Right there . . . yes. Yes—Griff!" she cries out as her pussy convulses around my cock, squeezing it so tight I think I might pass out. I ring out every ounce of pleasure from her, before gripping her hips tightly and finding my own release. White spots cloud my vision as I come down from the most intense release of my life.

Kenna doesn't move to get off me. She just pulls me up flush against her chest and kisses me. Her legs wrap around my waist, and my softening dick gets aroused at the feel of her still around me.

"It's seriously never been like this, never felt so good."

Kenna shifts, grinding her hips in circles, before she mockingly says, "Are you telling me that I just rocked the world of *the* Griffin Turner?"

"You fucking ruined me, Kenna," I admit truthfully. She slowly lifts off me, and I give her a quick kiss on her forehead before heading to the bathroom to take care of the condom.

When I get back into bed, Kenna is pitched up on her elbows, looking out the floor-to-ceiling windows that overlook the lake. Just as I join her, wrapping one arm over her back, the fireworks start booming over the lake. Ranger, who I didn't realize was in here during our lust-filled haze, jumps up onto our bed and nuzzles his head under Kenna's elbow.

"Oh, buddy. You're still scared of the fireworks, aren't you, boy?" she asks him before turning to me. "I didn't even know he was in here. Hopefully, he isn't scarred from what he just witnessed."

Laughter roars out of me when I see the worried look on her face. "Did you know dogs can smell pheromones? So any time we've been even remotely aroused by each other over the past month, Ranger has sensed what was about to happen. I wouldn't worry, baby. He's not scarred; if anything, he's jealous."

"My poor baby's been corrupted by us," she whines as she wraps her arms around his neck.

As we sit together watching the fireworks show with Ranger, I realize I've never been more at ease, never felt more at home than I do at this moment. I could get used to this little life, and even though we'll have years of distance ahead of us, there's no one else I'd want by my side than McKenna Wilder.

9

Griffin

JULY

I'm having the most intense dream. I think it's the after-effects of having sex with Kenna for the first time. The feel of her wet lips wrapped tightly around my cock is so realistic, I smile to myself as the hazy edges of the dream start to fade. Only, as I open my eyes and my vision begins to clear, I see the most divine sight in front of me.

I have to bite my lip to keep my loud groan from escaping. The sight before me is spellbinding. Kenna's on her knees, ass in the air, her lips wrapped around my cock, cheeks hollowed. I think I just discovered my newest addiction.

This is the best feeling in the world. No, that's not true. What would make this morning's surprise even better would be for Kenna to straddle me and sink down on my cock like she did last night.

"Did I just die and wake up in heaven?" I rasp, my voice thick with sleep and lust.

Kenna's lips literally pop off my dick—her sly smile spreads across her face, her eyes alight with mischief.

"Good morning, baby," she purrs as she straddles my hips.

The moment her wet heat meets my dick, I'm a lust-struck fool. I grip her hips and quickly roll her onto her back.

"Are you sore?" I ask, hovering my weight above her.

"Not really sore. It feels more like the good muscle fatigue you wake up with after pushing through a hard workout the day before. But that's never stopped me before, and it's not going to stop me today. Get a condom on and get inside me, Griff."

I love when she's direct and tells me what she wants. Leaning over her, I grab one of the condoms from the pack I placed on the nightstand last night.

I sit back on my heels while I roll on the condom, getting my fill of Kenna's gorgeously naked body, spread and on display for me. She inhales sharply as I continue my gaze down her torso.

I brace my elbows beside her head, tangling my fingers through her hair. Using my knee as leverage, I thrust so deeply inside her I'm not sure where I end and she begins.

Now that I've been inside Kenna, I'm not sure I'll ever get my fill of her.

She grips the sheets as I pick up my pace, grinding my hips into hers with each thrust. Her pussy begins to flutter around my cock, and it doesn't take much to bring me to the brink of my orgasm.

"Fuck, are you close? I don't want to come until you do."

"Then make me come," she demands.

As soon as the words leave her lips, I sit back and grab her ankles, placing them on my shoulders. I wrap my arms around her legs, almost as if I'm hugging them. This new angle allows me to fuck her so much deeper, and my girl loves that.

"Play with your clit for me, Sunshine," I command.

She complies as I begin fucking her ruthlessly.

"Griff, you're so deep. Right there, baby."

I deliver a few more punishing thrusts before I feel her pussy pulse and clench my cock. Her orgasm sends me spiraling, and I follow right after her.

I release her legs and pull out of her. "You're going to be the death of me, Sunshine."

Once I take care of the condom and clean us up, I pull Kenna into my arms. Her hair and skin smell like oranges, summer, and something entirely Kenna. It's intoxicating.

I smile to myself, basking in this moment. "Morning sex might just be my new favorite thing."

Kenna's head snaps up from where it was resting on my chest. "Am I supposed to believe you've never had morning sex before?"

"I have not. I've never spent the night with anyone but you, so the opportunity never presented itself."

"So you never spent the night with Emily over the nearly two years you were together?" she asks in disbelief.

"No, I didn't. I know this sounds bad, but she was mostly my girlfriend in name only. We were constantly on and off again. I think she liked the status that came with dating the big guy on campus. We didn't really discuss things beyond the surface level. Hell, I think we only went on three dates that whole time, and they were in a group setting. My relationship with her was superficial, but it was mutually beneficial. She got the status, and I had some of the puck bunnies lay off me."

"I'm not sure what to say to that. I mean, it makes me feel better knowing things with her weren't on the same level as they are with us. And I'm glad we were both able to experience what it's not supposed to be like before we got together."

"What do you mean by that?"

"Well, thanks to Drew, I now know what it's like to be with someone who projects all his insecurities and paranoia on me. He wouldn't accept me trying to end things several times, yet he was sleeping with other girls from the moment he moved into his dorm last year. I tried ending things before he left, but he kept saying we would make it work. I'm just glad I had checked out of the relationship long before I found him cheating on me."

"Wait, you found him cheating on you?" I ask, bewildered.

"Yeah. I went to visit him at his dorm. It wasn't even a surprise. He knew I was coming to visit that afternoon."

"He's such a fucking idiot for letting you slip through his fingers. But I've never been more grateful for another man's stupidity."

Kenna sits up, and stretches her arms above her head, causing the sheet to drop down and expose her bare breasts. After she finishes a yawn, she says, "I think I need a solo shower this morning. Sorry, baby."

"No need to apologize. I'm going to get some breakfast and start the coffee. Meet me in the kitchen when you're done," I tell her, giving her a quick peck on her shoulder.

I've just poured a second cup of coffee for Kenna when she enters the kitchen. I look up to find her wearing my favorite Emery Elites Hockey T-shirt. I'm so distracted by how good she looks, that I overflow the mug, spilling hot coffee all over the counter.

This girl will be the death of me. I'm so gone for her. I know I said I couldn't afford distractions, but she pushed me in ways I can't even begin to explain.

I leave the cup of coffee on the counter and wrap my arms tightly around Kenna, palming her ass before giving it a squeeze. Moving my scruff across her cheek, I gruffly say into her ear, "You look so fucking delectable in my favorite shirt. Welcome to the dark side. Emery red has never looked so good, Sunshine."

"I agree. But I look better in Abbott University maroon and white."

Removing my hands from her ass, I cup her face and cradle her cheeks. I stare into her eyes as if she's the most precious thing in the world—which, to me, she is. Every moment with her is better than the last. I didn't even hesitate to ask her to be mine the other day.

"I could get used to this—waking up to my girlfriend giving me the hottest head of my life, walking to breakfast in nothing but my shirt, letting me bend her over—"

She puts her hands over my mouth, cutting me off before I can finish detailing my next fantasy.

I lift her onto the kitchen island, spreading her legs so I can stand between them. Trailing my lips up her neck, I whisper in her ear, "I want to bend you over this island, push up this T-shirt," I say as I fist it in my hand, "run my hands over your tight ass cheeks, squeezing them before I spread them so I can slide my cock inside your dripping pussy in one, smooth stroke."

Kenna's breath hitches. Her gaze filled with lust. "You're insatiable," she whispers.

"I'm addicted to you, Sunshine. To your lips, the way you taste on my tongue, to your citrusy perfume, the way you come undone beneath me. I'm not sure I'll ever get my fill of you." It's true, I am addicted to her. She's turning me into the neediest man in the world. I can't stop thinking about her; craving a chance to see her, talk to her, touch her, kiss her.

Before we can take it any further, the front door opens. A very sweaty and shirtless Bennett walks in, pausing mid-way to take his AirPods out when he sees us. He shakes his head and goes up the stairs without saying a word. Bennett isn't much for confrontation, or conversation, for that matter.

Even though Bennett didn't call us out, Kenna still places her head in her hands to try to hide her embarrassment.

"Don't," I tell her, tilting her chin up to meet my eyes. Her eyes and nose wrinkle at me in question. "Don't for one second be embarrassed by us. I'm not and never will be."

"I'm not embarrassed by us. I'm mortified by the fact that I wasn't embarrassed at all." She shifts her gaze away from mine. "The idea of being caught kind of . . . excites me."

"Damn it, Sunshine. Now my nights in Boston are going to be filled with fantasies of my little exhibitionist." I skim the outside of her thighs and tell her, "Hop down before one of our siblings comes down."

Kenna hops down and follows me to the counter where I've set our cups of coffee and started prepping breakfast.

"Omelets sound good to you?" I ask her.

She looks up over her mug and nods in response. I start cracking eggs into a mixing bowl, and when I move to chop up the vegetables, Kenna hip-checks me out of the way.

"I've got the veggies. Will you start the bacon, sausage, and ham?"

I take the towel I always have slung over my shoulder when I'm cooking, and gently swat her butt with it. "Careful, Sunshine. This weekend has already got me fantasizing what it'll be like when we're living together."

Kenna's answering smile is damn-near blinding. "Is that right? Aren't you getting a little ahead of yourself, Hotshot?"

"No, just hoping for as many moments like this as possible over this next year when we're long-distance. I plan to put a very large dent in my bank account from Airfare."

"Same, baby. And I'm not even mad about it."

We leave it at that, knowing we're not ready to burst this bubble with talk of long-distance.

Kenna opens her Spotify app on her phone to play music. She absolutely refuses to cook without being able to sing and dance. She plays "Fearless (Taylor's Version)," and like everything when it comes to Kenna, I just can't help myself from singing along with her.

After a day full of wakeboarding, tubing, and wake surfing, my muscles are sore, and Kenna and I are both dead on our feet. We opted out of going to the carnival Jackson and Tae invited us to, so once we finished eating dinner, we headed to our room to watch a new Jason Statham movie.

"How about a bath first, Sunshine?" I call out from our ensuite.

"Mmm, I'd love that," Kenna responds from where she's perched on the end of the bed.

I fill the soaking tub with the bath salts, oils, and bubbles that are sitting on the ledge next to the two glasses of red wine I set there. The tub is big enough to comfortably fit the two of us. We've taken enough showers together by now that I know Kenna prefers to melt her skin off, so I fill the bath with scalding hot water.

Steam rises from the tub as Kenna enters the bathroom completely naked. Thankfully, the floor-to-ceiling windows have reflective film on the outside, so nobody else gets to see Kenna like this. I can't believe she's mine.

I strip down and sink into the hot water. Kenna follows me in, sitting in between my legs with her back against my chest. She rests her head against my chest, closes her eyes, and sighs in contentment.

"What would you do if you couldn't play hockey professionally?"

The question catches me off guard. Not many people are interested in asking me questions that aren't related to hockey.

"At first I majored in sports management as kind of a way to coast academically while still getting my degree. But I think if I wasn't able to play anymore, whether it be because of injury or retirement, I want to be an agent. I like working with Jared, and his story is what made me decide to sign with him. Did you know he used to play hockey professionally? He was drafted second overall in 2015, but he had to quit after only three seasons due to having too many concussions."

"I think you'd make a really good agent. You're smart, charismatic, and you can bullshit with the best of them, which means you could schmooze any young gun to sign you as their agent."

"What about you, Sunshine? What do you want to do after college?"

"I know it's a farfetched dream considering I'm only eighteen and the average age of the Women's US National team is somewhere in the mid-twenties. But I want to be a part of that team someday. I'd love to play professionally for a few seasons. But if those dreams don't work out, I want to coach and teach. I've always loved working with kids, especially young athletes."

"Dreams are meant to be just out of reach. If they aren't somewhat farfetched, how are you supposed to push yourself and work for them? Kenna, I've never met someone as determined and as passionate as you. This dream of yours is within reach, and I can't wait to cheer you on when it comes true. But, if for some reason it doesn't work out, I have to tell you that you'd be the hottest teacher and coach that ever existed. You should probably consider teaching at an all-girls academy, though."

She playfully nudges her elbow into my ribs in response to my antics.

I love getting to see these different sides of Kenna. She's not just confident; she lets me see her shy side when she's being bashful; she lets me see her playful, competitive side; she lets down all her walls, free from inhibitions around me. How fucking lucky does that make me?

"Do you ever think about the future? I mean, aside from hockey, do you ever picture what kind of life you want?"

Again, her question takes me by surprise.

Note to self: Kenna not only gets horny, but she gets philosophical after two glasses of wine.

"Of course. Honestly, at times, thinking of the future makes me angry because I know I'll be experiencing more firsts without my mom there to see. She won't see me sign my first NHL deal or play my first NHL game. She won't be at my wedding or meet any of her grandkids. It's hard to accept that. But, yeah, I picture my future."

"What do you see when you picture it?" This question comes from her as more of an unsteady whisper.

I intertwine our fingers together and pull her tighter against my chest. Then I nuzzle my head against hers while telling her, "I picture nights like these. You'll be wearing my ring on your finger—your *left* ring finger. You'll be a little tipsy from the wine we had at dinner with our friends. You'll still be asking me about our future, and I'll tell you I want to start making babies—lots and lots of babies. Then we'll start making those babies, or practice making them, at the very least. And I'll pull you against my chest and fall asleep with you in my arms every night, just like I will for the rest of our lives." I can so easily picture it—I *have* pictured it several times.

She closes her eyes and smiles. "I can see it too. Sometimes, I just wish we could skip to the good part, you know? But I love making memories like this weekend to look back on."

I hum in response, rubbing slow circles across her stomach and hip bones. The sheer fulfillment I feel in this moment is unmatched by anything else I've ever experienced.

"Are we crazy for taking on a long-distance relationship that will likely span like four years after only being together one summer?"

I tense at her question. I understand why she asked it, but I won't lie, it makes me nervous to think she's apprehensive.

"Sure, we're crazy. But think of how badass our story will be when Katie and Carson are recounting it at our wedding someday?"

"You're certifiable. And again, you're getting a little ahead of your-self. You're supposed to wait at least six months before you start showing all your cards."

I reprimand her by tickling her ribs. "Well, get used to it. You're stuck with me now, Sunshine."

Doesn't she see it? Realize it yet? She owns me. Every last piece of me.

10

McKenna

AUGUST

It's college move-in day tomorrow for campus athletes and I'm in my room putting the last few pairs of shoes in bins. There's a loud thump before I hear, "Oh, fuck!" from Carson's room.

Sighing deeply, I move down the hall and knock on his door. "Everything alright in there, Carse?"

I'm met with deafening silence, so I try the doorknob to find it's locked. "Carson, are you okay? I heard a loud noise, and I know you're in there. Will you just tell me you're alright?"

A few moments pass, the silence eating at me. Then, finally, Carson opens his door, seemingly out of breath and covered in sweat, before he replies with, "Yeah, everything is fine. Just had a trophy fall off the shelf."

"Right . . . well, I'm glad you're okay—" I stop short when I hear a light giggle from the other side of the door. A laugh that sounds *very* familiar.

"What the hell? Is that . . . is that *Katie*?" I demand.

Appearing from the other side of the door and looking quite disheveled, Katie says, "Oh, please, Kenna, as if you could talk! But before you get your panties in a twist, it's not what it looks like."

"Uh-huh . . . and what exactly does it look like?"

"Like I was just giving Kitty a life-changing orgasm?" Carse guesses. "He most certainly was not." She turns and swats his chest. "I was helping Carse pack some of his shit to avoid packing up my room. I was getting too emo packing up all my pictures. Anyways, a trophy did fall—the most prized one—the one from our wheelbarrow relay race."

"Show me . . . I'm having a hard time believing Carse wouldn't be crying in the corner if that were the case."

"Hey, I'm not that big of a pussy. Besides, we said it fell. It didn't break."

"Don't talk about parts of the female anatomy you know nothing about," Katie snarks, crossing her arms across her chest.

Carson rubs his palm across his chest, feigning hurt. "You wound me. But it makes me feel better knowing you're so obsessed with my sex life, Kitty."

"Oh, please. You'd have to actually *have* a sex life for me to be obsessed with it," she retorts.

"Delusion doesn't look good on you. In fact, neither does jealousy. If you want to know what it feels like to receive an orgasm from a man, I'd volunteer as tribute," Carson propositions.

Katie's face turns red before she snaps back, "I told you that in a moment of weakness. I'd rather get fucked in the ass by a cactus than receive an orgasm from you."

I think I might die from laughter. It's hard to breathe through the belly laughs. Sometimes I feel like I'm watching a ping-pong match with these two. The back and forth is both hilarious and exhausting.

"Do you see what I have to put up with now that you stole my best friend?" Carson gripes. "G never wants to hang out with me anymore because he's too caught up in you."

"Alright, alright. Katie, let's leave Carse to his packing. I just finished up, so why don't I come over and help you finish?"

"You're going to wish you didn't make that suggestion when you see the disaster that is my room," Katie says as she makes her way down the hall toward the stairs.

I hold back a second, looking at Carse. "Do I have anything to worry about here?"

He gives a chin nod in the direction Katie just retreated. "The only thing you have to worry about is Kitty eating someone alive with that mouth of hers."

Shaking my head I say, "That's not what I meant. Do I need to worry about you breaking my best friend's heart? I can see something has changed between the two of you. I'm not blind. We're all going to the same college. So I'm going to ask again. Do I have anything to worry about?"

He breathes out what sounds like a defeated sigh. "No, you don't, but you have to swear not to say anything."

"Okay, I swear."

"We kissed once over the Fourth of July. It was stupid. We were both drunk, and we agreed nothing else would ever happen."

I'm not really shocked by his admission. More so hurt that Katie felt like she couldn't tell me when that happened over a month ago.

"I'm not surprised that it happened. So I take it you're not the mystery guy she was seeing?"

He shakes his head. "No clue who that was. But, no. There hasn't been anything going on behind anyone's back. It was one kiss, and no offense, it was like kissing my sister."

I chuckle at that. "None taken. I'm going to help her pack up. We've got an early morning tomorrow. Are you ready?"

"Fuck yeah," he hollers, scooping me into his arms. "From diapers to dorms. Look at how far we've come."

Shaking my head, I reply, "You're such a dork. Now get packed so we don't miss our arrival time."

The next morning comes faster than I had imagined. Carson, Katie, and I each rode in separate vehicles due to the sheer amount of stuff we had packed. Carson rode to his dorm with my dad while I rode with my mom. Katie rode with her dad, but Griff's Jeep pulled in behind them, packed to the hilt with bins, bedding, and more clothes than Katie would ever need this year.

Today is move-in day for athletes on campus. From what I've heard, the fall and winter sports are the only teams moving in today. We were one of the earliest move-in times.

Katie and I requested to be roommates, and our dorm room is on a floor full of jocks, most likely because it's the closest to the practice facilities. Our dorm is co-ed, but from the sounds of it, only the men's basketball, golf, and wrestling teams are in ours. Carson's dorm is just across the road and houses the football and hockey teams.

"Are you planning to ever wear the same outfit or pair of shoes twice? I think you packed your entire closet. You do remember we live like fifteen miles away, right?" I ask her after taking the fourth trip full of just her clothes up the two flights of stairs to our dorm room.

A few girls from the soccer team are across the hall when we round the corner. Griff is in front of me and Katie, giving me the best view of his bubble butt in his athletic shorts and form-fitting T-shirt.

As we passed the girls in the hall, I heard one of them ask, "Oh my god, is that Griffin Turner?"

Then the girl next to her says, "He's easily the hottest college hockey player."

Finally, the third girl chimes in. "Didn't he get drafted? Wait, do you think he's transferring here?"

Great. As if I wasn't already nervous about when Griff goes back to school, now the last three weeks we have together are going to be filled with girls hitting on him whenever he visits me.

The NIL rules that were passed a few months ago have already allowed Griff to make a few lucrative deals with major sporting brands. He's made deals with Bauer, Gatorade, and Lululemon already. Which means his face is all over social media and ads. Therefore, Griffin Turner has turned into a poster boy athlete for women to fawn over.

I know he would never cheat on me, and the heightened notoriety hasn't gone to his head. But I'd be a liar if I said it didn't add to my nerves about our long-distance relationship. My ex, Drew, cheating on me while we were long-distance doesn't help either.

Once we get to our room, Griff sets down the bins he's carrying, grabs the hangers from my arms, and tosses the clothes on Katie's bed.

"Come here, Sunshine." He pulls me in for a hug, wrapping his arms around my waist. He bends his head to whisper in my ear. "I don't want you to worry about anything, Kenna. I'm crazy about you—some might say obsessed."

I smile at his attempt to reassure me. "I know you are, and I am, too. I know you'd never cheat on me, Griff. But I'm not going to lie and say I won't be jealous of the fact that other girls get to ogle my man when we're long-distance. But I'm sure that's nothing a little FaceTiming can't fix."

He sighs in relief, most likely because he's used to drawn-out fights with Emily over other girls. "What kind of FaceTime calls are we talking about?"

I pull away and innocently respond, "Oh, you know. The kind where you show me the goods no one but me gets the pleasure of seeing."

Griff chuckles and pulls me back into his chest. "Mmm—I think I can do that. As long as I get to see my girl like no one else does, too." He brings me in for a kiss that is far from innocent.

"Ahem!" Katie interrupts, breaking us apart. "G, I think we're all done with your muscle services for now. Why don't you lend me back my bestie for the rest of the day so we can get our room set up and do some girlie shit."

"Alright, alright. I'll take your not-so-subtle dismissal and leave," Griff replies before bringing me in for another quick kiss and a tight hug. "FaceTime me later, Sunshine?"

I laugh at his lack of subtlety—it's just as bad as Katie's attempt. "I'll call you later. We've got to figure out plans for Jackson's party on Friday, too."

Once he shuts the door behind him, Katie grabs my hand and sits on my empty bed.

"Can you fricken believe it?! We're freshmen in college. We're rooming together. And we're both starting training camp in a few days as college volleyball players on the same damn team. What a time to be alive, Mack!" Katie squeals with excitement.

I turn my head to look at her. "You're more than my best friend—you're like the sister I never had, Katie. Of course, we're doing this together!"

All of a sudden, and out of nowhere, Katie bursts into laughter. "Remember yesterday when you thought Carson and I were hooking up? That shit was hilarious."

I want so badly to tell her I know she and Carson kissed, but I'll let her come to me with that when she's ready. Instead, I suggest, "We could save a ton of money if we did a double wedding."

"Dear god, Mack! The only wedding I foresee happening between a Turner and a Wilder is you and my brother."

If that ever happens, I have no doubt it will be the best day of my entire existence.

Training camp began two days ago, and so far, it's been brutal as hell. It's been early mornings, two-a-days, hitting the weight room, team meals, team bonding, and meeting the coaches and training staff. Call me a masochist, but I've loved every second of it. Getting to compete at this level is what I've been working for since middle school. It's why I've sacrificed missing countless weekends with friends, school dances and events, and even dates with boys.

So far, the upperclassmen have been welcoming to me, Katie, and the two other freshmen, Alexa and Brooke. I've been surprised to find how tight-knit the team is already, even though we're all competing with each other this week—giving our all to stand out to make the final roster, get playtime, and become starters.

Coach Hendrix has already pushed me harder than any other coach has, and it's only the first week. Katie and I are both playing well. Our connection on the court shines through during every drill and scrimmage we compete in on the same team.

I was completely spent by the time our team dinner was over tonight, but when I got back to our dorm, a package was waiting for me at the security desk. I thanked Fred, the security guard on duty, and then headed upstairs to take a much-needed shower.

I nearly forgot about the package until I was ready to crash on my bed, where I set it before my shower.

My exhaustion wanes a little as I open the box and discover the contents. Inside the box is a card that reads:

Sunshine, I just signed a deal with this company, and I told my agent I'd only do it if I could get you one to use as well. I know you're crushing it at training camp. Hope this helps recover your sore muscles on days I can't be there to massage them for you. xx—G

My heart stutters the way it always does when it comes to Griff. I put the card on my nightstand table. It's probably weird, but I've kept every little card and note he's given me so far. I know I'll want to look at them when we're in the thick of our long-distance phase.

I turn back to the box and grab what looks like a hard shell carrying case. I open the case to find a rechargeable massage gun with several different detachable heads.

After putting the battery in and attaching a sphere-shaped tool, I FaceTime Griff.

He answers on the second ring, his shirtless chest and chiseled jaw filling my phone screen. "Hey, Sunshine."

"Hi, baby. Guess what?" I ask, but I don't wait for his reply. "I got a package in the mail today."

As soon as the little machine starts percussion, massaging my sore quad muscles, I moan. It probably sounds like I'm masturbating, but this might honestly be more satisfying than getting myself off.

"Jesus, Kenna. I think we're going to have to add FaceTime sex to our long-distance arsenal. The sounds you're making from just that massage gun touching your quads make me think I should get you something smaller to massage your clit while I'm away."

"I don't have any toys." I feel my cheeks heat as soon as the words leave my mouth. It's not that I'm opposed to them, I've just never been able to bring myself to purchase one.

Griff's smile turns devilish. "Consider it done. Now, tell me how training camp went today."

I continue to massage my sore muscles, practically purring from the relief I'm already feeling. "It went really well. Coach played me and Katie on the starter's side of the court for a few drills and our last scrimmage of the day. Hopefully, that means we'll see a little playtime in some of the games this season."

"That's my girl! You and Katie both worked your asses off this summer, so your coach was bound to see that. Mark my words. You'll be a starter by the end of the season."

I smile down at his face on my screen. "Your confidence is both sexy and slightly misplaced. I think Katie has a good chance of beating out Zoe for the starting setter position, but I've got two other girls vying for the same outside hitter position."

"I don't know if you've heard, but my girl is a beast on the court. Her nickname in high school was Mack Attack because every hit was a kill."

"You're a dork," I tell him, shaking my head.

"Yeah, but you still miss me like crazy," he retorts.

"You're right, I do. Why can't it be Friday night yet?" I whine.

Griff's answering chuckle plays through my speakers like a soothing melody. "Only two more sleeps until I get to fall asleep with you in my arms."

"Jeesh, I need to watch my back. I've got a stage-five clinger on my hands. Counting down the sleeps until we're together again?"

I can't wait to fall asleep in his arms and be cocooned in his warmth.

Griffin Turner has turned me into an addict, and I can't complain one bit.

Friday morning brings the first warning signs that I can't ignore. My back started aching as soon as I woke up, and my boobs felt heavy and sore like I've got two sacks of sand in my sports bra. I'm praying I can make it through this final day of training camp before Mother Nature drives a stake through my uterus.

I've been dealing with my endometriosis symptoms since they started progressively getting worse freshman year of high school. Unfortunately, the combination of being an early bloomer and my family history of endo means my symptoms have become intense—sometimes debilitating.

I've been on birth control since my freshman year of high school. My doctor suggested taking progesterone-only pills so my estrogen levels wouldn't get any higher. My periods have been irregular—sometimes, I can go up to three months without getting one. My last period was before graduation and lasted over a week, with cramps so intense I had to miss several days of school.

I barely made it through the second practice before returning to my dorm room to lie down. Griff and I were supposed to go out tonight with Carson and Katie, but I texted our group thread earlier, letting them know I wouldn't make it. Katie tried to tell me she was staying with me, but I told her she was not missing out on the end-of-summer party at Jackson's. It was most likely the last time everyone would get together before going to different colleges and down different paths.

The pain in my back and abdomen is crippling, so I put on my rattiest pair of sweatpants and grab one of the T-shirts Griff gave me now that we can't sleep together every night. I even sprayed some of his cologne on them. I bring the shirt up to my face and take a deep inhale of his signature woodsy scent. I'm still standing in my sports bra when a knock sounds at my door.

"Open the door, Sunshine."

Why did I think Griff would still go to the party without me?

I open the door, not surprised to find Griff on the other side. What surprises me are the grocery bags he's holding in his hands. I must give him a questioning look, to which he just shrugs in reply.

"I heard my girl was feeling under the weather," he says as he walks by me to set the bags on my desk.

"That may just be the understatement of the year," I state.

Griff grabs my hands and pulls me into his chest. "Come here. I can see just by looking at you how much pain you're in. Lie down and let me play hot nurse," he jokes.

He pulls back my comforter and I take his suggestion and lie down. "What's with the bags?" I probe.

Griff's hand goes to the back of his neck, the way it does when he's nervous, and he feels the need to tug at his hair.

"Oh, right. I-uh . . . got some supplies. I didn't really know what you'd want or need, so I just kind of winged it." He grabs the bags from my desk and sets them on my bed before sitting off the edge next to me.

"I didn't know if you had a heating pad with you or not, so I got one of those. Then I saw these heat therapy patches that I thought you could wear at practice. Well, that was probably a dumb idea. You'll be sweating at practice, so you probably won't want the added heat—"

I grab his hand to stop him from pulling out the next item from the bag and tell him, "Those look amazing. I'm definitely going to try those out. In the past, I've had to miss school, practice, and even a game because of my cramps. This is so thoughtful, Griff." I start to choke up.

"Of course, anything to make my girl feel better," he says before continuing to dig through the bags. "I got a mix of snacks . . . some kettle corn, pretzels, those chocolate-covered peanuts you like, Funyuns, Dr. Pepper, Gatorade, and sour gummy worms."

"So you basically bought out the entire pharmacy," I deadpan. "You didn't have to do that, but thank you. I love y—I love how thoughtful you are."

Oh my god. Did I just seriously almost blurt out that I love him in a hormone-induced haze?

Thankfully, he didn't catch my almost-confession, or he's taking pity on me. Either way, I'm relieved.

A little while later, we're watching *The Proposal* on my laptop that's propped up on my nightstand. Because rom-coms and Ryan Reynolds make everything better.

Griff has me cradled in his arms, my body curled around him, my head resting on his chest, while he rubs my lower back. The feel of his calloused fingers pressing into my skin feels so good that it distracts me from my pain, causing a quiet moan to slip out.

His deep voice tickles my forehead. "So, I was doing some reading and—"

"That's never good," I mockingly cut him off.

"Don't be a brat. Anyway . . . I was doing some light reading and came across something that piqued my interest. Did you know that having an orgasm helps relieve period cramps due to the oxytocin and dopamine that's released?" he asks in a casual tone as if this were just another random conversation.

"I didn't know that. Why were you reading about that?" I press him.

"Katie may have mentioned that your time of the month is more intense than most. I wanted to see if there was anything I could do. Hence, the supplies and, if you're up for experimenting, the orgasm I plan on giving you."

I shake my head furiously back and forth. "No. Not-uh. Not happening. If you see anything that is going on down there, you'll never want to give me another orgasm again."

113

"Chill out, Sunshine. I'm not going to eat you out."

Well, at least we're both clear on that.

"I've made you come plenty of times by just grinding against my dick," he says before adding, "and just so we're clear. I am not opposed to shower sex during your time of the month. I'll close my eyes or do whatever you want if it'll make you feel better."

I'm not sure I could get past the embarrassment I'd feel if we did have sex while I have my period.

Griff pulls me from my thoughts when he asks, "Where did you put that massage gun I got you?" The twinkle in his eyes leads me to believe he's up to something.

"It's in the case on the bottom of my side table. My back is pretty tender, so could you use the lowest setting?"

"Oh, I don't plan to use it on your back, Sunshine." He smirks. "Do you trust me?"

"Of course I do," I reply without hesitation.

"Roll onto your back and spread your legs slightly."

I comply, eager to see where he's going with this. Griff places two of his fingers over my clit, circling them over my sweatpants.

A rush of heat floods my core, the way it always does when Griff touches me. He kisses me deeply. The combination of the way he tastes on my tongue and his spicy scent fills the air—he consumes me.

He grabs the massage gun and turns it on the lowest setting, straddling my thighs. Placing his two fingers back on my clit, he uses his other hand to hold the massage gun. The moment he places the massage gun against his opposite hand and his two fingers begin vibrating against my clit, my hips jerk in response. The way his legs bracket mine in place keeps me from bucking off the bed.

The combination of the vibration and the way his fingers play my clit like a fiddle have me coming undone in under a minute. My orgasm takes me to new heights, and just like Griff read, as the high subsides, I notice my pain has, too.

Griff puts the massage gun back, then motions me to drape myself over him, just how he likes. But I don't want to receive without reciprocation. As I start to lower myself between his thighs, he stops me.

"Sunshine, tonight was about you and helping alleviate your cramps. Now get that fine ass back up here so I can snuggle my girl while we watch a movie together."

I do as he says because how could I not? I mean, in a hormone-induced haze, I almost spilled my feelings for him. I'm not sure he's ready to hear those three little words just yet, but damn, do I feel them with every fiber of my being.

11

Griffin

AUGUST

The Sports Pavilion, where the Bobcat's volleyball team is about to take the court, is packed. The band is playing, amping up the crowd of spectators, and Carson and I are seated in the front row of the student section, behind Abbott's service line. The crowd roars when the home team comes jogging out of the locker room and onto the court. Tonight is Katie and Kenna's first home game. They've both been working their asses off in practice and training camp for the past two weeks. After warmups are over, the Bobcats stand beside their bench as the lights dim and a spotlight is directed at the human tunnel they've made.

"Ladies and gentlemen, welcome to the Sports Pavilion, home of your Abbott Bobcats as they take on the Michigan Lakers!" I hear the announcer boom before he begins listing Michigan's starting lineup.

"And now, starting for your Abbott Bobcats . . . Starting at setter, a freshman, standing at five foot eleven inches from Edina, Minnesota, number twenty, Katieeee Turnerrrr," the announcer roars through the speakers.

"Holy shit, did you know she was starting tonight?" Carse smacks my chest when he asks.

"I had no clue," I confess.

"Staring at outside hitter, a freshman standing at six feet tall from Edina, Minnesota, number twenty-one, McKennaaaa Wilderrrr," the announcer says as the crowd cheers.

"That's my sister," Carson shouts so loud, I see Kenna's shoulders shake from laughter. "Please tell me you had no idea she was starting either." Carson looks at me accusingly.

"You know how it goes, Carse. Coaches sometimes make game-day decisions with lineups. I'm just as pleasantly surprised as you are to see that our freshmen sisters are in the starting lineup. Thankfully my old man and your parents were able to make it."

The announcer has finished listing off the rest of the starting lineup and Katie and Kenna stand beside one another at the service line during the National Anthem before running to the net to do the pre-match handshake. I can't imagine having to shake the opponent's hands before an intense game.

The Bobcats lost the coin toss, so they're on serve receive. Katie and Kenna did some elaborate handshake with each other before taking their positions on the court.

From where we're seated, Kenna is only a few dozen feet ahead of me, bent over in a ready position. I'm drawn to the way her black spandex shorts cling to her ass. Apparently, so are a few other guys standing behind us in the student section. And apparently, they have a death wish.

"Bro, look at number twenty-one's ass. If that's what the incoming girls look like, I'm going to have to reconsider my no-freshmen hookup rule," one of them declares.

Before I can say a word, Carson stands up, turns around and says, "Hey, asshole. That's my sister, so why don't you shut your damn mouth before me and her hockey-playing boyfriend rearrange your face."

117

The guy's face pales when he looks between the two of us, sizing us up and realizing he and his buddies are no match for us.

"Sorry, man. Just a bit of harmless hackling with my bros. No disrespect."

"Well, keep my sister out of it, or we'll have a problem. Got it?" Carson doesn't wait for a response. He turns back to face the court just as the first set starts off with a serve aimed right at Kenna.

She receives the ball with a damn near perfect pass to Katie. Katie sets the ball high and outside to Kenna. The opponent attempts to put up a double block against Kenna, but it does nothing to stop the punishing hit Kenna smashes right on the line.

The whistle blows, calling the play dead as the announcer says, "Point AU! That's Wilder's first career kill with the Bobcats."

Fuck yes. That's my girl.

The Bobcats dominated the first and second sets of the match. The third set is currently underway, and they're quickly on their way to sweeping Michigan. Watching Kenna and Katie live out their dream right before me fills my chest with pride.

A timeout is called by Michigan's head coach and Carson and I just took a seat when he says, "They're killing it, man. I honestly didn't think they'd get much playing time tonight, let alone start."

"I know. They don't even look phased that it's their first college game. I was so scared my first game that I threw up before it started. Then proceeded to puke between each period."

"No way. The cool and confident Griffin Turner had the anxious pukes?" he asks in disbelief.

When they take the court again, Kenna is up to serve. She tosses the ball up and slams a hard jump serve just over the tape of the net.

The announcer cuts in, "Point AU!"

"Fuck yeah! That's her third ace of the night!" Carson smacks my chest as if I could take my eyes off her.

I know what it takes to get where she's at—the chances of playing at the college level are slim, but dominating the game the way she is as a freshman—it's the next level.

A few points later, Katie ends up getting an ace of her own to end the match.

When Kenna emerges from the locker room, she spots me across the court and runs up to me, jumping into my arms, wrapping her legs around me, and crashing her lips against mine. Fuck, I'm going to miss not being able to do this after every single one of her games.

As I remove my mouth from hers, my entire body rebels, wanting—needing more of her.

Not here in front of everyone. Get her back to her dorm first.

When we get back to Kenna's dorm, it's just the two of us. With Katie's help, I set up a surprise for Kenna in her room earlier.

Kenna opens the door, inhaling a sharp breath when she looks inside. Above her bed are nineteen balloons stringing from the ceiling, with pictures attached to each one, and a balloon banner above her bed reads "Happy Birthday," with the gifts that I got her wrapped on her bed.

"Griff, are you kidding me? This is the sweetest thing ever! Thank you so much." She jumps in my arms, and I grab her ass as she wraps her legs around my waist.

After breaking from a tease of a kiss, I say, "Of course. I have to make sure my girl has the best birthday. Now that you've not only won your first game, but started and dominated, it's time to celebrate."

"How long did it take you to do this? When did you do this?" she asks as she wiggles out of my arms.

"Katie gave me her keycard to get in after the two of you left for your game. It didn't take long to place them in here. Katie is better at wrapping presents, so she came home yesterday to help me do that."

"This looks too pretty and heartfelt to touch." She brushes her fingers along the black wrapping paper and bows covering the gifts.

Kenna reaches for the balloons to look at the pictures. She gasps when she sees what's written on the back of each photo. Each photo has a number written on the back, one through nineteen, that describes nineteen things I love about her. I watch as she carefully peels the photos from the balloon strings and places them in order.

The first photo is a picture of Katie, Carson, Kenna, and me at the bus stop on their first day of kindergarten.

Kenna reads aloud, "One: I love that you still gave me a chance even though I used to pull your pigtails." Her answering giggle lets me know she's picturing the many times I used to chase her and then tug on her hair.

"See, I've tried subtly telling you my feelings since we've been kids," I playfully tell her.

Kenna shuffles to the next photo; it's the two of us cuddled with Ranger. "Two: I love that you're a package deal." Her eyes water when she looks up. "I miss having him snuggle me every night."

I exaggeratingly grab my chest, feigning hurt. "And here I thought it was me you missed snuggling up to each night."

Rolling her eyes at my theatrics, she shuffles to a photo of us making breakfast together at the cabin. "How did you get this one?" she asks.

"Katie took it one morning and sent it to me. I've been gatekeeping it for this surprise."

She shoulders me and continues, "Three: I love waking up beside you and making memories like this with you."

Kenna continues to shuffle through the photos, reading off things I love about her on the back of each one. "Seventeen: I love that when I look into your beautiful eyes, I feel at home." Shuffling to the next one she reads, "Eighteen: I love your passion and drive. You can do anything you set your mind to because of your determination."

As she gets to the last photo, a throwback to after one of my high school hockey games when she came to watch Carson, she reads, "Nineteen: I love that we're each other's biggest cheerleaders. I can't wait to be by your side as our dreams continue to come true."

As she finishes reading, she looks up at me, eyes full of unshed tears. "You're seriously the best, baby." She's looking at me with such awe that it makes me want to give her little surprises every day for the rest of our lives.

I'm hopelessly in love with her.

It's not like I was surprised at this revelation. I've been hooked on McKenna Wilder since we were kids. But seeing her face light up when she sees me, getting to see her first thing in the morning, convincing her to kiss me with morning breath, watching her come undone beneath me, getting to hear her hopes and dreams, and picturing myself beside her, cheering her on, all of it has made me realize I'm absolutely gone for this girl.

I'd do anything to make her happy, to keep this look of bliss and contentment on her face.

I think I may have always loved her. I just didn't know what to call it then.

"McKenna," I start but have to clear my throat. "I not only love all of those things about you, but I love *you*. So fucking much it hurts. It's always been you, Sunshine."

121

The unshed tears she was holding back fall down her cheeks, and I quickly move to wipe them away with the pad of my thumbs.

"I love you too, Griffin. God, do I love you. You've quickly become my best friend. I used to think my crush on you was one-sided. But after seeing all of this"—she points to the balloons and pictures now splayed across her desk—"I believe it's always been us."

I wrap her up in my arms, breathing her deep in my lungs. "I'm going to wait to break it to Katie that she's no longer your best friend."

Kenna's answering laughs help stop her tears, and when she tries to playfully swat my chest, I grab her hand and place quick kisses along each of her fingers before trailing them up her wrist, elbow, arm, collarbone, neck, and cheek before finally claiming her mouth in a deep kiss.

It doesn't take long for the kiss to deepen. I back Kenna up to her bed, stopping when I realize her gifts still litter it.

Breaking the kiss, I grab the gifts and set them on her desk. "Do you mind if we wait to open your presents?" I ask Kenna, giving her a devilish smirk.

"How do you know Katie won't be barging in here soon?" Kenna questions.

"Well, for starters, she doesn't have her key. Then there's the fact that I asked her not to come back here until after I give her an 'all clear' text."

With that settled, Kenna helps me move the presents to the desk. Once she sets down the last one, I turn her around and begin stripping her out of her T-shirt and sweats.

My cock strains painfully behind my zipper at the sight of Kenna completely naked.

"Get on the bed and spread your legs, Sunshine," I command. "I have one present I think you should open now."

Kenna readily complies, and I don't try to hide my groan of approval. I grab a small wrapped present off her desk and hand it to her.

Quickly tossing my shirt in the corner, I push my pants and boxers off in one go. I kneel on her bed and nudge my shoulders between her thighs.

"Fuck, Kenna. Your pussy is glistening for me." Leaning down, I give her clit a long, languid stroke. She answers by grinding down on my face.

She's fumbling to open the present, but I can tell the moment she realizes what it is.

"Griff, what is this?"

"It's a g-spot vibrator. I thought after the other night you might like to use this one when I'm in Boston and we FaceTime each other. Or just, you know, whenever you're missing me." I give her a wink before grabbing the vibrator from her hands.

"I charged and cleaned it before I wrapped it," I tell her, running the silicone through her slit, getting it nice and wet for her.

"Ready, Sunshine?"

Kenna bites down on her bottom lip and nods her head.

I turn it on, clicking through some of the different vibrating modes until I find one I think she'll like.

Circling her entrance first, I guide it up. The moment it touches her clit, her hips buck off the bed, and she moans loud enough to echo the halls.

I sit up and pull back my hand, leaving Kenna wanting and full of lust. "I'm going to need you to be a little quieter if you don't want your RA to interrupt us for a noise complaint. Do you think you can do that for me?"

She hastily nods in response.

"Good girl." I punctuate my statement by grinding my hips into her, sliding my cock along her pussy.

I place the vibrator between us, right against her clit. The combination of the vibrating and the noises she's making is sending me barreling toward an orgasm right along with her.

I'm so wrapped up in this moment that I don't even realize until I've thrust in and out for a few slow, torturous strokes that I'm not wearing a condom.

Quickly pulling out, I say, "Shit. I didn't put on a condom."

Kenna grabs my face, halting my movements to reach for my wallet. "You don't need to—I mean, I'm on birth control. I-if you've been safe before like I've been, we could—"

I look down at her, cutting her off. "I've never gone without a condom before. I'm negative. I got checked at my physical and haven't been with anyone but you since."

"I'm negative, too. I want to feel you with nothing between us," she says breathlessly.

"Are we really doing this?" I ask, hovering over her.

"We can be each other's firsts for something," she says sheepishly, pulling me down for a kiss.

I break the kiss so I can look into her eyes. "I don't care about being your first for anything, Sunshine. I want to be all of your lasts," I insist before lining myself up between her legs. I run my length up and down again, before slowly inching my way back inside her.

Nothing has ever brought me so much pleasure as the way her bare pussy suffocates my cock.

I want to drag this moment out as long as possible, so I slowly thrust in and out of her. Each time my hips meet hers, I grind my pelvis against her clit, driving her to the brink of climax.

We kiss with lazy, passionate strokes of our tongues, and the vibrator is long forgotten at this point.

This doesn't just feel different because I'm taking her bare. But because we're not just fucking. For the first time in my life, I'm making love, and, fuck, if that doesn't make my chest both swell and tighten . . .

Kenna has quickly become my everything. When you have almost a lifetime of history the way we do, it doesn't seem so crazy to free-fall, leaving all inhibitions in the wind.

It only takes a few more grinding thrusts for Kenna's pussy to clench violently around my cock. I ring out every last quake of her orgasm, finding my own release alongside hers. I come deep inside of her, my cum filling her. The sensation is so intense I almost pass out, and my vision blackens.

Trying to avoid slamming my full body weight on Kenna, I roll us over onto our sides without pulling out of her. I need to hold onto this feeling with nothing between us for as long as I can.

"That was the best birthday present ever," Kenna pants, looking blissed out.

"That was the best sex ever. Period. And it's not just because I fucked you raw, either, so don't even start with that."

She stares into my eyes. "I could feel everything so much more. It felt like I'd never come down from my climax once you came inside me," she admits.

"The feeling of your pussy clenching me without a barrier was incomparable to anything I've ever felt."

When I feel my dick softening, I pull out of her, but I can't stop myself from scooping up my cum that was spilling out of her and deeply fingering it back inside her pussy.

"I want to mark every inch of your skin. Does that make me sickly possessive?" The question slips from my lips against my will.

"It's probably a red flag, but I must be fucked up because it turns me on," is Kenna's shy reply.

"Let me get you cleaned up, Sunshine. We've got a reservation to make. And before you ask, no, I won't tell you where—it's a secret. But thanks for letting me have dessert before dinner."

She claps her hands together and whines, "Oh, come on. Tell me where we're going, baby. It's my birthday!"

"Nope. I'm taking the woman I love to dinner, and it's remaining a surprise."

"Say it again. Tell me you love me."

"I love you, Sunshine. So fucking much it's not even funny."

"I love you too, G. I don't think I've ever been happier than I am at this moment."

Her happiness is all that matters to me. I want to make each day the happiest of her life. Forever.

12

McKenna

SEPTEMBER

Katie and I arrived at Boston Logan Airport early on Friday morning. It's Labor Day weekend, so our coach gave us the weekend off, and we don't start classes until Tuesday next week. Our trip was a last-minute decision to surprise Griff, so we couldn't sit together on the flight here.

I know I said it was to surprise Griff, but as soon as we made the decision to come, we called him to see if he was okay with it. He moved in earlier this week, so aside from our daily FaceTime calls, I haven't seen him in five days. I know, I'm pathetic. But can you blame me for being insanely needy? We declared our love for each other before he came inside me for the first time, and then he moved across the country the next day for the start of our four-year long-distance relationship.

Now, Katie and I are waiting by the arrivals terminal for Griffin to pick us up. We're sitting on a bench, resting our ankles on our carry-ons.

"Are you excited to visit Griff?" Katie turns to look at me.

I can feel her gaze. "I am, but I can't help but have a minor case of PTSD when it comes to visiting my boyfriend at college now. Don't get me wrong, I know Griff would never cheat on me, but the fear from my past is still there."

"While I don't blame you, just know that Griff is completely obsessed with you. I know he's one of the top prospects for the NHL next year, but in Boston, everyone treats him like he's a god."

"I know. I remember you saying that when you and your dad spent Christmas break here last year because of his hockey schedule. And I saw it first hand the few times he visited me on campus."

She nods in acknowledgment. "I figured you already knew, but I didn't want you to feel blindsided by the amount of attention he receives here."

I nudge her shoulder and thank her for the head's up. The sound of a horn pulls our attention to the curb. Griffin gets out and rounds the hood of the vehicle. I don't waste any time, quickly hopping off the bench so I can leap into his arms.

"Sunshine. I missed you so fucking much." Griff squeezes me in his arms. His familiar scent fills me with longing. The feel of his arms surrounding me makes my heart swell in contentment.

"I missed you more," I say and instantly feel needy as fuck.

He pulls back and, as if reading my mind, demands, "Don't. We're mutually, pathetically, sickeningly in love with each other."

"You can say that again," Katie chimes in. Griff places me back on the sidewalk, and we both turn to look at Katie. "Oh, did you forget about me? Where's my big welcome hug, G?"

Griff opens his arms and motions for her to come give him a hug. Katie pulls away from the hug and jousts him on his side. "I'm just giving you two shit. You know I've shipped you two from the start. How else is my bestie supposed to become my sister-in-law and auntie to my kiddos someday?"

Instead of Griff outwardly freaking out, he just shakes his head at his sister and replies, "Just don't make us an aunt and uncle too soon, Katie Cat."

She beams at him, then turns to me, "So when's the wedding?" she asks, completely ignoring his comment.

"You're hopeless," I tease.

"Wrong. I'm actually full of hope. That's how I just *know* this is going to end up just like I've always envisioned. Kenna, in a beautiful white dress, walking down the aisle to my amazing big brother, who will be bawling like a damn baby."

Katie shakes her head and holds her hands up in surrender. "Alright, alright. I'll lay off for now. But promise me one thing." She looks over at me expectantly.

"That depends," I reply.

"Promise me I'll have the best seat in the place. I don't want to miss a single tear or snot bubble on Griff's face—" She hasn't even finished her teasing before Griff tackles her and tells her to get in the car.

"I'll let you take shotgun, Kenna," Katie calls over her shoulder. "After all, it's been five whole days since my brother got to hold his girl's hand." She turns on her heel and shouts, "Oh, G. You're *fancy*. Thanks for picking us up in style."

Griff shakes his head as he places our luggage in the back of the Mercedes he pulled up in.

"Whose G-Wagon is this?" my question comes out high-pitched, my voice laced with panic.

"This is my roommate's. He let me borrow it to come to get the two of you. I keep my Jeep in Minnesota, remember?" He answers.

"Right. I miss riding in your Jeep. Not going to lie, I was so excited to see you I didn't even notice this earlier."

"Good. I missed being the center of your attention," he says, grinning as his mouth covers mine.

I pull away and tell him we better get going. Once again, Griff opens the passenger-side door for me, gesturing for me to get in. I thank him, and then we're off.

"Where's your new house? Who are your roommates this year? Do I have to share a bedroom with the two of you? Fill us in." Katie rattles off and Griff takes her questions in stride, smiling.

"Same house as last year. We've got the same roommates aside from Slater. He moved out in the spring since he got signed after our season ended. We haven't voted on who gets his room yet, so that's where you can sleep, Katie Cat."

"Sweet. That way, I can finally get a break from hearing the two of you go at it," Katie says.

Wanting to detour that comment and curious to hear more about his roommates, I request, "Give me a rundown on your roommates. You've mentioned them here and there, but I don't think I can keep them straight."

"Alright, we've got the Russians, Maks and Nico. They're brothers. They were born in the US, but they're one hundred percent Russian and have slight accents; ergo, we call them the Russians. Maks is the one with black hair and a slight beard. Nico has lighter hair, is covered in tattoos, and he's six-foot-six. Then we've got Emmett, he's our resident nerd on the team. He's wicked smart and will probably win a Nobel Prize for curing cancer or something. Emmett will likely have his glasses on, he only puts contacts in to play."

Griff's house is only about seven miles from the airport; however, with mid-day traffic, it takes us closer to twenty minutes to get there. We pull up to the curb of a brownstone that's within walking distance of both campus and Fenway Park, according to Griff. He says he was looking into getting us tickets to a Red Sox game, but hadn't managed to snag them yet.

"I love it. It's so charming," I tell him.

"Yeah, it's alright. Not entirely what I'd choose for myself. But I can't beat free housing and getting to stay with some of my teammates. A lot of the team lives in the housing accommodations along this block. But most are only for two or three people. Ours is the biggest, with five bedrooms, so we host most of the team hangouts here," he says as he grabs our luggage from the back.

The concrete steps lead up to a gorgeous dark oak door with a full-length glass panel, on both sides and above the door are framed by glass windows. The exterior doorway is framed by an intricate stone that shows the character of these homes.

When we enter the house, however, we come face to face—well, face to *everything*—with one of Griffin's roommates, who I'm guessing is Maks.

Griffin

Maks is a total slut. He knows it, we know it, and he's completely unapologetic in his pursuit to fuck his way through campus. The guy has no qualms when it comes to his sexual escapades. I've seen him naked, buried deep inside nameless chicks, more times than I can count. Currently, Maks has a busty chick with fire-engine red hair splayed out on the dining room table.

I don't even try to hide my anger when I tell him, "Come the fuck on, man. You can fuck in every other inch of this place, aside from my room. But I'm putting my foot down when it comes to the place we fucking eat. Put your dick away, I told you my sister and girlfriend were coming this weekend."

Completely unashamed, Maks pulls out of the chick and nods his head toward the steps, signaling for her to head to his room. He doesn't even bother to cover his sheathed dick as he tells her, "Mine is the first door on the right. I'll be right up."

While she makes her way up the steps, he goes to the kitchen to grab a water bottle from the fridge. He stands in the middle of the kitchen, in all his naked glory, and chugs the entire bottle before tossing it in the trash. As he walks by us, he winks at Katie, whose jaw is still hanging wide open.

When he finally saunters his ass up the steps and out of sight, I turn to Katie and a blushing Kenna, "I'm sorry about that. Maks is, well . . . Maks. I'll talk to him again later and make sure he keeps himself in check for the rest of your stay."

Katie's shit-eating grin is followed by, "Oh, but I think I like him unchecked. That was something I wouldn't mind seeing more of, actually."

"Katie, don't even think about it," I warn.

"So, what? You can fuck and date my best friend but I can't ogle any of yours?" Katie huffs.

Not wanting to have this argument, I suggest we put our bags in our rooms and go out to lunch instead. Katie's stomach answers with a loud rumble, and we decide to go to an Irish pub a few blocks down, right off the Boston Harbor.

Later that night, there's a knock on my door.

As I open the door, I say, "You don't have to knock to come into our room, Sunshine."

Maks' smug face is not what I was expecting to see. "Hey, *Sunshine*, mind if I come in?" The way he mocks me amplifies his Russian accent.

I sigh. "What do you want, asshole?"

Maks, being the pain in the ass he is, shoulders his way into my room. I shut the door behind me and turn to face him.

"Look, I wanted to apologize for earlier, G. Fuck knows if any of you asshats ever pulled something like that when my baby sis was visiting, I'd hang you by your scrotums, slit your throats and watch as you bleed out, drip by fucking drip."

Well that's . . . oddly specific. Sometimes the shit that comes out of Maks scares the piss out of me.

He clears his throat. "Anyway, I wanted to make up for it. Here," he says as he places six Red Sox ticket stubs into my hand for I assume me, Kenna, Katie, Nico, himself, and Emmett.

I only catch a glimpse of the tickets before my head shoots up. "Maks, you crazy motherfucker, these seats are right behind home plate. How in the hell did you get these?"

"Let's just leave it at I know a guy who owes me a few favors, so I decided to cash in on one of them." His smirk is accompanied by a devilish glint in his eyes.

"Well, thanks, man. This almost makes up for me having to hear my little sister talk about your, and I quote, 'monster cock,' all afternoon."

Maks just chuckles. "I'm not even going to go there. Let your sis and your girl know we're pregaming tomorrow at the house before the game. Tell your sister not to worry, I'll get her there with plenty of time to watch the guys warm up in their tight baseball pants."

"Jesus." I shake my head. "I'm sure she'll appreciate that tidbit."

"I'm headed out. Later, G."

Once Maks makes his way down the stairs, I head across the hall and knock on Katie's door.

Kenna opens the door, biting her lip as she takes in my shirtless chest and light gray joggers.

133

"Maks just came by to apologize for earlier and gave me these," I say, handing the tickets to her.

"Are you for real? Katie, we're going to Fenway and we'll be right behind home plate!" she exclaims.

"Fuck, yeah! I can't wait to watch the catcher and the ump squat down in front of us all game."

"What the fuck, Katie Cat?" I groan. Turning to Kenna, I ask, "You just about ready for bed, Sunshine?"

Katie interjects before she can respond, "Griff, it's like ten o'clock. Are you seriously not taking us out?"

"Not tonight. We're going to pregame here tomorrow before we head to Fenway. Then Maks will probably throw an after-party, too. Get some sleep for tonight, and we'll save the shenanigans for tomorrow."

"God, you're such a buzzkill sometimes, you know that? Don't try to act like you're looking out for our best interest. You're trying to fulfill your need to have Mack in your bed for as many hours as you can before we fly out on Sunday."

"I won't even try to deny that's true. But can you blame me?"

"No, I can't. Now you two get the fuck out so I can relive that scene we walked in on earlier today."

"Seriously, Katie. What the actual fuck is wrong with you?" I whine.

Kenna and I make our way back to my room, and I'm on her as soon as I turn the lock.

"Finally, I thought I'd never get you alone," I tell her.

Her answering giggle gets muffled by my lips against her.

"I love kissing you, Griff. I could kiss you every minute of every hour of every day for the rest of our lives and it still wouldn't be enough."

"Fuck, Sunshine. I love hearing that. We've got a lot of making up to do. Five days without you has felt like an eternity. Come here." I sit at the end of the bed and pull her onto my lap.

My cock stirs as Kenna straddles me.

In a matter of seconds, our clothes are shed and scattered along the floor, and Kenna is resuming her position straddling my lap.

I run my cock along her pussy a few times before she pushes my hand aside and damn near impales herself on my cock.

Holy. Fucking. Shit.

"God damn, McKenna."

Her only answer is to quicken her pace. I match her pace, thrusting into her fervently.

"You're so tight . . . you're choking my cock, Sunshine."

"Choke me back," she insists. I pause her movements, staring into her eyes to make sure I understood her correctly in my sex haze.

Kenna pulses her pussy around me before pulling her hips from my grasp and slamming back down my cock. "I said. Choke me."

I only hesitate a second before wrapping one hand around her delicate nape.

"Oh, fuck!" she loudly moans.

"Shhh, Sunshine. I need you to be a good girl and keep quiet," I whisper, applying slightly more pressure around her neck. That does the trick. Within seconds, Kenna is staring into my eyes as her orgasm takes hold of her.

I feverishly pound into her pussy, nearly passing out as I spill into her.

Removing my hands from her neck, I pepper soft kisses atop the light pink marks they left.

"You're going to be the fucking death of me, McKenna."

"But what a way to go," she quips.

What a fucking way is right.

McKenna

Our flight back to Minneapolis was the latest flight we could get on Sunday evening, so we arrive in Minneapolis sometime around one in the morning.

Classes start on Tuesday, so we wanted to have as much of Monday to get ready for our first day of college. I've always loved the first day of school. The first day is like the start of a new chapter; the slate is wiped clean, and the possibilities for new beginnings are endless. That's even more true for the first day of college.

Katie and I are in the back of an Uber, heading back to our dorm when I place my hand on hers and look over at her. "I probably sound like a broken record, but I'm so excited to start our next chapter with you by my side."

Before Katie can even respond, blinding lights fill my vision. My responding scream is quickly cut off as another vehicle crashes into ours. The jarring sound echoes, mixing alongside the ringing in my ears.

Searing pain ricochets throughout my body, causing my vision to blur with black dots that quickly pull me into the darkness.

13

Griffin

September

I wake to my phone buzzing incessantly. It's nearly four in the morning, so panic seizes my lungs when I see my dad's name on my caller ID.

"Hello?" I raspily answer the phone with more of a question than a greeting.

"G-Griff. Y-you need to come home." I can barely understand my dad through his sobs. My stomach sinks. The only other time I'd ever heard him sound so broken was when my mom died.

"Dad, what is it? What's wrong?"

"It's your sister. S-she was in an accident. Oh god—" He's cut off, and I hear what sounds like a robotic voice calling for a code blue.

"Dad! What happened?" I scream into the phone.

There's a rustling on the other end. Then I hear another voice come through the phone. "Griffin? Is that you? This is Elizabeth."

Why is Kenna's mom with my dad? "Yes, it's Griff. Can you please tell me what happened, Liz?"

"Griffin, honey, I need you to get on the next flight back here, alright? There was an accident. The Uber Katie and McKenna were riding in on the way back to their dorms from the airport was t-boned by another vehicle. We don't have all the details yet, b-but you just

137

need to get here—" she chokes out, her sobs filling the other end of the phone.

"Are they okay?" I demand. *Please, god, let them be okay.*

"McKenna is still unconscious, but stable. They're doing a head CT now to rule out brain bleeds. Katie is still in surgery, her injuries were more severe since the crash was on her side of the vehicle. I'm so sorry I don't have more details for you, Griffin. We just don't know yet," Liz struggles to say through her tears.

"Can you let my dad know I'll be on the next flight out? Please keep me updated, Liz," I choke out, bile rising in my throat.

"We will. Be safe," I hear her say as I hang up the phone. My body begins moving on autopilot, going through the motions as I book my flight, quickly pack a bag, and wake up Maks and Nico to drop me off at the airport without any real recollection of how we got here.

"Keep us posted, G. Let us know if there's anything we can do," Nico says as he pulls me into a tight hug. Maks grips my shoulder and gives me a quick hug.

I nod in response, not wanting to speak, because I know I'll break. I can't even muster up the courage to thank them for the ride. Turning on my heel, I wheel my carry-on through the sliding glass doors.

I breeze through check-in but am frustrated when I find security lines are longer than I anticipated for a 6 a.m. flight, but I guess it is Labor Day.

Once I've boarded the plane, I take one last look at my messages to see if there's an update on Katie or Kenna. I have no new notifications, so I put my phone in airplane mode and pray that they'll both be okay when I land.

I turn my phone off airplane mode to arrange for an Uber, but before I can click the app, I get a call from Carson.

"Carson, how are they?" I ask right away, not bothering with a greeting.

"G, I'm about a mile away from the airport to pick you up. I'll meet you outside the arrivals by baggage claim."

"Thanks. Now, please tell me how they are," I insist.

I hear Carson take a deep breath on the other end of the phone. "Katie's had a lot of complications. She's still in surgery. Your dad has been given more updates than usual, due to his position at the hospital, so that's been nice. Mack's CT showed brain swelling but, thankfully, no bleeding. She's been put in a medically induced coma to try to combat the swelling so they can avoid surgery."

Fuck. Fuck Fuck.

"Look, man, I'm going to be there in a minute, and then we need to get back there to be with everyone. Let me know what you need from me. I'm here for you, G."

I break out in a sprint to get from the terminal I'm at to the baggage claim area where Carson will be picking me up.

I've barely made it outside when I see Carson's truck pull up to the curb. I quickly get in the passenger seat, tossing my travel bag into the backseat.

When we haven't started moving yet, I impatiently look over at Carson to find him staring ahead and tightly gripping the steering wheel.

"Carson. Go!" I yell at him.

He turns his head toward me, tears threatening to spill out of his eyes. He has the same eyes as Kenna. And with just one look, fear consumes me.

Carson's voice is hoarse as he whispers, "What if they aren't okay, G?"

"We can't sit here and think that way. We've got to get to the hospital, where they'll have answers for us. Where we'll be able to see them and be with our families," I try to appeal to him.

Carson wraps his arms around me, pulling me in for a hug that leaves me stiff at first. Fuck, this is exactly how people reacted when my mom died. I reciprocate his hug, patting him on the back a few times before asking him if he needs me to drive. After assuring me he's fine, we make the drive to the hospital Katie and Kenna were both brought to.

We're not even through the second set of glass doors before Kenna's mom, Liz, wraps me in her arms. "Oh, Griffin. Thank god you're here." She pulls away, taking my face in her hands and looking at me. "They're going to be okay. They have to be okay," Liz states, her chin wobbling, and her red eyes brimming with tears.

"Where's my dad? Is Katie out of surgery yet? How's McKenna?" The questions rattle out of me.

"Your dad went to speak with the Chief of Surgery just a moment before you arrived. I believe he wanted a more thorough update on Katie's condition than what the residents were providing. This must be even harder for him to sit back and wait when he feels like he could be helping."

"Okay, I'll wait for him to get back. And McKenna? How is she? Can I see her?"

"Griffin, she's in the ICU in a medically induced coma. Only immediate family is allowed to see her right now."

"He can tell the nurses and staff that he's me. They won't know any better," I hear Carson suggest from beside me.

I look over and nod my head in appreciation at his suggestion.

"I'll ask Theo to grab a coffee with me. He's in with McKenna now. You can sit with her for a little while until we get back," Liz offers, and I take her up on it.

"G, I'll call you when your dad gets back here," Carson assures me.

"Thanks, Carse. And thank you for picking me up. I appreciate it." I pull him in for another brief hug, then follow Liz to Kenna's room.

The monitor's beeping sounds like a haunting chorus. One I never thought I'd hear again after my mother lost her battle with cancer almost ten years ago.

Seeing McKenna hooked up to a ventilator, knowing she's in a medically induced coma, and not knowing whether or not Katie is okay . . . it fucking breaks me. I try to cover my mouth, but the sob still chokes out of me.

Theo squeezes my shoulder and tells me she's going to be alright, but nothing about this situation is right. He must not know what I overheard the nurses saying in hushed voices about the driver that hit them having failed his tox screening. They said he was nearly three times over the legal limit to drive.

A drunk driver. This happened to my sister and to the girl I love because of a goddamn drunk driver.

If they don't make it, and he's still in this hospital, he'll be a dead man walking.

I'm consumed with so many feelings—anger, rage, fear, regret—that I don't hear what Theo just said to me.

"What? Can you repeat that?" I ask him.

He sighs, not in frustration, but in exhaustion. "I said the doctors said she would likely be in a coma for the next twenty-four to forty-eight hours. After that, we will have a better idea of any long-term complications."

Jesus. I hadn't even brought myself to consider the long-term complications.

I nod in thanks to Theo, patting him on the back as I pass him, then pull up the chair beside Kenna and sit down. I enclose her hand in mine and bring my forehead to where our hands are joined.

"You and Katie both need to be okay, Sunshine. Please just be okay," I plead to her unconscious body—her chest only rising and falling steadily because of the tubes and machines pumping life into her.

I hear my dad's voice murmur something in the hallway before his footsteps sound through the door and then stop. Not willing to take my eyes off Kenna's sleeping form for a second, I stare at her while I ask him, "How much longer until Katie's out of surgery? God, it's been hours now. Is this normal?"

Deafening silence falls over the room before a deep wail sounds from my dad's chest. I snap my head toward him, "Dad?" I implore.

The shake of his head and his answering look hit me like a slapshot to the chest. Pain and loss radiate throughout my body.

"No. Please, god, no." I shake my head, petitioning the truth.

"Katie—" My dad's voice breaks. "She's gone, Griff." I watch him take a deep, steadying breath. "There was nothing they could do. There was a complication during surgery, and the resulting damage to her brain was too extensive. She was declared brain-dead. I was only allowed in the O.R. to see for myself before the transplant team took over."

"Don't you dare flip the switch on me," I shout at him, releasing Kenna's hand and standing up. "I am not a patient's family. You don't get to turn into the clinical, detached Dr. Turner right now. I am your son."

My heart is pounding out of my chest, my fists tremble at my sides, and I feel like I'm gasping through a straw. Panic seizes my lungs. Black specks dot my vision. I can't breathe. I don't want to.

It's been thirty-two hours since I found out my baby sister was declared brain-dead and donated her organs to save eight lives. My only comfort in those hours is knowing Katie would've been proud to have saved others.

When I boarded my plane yesterday morning, I never thought this would be the outcome—that I'd lose my beloved sister. Or that the girl I'm in love with would still be fighting for her life.

Earlier this morning, they stopped the medication that was inducing Kenna's coma. Her doctor said he anticipated her regaining consciousness within six to eight hours due to the swelling on her brain having been relieved significantly.

That was eleven hours ago.

My phone chimes again with incoming messages. I regrettably informed Maks, Nico, and Emmett what happened and that I wouldn't be back for the first week of classes. They said they would handle getting in touch with Coach, my advisor, and the dean if they needed to.

I appreciate them now more than ever, I do. But the constant string of texts to check in on me is beginning to grate on my nerves. So I don't bother checking my messages. Instead, I place my hands back on Kenna's right hand. I run my fingers over the tan line on her finger from where her ring typically is. They took it off her and placed it with her belongings when she was admitted.

A bag of Katie's belongings is all we were given yesterday. That and a pile of paperwork for my dad to sign and sort through.

Still rubbing that line on her finger, I begin humming "You Are My Sunshine" to Kenna. Tears flood my eyes, and the humming becomes difficult as my throat tightens.

"Please come back to me, Sunshine," I beg, struggling to get the words out through the sobs wracking my body. "I can't do this without you. Don't leave me. I can't go on without you and Katie. I won't. Wake up, baby. Please, I need you right now."

I feel Kenna's hand twitch in mine and my eyes shoot up to see her eyelids fluttering rapidly. Her monitors begin beeping more frequently before her eyes slowly open. Kenna looks like she's struggling to keep them open. She begins to cough as her conscious brain fights against the breathing tube.

I press the call light on her bed and yell for someone to help her.

"Sunshine, you're okay. I'm right here. You were in an accident. You were intubated. I need you to calm down until they can get that taken out."

A team of nurses and doctors rush into her room. One of the nurses grabs my arm, ushering me to the door. "Sir, we're going to need you to go to the waiting area."

"I love you, Sunshine. I'll be right back, Kenna," I raise my voice gently, only so she can hear me over the chaos.

I turn to the nurse and tell her, "You can't tell her about Katie. It has to come from me or her family. No one else should tell her."

14

Griffin

SEPTEMBER

I t's the morning of Katie's celebration of life. Katie has been gone for six days now. We wanted to wait until after McKenna was discharged from the hospital on Thursday to do anything. It's Sunday now. The day of rest. But I can't rest—can't eat, can't sleep, can't fucking breathe—knowing that my baby sister will never do those things again.

My teammates came from Boston and are currently filling every inch of my childhood home's living room. I'd normally make a witty remark to lighten the mood; that's typically my role on the team. But I don't know how to feel anything anymore. I'm broken beyond repair.

I feel nothing. Absolutely nothing. I'm numb, my head void of feelings, my heart a boulder in my chest.

The sound of McKenna's pleading cries as she choked and gasped for breaths between sobs has reverberated in my head since Carson and I broke the news to her. The agonizing symphony is like a ringing in my ears, drowning out everyone who tries to speak to me.

Like right now. Maks is talking to me; I know he is because he's facing me, making eye contact, and his lips are moving. But I couldn't tell you what he's prattling on about for the life of me.

"I'm sorry, what?" I ask him, not really caring if he repeats himself.

Maks doesn't get upset. He just repeats, "I said, do you want one of us to drive you and your dad to the gymnasium?"

"Oh. No, my dad said he got a car service to take us there and then to the burial after. But thanks."

"Of course. Just let us know what you need, G. We're here for you," Maks says before slapping me on the shoulder. He rounds up the rest of the guys, and together, they carpool to my former high school's gymnasium.

My dad and I decided to have Katie's celebration of life at a place she loved and where she spent most of her time. Abbott University offered for us to use their facilities, but it didn't feel right knowing Katie had only played there for a few weeks.

The ride to her celebration, if you can even call it that, is filled with uncomfortable silence. If it hasn't involved Katie's funeral, we've hardly spoken to each other since Monday.

Once we arrived at the school, my dad and I were ushered into the gymnasium by a few faculty members who were Katie's former teachers. The community has taken the news of Katie's death hard, and the outpouring of support has meant a lot to my dad and me. Once we got approval to have her funeral at the high school, there were dozens of volunteers offering their assistance to make this come together.

Before we took our seats, I looked around the packed gymnasium. It's at maximum capacity, meaning over two thousand people are in attendance today. It's heartbreaking to think the last time I saw this space look like this was at Katie's graduation ceremony. Now, *that* was a cause for celebration. How can we sit here and lie to ourselves by calling this a celebration of life? How can anyone *celebrate* the thoughtless murder of my only sister? One man decided to selfishly drive himself home when he was wasted off his ass instead of calling one of the dozens of ride-shares. The injustice is that he will likely only get three to four years in prison before he's back on the roads.

I follow my dad to the front row of seats and then sit beside him. My grandma, grandpa, aunts, uncles, and cousins are already seated on my dad's other side. I look over at the empty seats on my other side just as McKenna and her family are ushered into our row.

Kenna sits down beside me. She grabs ahold of my hand like it's her life preserver. In some ways, I feel like we are each other's life preservers. I'm not sure what I would've done had she not woken up—if we were laying two people to rest today. It's a revolting thought I can't bear to have.

McKenna

I can't help but envision my portrait next to hers, an urn full of my ashes beside hers. It's a sick world to have to wake up from a coma and find out you've lost your best friend. Katie was my person—she was so much more than my best friend. She was a living extension of myself. Now she's gone. And I had to fucking wake up here without her.

A part of me died with her that night. I'm barely hanging on. I wish I could take her place. It should've been me.

"Thank you for coming to join us in celebrating the life of Katie Anne Turner, who tragically passed away earlier this week at the age of eighteen. Katie was a beloved daughter, sister, granddaughter, niece, cousin, friend, and teammate." I hear the pastor's voice drown in and out of the chaos and guilt that have consumed my mind since I woke up earlier this week.

I faintly hear the pastor's sermon preaching about Katie finding peace in heaven with our Heavenly Father and her mother. But doesn't he understand? She had peace here with us—me, Jack, Griffin, Carson—her friends, and family. She's being laid to rest against her will.

"Now, the eulogy, which was written by her brother, Griffin, will be read by Katie's best friend, McKenna."

Taking a deep breath, I stand on shaky legs, giving myself a moment to get my balance. Without missing a beat, Carson stands and escorts me up the stage's steps to the podium set-up. It looks just like the night of our graduation ceremony.

I take one more steadying breath before reciting the words Griffin wrote about his Katie Cat. When he asked me to read the eulogy on his behalf, I jumped at the chance to support him, in an effort to lessen his burden. I'm only now regretting my hasty agreement as I stare out into the packed gymnasium to find a sea of people dressed in white, per Jack and Griffin's request.

As I continue to read Griffin's words, I realize I've recited almost the entire eulogy without getting choked up. In fact, I haven't felt anything since I came home from the hospital to a room full of memories of Katie.

After delivering the eulogy, I sit through the rest of the ceremony, holding both Carson's and Griffin's hands for dear life.

People continued to come up to me after the ceremony, telling me how lucky I am to be alive. But if they knew the kinds of intrusive thoughts that have riddled my brain the past few days, they'd never think I was lucky.

I know I should be thankful to be alive, but any gratitude for my life is washed away by grief and the guilt that consumes me.

If I hear one more person encourage me to live for myself and for Katie, I will lose it. Don't they understand that I can't fucking breathe, let alone live without her here with me?

We're in Griff's Jeep in front of my dorms early the next morning.

After the burial yesterday, Griff asked me if we could go up to the bluffs, just the two of us. He wanted to be together in a place that wasn't filled with Katie's things and memories of her. I agreed, and we spent the night wrapped in each other's arms beneath the stars.

But since we woke up this morning, Griff hasn't spoken a word. When I asked him if he was ready to bring me back, his only response was a single nod.

Unable to bear the silence any longer, and knowing this is my last chance to see him in person for almost two months, I plead to him, "Griffin, this is the hardest thing we'll ever endure. But I want you to know I'm here for you. I'll always be here for you. Just please lean on me, grieve with me. Please don't push me away. I love you so much, Griff—"

"No." He cuts me off in a chilling, detached tone. "You need to stop telling me that. Stop lying to yourself when you say or think those words."

My spine stiffens from his unsettling tone and hurtful words. "I love you, Griff. Did you hear me? I just told you I love you, that I'm here for you, and your response is to rip my heart out by telling me I'm lying?" I raise my voice at him, losing my patience. He's hardly spoken to me since I woke up this week. I understand he's grieving, but so am I.

"You can't love me, McKenna. Don't you understand? A part of me died with her! I can't feel anything. I've gone numb. I'm not even half the man you need me to be. I'll never be whole again," he yells back at me as he pounds his fist into his chest.

"And you think, what? That I don't feel numb? That I don't feel guilty for every breath I take? I wish I could take her place," I scream in agony as I let the darkness bleed out of me. "God, I've wished every second of every day since that horrible moment that I would've been on that side of the car. Or I would've called Carson or my parents to pick us up from the airport instead of waiting for an Uber. I drive myself crazy thinking of every different scenario that should have happened so Katie could still be here," I holler with such ferocity that my voice becomes hoarse and my throat burns. I shove my hands into his chest. He doesn't even move; he just stares back at me.

"Neither of you should have even been in that car. If you wouldn't have been so desperate to see me—if this relationship didn't blind us—then she would still be here," he breaks. Unwilling to look at me, he stares straight ahead.

My heart dissolves in my chest at his accusation. His words sink me, and I feel like I've been struck. He just confirmed my greatest fear: Griff blames me for that night—for the accident.

He must sense the gravity in his words because he tries to back-peddle. "It's just going to be too hard, McKenna. You should be focusing on your dreams and goals. Play in the Olympics. Win a gold medal. Dedicate your time to your studies, make new friends, and play the best volleyball you can."

I cut his rambling lies off when I say, "Tell me the truth. Don't feed me halfhearted excuses. Why are you doing this?"

His answer is the kill shot to our relationship. "I don't want you anymore. How can I be with someone who will remind me of everything I've lost for the rest of my life?"

Despair slices through my chest, shattering my already broken heart into pieces, his words cutting me like a knife.

We'll never be able to come back from this.

15

McKenna

OCTOBER

Nothing feels right. I'm on auto-pilot—going through the motions, completely numb from any feeling besides unrelenting heartbreak.

After Griffin broke my already-shattered heart into a million irreparable pieces, I had to come back to a dorm filled with Katie's belongings.

The pain I feel every day without Katie here feels like I'm walking on snow, and all of a sudden, grief strikes me like an avalanche, burying me alive.

I can't tell you how many times I've dialed her phone, just to have it go to her voicemail. She was my person. I went to her for everything, and she was always only a few steps, or a phone call away. Lately, I just call so I can hear her voice on the voicemail message.

Carson has been my rock; I'm not sure what I'd do without him. He even came by the dorm and helped pack up Katie's things. Jack told me to keep anything of hers that would bring me comfort and the rest he would go through.

After meeting with my coach and athletic director, we decided it would be best if I redshirted this season. Because I only played two games before the accident, I was able to qualify for a hardship waiver.

With the concussion that resulted from my brain swelling, combined with the grief, anxiety, depression, and survivor's guilt I'm working through, I was on board with my coach's suggestion.

Being a redshirt freshman means I'll still practice with the team once I'm cleared, but I won't travel or play any games. I also don't lose a year of eligibility. Due to the severity of my concussion, I've been out of practice for over a month, and it'll be another two weeks before I can return to light activity.

The extra time off practice has allowed me to catch up on my classes, go to some of Carson's pre-season games, and find a therapist to work with.

My therapist's name is Camila, and I've felt like I can open up to her so far. Today, I'm sitting across from her in her office, watching as she nods in understanding of what I've just said.

"Sometimes it feels like a betrayal to her if I get new friends. She's irreplaceable in my life."

"I can understand why it may feel like a betrayal. But, tell me, what do you think Katie would want you to do?" Camila asks.

"She was the most selfless person I know. Katie would want me to be happy, to meet new people, not close in on myself. But I don't know how to do that without her. She always pushed me out of my shell."

"Have you gone out with your team? Made any new friends?"

"Katie and I became friends with Alexa and Brooke when we trained with them this spring and summer. Brooke and I have become closer recently. She lost her brother three years ago, so she's been talking me through the waves of grief and guilt I'm feeling."

Camila adds notes to the legal pad that's always in her lap during our sessions while I recount one of the conversations Brooke and I had that's been weighing on me.

"Brooke said the first year will be the hardest. I'll be filled with moments where I think I'm okay. Then I'll see something, experience something new that makes me want to call her up, and grief will pull me right back under. There will be times when I'll be reminded that something was Katie's last. Or firsts that I'll experience that I realize she never will." Brooke's words really hit their mark with me when we spoke earlier this week.

I continue, "Typically, I love going back to school, so my first day of classes would have been something I looked forward to. I was looking forward to them before the accident. Instead, on my first day of classes, I not only felt unbearable sadness and heartbreak, I was riddled with guilt for being alive—for being able to attend classes when Katie never got the chance. Will it always be like this? Will I feel guilty when I'm proposed to, get married, or start a family?"

"I can't answer that for you. Each milestone may bring a wave of grief and possibly guilt. But instead of letting those feelings take hold of you, I want you to write in your grief journal what you would have said to her had she been there with you. Write what you would have texted her, or called her, and said."

Hearing Camila bring up texting triggers me to look down at my phone sitting on my lap. It makes me think of my text thread with Griffin—at the weeks of unanswered texts I've sent him.

Me:

Did you make it back alright?

I miss her so much.

I miss you.

> It feels like I lost both of my best friends that night.

> Say something, Griff.

Griff hasn't returned any of my texts or calls. I haven't been able to bring myself to stop trying, though. It makes me feel more pathetic each time my attempt to reach out goes unanswered.

"McKenna? Where did you go just now?" Camila questions.

I shake my head, knowing we don't have enough time to dive into my feelings about Griffin in today's session.

"These sessions are yours. Remember, we go at your pace," Camila reassures me, giving me the courage to speak about what's weighing on my heart.

"I'm already grieving Katie, but it feels like I need to grieve Griffin, too. I haven't moved past the denial phase of grieving him. I'm not even angry with him. After what he said to me—what he believes—I should have already accepted that we will never be together again. But I can't."

I wish he would give me something. A drunk text. A drunk dial in the middle of the night. Anything. I hate that I'm so desperate for an ounce of his attention. If it weren't for me being able to see that he's on the ice for each of his games, I'd believe he died that night, too.

Today was dark. I woke up, and grief kissed me with a feeling of despair I hadn't been able to shake. I wished I could cry inconsolably, but I couldn't. Instead, emptiness took hold of me.

I knew I needed to get out of my own head, so I called Brooke to see if she was free, and now we're currently grabbing dinner at The Eatery on campus before our late class starts.

"Do you want to come out with us for Halloween? We're doing a team costume theme. I guess they do it every year, and this year, the theme is Disney Princesses. You'd make the perfect Rapunzel," Brooke suggests. "Please come, Kenna. You can't leave me on my own. Alexa is visiting her boyfriend that weekend, so I'll be the only freshman." She folds her hands together, pleading for me to give in.

"Where are you guys going?"

"We'll probably hit up Greek Row."

I manage to hide my cringe. Drew pledged for a frat last year, and I hated every one of the parties he dragged me to until we broke up.

"Fine, I'll be your sober companion. I don't drink at frat houses," I tell her.

"I don't care if you drink as long as you're willing to shake it with me on the dance floor. I remember your moves from this summer, girl."

My heart sinks thinking about this summer. It was only a few months ago, and yet, I feel like these past few weeks have made it seem like a lifetime ago.

"I'll be sure to let my hair down, as they say in *Rapunzel*." My lame attempt at a joke hits the mark for Brooke. She squeals in excitement.

"Yes! Okay, we've got to go costume shopping. Can you go after your next class? We should take advantage of this afternoon without practice."

"Yeah, I'll drive us." That's another invisible scar I've picked up since the accident. I'm not scared to drive, but I refuse to relinquish control to others. So far, I've only been comfortable getting in a car with Carson driving. Well, and Griff, too, when he broke up with me.

Halloween weekend is officially here. Brooke and I joined our team-mates at one of the upperclassmen's off-campus houses to get ready earlier.

Now we're at one of the frat houses on Greek Row, dancing on a makeshift dance floor to "Thriller." I'm starting to regret my costume choice because my hair feels heavy and keeps getting tangled against my sweat-slicked skin.

After realizing my phone was buzzing, and it wasn't just the bass of the music, I grab it from my bra.

My heart stutters when I see his name flash across the screen.

I swipe to answer the call, covering my other ear so I can hear better over the noise. "Griff?" I answer with a question, unable to believe he's actually calling me. My feet move quickly from the dance floor. I need to get outside so I can hear him better.

Griffin's deep voice comes through the other end. "McKenna. Sun-shine, is it really you? Where are you?" His speech is slurred so much that I can barely understand him. Every butterfly that erupted in my chest at finally seeing his name on my phone is quickly laid to rest hearing him like this.

I get outside to the front porch of the frat house just as some guy says, "Hey, blondie. Who are you supposed to be?"

Griff cuts in before I can say anything. "Oh, I get it. Sorry for interrupting. Forget I called."

"No, Griff! Please don't hang up. I just had to get outside so I could hear you. You're not interrupting, ever. I promise."

"I hate the sound of your voice. Do you know that? It makes me feel. I don't want to fucking feel anything, McKenna." His voice cracks as he whispers, "Everything hurts, Sunshine."

His broken voice reopens every wound in my heart.

I cover my mouth to choke back the sob before it can leave my throat. Tears flood my vision. "I know, baby. I know the pain is unbearable. But I could never hate the beautiful sound of your voice."

God, I've missed hearing his voice.

His agony bleeds through every word as he says, "I miss you. So fucking much. Why did you have to make me fall in love with you? Don't you get it? The only two other women I've ever loved in my life are gone. Everyone I love fucking dies, McKenna."

My heart shatters with the realization that he pushed me away because, in his heart, he honestly believes it's what's best for me.

"Griffin, baby, please listen to me. I love you so much. I'm still yours—every piece of me is still yours. Don't push me away anymore."

"I have to. I can't lose you, too. Even if I can't have you with me, at least I know you're alive and thriving."

I can't help but scoff at that. "Thriving?" I ask incredulously, raising my voice. "In what alternate reality of yours am I thriving, Griffin? The one where I not only lost my best friend but also the love of my life in one go? I'm anything and everything *but* thriving," I damn near yell.

"Fine, fuck, fine!" he shouts back, slurring even more now. "You're right. Neither one of us may be thriving right now, but you sure look like you're making one hell of a go at replacing me. I saw those pictures, McKenna. I hope little Rapunzel finds her Prince fucking Charming tonight."

And with that, he hangs up on me. When I try to call him back, it goes right to voicemail.

How much longer can I fight a losing battle before I give up?

He doesn't want me anymore.

Griffin

The past few weeks have been a blur. I got so fucked out of my mind on Halloween I don't even remember calling Kenna. Maks had to tell me the next day.

Lately, my life has been a toxic cycle, repeating every day. If I'm not on the ice or trying to blow off class, I'm drowning myself in a bottle of liquor. I don't even have a preference. If it will drown out the pain, I'll drink it.

My coaches, teammates, and friends are all worried about me, but I can't bring myself to give a fuck. I've been bringing it on the ice. My sole focus and motivation is hockey. It's become more of an obsession—a fixation—than ever before. Hockey is the one thing that brings me a modicum of relief from the pain that consumes me.

I slam the front door shut behind me, making my roommates lift their heads from where they're playing *Call Of Duty* in the living room. Emmett nods in greeting to me. I nod back as I head up the stairs to my room. I need to take a shower and get ready before we head out.

I'm just tightening the Half Windsor knot of my tie when my phone rings. I answer on the third ring, hesitating when I see my dad's name flash across the screen.

"Hey, Dad."

"Griffin, I wanted to talk to you. Is now a good time?"

"Can you make it quick? I'm about to head to the rink for my game."

"Right. Sorry, who do you play tonight?"

"Harvard, it's rival night."

"If you can get something past Calvetti, you guys have a shot at staying undefeated."

"I'm not too worried about it. Calvetti's ego needs to be checked, and we plan to do so tonight."

"That's my boy," he says before clearing his throat. "Listen, Griff. I wanted to let you know I've accepted a job at Mass General in Boston as their Chief of Surgery. I originally turned them down, but with you on the East Coast and Katie gone, I changed my mind and accepted their offer. I'm selling the house and should be settled in Boston by the end of the month."

I'm having a hard time wrapping my head around what he's saying. He's moving here. He's selling the house. My childhood home. The place that's filled with memories of both Katie and my mom. I hear my dad getting emotional on the other end of the phone.

"What?" I barely choke out the question—my voice pinched with emotion.

I hear the pain in my dad's voice when he replies, "I'm sorry, Griff. I just can't do it. I'm not strong enough to stay in a house that reminds me of them every second of every day. I miss Katie. I miss your mother. I feel like I'm drowning in that house, and I'm all alone."

Taking a deep breath, I try to see his side of things.

"I could hardly stand sleeping in that house the night before her funeral. It's okay, Dad. We should let it go," I tell him.

And *I* should really listen to my own advice. I need to let everything go from that house and the one next door. I can't fuck up anymore by calling her—I need to let her go like I said I would.

In my heart, I know I'll never get over McKenna Wilder. She'll always be the one I pushed away. The woman I'll compare all others to for the rest of my life. She's Sunshine—just not mine anymore.

16

McKenna

DECEMBER

Our team lost in the first round of the post-season last week on our home court. To be honest, I'm surprised we got a playoff berth with how bad our record was in September and early October. And honestly, it's been difficult being a spectator on the sidelines during home games—unable to contribute.

But it's for the best. I'm still feeling the effects of my concussion. The headaches I still get cause waves of nausea to hit at the most inopportune of times.

Like now, for instance. I'd been in the library studying for my finals for the past few hours when a serious bout of nausea hit. I'm currently in a public bathroom stall dry-heaving. Talk about hitting a new low.

After a few more minutes, I think it's safe to conclude that I'm not going to throw up. I make my way back to the study room I reserved with Brooke.

When she hears me shut the door, Brooke takes out one of her AirPods. "Hey, are you alright? You don't look so great. Another headache?"

I nod, then shake my head. "Yes and no. My head doesn't even really hurt right now. Maybe I just need to grab a bite to eat."

Brooke stares at me for a few beats before she says, "Don't take this the wrong way, and feel free to ignore me completely, but I remember during training camp that you had like, the worst period ever. We've been hanging out a lot since then, and I can't remember that happening to you again . . ." She doesn't finish; she just lets her thoughts linger in the silent room.

A small bout of anxiety squeezes my chest at her insinuation. "I mean, my endometriosis typically makes my periods unbearable. But it also makes them irregular. It's not uncommon for me to go two or three months between my periods."

"Did you typically get headaches and nausea this much before the accident?" she presses on.

"No. But the doctors did say the recurring headaches could be a short-term side effect from the accident." I sound defensive—I know I do.

"Right, but you just said your head didn't hurt right now. Have you had your period since August?"

My stomach sinks. "I see what you're getting at. But I can't be. I haven't had sex since . . . like my birthday. Well, Boston, actually. But that was over three months ago. I think I would know something like that by now."

"Kenna, you've been grieving Katie and mending your broken heart. You've been understandably preoccupied. Not only are you grieving, but you've been focusing on studying and getting back on the court. Would you take one if I go to the pharmacy and get some tests?"

I shake my head. "That's not necessary. It's not possible, B."

"Then it's settled. There's no harm in confirming you're not pregnant. If the test is negative, you should follow up with your doctor. If it's positive, well . . . then I'll be there for you either way."

Her words are both soothing and unsettling. Brooke has been a really good friend to me. Could she be right? It sounds bad when she lays it all out. But I've always had unpredictable periods.

I cave, knowing I'll feel better once I confirm I'm not pregnant. "Alright. Let's go to a drugstore off campus. I'd like to avoid being recognized by anyone we know."

Brooke barely has the door to my dorm room open before Carson comes barreling into my room.

"What the fuck happened?" he grinds out.

He stops short when his eyes land on the three pregnancy tests lying on my desk. The three *positive* tests.

His head slowly turns to look at me. I'm on my bed, cradling my stomach in the fetal position. When his confused gaze meets mine, it turns to concern. I throw my head in my hands as the sobs rake my body all over again.

Brooke clears her throat and grabs her jacket. "I'm going to give you guys some space. Kenna, call me if you need anything. Please. Actually, you know what? Just call me when Carson leaves, no matter what. I'll plan on staying the night in here."

I hear Carson's tender voice tell her, "That won't be necessary. I'll stay here. I'm not letting her out of my sight tonight. Thank you for texting me, Brooke."

"Of course. Kenna is the one who asked me to text you," she informs him before quietly closing the door behind her.

I feel the weight of Carson's stare. "Mack, talk to me."

"I can't bear to look at you, Carson. This is so fucking bad," I choke out.

He sighs. "Mack, come on. It's going to be okay. You haven't even confirmed you're pregnant yet, have you?"

I turn to look at him. "I think three positive tests suggest I'm very clearly pregnant, Carse."

He shifts on his feet. "Aren't there false positives? I mean, maybe you got a bad box."

I scoff at his suggestion. "I don't need to go to the doctor to confirm anything."

Carson's brows furrow. "No, but you do need to go to the doctor to confirm how far along you are and make sure everything is okay. You have been really sick, but I guess I just thought that was from the accident."

When I don't respond right away, he adds, "I have to ask. Is G the dad?"

My chin begins to wobble. "Yes. I haven't even talked to another guy."

Carson hangs his head and takes a deep breath. "Well, that's good. Griff is a good guy. I know you guys are going through a lot right now. But he would never abandon you."

Angry tears sting my eyes. "I wouldn't be so sure. He already abandoned me when things got hard. He won't speak to me, won't return any of my calls, or reply to my texts. I'm not even sure how I'd tell him. This isn't exactly something you say over a text or leave in a voicemail."

Carse pulls me in for a hug. "It will all work out, Mack. You're the strongest person I know. I'll be by your side, supporting you no matter what you decide to do. Let's tackle step one together. Where's your computer?"

I point to my desk, where my laptop rests next to the tests.

"Alright, we're going to find you a doctor to see. If they have any appointments available that I can make, I would like to go with you if you're okay with it."

"I don't think I could go without you at this point."

Carson's unwavering support causes the floodgates to open—I cry in his arms until I can't physically cry any longer. He doesn't lecture me. He doesn't tell me I was irresponsible. He just holds me in his arms and lets me get it all out.

It's Friday mid-morning, and Carson is sitting with me in the waiting room of my new OB's clinic. Dr. Bahati had great reviews online, and she's a woman, which made me more comfortable. I've got a lot of questions about if and how my endometriosis will impact my pregnancy and if the baby is okay after the accident.

Carson's leg continues to bounce up and down next to me, so I ask, "Are you anxious?"

"One hundred percent. Aren't you?"

"I have so many thoughts, questions, and concerns running through my mind at a constant rate that, at this point, I think my brain is too exhausted to be anxious."

"I get that. Did you write down your questions like the article we read suggested?"

"Yes, brother bear." I shoulder-check him, and he rubs his upper arm, pretending like I could actually hurt him.

"Good. I wrote mine out, too." He proceeds to show me a note on his phone with twelve questions.

"Twelve? How do you have twelve questions about *my* pregnancy?"

"It's not just about you now, Mack. I have questions about how my little niece or nephew is doing, too. Speaking of . . . question number two: when do we get to find out the gender?"

"From what I read online the past few days, I think I could find out today if they do an ultrasound. But I decided I don't want to find out the gender right now. Maybe not until the baby is born."

"What? How are you going to plan? Can I have the doctor slip me a piece of paper with the gender on it? I don't think I can wait until the baby is born."

"Well, I was thinking that if I do find out the gender beforehand, I should probably wait for Griff to be here, don't you think?"

"Yeah, that makes sense. Have you thought more about how you want to tell him?"

"Like I said before, it's not something I can say in a text or leave on his voicemail. I guess I'll have to wait until he's home for Christmas."

Carson stiffens beside me. "Didn't Mom and Dad tell you? Jack sold their house and moved to Boston right around Thanksgiving."

"What?" I ask in disbelief. "I just thought he went to see Griff for Thanksgiving because he had games that weekend that wouldn't allow him to come home."

"Nope. Mom said Jack took the Chief of Surgery job at a big hospital in Boston so he could be closer to Griff. I don't see why, though. G is only going to be there for another year before he signs with Colorado."

"And he already sold their house?"

"Yeah. He's already moved out and everything."

I can't believe I'll never step foot in that house again. It feels like my childhood home has been taken out from under me. I feel cheated that I didn't get to see it one last time before he sold it.

"So how the hell am I supposed to tell Griffin he's going to be a dad?"

Before Carson can answer, I hear my name called by a nurse in mauve scrubs holding a clipboard.

"Hi, that's me," I say and hold up my hand. "Is it okay if he comes back with me?" I ask and point to Carse.

"Absolutely. Dad is welcome to join you for any of your appointments."

"Oh, no. He's not the dad. He's my twin brother." I quickly correct her.

The nurse's cheeks tinge with embarrassment. "My apologies. Yes, your brother is welcome to accompany you."

We walk down a hallway, stopping when the nurse asks me to step on a scale. Once I get weighed, I realize I've only gained two pounds. I wonder if that's normal. I'll have to remember to ask the doctor. I do have a small swell to my lower abdomen, though I wouldn't necessarily call it a bump yet at this point. The nurse also has us stop by the lab to get a urine and blood sample from me.

We're taken to a room that has photos on the walls of a woman's bump, a woman holding a newborn baby on her chest, and a woman nursing her baby. There are also diagrams hanging on the wall of the female anatomy. I don't miss how Carson's eyes widen as he takes in the room's decor. Leave it to Carse to make me laugh during a stressful situation.

The nurse asks some standard health history questions, takes my vitals, and then says, "It looks like your urine test is already in the system. Congratulations, we can confirm you are definitely pregnant. Your hCG levels are in range for when you said your last period was, but we will do an ultrasound to get a better measurement of your due date. Do you have any other questions for me before I grab Dr. Bahati?"

"No. Thank you."

Once the door is closed, and it's just Carse and I in the exam room, he turns to me. "Are you freaking out? They're not going to like, look down there while I'm in here right?"

Just as the words leave his mouth, there's a light knock on the door before my doctor peeks her head in. "McKenna?" she asks, then holds her hand out for me to shake when I nod. "Hi, I'm Dr. Bahati. Nice to meet you." She then looks over at Carson and holds her hand out for him to shake. Instead, he grabs her palm in his and smacks a kiss on the top of her hand. Dear lord, please help me.

"Hi, I'm Carson, Mack's twin brother. I'm the funcle."

"The what?" I squeak.

"Funcle. The fun uncle." He rolls his eyes as if that should have been obvious.

"Nice to meet you, Carson," she says politely before turning to me. "So, McKenna. I hear congratulations are in order. I saw in your chart that you weren't sure of the exact date of conception due to your irregular cycles. Were those caused by your endometriosis?"

"Yes. It isn't uncommon for me to go two to three months without a period."

"That can be common with endometriosis. When, then, did you find out you were pregnant?"

"Well, I didn't think I was. I only took a test earlier this week. I was in a bad car accident about three months ago, and I thought the nausea and headaches were a result of my concussion."

Carson cuts in. "It was more than a concussion. She was in a medical coma for almost two days due to her brain swelling. If she was pregnant then, shouldn't they have caught that with all of the bloodwork and testing they ran?"

"That depends on whether or not McKenna was far enough along at that point for the pregnancy to show in bloodwork," Dr. Bahati explains. "I would like to do an ultrasound today to get a better idea of how far along you are, and to ensure all is well. Because we know that you're at least three months along, we can do an abdominal ultrasound."

I nod my head in agreement, my anxiety spiking with each step as I follow Dr. Bahati down the hall to the room where the ultrasound scans are done.

As she washes her hands in the sink, Dr. Bahati tells me to hop up on the exam table, lift my shirt up, and tuck it into my bra.

"You'll feel some cool gel, and then you can look up there at the TV to see your little one."

Carson and I gasp in unison as we watch the screen's display—it's the twin connection. I'm not sure what I was expecting, but I didn't realize I would see anything that resembled a baby. Weren't they supposed to look alien at this point still?

But instead of a blob in front of me, the most beautifully developing baby is on the screen.

After doing some measurements, Dr. Bahati says, "Alright, McKenna. It looks like you're right about seventeen weeks pregnant, and the baby is looking great. I'm just going to take a listen to baby's heartbeat."

Just then, the most amazing sound floats through the speakers. Tears flood my eyes as I listen to my baby's heartbeat for the first time.

"Baby's heart rate is 155 beats per minute, which is great. Did you want to learn the gender today?"

I say no, just as Carson says yes. Dr. Bahati chuckles and shakes her head. "We can wait on that for now, McKenna."

She continues to take some additional measurements while Carse and I both stare at the screen in awe.

"Hmm," Dr. Bahati says to herself as she takes a few more measurements below the baby.

"What is it? Is something wrong?" I ask, my voice pinched in fear.

"Nothing is wrong, McKenna. But your cervix is measuring shorter than I would anticipate at this early stage in the pregnancy. I would like to place you on light activity restrictions throughout your pregnancy so we can monitor this. A shortened cervix can lead to preterm labor, and we want to avoid that as best as we can," Dr. Bahati informs me.

"Is this because I was too active when I didn't know I was pregnant? I play college volleyball, but I've only recently been cleared for normal activity after my concussion. The season just ended, so light activity shouldn't be a problem once I talk to my coach."

"A shortened cervix is not uncommon. There has been no research to show that overexertion or heavy exercise causes a shortened cervix. However, I want to stress how important it is to remain on light activity—drive instead of walk when you can, take the elevator instead of the stairs when able, and try not to lift over fifteen pounds for the time being." Her response is reassuring.

She hands me a towel to clean my abdomen before she continues, "I saw on your intake paperwork that this was an unplanned pregnancy. Do you have any questions for me? We have materials I can send home with you so you can be informed about your options."

Carson squeezes my hand beside me, letting me know he's here for me.

I clear the tickle of anxiety in my throat before responding, "Thank you. It wouldn't hurt to learn more about adoption, though I don't foresee myself going that route."

She places her hand on my arm in a gesture of endearment. "Of course. I will grab those materials and the prescription for your prenatal vitamins and be right back."

As soon as she's out of the room, Carse turns to look at me. "That was amazing, Mack. I'm sorry if I pushed you into thinking I wouldn't support your options. I'm here for you no matter what. I shouldn't have assumed you would keep the baby."

I shake my head at him. "No, Carse. You don't need to apologize. I want to keep the baby. It's just all still so new. I haven't told Griff, or Mom and Dad. I have no idea if they will all react the same as you did, with unwavering support. I just want to educate myself on all the possible options."

He nods in understanding while I untuck my shirt and sit back up.

A few moments later, Dr. Bahati comes back in the room with the materials and says, "We will have you back in about a month to do another ultrasound. That one will be the full anatomy scan. In the meantime, take your prenatal vitamins, drink plenty of fluids, try to eat small, frequent meals to help with the morning sickness and curb the nausea, and take it easy."

"You got it, Doc. I'll make sure to keep her in line," Carson replies with his hand across his chest. "I take my duties as funcle seriously. I won't let you down."

Maybe telling my parents won't be so bad. That way, maybe my mom can come to some of these appointments instead of Carse. He's going to get me in trouble with my doctor.

I'm woken up by one of the best feelings in the world—Ranger's wet nose nuzzles mine before he lays on a long lick across my cheek. I giggle in response and he paws at my hand, his way of telling me to pet him. He's always so needy first thing in the morning.

As the sleep clears from my brain, I realize it's Christmas morning. That means I'm nineteen weeks pregnant. As the thought crosses my mind, my phone chimes with an incoming text.

Carse:

> Merry Christmas, Mack & Uncle's little mango. I miss you!

Me:

> Mango?

Carse:

> Yep. 19 weeks. According to my app, the baby is the size of a mango.

> Knowing the size of mango's parents, we probably should skip ahead a week...

> Merry Christmas, little sweet potato.

Me:

> Merry Christmas, Carse. We love you and miss you too! Good luck tomorrow—kick some ass!

Carse:

> Good luck to you, too, sis. It will all be okay.

I quickly brush my teeth, put my hair up in a bun, and wash my face before heading downstairs to breakfast. Nerves fill my belly, making me second guess if it's nerves or if I'm finally feeling the baby move. I place a hand on my lower abdomen, the move soothing some of my anxiety.

Alright, little one. It's time to tell grandma and grandpa about you.

Just then, I feel another flutter in my lower stomach and decide it must be the baby nudging me to let me know I'm not alone.

How does one really tell their parents they're about to become grandparents far earlier than they were planning? If things had gone as planned, they wouldn't be grandparents for at least another decade.

I take a deep breath as I round the corner and enter the kitchen.

"Good morning, Princess. Merry Christmas," my dad says to me as he flips pancakes on the griddle.

"Merry Christmas, Daddy."

"Merry Christmas, hun. How did you sleep?" Mom asks me when she comes out of the butler's pantry.

"Good. I always get my best night's sleep when I'm home. I miss Ranger so much when I sleep in my dorm. I'm excited to get to sleep with him every night over winter break."

We sit down for Christmas morning pancakes together, and I know I need to just tell them already.

"Honey, I saw a bill the other day from a women's clinic. Is your endometriosis flaring up? You should've told me you were going. I would've gone with you," my mom says as she places her hand on mine and gives it a gentle squeeze.

"I uh—went to the doctor to have some tests run." I hesitate. God, this might be the hardest thing I've ever done.

"What kind of tests? Are you still having the headaches and nausea from the accident?" she asks, worry etched on her face.

"I am, but it turns out it's not because of the accident." Just then, I decide to take a giant bite of pancakes. I try to chew quickly, but when I swallow, the sticky stack gets caught in my throat.

Holy awkward as fuck.

My parents share a look, and then they both stare back at me, waiting for me to finish chugging my glass of orange juice to clear my throat.

Buying more time, I don't just take a few sips. I chug the entire glass. When I go to refill my glass, my mom places her hand on my arm to stop me.

"McKenna, talk to us. You can tell us anything."

Well, hopefully, I don't make her eat her words. Here goes nothing.

Looking down at my pancakes, I avoid making eye contact as I blurt, "I went to the doctor to confirm that I'm pregnant."

I look up to see both of my parents' eyes widen. They definitely were not expecting that. Dad's grip on his fork tightens momentarily, and Mom's eyes well with tears.

"I'm going to guess it's Griffin I need to have a talk with?" my dad questions, breaking the tense silence.

What happens next completely throws me off. My mom jumps out of her chair and pulls me in for a hug. "I'm going to be a Grammy! Oh my goodness, I can't tell you how lonely I've been since you two flew the nest. Please tell me I get to watch the baby while you're at class and practice. When are you due?" she practically squeals.

What the fuck is happening?

My stomach sinks thinking about volleyball and school. I know there are plenty of people who go on to get a degree after they have a teenage pregnancy. But my dreams of volleyball and Team USA are shot.

"I'm still not sure what I'm going to do. My due date is May 18th. I haven't even told Griffin yet. I'm going to try to finish school still, but I won't be able to play volleyball next season. I can't possibly think that after this season, in addition to being a mom, I'll have a spot on the roster."

My dad joins the hug, wrapping us in his arms, before he says, "You never know, Princess. Why don't you go speak to your advisor and Coach after the New Year? As for Griffin, when do you plan on telling him?" I can't help but notice my dad's tone change when he asks about Griff.

"We aren't really speaking right now. Well, he hasn't been replying to me. It's not something I want to text him or leave on his voicemail. Carson thought maybe I could fly to Boston for the game they play versus each other. It'll still be my winter break."

Mom's gaze turns sympathetic, but Dad's face reddens with anger.

"I don't want you to fly there by yourself, Princess."

"I'll be fine, Dad. I promise."

"Tell me your flight times, and I will bring you to the airport and pick you up."

With just that one gesture, grief's riptide pulls me back under. Making me wish that would've been the case on the last trip I took to Boston.

17

Griffin

JANUARY

My skates hit the ice for warmups, and I inhale deeply as I take a few laps around our zone. Being on the ice is the only thing that makes me feel anything. It's my only escape from the darkness of grief that threatens to pull me under every waking moment. Well, hockey and whiskey. But lately, even drinking myself into oblivion isn't easing the pain—the anger—I feel. That's why I started taking the pills a few weeks ago.

My birthday is this weekend, which means next week would've been Katie's nineteenth birthday.

I'm striding toward the middle of the ice when I spot number twenty-two on the opposing team.

Carson.

I knew the game against him would bring memories rushing back that I'd been trying to repress. Memories of games of mini hockey, pond hockey, and street hockey, all with the four lakeshore kids—me, Carse, Kenna, and Katie. My stomach still sinks every time I even think of her name; both of their names, if I'm being honest.

I didn't just lose Katie that night. I lost part of myself, too. I had to push Kenna away, and in doing so, I lost the love of my life.

It's so weird. I know she's halfway across the country, but every time I look in the crowds at one of our games, I'll see a girl with long blonde hair and swear it's Kenna.

Like right now, as I turn away from Carson, I could swear the girl behind the penalty box is Kenna. The girl has her back turned to me, but her honey-blonde hair falls over her black parka jacket and down to her waist.

I shake my head, about to turn away, when the girl takes off her jacket, making my chest constrict with more emotion than I've felt in months.

It's her. I know even before she turns and I make eye contact with those hauntingly beautiful blue eyes.

I snap out of the trance that her eyes put me in and take her in. Now that her jacket is off, I can see that Kenna is in a jersey split down the middle—half red with a nine on one side and half white and maroon with a two on the other side. It makes my stomach bottom out.

Have all the school spirit you want, aside from the games we play versus each other. Come on, Katie Cat, I need a fan in the crowd. Kenna will wear Carson's jersey—I need someone supporting me.

Alright, I promise I'll always be your number-one fan whenever I'm at one of your games.

Kenna shouldn't be here if Katie can't.

My games, the ice, and hockey are supposed to be my one escape from the pain.

Seeing her after all this time, here . . . wearing *that* . . . well, it fucks me up.

It takes everything in me to pull myself together and turn my back on her.

Fuck.

Skating across the ice to our bench, Maks holds his gloved hand out for me to bump.

"You good, brother? You look like you've seen a ghost," Maks says.

I shake my head. "No, my head is fucked right now. Kenna is here."

His eyebrows disappear under his helmet. "You sure? You've thought you saw her before."

"I'm sure. She's wearing my jersey. Well, half of my jersey and half of her brother's jersey." I nod my head toward the penalty box she's sitting behind.

"Shit, G. Do you want me to get someone to bring her down to talk to you before the game? We need your head in the right place."

"Hearing her voice would fuck me up worse than seeing her is. I'll be good, Maks. I just need to take a few laps to clear my head."

I take off at a leisurely pace around our zone. I nod to a few of my teammates and then let the music flow through me, amping my adrenaline.

After we warm up, we go to the locker room while they resurface the ice. My hands shake as I reach into my jacket pocket and feel for the small baggy I bought earlier today. My nerves are shot.

I slip the baggy into my fist before heading into one of the bathroom stalls. I've only taken Adderall a few times recently when everything became too much, and right now, things are too much. So I slip two pills into my mouth and dry swallow them.

I've never fucked around with drugs prior to these past few weeks. But seeing Kenna tonight has my head fucked, and I need to focus.

It's early January, which means Carson and a few guys from each team just got back from the World Juniors tournament, which was in Canada this year.

I was too old to play this year, but I'm proud of the guys who played on the U.S. team. They beat Canada in the finals—it was a barn burner.

I have three Emery teammates who played for Team Canada, but they all seem to have put the game behind them, ready to focus on our season again.

But tonight our team isn't the only undefeated team on the ice. This game is big for both teams. I need to get my head in the game.

Abbott University has more young guns trying to prove themselves. We have more seasoned players desperate to win a National Championship.

I've reviewed countless hours of film over the past two weeks in preparation for this game.

But one glimpse of Kenna has me in a tailspin. My only hope is the pills will help me focus and I'll be able to zone her out. I have to.

It's nearing the end of the third period, the game is tied two to two, and I've got a goal and an assist. The game has gotten chippy—I took a hard one against the boards last shift. Carson just got tossed to the ice in front of our net by my teammate, Schmitty.

We're at the face-off circle when Schmitty decides to try to get a rise out of Carson. "Hey Wilder, your sister looks like she's ready for a wild night. Feel free to let her know she can get a ride home from me tonight. Maybe she can take me for a ride later."

Fucker. Doesn't he know about my history with Kenna? Instead of just getting in Carson's head, he's fucking with mine too.

"That's enough," I bark at him.

Just when I get Schmitty to shut the hell up, one of Carson's teammates, Ian Nelson, decides to clip the last thread of patience I had for tonight.

"Sorry, Schmitty. She's rooming with me tonight." Then he looks right at me, smirking as he positions himself for the face-off.

My skin feels like it'll burst at the seams if I don't expel this rage inside of me.

Nelson lowers his voice so only I can hear, "I should thank you, Turner. Chicks do the hottest things when they're a little broken."

I clench my jaw so hard I think I'll crack a tooth.

"And you didn't just break her a little. You fucked her pretty little heart up, just like I plan to do to her pussy—"

Before he can finish, I drop my gloves, grab his jersey, and start throwing blows to his head. His helmet comes off after I connect with the side of his head the second time.

Nelson lays a few on me before my fist connects with his nose. I feel his bones crunch beneath my knuckles. Nelson falls back on his ass, cradling his face as blood seeps through his hands onto the ice. He looks up at me, and the sadistic fucker must have a death wish because he says, "I can't wait for her to kiss it all better."

I lunge toward him, ready to go again, but I'm pulled back by Emmett. "Get in the locker room, G. You're done." He's right. Fighting in college hockey is frowned upon and heavily penalized, which means it's not surprising when I'm ejected from the game and told I will have to sit for the next one.

What the fuck did I just do? I'm our team's leading scorer, and the game is tied with only a few minutes left.

After I got a verbal ass-kicking from Coach, I put my headphones in, grabbed my shit from my locker stall, and stormed out of the locker room.

Ignoring the fans in the hallway, I walk straight to the player exit. Just when I'm about to round the corner, someone yanks my elbow.

Taking out my AirPods, I turn, about to tell whoever it is to fuck off.

But when I fully turn, I'm met with Kenna's mesmerizing, pleading eyes. "Griffin, can we please go somewhere to talk? There's something we need to discuss."

My heart sinks at the sound of her voice. I've missed her so fucking much. But instead of telling her that, my response comes out cold and rigid. "I have nothing to say to you, McKenna. You need to walk away. Get on the next plane out and go back to Minnesota."

"I can't go back without having this conversation with you. Please," she begs, her eyes brimming with tears. I soften when I see the emotion on her face.

Seeing Kenna in front of me—looking so beautiful it hurts—is messing with my intentions.

You can't be with her.

I'm about to say fuck it and give in when a familiar and very unwelcome voice interrupts, "Oh my gosh. Desperate much? He said he doesn't want you. Get over it and move on." Emily, my ex, slinks her arm through mine. I can feel her claws grip me through my wool dress coat.

Fuck, this looks bad. I know it does.

Kenna doesn't say anything, but the look of agony on her face hits me like an ax through the chest. Then, it dawns on me that maybe this is what she needs to see. I need to hurt her now, make her understand that it's done between the two of us. That way, she can move on, and I don't have to ever feel the pain that comes with seeing her again. I'd rather feel the emptiness from her absence in my life than the pain and anger that seeing her brings.

Pain because I miss her with every breath I take. She very well may be the oxygen I need to survive.

Anger because I hate myself for pushing her away, and her presence is enough to bring me to my knees.

Hurting her is the only way she'll finally cut ties with me. It's what's best for her.

I remove my arm from Emily's grasp and wrap my arm around her shoulders instead.

Kenna visibly flinches at my gesture. I know what she's thinking. The betrayal is written all over her face.

Even though I haven't spoken a word to Emily this semester, I look at Kenna and lie straight to her beautiful face. "Like I said, I have nothing to say to you. You need to move on. Your attempts to reach me have all gone unanswered. It's starting to look pathetic. Now, if you excuse us, we've got a victory party to attend. Be sure to send Carson my condolences on his loss tonight."

"No need. I'm right here," Carson chips in as he sidles up beside Kenna. "What the fuck, G?" His voice drips with anger, matching the rage fueling me.

"Don't take it personally, Carse. I'm sure there will be plenty more losses in your college career. The first one always stings the worst." My tone is detached—condescending.

Carson's eyebrows furrow beneath his beanie. "Jesus, G. Do you think I give a fuck about the game right now? Why the fuck are you talking to my sister like she's a desperate bunny?"

Kenna cowers at his question.

"If she's going to act like one with Nelson, then I'll treat her as such." I don't wait for a response from either of them. Grabbing Emily's hand, I drag her after me. I need a stiff drink. Better yet, I need to drown in a bottle.

McKenna

I feel self-conscious wearing my jersey to the party Carson said Griff would be at, so I put on one of the oversized sweatshirts I purchased last week. My bump is still barely visible, but I don't feel like drawing more attention than I'm already going to.

Besides, I don't think Griff liked that I wore the jersey in the first place. Even though we aren't together, I will always love and support him, and I just wanted him to feel a little less alone tonight—that he had someone there to cheer him on since Katie couldn't be. How naive of me to believe he wouldn't already have hundreds of fans with his name and number on their backs.

My heart aches thinking of how he looked at me outside the locker rooms. I don't even recognize this version of Griff—arrogant, detached, rude, empty.

Carson and I are walking to the house party. "How did you know where he was?" I question Carson.

"One of his teammates, Tanner Miller, played on Team USA with me, so I texted him and asked where the party was at tonight," Carse replies.

"I just don't understand why he wouldn't give me five minutes to talk alone. Even if he is with Emily again, he could talk to me. He acted as if I meant nothing to him—like we hadn't known each other for over fifteen years." I quickly swipe a fallen tear from my cheek.

Carse takes a deep breath and then blows out a white cloud into the cold Boston air. "I can't say I would be recognizable if you had died that night, Mack. I'm not excusing his actions or words—I've never been more pissed off and disappointed than I was tonight." He pauses, gathering his thoughts. "I think you've got to go in there and not take no for an answer. You've got to do it for my little papaya." He points to my stomach and then adds, "But seriously, who even knows what the fuck a papaya is? I had to Google it once it came up on the app yesterday."

Laughing at his antics, I wrap him in a tight hug. Well, as tight as my little bump will allow.

"This is the place." Carse nods to the house in front of us. It's a brownstone, similar to Griff's, just a few blocks down from his, actually.

We walk through the front door, and I'm surprised to see how spacious it is. We walk toward the large kitchen island that is filled with alcohol and mixers.

Loud music makes hearing what Carson is saying hard. Leaning in, he shouts, "Go find G. I'll be right in here with Miller if you need me."

I nod back at him before leaving the kitchen in search of Griffin. It doesn't take long to find Griff. He's in the back corner of the living room, flocked by a group of guys whom I'm guessing are teammates and a few girls.

Taking a deep breath to ease my nerves, I shift through the crowd to get to him.

I tap Griff's shoulder. When he turns and sees it's me, his face surprisingly lights up with one of his signature smiles I've missed so much.

I'm so thrown off by his reaction to seeing me that it takes me a moment before I say, "Griff, I need to talk to you. Can we go into another room?"

He quickly nods his head up and down. "Sure, anywhere you want. Anywhere. Do you want something to drink?" I'm thrown off by the complete one-eighty he's taken since we talked a few hours ago at the rink.

Griff stares back at me with blown pupils and sweat coating his forehead then rubs his hand up and down my arm, before grabbing my wrist and dragging me down the hall to what looks like a den.

There are a few guys sitting together and taking drags off a joint. "Out, now," Griff commands.

"Who's the bunny you've got there, G? Think I can take a turn later? I don't mind Turner's seconds," one of them says.

Griff's grip on my wrist tightens, causing me to wince in pain.

"Griff, stop. You're hurting me."

"Don't *fucking* call her that. Don't even *fucking* look at her. Get the fuck out. All of you, now," Griffin growls.

The guys seem to get the message because they quickly leave the room and shut the doors behind them.

Griff moves toward me, stumbling a little bit on his feet.

"What are you doing here, Sunshine?" he asks, taking my face in his hands. "I have to touch you to know you're really here."

I close my eyes and lean into the warmth of his touch. My heart swells from the familiarity and comfort his caress brings.

That is until he grinds his erection into me and groans. I take a huge step back, breaking our embrace.

I feel like I'm getting whiplash from his intense mood swings. He went from being annoyed with me being at his game, to ecstatic to see me here, to being ready to throw down with one of his teammates, to grinding with me in a matter of minutes.

I come right out and blurt, "Griffin, I'm pregnant."

A look of agony passes across his face before his mask of indifference slips back into place.

"You sure moved on quickly. Not like I can blame you. It's been easier to numb the pain of losing Katie by blowing my load with a random here and there. But I didn't take you to be so careless. It was one thing to go bare with me, but to trust some random guy—"

I don't let him finish that statement. "I haven't been with any random guys. Jesus, Griff. What is wrong with you?"

"What is wrong with me? What the hell is wrong with you? You come here, ask to get me alone, rub up on me, then drop a bomb that someone knocked you up?"

"Not someone. *You.*"

"Me, what?"

"You. You got me pregnant, Griffin."

He lets out a low, menacing chuckle. "Get the fuck out of here with that shit, McKenna. I haven't touched you in months. You can't pin your mistakes on me. You probably can't remember who the real dad is, so you're trying to trap me with it so I'll feel obligated to take you back."

My head snaps back as if I've been slapped.

"I haven't even looked at another guy."

"Is that so? What about Ian Nelson? He seemed to know you pretty intimately," he practically growls.

"Ian is Carson's roommate. I don't know much about him, so I'm unsure how he could know me intimately."

"Don't be obtuse. You don't have to know someone to fuck them. I clearly didn't know you."

Unshed tears blur my vision. "Why are you being so cruel?"

"I'm not the one being cruel, Sunshine."

"Please don't call me that."

"Yeah, you're right. I suppose our time for niceties and nicknames passed the second you tried to trap me with a baby. How convenient that you get pregnant and then try to pin it on the nation's top NHL prospect. I didn't take you as one for a free meal ticket when you always have your mommy and daddy dearest to ride home to."

Out of nowhere, Carson charges up to us and slams his fist into Griffin's face. "You motherfucker!" Carse yells at Griff. I scream for Carson to get off him and bring myself between the two of them.

"I can't believe I ever trusted that you'd take care of my sister. You can't even take care of yourself," Carson shouts.

Griffin is breathing rapidly; his eyes are gazing at me ferally, which puts me on edge.

"You need to stay the fuck away from me, McKenna. I mean it. Don't make this ugly."

"I can't imagine this getting any uglier than it already is, Griffin. But the message was received loud and clear. I just thought you had the right to know. How *obtuse* of me to think you'd actually want to be involved in your child's life after knowing they exist."

His wide eyes soften for just a moment. "Stay away from me, Sunshine. Please. Everyone I love dies. I can't lose you too."

I shake my head, tears streaming down my face. "If you ever truly loved me, you wouldn't be sitting here breaking my heart into a million pieces, again."

And with that, I grab Carson's hand and turn my back on the only man I've ever loved—promising myself that my baby deserves better than this version of Griffin.

18

Griffin

JANUARY

My head feels like it's been split in two, right down the middle, and I sit up too quickly when my door flies open, causing my stomach to clench with nausea.

"How long?" My dad asks, his voice stern and louder than he's ever directed toward me.

"What?" I croak out. My throat feels like I ate a bag of cotton balls.

He slams my bedroom door shut, pulls my desk chair beside my bed, and sits down before he demands, "Tell me how long you've been using."

I surprise myself, doing a decent job of hiding my fear of being caught. I look him right in the eyes and lie. "I don't know what you're talking about."

"Don't bullshit me, Griffin. My last surgery got canceled, so I was able to make it to your game. Imagine my surprise when I show up and find my son is high right before he gets in a fight. His first-ever fight on the ice. What are you taking? Adderall? Ritalin? Oxy? Cocaine?"

I think about coming clean—being honest with him—but I guess I just don't have any fucks left to give. I double down on my lie. "Dad, I'm not sure what you saw last night, aside from me delivering Abbott an absolute ass-kicking. You haven't seen me play in a while. I'm not taking anything. I'm just that good."

Standing, he places his hands on his hips and shakes his head at me. "I can't believe this," he says without looking at me. "How could you do this, Griff? Don't you know you're all I have left?" His voice breaks, and fuck.

Fuck! How can I be so reckless?

I swore I would never do this to my dad after we lost our mom. But losing Katie? The pain I have to live with every day is too unbearable. Some days, I lie in bed and picture it all ending. I imagine what it would feel like if I didn't have to wake up each morning with grief's licks of pain, or if I didn't have bouts of insomnia—grief's stronghold refusing to let me escape in my dreams for even just a few hours.

Swallowing the lump in my throat, I whisper, "Adderall. But I'm fine, Dad."

"Griffin, you're not fine. I just got off the phone with Emmett. He said you got really drunk last night and yelled at McKenna."

I cut in. "Kenna was here last night?" My stomach churns at the thought of what I said to her in the hallway outside the locker rooms.

"Jesus, Griff. You can't mix alcohol and amphetamines, even when prescribed. How much did you take?"

Shaking my head, I don't want to admit this to him. I know I overindulged last night. When I saw Kenna after my game, I couldn't handle all of the feelings that came rushing out. I got two more pills, crushed them up, and snorted them for the first time right when I got to the party. I then proceeded to drink myself stupid to try to numb the ache in my chest.

Avoiding his question, I answer with one of my own, "Was Kenna really here last night?"

"That's what Emmett said, and by the looks of it, whatever you said must not have been good," he says, gesturing toward my face. "Someone gave you a hell of a shiner. If I had to guess, I'd say that was likely Carson's doing."

Shit. So that's why my head is pounding and my eye is swollen.

Dad clears his throat. "I've been seeing someone recently, Griff, and I think you should too."

My chest tightens. "You come in here and yell at me for allegedly using drugs, and now you want me to start dating someone?"

"No, I'm not dating anyone. Shit, that's not . . ." He pauses to take a deep breath. "What I meant to say was I started seeing a therapist to help me process Katie's death. I would like it if you would start talking to a therapist, too. All I'm asking is for you to try it out. If you don't like my therapist, we can find you a different one."

I look into my dad's pleading eyes. As much as I don't want to talk to a stranger about my little sister, I know I need to. If not for myself, then for the man standing before me.

"I'll do it."

Relief flashes across my dad's face. "Thank you, Griff. I love you, Son. So much. I can't lose you too. I want to fight these demons with you. Please don't shut me out."

After I told him about the intrusive thoughts I'd been experiencing and how I took Adderall to try to drown them out, he texted his therapist and asked for an emergency session. That afternoon, my dad and I went to my first therapy appointment.

The therapist recommended trying to disconnect from some of the factors that are heightening my anxiety. To start, I gave my agent, Jared, my phone and told him to contact me on a flip phone I picked up. It's perfect—no social media, no one aside from my dad, my roommates, Coach, and Jared have the number.

Then Jared recommended hiring a publicist to handle my social media and contractual obligations for my NIL deals for the foreseeable future, and I agreed.

My regular phone was triggering. Memories and daily photos titled "On This Day" would pop up of Katie and I, or Kenna and I, and the anxiety would suffocate me. It got so bad I was having daily panic attacks before I started coping with Adderall and alcohol.

I pray to a god I'm not sure I believe in that tomorrow will be better. Maybe these changes I'm making will make me want to wake up tomorrow morning instead of wishing I don't.

McKenna

The minute the wheels touched down again in Minneapolis, I scheduled a meeting with my advisor to set up online classes for the spring semester. The doctor had told me the due date was May 18th, so I could potentially go to in-person classes, but I'm not sure I want to deal with the pitying looks and questions I'll be bombarded with.

I then set up a meeting with my coach and told him about my pregnancy.

My coach told me that even though I won't be able to participate in spring training, I will be expected to attend summer training sessions with the team if I want to keep my spot next season. I'm not sure how that will look with a newborn, but I want to try.

Thankfully, both my coach and adviser have been really supportive. To say I'm shocked that Coach didn't take my spot away is an understatement.

My parents and Carson helped me move out of my dorm room after I got back from Boston. I'm going to be living with my parents and taking the short drive to campus from their house come the fall. For now, I'll be taking my online classes while living here and getting ready to have a baby.

My mom has graciously offered to watch the baby while I'm at school or practice. I feel like such an imposition on my parents. They finally became empty nesters, my dad is set to retire in a few years, and I know they were looking forward to traveling more as he lessens his caseload to prepare for retirement.

I've looked at the adoption pamphlet from Dr. Bahati's office dozens of times since I returned from Boston—since I realized I was going to be a single mom. Being a young mother is going to be challenging enough, but knowing I'm going to be doing it on my own—well, without a partner to lean on—is something that scares the shit out of me.

Sure, I'll have the support of my family, but I won't have a teammate to lean on for the next eighteen-plus years of this little baby's life.

I feel like I can barely keep my head above water right now. Each day, when I wake up, grief and guilt threaten to pull me under. I can't imagine how I'm going to have a newborn and tackle these feelings of helplessness and sorrow.

But if there's one thing I know Katie would say to me in this moment, it'd probably be something sassy like, "Perk those swollen tits up and get to fucking work, blondie." She was the yin to my yang. Most of the time, she knew what was wrong with me without me even having to say a word.

Goddammit, I miss my person. She would tell me I've got this.

Now, I've just got to believe in myself.

I've got this.

19

McKenna

MARCH

I don't have this.

Holy fucking shit, I don't have this at all.

Why in the fuck did I think I could do this?

I always imagined having my first baby with my husband by my side. Holding my hand. Feeding me ice chips and telling me I look beautiful even though I look like a hot mess.

Instead, I have a panicked Carson stuck to my side like glue. He keeps telling me to breathe through the pain, trying to coach me through the breathing techniques I learned in my online birthing classes last week. But I don't give a flying fuck about breathing techniques when I feel like someone has lit me on fire from the inside out.

Because of my shortened cervix and, up until I was hospitalized a week ago, unknown placenta previa, the nurses are prepping me for an emergency C-section.

This isn't supposed to be happening yet—I'm only thirty-three weeks along. I'm supposed to have at least another month, if not two.

Taking a deep breath through my nose, I try to breathe through the pain. But that isn't doing jack shit.

"Can I get the epidural yet?" I scream at the nurse, who has been nothing but nice. Shit. I'm being a massive bitch.

"I'm sorry, McKenna, not yet. Once you're in the OR, the anesthesiologist will be giving you a spinal block. After that's in, it will help alleviate the pain you're feeling."

"I can't do this." I look to Carson, shaking my head. The same panic on his face is mirrored on mine.

He takes the hand I'm not gripping and rubs the back of his head. "It's uh—a little too late for that, Mack. Besides, nurse Jacqueline said I could be right there with you. Isn't that right, Jackie?"

"As long as McKenna agrees to have you in the OR, and she remains stable, you may be her support person during the procedure."

Poor Carson. He came to visit me earlier, just like he has every day since I was hospitalized a week ago. When my contractions started to pick up, they declared me in labor after checking my cervix.

Due to the placenta previa, a vaginal birth isn't an option, so a C-section is the safest option for both the baby and me.

Things have moved quickly since then. So quickly, that it looks like Carson will be in the OR with me instead of my mom.

"Alright, sir. I'm going to need you to change into these scrubs and put this fashionable scrub hat and shoe covers on," the nurse says as she hands the items to Carson.

He swallows hard. "This is really happening, isn't it?"

"It is. We need to get moving to keep both baby and mama safe," she says.

With that, Carson goes into the ensuite and changes. Meanwhile, another contraction hits me. This one pulls at both my stomach and back, feeling like I'm being squeezed to death.

After another thirty seconds, the contraction begins to subside. I take a deep breath and ask the nurse, "I'm feeling a lot of pressure down there. Is that normal? I also might have peed on the bed a little bit with that last contraction." Embarrassment heats my cheeks. The discomfort of having multiple people checking my cervix and taking a peek under my blankets the past week has been a humbling experience.

"Let me take a look," Jaqueline says as she lifts up the blanket. "I don't believe that is urine. Your water may have partially broken. I'm going to go get Dr. Bahati."

Before she can leave the room, the bathroom door swings open. Carson comes out and asks, "Hey, Nurse Jackie, am I more of a McSteamy or McDreamy?"

She takes him in, then declares, "McSteamy. No doubt about it." Then she swiftly leaves the room.

I barely get out a chuckle before another contraction clenches my abdomen in a vice grip. This one is stronger than the others, and tears stream down my face from the pain.

Moments later, Nurse Jackie, as Carson calls her, comes back into the room with Dr. Bahati and a few others.

"Good evening, McKenna. The team is going to be wheeling you to the operating room, and I'll be completing your C-section. Once the baby is delivered, the NICU team will take over care of the baby while I close you up. Do you have any questions for me?"

Before I can get anything out, Carson intercepts. "Will the baby be okay? Will Mack have to be put under since this is an emergency C-section?"

Dr. Bahati gives Carson a small smile. She's familiar with him and his inquisitive nature by now—if my mom couldn't make it to an appointment, he was usually there with me. It's only fitting that he be by my side tonight as I bring my baby into the world.

"Hello, Mr. Wilder. McKenna will be able to stay awake as long as she remains stable. McKenna, you will be receiving a spinal block when you get into the OR. As far as the baby goes, we really won't know more until he or she is with the NICU team. But I assure you, the baby will be in the best hands. Our hospital has a level four NICU, which is the best of them. I would anticipate that the baby will need breathing assistance at this point in the incubator. You did receive two rounds of steroids to help the baby's lung development progress, but each day the baby can get closer to term helps their odds drastically. The baby is very lucky to have been able to continue developing for the past week. McKenna, do you have any other questions before we wheel you down?"

Feeling another contraction starting up, I quickly shake my head and ask the nurses how quickly they can get me to the anesthesiologist.

The operating room's sterility is stifling. Sounds of equipment reverberate off the walls.

A blue medical curtain blocks my view of my abdomen, but I'm not in pain anymore. They were right about the spinal block working like magic. However, I do feel some slight pressure. *It's the strangest feeling.*

As soon as that thought crosses my mind, I feel a large bout of pressure and then immense emptiness.

"It's a girl!" I hear from the other side of the curtain.

A girl? Oh my god. A girl!

I don't hear any cries.

"She's not crying. Why isn't she crying?" I frantically ask. Turning my head, I see the NICU team gathered around the baby off to the side of the OR that is barely visible to me.

"We need to help baby girl breathe. Until we know how her lungs will do on their own, we are going to intubate her to ease the burden on her lungs. We're going to take her to the NICU now, mama," I hear someone say, though I'm not sure who says it.

Mama. I'm someone's mama. A baby *girl's* mama.

I wish Katie were here. I wish Griff were here. I wish I didn't have to feel this unbearable pain that comes with this joyous moment.

Dr. Bahati tells me she's going to start stitching me up, and that after I'm out of recovery, I can be escorted to the NICU to see my baby girl.

I look up to see Carson with tears streaming down his face. "She's so beautiful, sis. I'm so fucking proud of you, Mack." He squeezes my hand that's strapped to the operating table.

Carse catches a few stray tears from my cheeks with his thumb. "She's going to be okay, Mack."

I silently nod my head in agreement. She has to be okay. My sweet girl.

After I'm out of recovery and the spinal block has worn off, Carson wheels me to the NICU to see my *daughter*.

The NICU nurses assist us in donning the proper personal protective equipment, or PPE as they call it, to keep the baby safe from as many germs as possible.

Because of her breathing tube and the warming blankets helping regulate her body temperature, I won't be able to hold her for at least a few days.

I was told I would be able to stick my hands through the two ports on the side of the incubator to touch her, though.

So when Carson wheels me right up to the side of my daughter's incubator, I stick one hand through and place my pinky in her tiny hand.

I take her in. She's bigger than I thought she would be at thirty-three weeks—though that shouldn't surprise me, knowing how tall Griffin and I both are. She has the faintest dusting of hair on her head and eyebrows. Her small hand barely encompasses the tip of my pinky finger, though she's able to grip it.

A girl. I wasn't sure what I was having, but all this time, I pictured I'd have a little girl.

It isn't until now, at this moment, when I'm touching her, and she's in front of me, that a name finally comes to me.

"Cadence. After your Auntie Katie and your grandmother Catherine, who are both no doubt watching over you right now."

Carson clears his throat before he rasps, "I love it. Do you have a middle name?"

I look over at him and think for a few moments before responding. "Aelia."

"Aelia? Hmm . . . I like it. Never heard it before."

I'm not surprised. It isn't a very common name. I found it when searching for names with different meanings. The meaning of Aelia is "sunshine." Even if Griffin doesn't want to be a part of her life, a piece of each of us exists in her—Cadence Aelia.

"I think I'm going to call her 'Cadey Cat' if that's okay with you," Carson whispers.

"I think Katie would love nothing more than for her niece to have a piece of her." Even as I say it, I'm not sure I'll be able to bring myself to call her by that nickname. But I love that Carson wants to.

Hearing Carse call Cadence "Cadey Cat" makes me think of Griff again. My heart hurts with the realization that he doesn't even know he has a daughter. Sure, I told him about my pregnancy, and even though he told me he wanted nothing to do with me, he still deserves to know she exists.

"Carse, I need to call him. I don't have my phone. Do you have yours?"

Carson doesn't even ask who I'm referring to—he knows as well as I do that Griffin needs to know this. He hands me his phone, and I take a steadying breath before I dial Griffin's phone number. I've known it by heart since I was a teenager. It is only one digit different than Katie's was.

The phone rings twice and then goes to voicemail. Great, he's still rejecting Carson's calls.

Instead of leaving a voicemail, I text him.

Carson:

Hey, this is Kenna. I know things were a mess when I left Boston, but I thought you deserved to know. I had a baby girl. Her name is Cadence. Please call me.

The NICU monitors create a symphony of noises that echo and haunt my every dream.

Cadence is hooked up to so many chords and tubes, I can hardly see her beautiful face.

This first week has been hard. It feels like every step forward is met with two steps back. Progress in the NICU is slow, and each day feels like an uphill climb—though I'm told that she's doing incredibly well. My baby girl is a fighter, and it kills me to see her struggle.

I'm pulled from my thoughts when my phone chimes with a notification. I swipe and see it's an update on Carson's game. Today, he plays in the national semi-finals. The Frozen Four is here in St. Paul, and he's playing against Griffin's team, Emery University. Both teams have been so steady all season, and I can hardly believe I'm not there to cheer Carson on.

He told me yesterday he wanted to speak to his coach and not play today. Carse said he couldn't bear the thought of playing when Cadence was still in the NICU, especially since her status differs so much each day. I told him that if he didn't play today, I would tell the nurses that he needed to be removed from the approved visitor list.

Carson pouted but eventually relented. He said he wasn't looking forward to playing against Griffin, knowing the last time they saw each other ended with Carse punching Griff. Carson is also just as upset and disappointed in Griff as I am that he still hasn't responded to my text.

I was worried maybe his phone was broken, but he's been pretty active on social media this week leading up to the Frozen Four tournament.

I've come to accept that he doesn't want anything to do with me. What I can't accept? That he doesn't want anything to do with our daughter. Cadence is an innocent accident that came from two people who were in love. She doesn't deserve his neglect and abandonment.

My phone chimes again, and I see that the game is tied one-to-one after the first period.

Just as I'm about to text my mom for an update on how Carson's playing, a monitor starts dinging loudly, alerting the nurse in the hallway to come in.

"What's going on?" I ask her frantically.

"Your daughter's oxygen levels have lowered, causing the alarm to sound. I paged the on-call doctor to come see her."

The doctor comes in a few minutes later and says they need to run some additional tests on Cadence's heart and lungs.

After an echocardiogram is completed, they determine that Cadence has patent ductus arteriosus, which is a heart defect that is sometimes found in preemies.

Even though I'm not sure if the game is done or not, I call my mom to tell her. She says the game just finished and that Carson's team won in overtime. Carson had the game-winning goal.

I don't have the capacity at the moment to be happy for my brother. All I can focus on is what the doctor just told me.

I choke on the sob stuck in my throat. "There was a complication with Cadence. She has a heart defect, and they want to do a cardiac catheterization tomorrow morning to repair it."

"Oh my gosh, McKenna. I will have your dad bring me to the hospital now. Do you need us to bring you anything?"

"No, but thank you." I take a deep breath, hesitating, before I add, "Do you think we could avoid Carson finding out? I don't want to mess with his head before the big game. If he finds out Cadence needs to have a procedure done, he will refuse to play in the National Championship game."

There's a pause on her end. "I don't know if that's a good idea, honey. Your brother cares and loves fiercely. He will be hurt if we keep this from him. Besides, the game isn't tomorrow. It's on Saturday."

She's right. I know she is. Carson will probably never forgive me if I keep this from him.

"Okay. But can you please tell him? I'm not sure I can get through it again." Tears fill my eyes, and my throat tightens.

"Of course, honey. I'll be there soon. I love you."

Hanging up the phone, I let the tears that I was holding back fall.

I never imagined having a baby on my own. And I certainly didn't expect to have that baby in the NICU, getting prepped to have a heart procedure at only eight days old.

A half-hour later, there's chatter coming from the hallway before Carson comes into the room donned in PPE.

"What are you doing here?" I ask incredulously.

"I came as soon as I heard. Tell me she's going to be okay," Carse demands.

"The surgeon who will be performing her procedure tomorrow morning seemed very positive about her prognosis. He said the PDA she has is sometimes seen in preemies and that sometimes they close on their own. However, Cadence's is larger, causing her oxygen levels to lower, so they need to do a cardiac catheterization procedure."

"I'm so sorry I wasn't here, Mack. This is exactly why I didn't want to play tonight."

"Stop. If you wouldn't have played, I wouldn't have forgiven you. You didn't need to rush here. Cadence is stable for now, and the surgery isn't until tomorrow morning." I pause, then ask, "Did you say anything to him—to Griff, I mean?"

"No, I didn't say a word. He kept his distance and acted like we were strangers. Figures since he's ghosting my sister and abandoning his daughter."

"God, I know he misses Katie. I'm lost without her, too. But I don't understand how he can know he has a daughter and not want to know more about her, or see her when he's in the same state as her!" I raise my voice. Cadence stirs, so I quickly lower my voice. "This is so unlike him. Sure, it was unexpected and an accident that I got pregnant, but it isn't like Griffin to turn his back on his responsibilities."

"I don't think there's much left of the Griff we both knew growing up, Mack. Besides, now that Emery lost, there are rumors that Colorado is calling G up for the playoffs. He's probably on a plane back to Boston to pack his things now."

"It happens that quickly?"

"Yeah, it's not uncommon. Especially for someone who had as good of a last half of the season as Griff did. He was the leading point-scorer in all of college hockey."

I already knew this. Even though Griff had made it clear he wanted nothing to do with me, I still kept tabs on him. I needed to make sure he was doing okay. And by the looks of his stats, I'd say he was doing more than okay.

It shouldn't surprise me with how he behaved the last time I saw him that he would ignore my attempts to reach out to him. But there was still some small part of me that held out hope that he'd have a change of heart—that he'd want to be in his child's life.

The following day, the surgeon comes into Cadence's room just after seven in the morning.

"Good morning, Mr. and Mrs. Wilder. My name is Dr. Jordan. I'll be the cardiologist performing your daughter's procedure."

I don't correct the doctor, fearing they may make Carson leave the room if he isn't a parent of Cadence.

"Thank you, Dr. Jordan," I say, and he shakes both of our hands before leaving the room.

"Well, he has a strong handshake, so that makes me feel like he'll have steady hands during the operation. That's a good sign." Carson attempts to put me at ease.

I love him for trying, but there's no reassuring me right now. I'm a complete mess. Signing paperwork stating I consent to a medical procedure that could cause injury or even death to my daughter is not something I envisioned doing when I thought about what it'd be like to be a mother someday.

A nurse comes in and says, "I'm going to be taking your daughter to the operating room. Can you please confirm her name and date of birth?"

I do. Then the nurse states Carson and I can go with Cadence until we get to the entrance of the sterile field. I wish I could take her out and hold her just one time before they take her away.

The moment the nursing staff wheels Cadence's incubator past the sterile field, I crumble into Carson's arms, sobbing uncontrollably for so long my tears run dry. I pray with every fiber in my being for my daughter to make it through this procedure and, hopefully, into my arms.

Watch over her for me, Katie.

PART 2

After

Almost a year and a half later . . .

20

McKenna

JULY

I'm panic cleaning our new place. It's not a mess, but I want everything to be as tidy as possible for when the woman I'm interviewing gets here.

Carson just purchased a house a few weeks ago with his rookie signing bonus. I told him not to, but he said between his trust and the signing bonus, he had more money than he knew what to do with and that investing in real estate was something his agent suggested.

Speak of the devil, I remove Carson's noise-canceling gaming headset from his head. He peeks up from his spot on the couch with a what-the-fuck look on his face.

"Carse, can you help me pick up quickly before she arrives?" I ask.

He answers me with a question. "Before who arrives?"

"You haven't been listening to a word I've said, have you?" I question with a huff. "The nanny I'm interviewing to help watch Cadence a few days a week."

"Wait, you're hiring a nanny? Is she hot?"

"Seriously? No. Nope. You're not messing this up for Cades and me. I need someone I can trust to take good care of my daughter and not bone my brother!"

"I mean, multitasking is a great skill to have on a resume—definitely comes in handy while nannying."

"You're incorrigible. I wonder why you're still single . . ."

"Coming from my very single twin sister." He flashes me the sassiest of smirks.

I roll my eyes. "Can you just help me? Quickly. She will be here any minute. Just pick up the wrappers from the coffee table and fold the blankets on the couch. I'll do a quick sweep of the kitchen."

Just as I'm putting a few of Cadence's toys away, the doorbell rings. I jog to the front door and swing it open to find a beautiful brunette woman in front of me. She's got the brightest smile that reaches up to her emerald-green eyes.

"Hi there. I'm McKenna," I say, reaching my hand out for her to shake.

"Hello, I'm Dakota. It's so nice to meet you."

"You too! Thanks for being flexible with me. I didn't have much time in my schedule to meet up at a coffee shop. Come right this way. We can chat in the kitchen."

Dakota steps through the door frame, and I guide her to the kitchen.

"Sorry, we can just sit on the barstools. We just moved in, so not all of the furniture has been unpacked yet," I clarify.

"Oh, that's okay. I don't mind." She has the slightest Southern twang to her voice.

"Alright, well, I suppose I'll just jump right into it. I'm looking for a nanny for my daughter, Cadence. She's sixteen months old. She hasn't started walking yet, but she crawls everywhere."

"What a beautiful name that is. I love that stage, where they're learning something new each day!" Dakota sounds so genuinely kind—I can't help but smile.

"I know, it's so much fun to watch. But please, tell me a little bit about yourself and why you applied for the position."

"Right, I have to apologize in advance. I'm a bit rusty when it comes to interviewing."

"That's okay. I've never conducted an interview before. Think of it as a chance to get to know one another."

"Well, I graduated from college a couple of years ago with a degree in English. I've always loved working with kids of all ages. I babysat my younger cousins from the time I was twelve until I moved away for college. When it comes down to it, I'm looking for something to occupy my time while I figure out what I want to do next with my degree."

Just then, I notice Carson has come out of the pantry with an armful of snacks. He's stopped dead in his tracks, staring at Dakota.

"Oh, hello! I'm Dakota. I'm here to interview for the nannying position."

Carson's eyes literally smolder when she smiles his way. Setting his snacks on the island, Carse tries to look casual, crossing his arms and leaning against the edge of the counter.

"You must be Mr. Wilder," she continues, holding out her hand for Carson to shake.

"Carson, McKenna's twin brother. But you can call me Mr. Wilder if you'd like." He untucks one of his arms to shake Dakota's now outstretched hand.

"Oh my goodness, my apologies. It's nice to meet you, Carson." Dakota's breath hitches when her hand meets Carson's. She quickly pulls it away as if she's been burnt.

Trying to steer away from the awkward tension that Carson brought into the room, I ask Dakota, "What's your availability for weekends and evenings? I'm on Abbott University's volleyball team, so I may need the nanny to watch her during games if my parents decide not to bring her."

"Honestly? I have practically no life. Most of my friends and family live out of state, so I rarely have plans that will conflict with your game or practice schedule. I'm assuming you're also looking for someone to watch her while you're in classes?"

"Just two days per week while I'm in class. The rest of the nannying position would come for practice times and games. There may also be the occasional nights where Carson plays that I might want to watch, but the games would be too late for Cadence."

"That all sounds great." Then Dakota turns to Carse and asks, "Do you also play a sport for Abbott?"

"I did last season. I just signed my rookie contract with the Minnesota Wolverines." When she continues to stare at him blankly, he adds, "I am a professional hockey player."

"Oh my gosh, how silly of me. My apologies, I don't follow any sports aside from football. I don't have much of a choice there."

"Why is that?" Carson questions.

"Well, growing up in Texas, it's ingrained in our way of life."

"Ah, so that's where that slight drawl comes from. I like it." Carse flashes a smirk at her.

Dakota's cheeks turn crimson as she continues, "Then there's the fact that my older brother plays football for the Denver Mustangs."

"Shit, really? What's his name?" Carse asks, leaning forward with intrigue.

"Brody Meyer, he plays—"

Carson interrupts, "Are you kidding me? Brody Meyer, one of the league's all-time greatest quarterbacks, is your older brother?"

Her cheeks heat darker, if that's possible.

"My one and only."

Knowing I need to put Dakota out of her misery, I ask, "Hey, Carse, could you go check on Cadence? I think I heard her just now. She might have woken up from her nap."

Without another word, Carson runs from the room. "I'm coming, Cadey Cat!" If there's one person he loves most in this world, it's Cadence.

Shaking my head, I turn back to Dakota. "I'm sorry about him. He's a great guy, I swear. He just—he can be like a puppy dog sometimes."

She covers her mouth to hide her chuckles. "I think he and I will get along just fine. If I get the job, that is."

"I'm going to cut to the chase. I'm very much a person who picks up on vibes others put off. And I sense you're wanting this job for more reasons than just to occupy your time," I pause, and Dakota looks down at her hands folded in her lap.

"When it comes down to it, I'm looking for something to do while my husband works. He has a very demanding job, working long hours, and I'm bored of only being a housewife." Her tone shifts, and maybe it's just that she's shy, but she sounds hesitant to admit that aloud.

"Well, I'm just glad you applied for the job. I'd love to have you meet Cadence when she wakes up. If you pass the final test—getting her approval—then you're hired."

"Oh my goodness, I was not expecting this. I mean, I had hoped it would go well. But I thought my interviewing skills were so rusty you'd pick someone else for sure."

Just then, Carson enters the room with a smiling Cadence on his hip.

"What'd we miss?" He raises a brow. Cadence looks from me to Dakota and smiles so big her little dimple pops. Cadence claps her hands together, wiggling her body excitedly in Carson's arms.

"I offered Dakota the position. And I'm hoping she's about to accept the offer."

She stands up and heads over to Carson and Cadence. "Of course, I accept! Look at this darlin'. How could I say no to this smile?"

Carson's face lights up. "I do have a great smile, don't I? I had braces for two years in middle school and haven't lost any teeth on the ice yet."

"I wasn't talking about you, Golden Boy," Dakota taunts so quietly I barely hear it.

"Hear that, Mack? She's already got a nickname for me." He ruefully wiggles his eyebrows, then looks at Dakota, "Careful, Austin, I might develop a crush."

"I'm actually from Dallas."

Carson just shakes his head and smiles at her. I haven't seen this look from him before. It's like he's enamored. I'll have to break it to him later that she said she's married.

It's Carson's and my twenty-first birthday today. We didn't go out last night at midnight because I had a match earlier today. But Carse is refusing to let me back out of going out. He even arranged for Dakota to watch Cadence for me.

Our parents are joining us tonight at the bars. It might seem strange to have your parents join your twenty-first birthday, but we're both so close with them that it wouldn't feel right to celebrate this milestone without them.

A group of our friends met us downtown tonight to celebrate and we're at a bar by the arena Carson plays at, The Wolf Den. Brooke, Alexa, and a few of my other teammates are on the dance floor while I'm at the long table we reserved for the night, taking a shot with Carson and Ian.

Ian was Carson's roommate for the past two years, up until Carson signed with the Wolverines and bought his house this summer.

When I grabbed a shot from his hand earlier and took it, Ian teased me, "You already stole my roommate. Now you're stealing my liquor? That's it. You owe me a dance."

Ian and I have had an easygoing friendship since Carson introduced me to him. Over the past few months, though, he's turned up the charm and flirted endlessly with me. I can't say I hate the attention though. It's been almost two years since I've danced with a guy.

I'm laughing, and my cheeks are flushed as Ian leads me out onto the makeshift dance floor. Wrapping his arms around my waist, Ian pulls my back flush to his chest and before I know it, we're getting lost in the music, finding our rhythm together. After a few songs go by, I'm buzzed from the liquor and the music flowing through me.

Wait, I'm literally buzzing.

I realize then that it's my phone vibrating in the back pocket of my jeans.

Looking down at my phone, I see it's a call from an unknown caller. I'm not even sure why I do it, but I pull away from Ian before hitting the green button.

Bringing the phone to my ear, I hold my other hand over my other ear so I can hear over the loud bar. "Hello?"

I'm met with silence on the other end. This is giving me a sense of Deja Vu.

"Helloooo. This is McKenna. Did you get the wrong number?"

"No, I didn't."

My breath hitches when I hear Griffin's deep tone.

"Happy birthday, Sunshine."

Click.

That's it? After almost two years of silence, that's it?

But . . . he didn't forget.

Why does he do this to me?

He called me as an unknown caller, meaning I couldn't call him back or text him if I wanted to.

How dare he call me Sunshine and then just hang up.

It's as if he could sense I was having fun with another guy for the first time since he shattered my heart.

With one short phone call, with just one *word*, he's thrown my heart from my chest and sent it free falling.

Fuck you, Griffin Turner.

21

Griffin

September

The Mile High City has done wonders for my mental health. My heart broke in Boston, but I began to heal in the mountains of Colorado.

It's the beginning of September, so I need to report to training camp in a few weeks. This will be the start of my second full season with the Colorado Summits.

Last season I was a rookie, but I made sure my spot on this team was undeniable. I put up record points and won The Calder Memorial Trophy, which is the Rookie of the Year award.

Nights spent beneath the stars have replaced nights I used to party and close down the bars. There's a reason I had such an amazing year last year. I don't drink alcohol during the season, and I haven't touched any drugs since I began therapy almost two years ago.

Being outdoors has been so healing. I can't ski or snowboard due to my contract, which sucks when you live in a place that's known for being the best place in the country to go for that. Instead, I've rekindled my love of hiking, camping, fishing, and hunting. And there are truly not many places in the country better to do those things either.

This weekend is Labor Day weekend. It will mark the two-year anniversary of Katie's death. It feels like it's been an eternity since that day, while also feeling like it was just yesterday.

The grasp grief held on my life has loosened, but I still feel the squeeze of its presence at the most random times. Grief is a bitch that way—just when you think you've moved on to acceptance, the anger, anguish, and pleading rush back and bring you to your knees.

Dealing with the loss of my mother at such a young age was difficult. But losing Katie broke me in a way I hope to never feel again. I haven't let many people into my life since I lost Katie. No matter how much my therapist and I discussed it, I couldn't bear it when I lost my sister and pushed away the love of my life. It didn't seem fair—I could never replace them.

My life in Colorado isn't lonely, but I'm more of a loner. The guys on the team deemed me the recluse rookie last year. They'd give me shit for never going out at the beginning of the season, but they stopped once I proved myself out on the ice.

I'm currently on my way to the airport to pick up my dad. He stayed in Boston, where he's still the Chief of Surgery at the hospital. I tried to get him to move to Colorado with me, but he said he didn't want to leave his job after only a few months. It may have also had something to do with the woman he started seeing shortly after I left for Colorado. Her name is Bethany, and she's also a cardiologist at the hospital he works at, though she specializes in pediatrics. I'm happy for him, but I miss the shit out of him.

This weekend is a hard one for both of us. Last year, we went on a camping and fishing trip together out here. This year, we decided to make a tradition out of it and honor Katie the only way we know how: by spending time together.

Even though Katie mostly read books in a hammock on our camping trips growing up, she always loved to be outdoors. She would've loved Colorado as much as I do.

Two years has allowed me the time my heart needed to heal. I'm not sure I'll ever be able to think of Katie without a wave of sadness flooding me, but I've moved past the anger and despair I felt every time I heard her name or thought of the life that was stolen from her.

I pull up to the departure terminal, where my dad said he'd be waiting for me. Going to the departures instead of the arrivals is a weird quirk my dad swears by. He must be on to something though, since there is minimal traffic here compared to the line I saw for arrivals.

My dad is waiting, leaning against a cement pillar with his hiking backpack and a duffle bag. I pull up to the curb and get out to give him a tight hug.

We've come a long way in two years—a testament to the weekly virtual therapy sessions we complete together.

"How was the flight, old man?"

He lightly smacks my arm. "Who are you calling old? I'm still a spry and steady surgeon. I've still got a few decades before you can justify calling me that."

I shake my head at his nonsense. "Steady, maybe. Spry? We'll see if you can put your money where your mouth is when we're hiking to our fishing spot tomorrow," I tease as I toss his bags in the back of my Jeep.

Our plan is to drive to Black Canyon of the Gunnison National Park today, which is almost a five-hour drive. We'll stay at a hotel tonight and then get up early, get our campsite set up at the park, and hike to one of the trout streams. We like to fish as much as we can, and this National Park is supposed to have good trout fishing this time of year.

We're about thirty minutes into the drive when my dad finally brings it up—the discussion I was hoping to avoid for at least a day or two.

"Did you hear Carson signed with Minnesota?"

"I did." I grip the wheel a little tighter trying to ease the ache in my chest that comes any time I think of my former childhood best friend, which inevitably makes me think of his twin sister.

"They're going to have a hell of a team this season. Carson will fill the gap they had on the second line after they traded Fuller."

I hum in response, hoping he'll get the hint that I don't want to talk about this.

Clearly, he doesn't pick up what I'm putting down because he continues, "It was just announced yesterday that Bennett Wilson will be the team captain this year for the Wolverines. I'm glad Carson will have him to look up to. Bennett has always had a good head on his shoulders."

"He has," I agree. Bennett is a year older than me, and his brother Jackson is Carson's age. "Have you heard anything about Jackson signing with Minnesota? Or is he going to play another season for Harvard?" I ask.

"It sounds like they're going to see how training camp goes before making a decision," my dad replies.

I love playing for Colorado—it's always been my dream team to play for. When I was drafted by them, I was ecstatic. But I can't help but feel a pang of jealousy that Carson gets to play with Bennett and possibly Jackson, in our home state.

No matter where I live, Minnesota will always be home. How could it not be when I left my heart and soul there two years ago?

22

McKenna

OCTOBER

Today is by far the biggest moment of my brother's life. Carson is playing in his first, regular-season NHL game this afternoon. He was drafted to the Minnesota Wolverines shortly after Cadence was born, but they wanted him to play another year of college hockey before signing him.

My parents, Cadence, and I are all here today to support him, and today's game is an afternoon game. The 3 p.m. start time is great for Cadence's current nap schedule.

We're at the arena early, in our black and lime green jerseys with Wilder on the back, waiting for Carson to come on the ice for his rookie lap. It's a tradition the league does with rookies at their first regular-season game. I know Carson has been waiting for this moment for his entire life.

Even though this is the biggest game of my brother's career, a part of me is dreading being here. Not because I don't want to support him, but because Carson plays the Colorado Summits—the team Griffin now plays for.

After almost two years, I wish I could forget that man exists. Or at least stop the butterflies from taking flight in my stomach when I think of him. Even after he shattered my heart and abandoned his daughter—not even acknowledging her existence—my body and heart still betray me.

Griffin Turner had the nerve to call me on my birthday and then just hang up. Where does he get off?

I wish he wouldn't have hung up so I could've let him have it.

Oh, you want to wish me a happy birthday and call me by the name of endearment you gave me? How about you call me to ask how your daughter is doing? Or ask anything about her, since you know jack shit!

Instead, he took the coward's way out. He used a blocked number, knowing I couldn't contact him in return. And his old number? No longer in service. I've tried. I thought maybe he had blocked my number, but that wasn't the case. He just disconnected the number altogether. Conveniently, right after I texted him telling him he has a daughter.

But today isn't about Griffin. It's about Carson.

I've prepared myself, knowing I'll see Griff out on the ice. Thankfully, after we watch Carson's rookie lap, we get to watch the rest of the game from the family and friends suite they set us up with, so seeing Griffin Turner from a distance won't be as difficult to get through.

The buzzer sounds in the arena.

"Oh, look! Here he comes!" Mom jumps up and down.

Carson steps out onto the ice from the home team's bench, grabs a puck with his stick, and fires it into the net. He takes a deep breath, and the biggest smile breaks over his face. He's never looked more joyful than he does at this moment. Tears fill my eyes as Carson makes his way over to the glass where we're cheering for him. He holds his glove up and waves at Cadence, who's wearing a mini version of his jersey and noise-canceling headphones that take up most of her tiny head.

"Uncle Car Car loves you so much, Cadey Cat!" He blows her a kiss, and I hear girls screaming behind us.

219

Then the announcer's voice sounds through the arena. "Make some noise for your Minnesota Wolverrriiiinnneeesssss!" And just like that, the ice is filled with players in black and lime green jerseys.

Carson skates away to begin his warmup, and I quickly turn to head up to the suite. The last thing I want is to be ice-level when I see Griffin for the first time in twenty-two months.

Right as I turn the corner for the suite, I run into Ian.

"Oh, hey, Ian. I didn't know if you were going to make it today or not."

He wraps his arms around Cadence and me, embracing us in a hug. "And miss out on my best friend's rookie debut? Not a chance. How are you, Kenz?"

I slightly cringe inside every time he calls me that. He's not the first person, nor will he be the last, to call me that. But there's just something about the way he says it. Like it's some cute nickname only he's given me. Little does he know, no one else really calls me that because they all know I can't stand it.

"I hope you don't mind. Carson invited me to sit with you guys and join you for dinner and drinks after to celebrate," Ian explains.

"No, not at all. I'm sure he'll love to have you there."

"I was hoping maybe he wouldn't be the only one happy to have me here."

Oh boy. This is awkward. I absolutely *loathe* awkward situations. Like, I straight up get hives from awkward shit.

Before I can say anything, he continues, "Look, I know today isn't easy on you. Turner is here parading his bachelor lifestyle in your face. Just know I'm here for you . . . feel free to use that to your advantage . . . however you want."

Gulp. What the hell? What is that supposed to mean? Does he mean I should use him to make Griffin jealous?

Ha! Even if I tried that out, Griff wouldn't get jealous.

"I appreciate the offer, Ian. But I'm good, honest. Today is about Carse and celebrating his biggest achievement on the ice."

Ian just nods his head before placing his hand on my lower back and guiding us into the suite.

Apparently, my delivery needs more work.

Note to self: Be far more blunt in my future rejections.

The moment I see him coming down the player's hallway, I run up and jump into his arms.

"Great game, Carse. I'm so unbelievably proud of you. Scoring a goal in your rookie debut? Amazing!" I tell Carson as I bring him in for another big hug.

"Thanks, Mack. I think it's because I had my good luck charm here tonight," he says, letting go of me before making grabby hands at my mom. "Come here, Cadey Cat. Let Uncle Car Car hold his little lucky charm."

Cadence practically throws herself out of my mom's arms and into Carson's outstretched ones. "How did she do?" Carson asks me.

"She did surprisingly well. She even tracked the puck and said Ca-Ca a few times," I gush.

Ian slaps Carson's shoulder. "Hell of a game, man."

I stiffen as Ian wraps his arm around my shoulder, giving me a gentle squeeze that I'm sure is supposed to be reassuring; however, tonight, it just brings a wave of uneasiness.

"Ca-Ca," Cadence exclaims, slapping Carson's cheeks.

"Ouch!" he fakes being hurt, rubbing his cheek.

Cadence's responding giggles make us all ring out in laughter, the sound echoing off the walls.

My laughter quickly dies as the hairs on the back of my neck stand up, but it's not from Ian's embrace. It's from *him*.

I turn my head in time for my eyes to connect with chocolate-colored eyes. The same eyes I'd stared into every night as I read bedtime stories and sang countless lullabies until they peacefully closed. Only the eyes I'm staring into now don't belong to my daughter. They belong to her father, Griffin Turner.

23

Griffin

OCTOBER

After I finish the post-game press, get showered, and change, I put my headphones in and head down the player's hallway that leads us out to where the team bus is waiting.

I'm just about to press play on my postgame playlist when I hear a voice that jump-starts my heart. I knew with tonight being Carson's first game, there was a chance she'd be here if she wasn't playing her own game. I quickly place my headphones back in their case and take a deep breath.

My heart rate quickens, and my chest tightens when her laughter echoes down the hall. The melodic sound awakened something inside of me that I hadn't felt in so long. Flashbacks of what it was like to be the cause of that beautiful laugh hit me all at once.

Turning the corner, what had my pulse thundering only seconds ago suddenly causes my heart to stop dead in my chest.

I stand in shock as I stare into the icy-blue eyes that have haunted me for the past two years. Her face has paled into a ghostly shade of white, and she looks like she's about to faint at the sight of me.

"Mama! Look! Mama!"

The fact that I can hear anything over the ringing in my ears is a miracle. This has to be a sick joke, because the scene playing out in front of me isn't real life—it can't be.

I try to gather myself, but I can't. I'm stunned, frozen at the sight of Kenna, *my Kenna*, shrugging away from the guy with his arm draped over her shoulders.

And Carson is holding the blonde baby girl who just called her "Mama."

Kenna goes to grab the baby girl from Carson and wraps the little girl into her arms, nuzzling her neck—breathing her in.

"Hi, baby," she coos to the girl.

I watch as the little girl pulls back and grabs Kenna's cheeks, placing a big, sloppy kiss on her face before giggling.

How is this happening? I knew it was over. We hadn't spoken since that night in Boston, the night that changed everything.

But now it's *really* over . . . for good. Kenna has moved on. She created a life with someone else. They started a family.

A family you'll never be a part of.

My stomach sinks at the thought, my throat clogging with the realization.

Kenna turns her back to me, leaning in to whisper something to her brother.

The next moment happens as if in slow motion. The little girl peeks up at me over Kenna's shoulder and the moment her dark, coffee-colored eyes meet mine, *I know*, beyond a shadow of a doubt, that's my daughter.

My shock quickly transitions into confusion as the realization sinks in.

"Can someone please explain what's going on?" I growl.

I watch as Carson winces, Kenna turns an angry shade of red, and Kenna's parents go to grab the little girl—my daughter—from her arms.

"We'll take her to the restaurant and meet you both there," Liz says to Kenna and Carson.

"Ian, why don't you ride with us," her dad suggests.

"Works for me," Ian replies. That's when I realize Ian-mother-fucking-Nelson is the guy who had his arm slung over Kenna's shoulder.

Carson goes up to his mom and wraps her and the little girl into a hug. "Uncle Carse loves you so much, Cadey Cat," I barely hear him say to the girl before she's swept away by Kenna's parents.

I feel my vision blurring and my breaths starting to come out staggered. Did Carson just call her "Katie Cat?" As in, the same nickname I used for Katie?

"What's her name?" I demand.

Kenna stutters her response, "Wh-what? Whose name?"

"Cut the shit, McKenna," I command in a chilling tone, one I've never used before. "What's my daughter's name? She's mine, right? Jesus—of course, she's mine. Look at her eyes. They're a carbon copy of mine."

"Alright, let's take this conversation back here. There's no one in the film room right now. We can talk away from where the media may overhear," Carson suggests and leads us to a room down the hallway.

Once we're inside, I turn to find Kenna staring back at me with a thunderous expression. "Is this some sort of fucked up game you're playing, Griff? What is wrong with you?" she shouts.

"What is wrong with me? Who has a secret child and doesn't tell the father? Is she mine? Tell me right now."

"Yes—dammit! Of course, she's yours. Why are you acting this way—as if you're shocked? As if you didn't look me right in my eyes and tell me that you didn't care that I was pregnant and to stay the fuck away from you?" Her eyes are glassy now, filled with unshed tears.

"You're lying. You've never said a word to me about a baby—a pregnancy."

"What are you talking about? That night in Boston, when you played against Carson, I came to the after-party to tell you."

I physically recoil at the mention of that night. "And you clearly forgot to tell me—hence why I had no clue I've had a daughter for the past two years—"

Carson cuts in, "She's eighteen months. And I was there with Kenna."

Is he serious right now? The six-month difference doesn't matter much when I missed out on the entire two years.

Carson places his hands on my shoulders and says, "I was there that night with Mack when she told you. After seeing you when we got there, I should've never let her tell you by herself. I'd never seen you like that, man. It was like you had taken everything under the kitchen sink—you were crazy. She said she told you everything, and you laughed in her face and told her to get the fuck out of there."

My stomach churns, bile filling my throat. The visceral fear that they're telling the truth hits me like a truck.

I was so fucked up that night. It was the week of my twenty-first birthday, the same week that Katie would have been nineteen. I took too many Adderall and mixed it with alcohol to try and drown out the shock from seeing Kenna.

The only recollection I have of Kenna being there that night came from what Emmett and my dad told me. I can remember how seeing her again at the game—in a jersey that was half mine and half Carson's—made me feel something for the first time in weeks. I know that when I got to the party, I snorted more Adderall and drank my weight in alcohol, needing to drown out the pain I was riddled with. Anything to pierce through the veil of pain I felt when I saw the look on her face.

I have pieces of what that night consisted of, but clearly, I don't remember the essential piece they're talking about. The part I do recall is the look of anguish and disappointment on Kenna's face as I walked away after the game with Emily.

"You were in no place to bring a child into this world. Mack was so terrified after that night that she contemplated giving the baby up for adoption instead of keeping her." Carson takes a deep breath and continues, "I got her out of there and got her home as quickly as we could. The moment she saw Cadence, the light came back into her eyes. Shit, she changed all of our lives for the absolute best."

Cadence.

"Apparently, everyone but me—her father. Jesus Christ, I have a daughter," I choke out the words that haven't fully sunk in until this moment. "After everything we'd been through, did you think I didn't deserve another chance to know?"

Her dark expression tells me precisely how she feels about my remark.

But I can't waste another second hearing her reasons at this point. I need to see my daughter and get to know her.

"Can I see her?" I plead.

McKenna

Griff stands so close to me that we're almost touching. Over time, I forgot how tall and broad he is—though it looks like his muscles are

227

bulging more than ever. The league has done wonders for his athletic frame.

I take a deep breath to steady myself but groan when the smell of laundry detergent mixed with his cologne and mint overwhelms my senses. Why does he have to smell so intoxicating? The notes of cedar and spice spring me back in time to memories of being wrapped in his arms, feeling loved and cherished.

Seeing him again after two years is a heady feeling. I almost forgot how beautiful the gold flecks in his deep brown eyes are. Okay, that's a lie. I've seen these eyes, this jawline, this immaculate man every night in my dreams for the past two years. The sound of his voice now is just as haunting as the words he's spoken.

What does he mean he didn't know? The fucking audacity of this man. And he wants to see her? He's had a year and a half to come see her.

"That wasn't the only attempt I made to tell you about her. I called you on the night she was born," I state, my voice trembling.

"When? If you called on the day she was born, I would have remembered. I got my shit together after that night in Boston. My dad came the next day, took one look at me, and I started therapy that same day. I haven't touched drugs or drank in excess since that night." His admission takes me by surprise.

What does that mean if, after all this time, he hasn't reached out to me? I had convinced myself it was because he was still drowning himself in liquor and bad decisions each night. But I should've known better. An elite athlete, which is what I've heard Griffin be called by broadcasters, can't dissolve their problems in booze and drugs and still play at this level.

"I did tell you again. I called you from Carson's phone on the night she was born, but like every other attempt, it went to voicemail. So I texted you and told you that I had a girl and to call me. I took one look at her beautiful face inside the incubator they had her in, and I knew I had to tell you at least she existed. That you had a daughter who was a perfect little fighter."

"Fuck. Goddammit."

"What?"

"When was she born?"

"March 29th."

"As in right before the Frozen Four?"

"Yes, Griffin."

"McKenna, shit, I'm sorry. I can't say for certain if I was in the right headspace to pick up the phone or not at that time, but I honestly didn't have my phone anymore. I gave it up after that night in Boston when I started therapy. My agent, Jared, had it, and he hired a publicist to take over my social media accounts. I still haven't been on social media in almost two years, which explains how I didn't know until today that you even had a child."

Not that he needs to know, but I don't post anything about Cadence on my social media. It's important to me to keep her out of the media.

"I'm having a hard time wrapping my head around everything. Why did you choose to disconnect your phone?" I question.

"My therapist suggested blocking out things that triggered my anxiety and panic attacks I was having at the time. One major trigger for me was my old phone because of the photos on it and the social media memories that would come up. Every time I felt like I was coming up for a breath of air, a memory popped up on my phone, letting the grief resurface and pull me back under. So, I handed it over to Jared. He would tell me if anything major came up, but my dad, my coach, and my teammates all had my new number, so I didn't really use it much. I disconnected my old number when I signed with Colorado after the

Frozen Four. I didn't think to check my messages with the chaos of moving."

"I'm sorry, but it's hard for me to believe you when the timing came literally days after I called to tell you about her, Griffin."

"And you don't think I'm having a hard time wrapping my head around the fact that I just now found out I have a daughter?"

"If I have to try to be understanding of your situation, you need to try to put yourself in my shoes."

Griffin

I take a deep breath, and as my anger begins to subside, I curse myself for my stubbornness. "I'm sorry, McKenna. You're right. I apologize. That was unfair of me. I just don't want to miss another second of her life. Please, Kenna. I've already missed so much."

Seeing that she's not ready to discuss whether or not I can see Cadence yet, I look into Kenna's eyes and plead. "Will you tell me about her, please?"

She's still visibly upset, which is understandable. But she takes a calming breath, and then it's as if she can't help but smile as she begins to tell me all about Cadence.

"Well . . . her name is Cadence Aelia Wilder. Like I said earlier, her birthday is March 29th. She was born at thirty-three weeks, so we had to stay in the NICU for a little over a month. She was four and a half pounds and eighteen inches long. From the moment she arrived into the world, she's shown she's a fighter. She had a heart procedure at only eight days old."

Kenna must see the panic in my eyes because she reassures me quickly. "Cadence is okay now. You'd never even know she had a heart condition. Now she's at the top of her growth charts, which isn't typical of a preemie-baby." I watch in awe as she continues with sheer pride and joy, which is evident in the way she talks about her daughter. *Our daughter.*

"She's an absolute spitfire . . . no clue where she gets that from. It seems like she learns a handful of new words each day. She possesses enough sass in one pinky to take down a grown hockey player," Kenna jokes.

I know exactly where she got the spitfire attitude.

"Why did you name her Cadence? Did you know you were having a girl?"

"She's named after your mom and sister. Carson calls her Cadey Cat, though I can't bring myself to call her that. Even after all this time," she says, looking down at the ground. "I didn't know the gender until she came. I was still trying to wrap my head around being nineteen and pregnant. I didn't even know I was actually pregnant until almost halfway through the pregnancy."

Shit, I should've been there. She was all alone in this.

"You said her middle name is Aelia. What's that after?" I think I hear Kenna's sharp intake of breath in response to my question.

"Aelia means sunshine," she whispers so low I think I hear her wrong. *Sunshine.*

***

I haven't cried much in the two years since Katie died. But tonight, as I sit in my hotel room, trying to come to terms with the fact that I have a daughter, all of my emotions and grief wash over me in unruly waves.

I go through every stage of grief all over again. Not that I'll ever accept Katie's death, but now I have to grieve the fact that I wasn't there for my daughter's first year and a half of her life—for her birth, for the months she was growing inside Kenna's belly, for the moment Kenna found out she was pregnant. I wasn't there for any of it. I missed it all.

There's still so much I don't know about her or the time Kenna and I spent apart. Can Cadence walk? She was being held the whole time I saw her. And then McKenna mentioned she could talk and was learning new words each day.

I should have been there—not Carson, not her parents—me. I should've been there to rub Kenna's swollen feet and ankles. I should've been there to take her to her doctor's appointments. I should've been there to support her through labor, to cut the cord, to assure her our daughter, who was in the NICU, was going to be okay. I should've been there to help her through it all.

I can't get back those moments I missed, but I can make sure I don't miss out on any more than I already have.

I don't even hesitate as I pick up the phone and dial my coach's number.

Coach grants me a two-game leave to spend time here with Cadence and come to terms with being a father. Even though I know I won't be able to wrap my head around the fact that I have a daughter in a matter of five days, it's definitely a place to start.

The first step in coming to terms with being a father would probably be meeting the little girl who made me one.

I start a new text chain and enter a number I've memorized since I was a teenager.

Me:

> Hey Kenna, this is Griff. This is my new number. Where would you like to meet tomorrow? What time works best for you two?

232

Sunshine:

You can come to the house. I'll send you the address. Is tomorrow at 11:30 a.m. okay for you? When do you fly out?

Me:

Tomorrow at 11:30 works great. See you then.

I don't let her know I won't be flying out tomorrow with the team. I don't want to scare her any more than I already did tonight.

I hadn't realized until the moment I saw her how lonely I had been the past two years. Having her back in my life has awakened a part of me that had been dormant.

It's like I've been walking around in a catatonic state—unfeeling, completely void of emotions. But tonight, I'm feeling everything. Joy at the fact that I have a daughter. Sorrow and regret that I missed out on moments in her life that we'll never get back. And hope for a future I hope will be filled with a lifetime of memories and love for my daughter.

24

McKenna

OCTOBER

Once we finished Carson's celebratory dinner, I couldn't leave with Cadence quickly enough. I needed to get home and feel a sense of normalcy.

Going through Cadence's bedtime routine always grounds me, giving me a sense of relief when I'm feeling overwhelmed. And nothing has overwhelmed me in the past eighteen months quite like seeing Griffin Turner realize he's a father.

I'm flooded with guilt when I think of all the ways I could've tried harder to get through to him. Instead of forcing him to take responsibility for Cadence by serving him a request for child support, I chose to give up on him, therefore cutting him from her life.

But rather than beating myself up over the past, I choose to focus on the beautiful reality that is my present.

Cadence is filling her bathtime cups with water before splashing it all over. Her giggles echo off the walls of the bathroom, filling my heart with warmth and putting me at ease.

I finish washing her before draining the water and drying her off. After I lotioned her body and added essential oils to her feet, I put a new diaper and footie pajamas on her.

Cadence makes grabby hands toward her bookshelf and I grab two books before we sit on the glider in the corner of her nursery. We read *Chicka Chicka Boom Boom* every night, though the second book is always different. She gets so excited now when I read the "boom booms" and she recently learned the word, so the highlight of my day is when she joins in.

Once we've finished reading, I dim the lights in her room, turn on her noise machine, and begin singing her the same song I've sung every night since she first heard it in the hospital after her surgery.

Typically, when I sing this song to her, a string of memories flash through my mind like a movie reel. Memories of Griffin and I. Memories of Cadence's first year.

Tonight, as I rock my sleepy girl to sleep and sing "You Are My Sunshine," it is no different; however, I'm brought back in time to one specific memory—the first night she heard this song.

The monitors in the NICU beep quietly as Cadence's chest steadily rises and falls.

Her heart procedure three days ago was a success. Thankfully, the surgeon said he was hopeful for a full recovery and that Cadence shouldn't have any long-term adverse effects from the repaired defect.

My phone vibrates on the side table and I reach around the tubes of my breast pump to grab it before it wakes Cadence.

Unfortunately, I'm not quick enough, and she stirs before a high-pitched wail rings through the room.

I quickly remove the breast pump from my nipples, placing the parts on the table, before adjusting my nursing tank and picking up Cadence from her crib.

The day after her procedure, she graduated from the incubator to a crib. I got to hold her for the first time right before they wheeled her to the cath lab. I've never cried so many tears of joy and fear at once.

Now, as I try to soothe my upset daughter, tears of anxiety and doubt flood my eyes.

The past two days have been filled with Cadence's shrieking cries, causing very little sleep on my end. Sheer exhaustion has taken over my body, leaving my mind in a state of absolute chaos.

I'm rocking my hips side to side, trying to soothe her, when a nurse comes into the room.

"Have you tried any music to try to calm her down yet? If not, I can get you a little speaker from our nurse's station," she suggests.

"At this point, I'll accept all the advice you've got."

She returns moments later with the speaker. "Here you go. It has Bluetooth, so you can just connect your phone. There's a good lullaby playlist on Spotify. I can hold her while you connect your phone if you'd like."

I carefully place Cadence in the nurse's arms, then connect my phone to the speaker. I play the lullaby playlist the nurse suggested, then sit in the rocking chair with Cadence.

She's still fussy as the second song comes to a close. The start of the third lullaby comes on the speaker, and the acoustic guitar opening almost instantly calms Cadence from a shrieking cry to a whimper. As the opening lyrics fill the room, tears flood my eyes.

By the time the chorus of an acoustic version of "You Are My Sunshine" comes through the speakers, Cadence is no longer fussy. Instead, she's passed out peacefully in my arms.

I place her back in the crib before reattaching the pump parts to my sore nipples, and then I silently sob in the rocking chair while staring at the most beautiful gift in the world.

The next morning is Monday, and Carson comes to check on Cadence bright and early since he doesn't have classes until later that afternoon.

"Go take a shower and try to get some rest, Mack. I've got her. If I need any help, the nurses are just outside in the hallway."

"I can't bring myself to leave her side, Carse."

"Cadey Cat is okay now. You've got to accept our help, Mack. You don't need to do this alone."

Easy for him to say. He's not the nineteen-year-old single mother who feels like her every move is being judged. I'm so grateful for the help that my family provides Cadence and me. But I also feel guilty—like I'm failing when I accept their help.

I'm brought back to the present as I finish singing the last lyrics of our song—what was once mine and Griffin's but is now mine and Cadence's—to our daughter. I peer at her perfect sleeping form.

I can't tell you how many nights I'd rocked her to sleep, completely in love with her while completely hating myself for the failure I'd become. I would sit there and let the intrusive thoughts eat me alive.

She's better off without you.

Another family could give her more love and support.

You're the reason your family feels like they need to help you nonstop.

You couldn't even make the one person who said he'd love you forever stay. What makes you think you're good enough for this perfect little girl?

The postpartum period was a real bitch. But with the help of my therapist, I've been able to push those negative thoughts out of my head.

I sit here tonight, in her nursery, and focus on Cadence's perfect little lips, her dimpled fists, and her soft head of blonde hair. She has Griffin's coffee-colored eyes and one heart-stopping dimple on her left cheek.

I'm so thankful to be her mama. I'm grateful that Griffin helped make her. I'm sad that he honestly doesn't remember me telling him she exists. I'm mad that he changed his phone number and gave his old one away during the months I tried to contact him. I'm disappointed that Griffin and Cadence will never get those moments back that he missed out on.

I know I can't live in the past and stew on regrets. So, I give myself a few moments to reflect on how things could've been different before closing that chapter. I'm ready to turn the page and see where this new chapter takes me and Cadence.

The next morning, I woke Cadence up early, hoping maybe she would go down for her morning nap. Lately, it's hit or miss whether or not she will take two naps. On the days when she does take two, she's often in a better mood. I'm hoping, for Griffin's sake, that if she takes two naps, their meeting today will go smoother.

Thankfully, Cadence fell asleep about fifteen minutes ago for her first nap, and I've just finished changing into a pair of gray leggings and a cropped white T-shirt when the doorbell rings.

Not really thinking it's going to be Griffin at the door, I swing it open and am surprised to find him there. Griff is wearing jeans and an olive green hoodie that compliments his skin tone and brown eyes. His dark hair is longer, something I didn't pay much attention to last night. It curls at his neck, flaring out from under his backward baseball hat. I'm a sucker for a guy in a backward hat.

"Sorry, I know we said I'd come over at eleven-thirty, but I just couldn't wait around any longer."

"That's okay. Cadence just went down for her first nap. You can come in, though, and we can talk while she naps."

"Thanks, that'd be great."

"No problem. A word of advice?"

"I'll take all the advice you've got for me." He looks genuinely curious for any tips.

"Don't ever ring the doorbell to a house where there could be a sleeping baby. Like, ever. Just don't do it."

He chuckles. "Noted. I will never ring the doorbell again. Is it safe to text?"

"Depends. If I were still rocking her to sleep, definitely not."

"We'll just communicate telepathically."

"Deal." I deadpan, keeping a straight face for a moment before my cheeks turn up in a smile.

Griffin's responding chuckle sends goosebumps down my arms.

It's so strange to be here with him, smiling and laughing as if there hadn't been two years where we didn't speak to one another. Resentment stings my throat when I think of all the time that was wasted because of miscommunication and misunderstanding.

I clear my throat. "Do you mind if we talk in the kitchen? I was just about to start prepping lunch."

"Yeah, that's fine with me. This is a nice place. How long have you lived here?"

"Carson closed on it this summer. It's only been about two months now."

"Woah, he must've got a hell of a signing bonus."

"I guess. He said between that and the trust we got access to when we turned twenty-one, he had more money than he knew what to do with. I think he felt obligated to get something bigger than he needed so Cadence and I would move in with him. He knew it was hard for me to live with my parents."

"That sounds like Carson. How are Liz and Teddy doing?"

"They're doing really well. Dad is getting ready to retire in the next year, hopefully. Mom is absolutely obsessed with Cadence. I always thought they'd become snowbirds once my dad finally retired, but Mom refuses to live away from Cadence for the entire winter."

"Your dad didn't look too pleased to see me at the game."

"The circumstances could've been better."

I start taking ingredients out of the fridge for a Greek salad and grilled chicken I had planned to make for lunch.

As I grab a knife and cutting board, Griff asks, "Are you bringing Cadence trick-or-treating?"

"Yeah, Carson and I brought her trick-or-treating around my parent's neighborhood last year."

"What did you dress her up as?"

Shaking my head, I laugh at the memories from last year. "You know how Carson gets with Halloween—always so over the top. He got her a little shark costume, then I was the lifeguard, and he was a shark attack victim."

"Oh my god. Are you serious?"

I nod and grab some cherry tomatoes to cut for the salad. "I am. It was either that or he wanted me and him to dress up as bags of ice so we could be 'ice, ice, baby.'"

He shakes with laughter. "Do you have any pictures?"

"Yeah, would you mind grabbing my phone over there?"

He looks down at my phone, shaking his head before passing it to me. "Sorry. It looks like you've got a text. I didn't mean to look."

"Oh, that's okay. It's probably just Dakota. She's Cadence's nanny."

"It wasn't. Looks like Ian wants to know if you want to grab drinks later, *Kenz*."

Ugh. Kill me. Just literally dig my grave and bury me right now.

Out of anyone who could've texted me right now, why did it have to be Ian? And Griffin, of all people, knows that I hate being called "Kenz."

"Did you let Carson choose her costume for this year?" Griffin asks, brushing aside the fact that I was just asked out by another man. He seems completely unphased. I guess he should be. We're not together. We're not even friends. I'm just his . . . baby mama. God, I hate the way that sounds.

I nod my head while I finish cutting up the cucumbers for the salad. "Yes," I sigh. "He wanted to do DC superheroes. Cadence is Wonder Woman, Carse is going to be the Joker, and I got stuck with Catwoman."

"Do you still need a Batman?"

"Halloween is on Tuesday. That isn't for another two days, Griff. Don't you fly out to Detroit tonight for your game tomorrow?"

"I asked my coach for a leave of absence. He said I could have a two-game leave, so I don't need to be back in Colorado until Thursday evening for our game day skate on Friday morning."

I place the knife down on the cutting board and look over at him. "Why would you do that?"

"McKenna, how can you ask that? I just found out I have a daughter who is eighteen months old. I missed the first year and a half of her life. Her birth. Her first Halloween, Christmas, and birthday. I missed her first words, her first tooth, her first steps. I couldn't get on a plane with my team and play as if my whole world didn't get turned upside down."

"You haven't missed her first steps," I inform him, wanting to reassure him that he hadn't missed everything. At least, not yet, anyway.

I take him through the years he missed while Cadence naps and I make lunch. The walk down memory lane has me nostalgic. A sense of melancholy spreads over me as I think of all the moments Griff has missed out on.

25

Griffin

OCTOBER

C adence took her first steps. She took her first steps, and I was here to witness them.

God, today has been the best day of my life.

It started when I got to meet my daughter for the first time. She woke up from her nap about an hour after I got to Carson's house. Kenna had gone into her room to help her wake up, because I guess my daughter is like her mother and likes to take her time waking up, or things get dicey.

Once she was properly woken up, Kenna brought Cadence into the kitchen. I took one look at my daughter, and my world stopped, only to start again. This time, revolving solely around Cadence Aelia. My little ray of sunshine.

My same brown eyes stared back at me in curiosity when Kenna sat her in her highchair next to the stool I was sitting at.

Cadence's light blonde hair was a happy surprise. With how dark my hair is, I never really imagined any of my kids being blonde. I know that probably sounds stupid, but it's not like I used to sit up at night and imagine what my future kids would look like. Well, not unless you count the endless nights I spent thinking of Kenna and what our lives would've looked like had I not fucked everything up and pushed her out of my life.

I watched in amazement as Kenna and Cadence went about their routine. It might seem like a mundane thing to be amazed by, but McKenna is a really good mom. Like, really fucking good.

Kenna made lunch for the three of us and it was delicious. I ate like a starved man, and Cadence turned into a feral little monster as soon as Kenna suction-cupped her plate to her highchair tray.

After we cleaned up from lunch, Kenna said Cadence typically liked to play in either the living room or her playroom upstairs. I asked if it was okay for us to play in her playroom, so Kenna gave me a tour of the house. I can tell she did a lot of decorating throughout the house after seeing her bedroom and Cadence's nursery and playroom.

After about ten minutes of playing on the floor with Cadence, she crawled over to her play table, used it to help her steady herself when she stood up, and then she turned to show me a block she was holding. She drooled all over it before holding it out for me to grab. I asked her to bring it over to me, so she squared herself up to me and took one unsteady step before falling down.

Kenna gasped. "Oh my gosh. Did she just do that? I've got to get a video, or Carse will kill me. Stand back up, sweet girl!"

I threw my phone over to Kenna to get a video. Then I held my arms out for Cadence to walk into. She stood back up on shaky legs, then took one unsteady step right before taking another.

She walked for the very first time, and I was there to witness a milestone of hers.

Cadence only made it about three steps before she dropped down and crawled as fast as her body could take her right to Ranger. He just laid on the rug in her playroom, letting her fall all over him, tugging his ears and laying sloppy kisses on his nose.

Playing and taking her first steps wore Cadence out, and while she took a second nap, I asked Kenna if I could make them dinner. When she said yes, I ran to the grocery store to pick up some ingredients.

I just got back from the store, and Kenna has offered to help me make dinner.

I look around the entryway and living room as I take off my shoes. She's made this house into a home. There are touches of Kenna in each room. Fuck, now I'm jealous of her brother getting to live with my girls and witness the ordinary moments, day in and day out.

I shake my head to clear those thoughts.

We're currently in the kitchen, cooking together for the first time in over two years. It feels domesticated. It feels natural.

Kenna still refuses to cook without listening to music and she still can't sing a song on key to save her life.

And she still takes my breath away just by doing the simplest things.

I'm not sure how I'm supposed to go back to Colorado in a few days, knowing I'll be missing out on even more of these simple moments.

"Will the music wake up Cadence?"

"No, she's a pretty sound sleeper. Plus, she has her white noise machine on."

"Oh, right. Do you think maybe I could stay for her bedtime? I'd like to see what this big bedtime routine you mentioned looks like."

"I'm not sure that's a good idea tonight, Griff. I've got midterms to study for, and she might not go down easily since she napped twice. You might also distract her if she sees you."

I turn to look her in the eyes. "I know you've had to do this all alone, Kenna. But I'm here now. I want to help. I want to get to know my daughter. I want to know her bedtime routine so I can help her, too. I want to know what makes her upset and how to soothe her the way

244

you do so naturally. I want to be a part of everything. Will you please teach me?" I plead.

"Of course, I want you to get to know her, Griffin. It's not that I don't—we're just used to our little routine and it being just the two of us."

"You're truly amazing. I don't know how you did it the past two years. Being pregnant at nineteen by yourself."

"I wasn't by myself. Carson refused to leave my side, not that I'd expect anything else. My teammate Brooke has become a good friend, too. And once I told my parents I was pregnant, they were really supportive. Mom watched Cadence last year while I was at classes and volleyball. This year, I hired Dakota, Cadence's nanny, to help while I'm at volleyball and classes. I felt too guilty, always leaning on my mom to watch her. Dakota is great with her, so that makes things easier."

"I want to respect your boundaries, Kenna, I do. But I missed so much already. Unfortunately, I don't have the flexibility in my schedule to be here every day, or I would be. When I am able to see Cadence, I'd like to try to make the most of that time with her. So can I please stay for her bedtime routine? You can study while I play with her in her high chair and finish making dinner."

Her shoulders relax as she lets out a sigh. "I'd like that, Griff. Truly, I would. Yes, you can stay. Thank you for offering to let me study."

"I know I've only just met her, but she's perfect. You've done an amazing job with her, Sunshine."

Kenna's breath hitches at the term of endearment, and I mentally smack myself for letting it slip.

At the same time, I don't exactly have time to waste tiptoeing around her. I need to take advantage of every moment I have while I'm back here. I need to wise up and get it through my head that Kenna and I being together isn't a good idea. At least, not right now. We need to focus on learning how to co-parent Cadence first and foremost.

That's easier said than done when she looks so good, and being in her orbit again feels so right.

Besides, I don't even know if she's single at this point. It's been killing me not knowing.

So, I casually ask, "Are you seeing Ian? He seemed pretty friendly last night. I mean, it is what it is. I just want to know who is involved in my daughter's life."

"Are you sure that's the only reason you're sticking your nose where it doesn't belong?"

"Honest." *Yeah, right.* I'm acting like a jealous fuck, and she sees right through me.

She rolls her eyes at me. "He isn't really in our daughter's life at all. Has he seen her when he comes over to hang out with Carson? Sure. Are he and I involved? No. Much to his regret."

"So, you two have never . . ."

"Aside from a few dances on my twenty-first birthday, no, nothing has happened between us. Not that it's any of your business."

I hold my hands up in surrender. "Noted. I'll stay in my lane."

"Mhmm, I'm sure." She clears her throat. "So, I forgot to ask earlier, where are you staying while you're in town?"

"I just extended my reservation at the same hotel the team stayed at."

"Griff, that's almost a half hour away with traffic. Why don't you stay here? Carson has two spare bedrooms. There's only a bed in one of them right now, but it beats staying in a hotel. He has an away game tomorrow, but he will be back for Halloween."

"Are you sure?"

"Yeah, I am. This way, you can see Cadence more while you're in town for the next few days."

"I don't know what to say. I wasn't expecting this. Thank you. This means a lot to me, Kenna."

A few hours later, I tiptoe out of Cadence's nursery and pull the door closed. I have the absolute biggest smile on my face right now just thinking of how amazing it was to be a part of her day.

I walk down the hallway. Seeing Kenna's bedroom door cracked, I pop my head in to let her know I was able to get Cadence down. I realize my mistake instantly. The sight in front of me nearly kills me—Kenna is in nothing but a lacy bralette and a tiny pair of sleep shorts. She's just about to pull on a T-shirt when I see something that has my blood pumping even harder than seeing her like this does.

"What does that say?" My voice is raspier than it's ever been, dripping with desire.

She gasps, clearly caught off-guard. "Griff, what are you doing in here? You can't just barge in my room."

"The door was cracked. I came in to tell you I got Cadence to sleep." Taking a step into her room, I close the door behind me.

Her answering intake of breath might've made me realize I shouldn't close the space between us, but the curious desire in her eyes tells me otherwise.

"What does it say, Kenna?"

"What are you talking about?"

"The tattoo on your ribcage. What does it say?"

"Griffin, you're crossing a line we shouldn't cross again. Thank you for getting Cadence to bed. Please go to sleep in the guest room."

"What does it say, McKenna?"

"Griff," she whispers. We're so close, her breath fans across my chin, and I want more, but I know we shouldn't.

"Tell me, please."

"Take a look for yourself."

Right below her bralette, on the left side of her ribcage, written in script, is the word *Sunshine*.

I have the strongest desire to scrape my teeth over her tattoo before leaving open-mouth kisses along each letter.

Instead, I ask, "You permanently marked me on your skin?"

"I didn't mark you on my skin. I marked a word from a song that our daughter loves."

"I don't believe you. You'll always be *my sunshine*, McKenna," I whisper, staring into her blue eyes. I'm transfixed.

"We can't do this, Griff," she breathes.

"Why not?"

"Because so much has happened between us." A look of anguish takes over her face as tears flood her eyes.

Kenna steps around me, stopping when she gets to the door of her ensuite bathroom. "I just need us to focus on Cadence right now, Griff. We haven't talked in two years. Even though there were times tonight when it felt like no time had passed at all, that's not the reality of the situation. I need reliability. Cadence needs consistency. The version of you that I last saw in Boston is neither of those things. I'm willing to be proven otherwise, but it will take time. There's also the fact that you broke me when my heart was already broken."

I'm at a loss for words. I knew I broke the only beautiful thing left in my life, but realizing everything I missed out on, and all of the pain I caused Kenna because I was too scared to lose another person I love, it damn near brings me to my knees.

Kenna cuts off my spiraling thoughts. "Goodnight, Griffin."

I nod my head and find my words. "Goodnight, Sunshine."

With that, I head down the hall to my room. She's right; we need to focus on Cadence right now. We also need to get reacquainted with these new versions of each other. But I'm under no illusion that what we had between us is over. I'm going to prove myself to her. I'm ready to fight for the life I want—a life with my two girls.

26

Griffin

November

The plane's tires touch the tarmac, and I rush to take my phone off Airplane mode.

Once I have service again, I see a photo has come in from Kenna. I click and zoom in on a photo of Cadence and Ranger snuggled up and sleeping next to one another on the couch.

Sunshine:

photo message She rebelled against our naptime routine . . . she's lucky she's so cute!

Me:

I wish I could be snuggled up with them right now. We just landed in San Jose.

I pocket my phone when she doesn't respond after a few minutes. I've become desperate for any communication from Kenna.

"How's it going, Turner?" Thomas Jones asks as we're lining up to get off the plane. Everyone calls him TJ or Jonesy. He's one of the oldest veteran players on the team and someone I've looked up to even before I signed with the team.

"It's going really well, Jonesy." I take my phone out of my pocket and show him my lock screen. It's a photo Kenna took of Cadence on my shoulders from Halloween. I haven't had a chance to talk to Jonesy since

I got back to town last night. We had our game tonight, then boarded a plane to San Jose right away for our game tomorrow night.

"When we played in Minnesota, I found out I have a daughter. Her name is Cadence, and she's nineteen months old. That's the reason I was out for two games."

"Shit, rookie. What have you made of that news?"

"I'm not a rookie anymore. And while it shocked the shit out of me"—I pause with the biggest smile on my face—"I'm the luckiest guy in the world."

"Is the mom a puck bunny, or did you know her? You're from Minnesota, right?"

"McKenna is definitely not a puck bunny. We lived next door to each other practically our whole lives. Cadence came from two people who were in love."

I still love her. I'll never not love her.

He takes his hat off and scratches his scalp. "So, how did you just find out you've got a kid together?"

"Let's just leave it at I was at the lowest point of my life, and I take full responsibility for being the reason behind me missing out on the first year and a half of my daughter's life."

He slaps me on the back. "Congrats, man. She looks adorable, and fatherhood suits you. Is the mom planning to move to Colorado?"

I shake my head. "No, McKenna goes to school in Minnesota. She plays volleyball for Abbott University. Her whole family is there. Actually, her twin brother is a rookie for the Wolverines, Carson Wilder."

"Ah fuck, rook. Are you trying to tell me you're going to end up signing with Minnesota after your rookie contract is up? Hopefully, I'll be retired by that point."

"I have no idea. What I do know is that it's hard being so far away and missing out on even more time than I already have. How do you do it with the long road game stretches?"

Jonesy is thirty-five, and he and his wife, Becca, have four kids. If anyone can give me advice, it's him.

"It gets harder the older they get. JJ is ten now. Becca is busy traveling all over with the kids for his hockey tournaments. It makes it really hard to want to continue to play when I'm missing out on so many moments back home with them."

He must sense the anxiety rolling off of me from his words, so he gives me some words of encouragement. "What I meant to say was that Cadence is so little, she won't remember that you were away. I suggest a lot of FaceTime calls. Pay for them to come visit when they can, and look into getting a place there for the offseason if she isn't able to move to Colorado."

I would never ask Kenna to give up her dreams and move away from her family to be closer to me. This is my burden to bear. I just have to make the most of it, as Jonesy suggested. I'm willing to make sacrifices if it means there are fewer obstacles standing between me and Cadence.

My phone vibrates with an incoming text just as we're getting off the team bus at the hotel. It's late, so I'm surprised to see it's from Kenna.

Sunshine:

Just them?

My eyebrows shoot up so fast I think I may have pinched a nerve in my face. Is she . . . is she implying that I should want to snuggle up with her as well? Fuck, how do I respond to that? Of course, I wish I could be with Kenna. She will always be the one that got away. And I'll always be the idiot who pushed her away because I was too scared to taint her.

By the time I close the door to my hotel room, I bite the bullet and hit send on my response.

Me:

> Family snuggle session? Definitely count me in.

Sunshine:

> Don't say that. Not when I've dreamed of you saying things like that for the past two years.

I was damned if I did and damned if I didn't. Before I can think of how the hell to respond to her text, a FaceTime request lights up my phone.

McKenna Wilder is FaceTiming me at 1 a.m. her time. Nothing good can come from hitting accept. But what if something is wrong with Cadence?

I quickly hit accept. "Is everything okay with Cadence?"

Kenna's answering giggle-fit puts me at ease that Cadence must be okay. Though, now I'm confused as to what's got her giggling like that.

"I'll take that as a yes. Care to fill me in on what's so funny?"

"I just realized what time it is!" She wipes tears from under her eyes. "At this time, you probably think I'm booty calling you. I'm not doing that. But I do have a great ass. Don't you agree?"

I run my hand over my face, but she catches my answering groan.

"I'll take that as a yes. I had a couple of glasses of wine with Brooke tonight. Wine makes me so horny, did you know that? Of course, you don't know that. You left me high and dry before I developed that acquired taste."

"I very clearly remember a bath and wine glasses when we were together. I know what you're like when you drink wine, Sunshine. What I don't know is why you decided to call me if you're horny."

She scoffs. "Forget I called."

"McKenna, please don't hang up. I'm sorry. It's just confusing when you say we can't blur the lines."

"I still have it, you know."

253

Her change of topic throws me off. "Have what?"

"That present you got me on my nineteenth birthday. The one you said I should use whenever I'm missing you."

Is she talking about the vibrator I got her?

"It's pink, made of silicone, and oh my god, does it work wonders."

"McKenna," I say her name like a warning. I'm hesitant about where to go from here. She's clearly buzzed, and this feels like we're playing with fire.

"Oh, come on. Have a little fun! Am I turning you on, Griff?"

"Is that even a question? Everything you do turns me on."

"I'm so worked up right now, G. I need your dirty mouth to tell me what to do."

She sounds so desperate and needy. My cock stirs in my suit pants, but I won't have her like this.

"The only thing I'm going to tell you to do tonight is to get some rest, Sunshine."

"Prude," she taunts.

"You say prude; I say gentleman with extreme restraint that is being tested to the limit."

Her answering chuckles quickly fade into even breathing. I don't hang up as I get myself ready for bed and slide under the sheets.

When I'm sure she's asleep, I softly sing "You Are My Sunshine" to her and whisper all of the sweet nothings I've been dying to tell her.

"I've missed you so much. I'm going to be the man you and Cadence deserve. I'll never stop trying to prove how much the two of you mean to me."

I'm not sure how long I stare into the phone, watching the only woman I've ever loved sleeping peacefully. But when I wake the next morning, I know it's the best night of sleep I've gotten in years. Probably since the last time I slept with my Sunshine in my arms.

The next day, I got a call from my agent bright and early. He's on the East Coast, and he probably forgot about the time difference with me in California.

I swipe to accept his call. "Jared, just the man I wanted to talk to."

"How's it going, Griffin? I'm glad I caught you. I feel like you've been avoiding my calls lately."

"A lot has been going on. I just flew back to Colorado a few days ago, and we've been on a string of road games. I've been busy FaceTiming or calling Cadence every spare moment I get."

"About that. Have you decided on the paternity test? Then Andrew wanted me to ask you about having McKenna sign an NDA due to the events that surrounded her trying to tell you about Cadence."

Andrew is the lawyer Jared's agency uses for their clients. After I called my coach on the night I found out about Cadence, the next person I called was my dad, then my agent, Jared.

"No, I told you, I don't need a paternity test. Cadence is mine. As for the NDA, Kenna and I are both in agreement that we never want the circumstances surrounding our daughter's first years of life to be in the media. We want to protect Cadence from seeing any articles or interviews about us when she gets older."

"Griff, that's great to be on the same page now. But what happens if the two of you get in a big fight or if there is a drawn-out custody battle? Things happen, and shit turns ugly quickly. My job is to protect you. I'm trying to be proactive, stay ahead of things."

"I hear you, Jared. I do. But you've got to trust me on this one. I know Kenna better than I know myself. There's nothing to stay ahead of as far as they're concerned."

"Alright."

"There is something I wanted to ask you about." I take a deep breath. "How hard would it be to break my rookie contract with Colorado and be picked up by Minnesota?"

"It'd be damn-near impossible, Griff. Not to mention, you'd be labeled as the high-maintenance rookie that no team in the league would want to touch."

"That's weird. It's almost like my agent forgot I won Rookie of the Year last year. I feel like that's something an agent should know."

"I didn't forget. It's just not relevant to the conversation at hand. You asked about getting out of your contract. What makes you think Colorado would want to give up their Rookie of the Year?"

"I knew it was far-fetched, Jared. But I had to ask. Just know this now, I won't sign a long-term deal anywhere other than where my daughter is once this contract is up. I could give a fuck about the deal or the money. I refuse to miss more years of Cadence's life."

"Noted. You do realize that goes against everything I would normally fight for as your agent, though, right?"

"I get it. Listen, I've got to get another hour or two of sleep before our pre-game skate. Talk later."

"Later, Griff."

It's just getting dark out as I pull up to Carson and Kenna's place. I'm here for Thanksgiving. It's a big deal. They decided to have Thanksgiving dinner at their place instead of their parents because they weren't sure if my dad and I would be comfortable being next door to my childhood home. I haven't been back there since the weekend of Katie's funeral.

But my dad ended up not being able to fly out due to a big surgery he had scheduled.

I feel like a teenager taking a girl out on my very first date again. I'm nervous as hell to see Liz and Teddy after the look he gave me at Carson's first game. Honestly, I don't blame him for not giving me the benefit of the doubt. In his eyes, I not only ghosted his daughter, but I abandoned her and his granddaughter when they needed me most.

Of course, I'm not even going to try to bring up the fact that I didn't know Cadence existed, or I never would have abandoned either of them.

As for leaving Kenna, I honestly thought I was doing what was best for her then.

I take a deep breath and let the nerves roll off me. Then I pick up the bouquets of flowers I got for Kenna and her mom and the bottle of Maker's Mark I got for Carson and Teddy.

Knowing Cadence isn't napping, I think it's safe to ring the doorbell.

I do, and when Kenna opens the door, I literally have to rub the ache in my chest that comes from the sight of her. It's been a long three weeks since I've seen her in person. She's got her hair pulled up in a bun, and she's wearing a Wolverines sweatshirt with black leggings. Her face is free of makeup. She looks relaxed and carefree. She's pure perfection.

Nothing has changed when it comes to my allure for Kenna. If anything, seeing her with our daughter has heightened my attraction to her.

"Happy Thanksgiving," she says in greeting.

I stand there awkwardly for a beat before I pull myself together.

"You're so gorgeous it hurts, Sunshine."

Her breath hitches at my statement.

"Your pickup lines have not aged well, G," Carson teases from somewhere inside the house.

Ranger comes trotting around the corner when he hears the door. When he sees me, Ranger jumps into my arms and whimpers.

"Hey, buddy! How's my Goodest Boy doing? Did you miss me as much as I missed you?"

"It's only been a few weeks," Kenna teases.

"Any length of time without Ranger is like a lifetime."

"Trust me, I know. The semester I lived in the dorms was the loneliest I've ever felt, and I couldn't even have my support pup with me."

Her confession hits me like a punch to the chest. She was lonely because I wasn't there for her. I wasn't there because I chose not to be. Katie was her support person, and she lost her.

I need to take Carson aside and thank him for being there for Kenna when I couldn't be.

"Happy Thanksgiving," I tell her as I pull her in for a side hug. It's a timid move on my part—I'm not sure what she's comfortable with. Kenna stiffens at first, then softens, wrapping her arms around my waist. I breathe her in and place a chaste kiss on her forehead.

"These are for you." I hand Kenna one of the bouquets of flowers.

"Thank you, Griff. You didn't need to do that."

"I know, Sunshine," I whisper over her temple, causing a shiver to slide down her spine.

She grabs the flowers but pulls from my embrace when her mom, dad, Cadence, and Carson come into the room.

"And these are for you, Lizzie," I say as I hand her the other bouquet.

Liz doesn't hesitate as she pulls me in for a tight hug. She smells the same as always, like vanilla and cinnamon, wrapping me in a comfort only smells from your childhood can.

"It's so great to see you, Griffin. It's been too long." She squeezes my arm before stepping away to grab Cadence from Carson's arms.

"Should we go put these beauties in some water, Cades?" Liz asks Cadence as she carts her off to the kitchen.

Carson brings me in for a bro hug, patting my back. "G, it's good to see you. Happy Thanksgiving."

"Thanks for having me. I'm sorry my dad couldn't make it. He's been eager to meet Cadence, so he was disappointed this surgery came up."

"It's no problem. We're happy you could make it. A nice surprise that our schedules lined up for a day off," he replies.

As Carse steps back, Teddy stands off to the side, hands in his pockets, rooted in place.

I take a shot at clearing the awkward tension that's fallen over the room. Offering him the bottle of Maker's Mark, he just shakes his head once to himself.

"I told my little princess not to get her hopes up. It might not be drugs this time, but bringing around the hard stuff?" Teddy tsks me.

I'm about to drop my hand with the alcohol, but Carson scoops it up.

"What my dad meant to say is how thoughtful of you to bring the host a gift you know he enjoys, even when you don't drink during the season." Carson tries to come to my rescue.

Teddy scoffs. "It'll take a lot more than my drink of choice to soften me."

"I understand that, Theo. I wasn't trying to placate you. I can't eradicate the past. Unfortunately, I missed out on time that I can never make up for. But I intend to do right by your granddaughter and McKenna."

"What sweet words. Only your actions and time will tell. Until then, don't expect me to let up," Teddy practically growls the last sentence out.

"I look forward to proving myself to McKenna and Cadence. If, in turn, that changes your opinion of me, all the better."

With that, Teddy turns to the kitchen to help Liz with Cadence and I overhear her lecturing him to let go of his tough-guy act.

I've got my work cut out for me to prove myself to everyone—but I was honest with her dad. My first priority is to make sure Kenna and Cadence know they can depend on me and not worry about what her father thinks of me.

27

McKenna

DECEMBER

I 'm in so much trouble. Griffin Turner has flipped a switch inside my brain that makes me lose my head when he's near.

I'm just getting ready to leave my house to meet at the team bus. We'll ride together to the arena we're playing at today. The National Championship for volleyball is in St. Paul this year, and we made the final four. We won our game on Thursday afternoon, and today is the championship game.

Griff flew in for today's game. He has to take a red eye to get back for practice tomorrow, but he showed up for me. My walls are slowly coming down, and I've never felt more vulnerable.

Griff just got to my house to spend time with Cadence before they go to the arena we're playing at.

Instead of shrugging off his jacket when he comes inside, he picks up Cades and asks, "Can Cadence and I drop you off, Mama?"

Holy shit. Never in my life did I think being called Mama would make me so wet I would need to throw out my panties, but here is this sexy-as-sin man calling me Mama in that low, raspy voice of his, and I'm soaked.

As if he knows what calling me that just did to me, he sends me an ovary-bursting smile and accompanies it with a rakish wink.

"That'd be great, thanks." My voice squeaks. I know it does.

Griff knows I don't prefer to drive in the city traffic, but I still refuse to take an Uber or rideshare since the accident. We talked about it the other night when he FaceTimed us for Cadence's bedtime. Once she was asleep, he didn't rush off the phone. Instead we stayed up talking for almost two hours before I told him I had to finish a project for school.

That's been happening more and more lately—he and I FaceTiming and texting about more than just Cadence.

"I thought maybe we could take my truck if that's okay with you?" Griff requests.

"We could, but you don't have a car seat installed for her," I regretfully reply. I'm not sure if he didn't hear me or if he's choosing to ignore me as he guides me outside to the passenger side of his truck.

"Oh, that. I picked one up when I was in town last time."

He what?

"What? When?"

"When I came for Thanksgiving, I had Carse help me pick one out and teach me how to install it."

Griff flashes me that panty-melting smile with his dimples on full display, and I suddenly have this desperate need to feel his lips on mine.

Pulling myself from the lust-filled thoughts, I watch as Griff places Cadence in her car seat with ease. He shuts the rear door of the truck before opening mine.

He runs his hand through his hair, and I'd be surprised if I weren't literally drooling from how hot he looks doing that.

Get it together.

Clearing my throat, I thank him for opening my door. Once we're buckled, he backs out of the driveway and heads to campus, where the bus is picking the team up.

262

"It's weird seeing you drive something other than your Jeep. Do you still have it?"

He chuckles. "I do. I'm not sure I'll ever give that beaut up. Maybe it can be Cadence's first vehicle someday."

"I'm not sure we want her to have a vehicle with that much . . . legroom in the backseat." My cheeks flush a deep scarlet red as memories of what we used to do in his Jeep resurface.

Griff throws his head back and does a mix of a sigh and a groan. "Kenna, why? Why did you have to remind me that I'm going to go to jail someday for having a teenage daughter who will be dating little asshole punks?"

I laugh at the fact that he's just realizing this. "Oh, I'm sorry. Are you just realizing this now?"

"Well, I haven't really thought beyond the next few years yet."

I can't say I'm not curious to know what he's thought the next few years will look like. Does he hope Cadence and I will move to Colorado after I finish school? We haven't talked about the future at all, and the fear of the unknown has been weighing on me. I know now isn't the ideal time to bring it up, but I can't stop myself from asking, "What do you think the next few years will look like?"

Griff looks over at me before blowing out a deep breath. "I want to have this conversation more than anything, Sunshine, I do. But I don't think it's the best timing right before you're off to play the biggest game of your volleyball career."

I know he's right. But I was hoping he would give me something.

He must sense my need for reassurance. "Look, we will be having this discussion soon. Hopefully, next time I'm in town to visit, because I don't want to talk over the phone."

I'm glad we didn't start the conversation now, though, since we turn onto campus only a few moments later.

Once the truck is parked, Griff hustles to my side and opens my door. He wraps me in a tight hug and wishes me good luck. I reluctantly pull away and head into the athletic facility to meet the rest of my team.

It would be so easy to throw caution to the wind and to fall back into the safety of his arms. But I can't do that. It's not just about me and what I want for my future. It's about Cadence and what she needs for her future. She needs two parents to love, support, and adore her. She needs two parents committed to putting her wants and needs before their own. There hasn't been a day in the past two years that I haven't desired Griffin. And I doubt I'll ever go another day in my life not wanting this man. Does that mean I should just give in to my most basic desires and be with him? *Yes.*

No. Because I can't afford for this to go wrong again and have Cadence heartbroken if he abandons us again.

During warmups, I look at where my family sits and see Griffin holding Cadence. I can literally feel myself ovulating whenever I see him with her. He's so attentive and genuinely grateful to be her dad. The way he is with her is such a turn-on. But apparently, I'm not the only one turned on by his devotion to our daughter. I spot two girls a few rows back pointing and taking pictures of Griffin holding Cadence. I shake off the jealous thoughts that begin to cloud my vision.

I watch as Cadence tries to grab Griffin's hat for the dozenth time. He takes it off and flips it backward. Griff sets Cades in Carson's lap so he can take off her little jacket then he takes off his own.

Holy shit.

Griffin Turner is wearing matching maroon shirts with our daughter that say "MOMMY'S #1 FANS."

264

He grabs Cadence from Carse and then takes her hand in his, and begins waving to me.

I wave back enthusiastically, my heart swelling in my chest. I guess we're hard launching the fact that we have a daughter together.

Brooke nudges me. "Damn, girl. I feel like I might get pregnant just from witnessing the way he looks at you. He looks like a starved man, and you're his next five-course meal."

My face is bright red, and it's not from sweat or the warmup. "Brooke, don't," I warn.

"What? I'm just stating facts. He looks like he wants to make up for lost time later tonight."

"Well, then it's a good thing he has a red eye back to Colorado. I told you he and I need to focus on finding a way to co-parent Cadence, not jump into a long-distance relationship." It doesn't matter that my body practically sings when he's near. I know jumping right into bed, or a relationship, or whatever it is Griffin Turner wants from me isn't a good idea right now.

Speaking of right now, I need to focus on the most important game I've ever played in. My team needs me, and I need to perform to the best of my ability to prove to myself that I'm deserving of all the risks my coach took by keeping me on the team.

We're in the fourth set of the match. Our team is ahead two sets to their one. If we win this set, the match is over, and right now we're winning twenty-three to twenty-one. The Texas server sends the ball over the net. Brooke is our libero this season—she receives the ball and sends a near-perfect pass to our setter. I call for the set on the outside. The ball is set high to me, giving the double block time to set up. But I don't let that stop me. I send a punishing hit down the line for a kill. My fortieth kill of the night. I've never played this well in my life. Match point.

I can hear Carse and Griff's voices cheering me on above the rest of the crowd.

It's my rotation to serve. Standing a few feet behind the service line, I catch the ball one of the ball girls tosses to me, bounce it three times, and take a deep breath as the referee blows her whistle.

I get five seconds to focus on getting my serve over the net, but this is always the moment I take to think of Katie. I can feel her here with me as I toss the ball up and jump-serve it over the net.

The ball hits the tape of the net, and my breath catches in my chest as I watch it land on the opposite side of the court without any of their players touching it.

An ace. Meaning we just won the National Championship. Oh my god.

My teammates swarm where I stand on the court.

Confetti rains down on us from the rafters. This is the most amazing moment of my volleyball career.

After a few minutes of hugging, tears, and screams of celebration, our team breaks apart to shake our opponent's hands.

I look back to where my family is all standing and cheering for me. My mom and dad are hugging, Carson is clapping his hands with the biggest grin on his face, and Griffin is standing, holding a sleeping Cadence on his shoulder, wearing the sexiest smirk on his face—winking at me when our eyes connect.

By the time I finally break away from the team's trophy celebration, I run over to my family to thank them for coming.

Dad scoops me in his arms, and I tell him I couldn't have done it without their support.

Carson squeezes me so tight I think I'll suffocate. "That's our first team All-American right there, ladies and gentlemen! You fucking did it, Mack Attack."

Mom cries tears of pride. When I step out of her embrace, Griffin steps up next in line.

He wraps me in an embrace that threatens to bring me to my knees if he weren't here to hold me up. Cadence is now awake in his arms—I'm not surprised she was unable to sleep through the chaos of the crowds cheering.

"I'm so proud of you, Sunshine. You were on fire out there," Griff says before placing a kiss on my sweat-soaked forehead. He's still got his arms wrapped around me when he adds, "She would be so proud of you too."

"She is. Katie is always with me. No matter where I go or what I do, I feel her with me everywhere."

I hear Griff get choked up, so I pull my face away from where it was nuzzled on his chest. He grips my hip to keep me from fully pulling away from his embrace.

I look into his eyes, surprised to see them dry and clear. His face breaks into a dazzling smile. "I feel her here, too."

Cadence takes that moment to grab Griff's cheeks and say, "Dada, look, Mama!"

Griff's eyebrows shoot up to the snapback of his backward hat. "Did she just?"

I nod my head, tears filling my vision. "She did."

The most radiant, devastating smile spreads across his handsome face. "My sweet, smart Cadeygirl just called me Dada for the first time. And her gorgeous, talented mama just won the National Championship. I think this is cause for celebration. What do you say, Sunshine?"

I hardly remember to breathe when he looks at me like this—like he's undressing me with his eyes. I'm so entranced that I'm just about to kiss him when a reporter comes up and taps me on the shoulder, asking for an interview.

Barely able to blink out of the haze Griff just put me in, I turn and smile at the reporter. I don't remember a single word I said during the interview, too distracted by the hum of my body. I'm wound up, not just from the game but from the way only he can make me feel.

My control is hanging by the loosest of threads. I'm so screwed.

28

Griffin

December

Being Cadence's father brings me so much contentment and fulfillment. I got to Carson and Kenna's place a few hours ago to visit my girls for Christmas Eve.

Yes, I said my girls, as in both Cadence and Kenna. She's been keeping things platonic between us, and I'll respect that for now. But it doesn't change that I'm hers, and she's still mine. Even if she's not willing to admit that to herself quite yet.

We just finished clearing the dishes from dinner when I walk up behind Kenna, brush her hair off her neck, and whisper in her ear, "I want to take you somewhere before Cadence's bedtime. What do you say—are you up for a little Christmas Eve adventure?"

She softens into my embrace for a moment before pulling away to draw the imaginary line in the sand between us once again. "Sure, let me just grab her diaper bag and replenish her snacks."

"Ah, yes. We wouldn't want our little Cadeygirl to get hangry. I'll start my truck and get her bundled up."

We're out the door a few minutes later and we make it to the end of the street before she cracks.

"Griff, come on. You've got to tell me. Where are you taking us on this little adventure?"

I know curiosity is killing her. But she will just have to wait.

I'm headed toward her parent's house, and I wonder if she's going to be disappointed that the surprise I have in store isn't a visit to them. We're going over there tomorrow morning to spend Christmas Day with them and Carson. They gave us tonight to celebrate the holiday, just the three of us. Our first Christmas Eve as a family.

A couple of minutes later, we pull up to a gated community that's a few miles away from her parent's house. I punch in a code, and the gates swing open.

Pulling into a long, circular drive, I put my truck into park.

"What's going on? Is this one of your friend's houses?"

"No. Come on, let's get out. I want to show you something."

"Well, you can't just pull up to random houses on Christmas Eve, get out of your vehicle, and walk up to the front door."

"We're fine, Kenna. I know I can come here any time I want." I take a sleeping Cadence out of her car seat and carry her to the front door.

"Oh, yeah? What do you think, you just own the place?"

"Matter of fact, I do." I quickly enter the pin on the front door. The turn of the lock sounds, and Kenna's face turns ghostly white.

"I'm sorry, I'm having a hard time following. You do, what?"

"I do own the place. I walked through the house when I came to visit over Thanksgiving and made an offer as soon as I saw it. I figured I need a place to live in the summers and a place to stay when I come to visit the two of you."

"I don't know what to say, Griffin. This is just a lot to take in."

I rub her arm with my free hand in a way that reassures her that I'm here for her. "I get it. I just bulldozed you with my excitement and didn't stop to think about how overwhelming this may be for you. Can I show you around? Maybe a tour will take your mind off things."

"That'd be great."

I walk further into the open living space of the main floor with Cadence still asleep on my shoulder.

Kenna looks around, taking in the space. "It's beautiful, Griff."

"Thanks. I liked that it's an open concept, so I can see everything this little monster is getting into when I'm cooking or folding laundry or whatever else is going on. I swear, it feels like I take my eyes off her for a second, and she's clear across the room. Then there's a main bedroom with an ensuite down here, but I think I'll take the primary bedroom that's upstairs so I can be closer to her nursery."

I'm rambling. I know I am. I'm nervous as shit that Kenna won't like it. Turning around to face Kenna, I question, "Do you still call it a nursery when they're twenty months? I feel like before we know it, she'll be in a big girl's bed."

She nods her head quickly, tears welling in her eyes. *Shit.*

"Sunshine, what's wrong? Please don't cry. Your aquamarine eyes are too beautiful to gloss over with tears. If you hate it, or you think it won't be a good home for Cadence, I can get a different one. Fuck, I should've just had you come with me, but I wanted to surprise you and show you how serious I am."

"I'm sorry, I can't help it. What does this all mean, Griffin? Are you going to try to get custody of Cadence? Because I was hoping that if this day ever came, we would be able to talk this out amongst ourselves. I don't want to get any lawyers involved if we can avoid it. I know that's not fair of me to say, considering who my dad is. But—"

Before she can finish, I cut her off. "McKenna, stop. Here I go again, not making myself clear. I have no intention of getting lawyers involved in our lives. I want this to be a home that Cadence feels comfortable in when she comes here. But, yes, eventually, I would like her to live here full-time. The schools in this neighborhood are excellent. I made that one of my non-negotiable items on my wishlist."

"I think I heard you wrong. Did you just say Cadence would be living here full-time?"

"Of course. The three of us will all live here full-time. Well, the four of us. We can't forget about Ranger."

"Griffin. What are you talking about?"

"Well, I'd only live here full-time in the off-season. But my rookie contract is only through next season, so who knows where we'll be at that point. But you and Cadence deserve a home that's entirely your own."

"We can't live together, Griff. We haven't even figured out how to co-parent yet. We-we're barely even friends."

Ouch. I rub my chest, trying to ease the ache from her words.

"You're right. Sorry, I'm getting ahead of myself. I bought this house to have a place to live when I'm here in the off-season. That's not for another six months, so we will cross that bridge when we get to it. In the meantime, I wanted to show you the place and let you know my intentions. You may think we're barely friends, but that's not how I feel. In fact, I'd say you've quickly become my best friend again."

"I'm sorry. I didn't mean it. We're friends. But we're also not. Some-times, the way I still feel isn't friendly."

"Look, I know there's probably still a lot of hesitation or resentment on your end that will take time to work through. It just makes me want to try that much harder to prove that I'm in this. That I will never turn my back on the two of you again."

Kenna doesn't respond with words. She brings her hand to her mouth to cover a sob, tears falling down her cheeks as she shakes her head in acknowledgment.

I may only be half a man, but these two girls—Kenna and Ca-dence—have picked up the pieces and made me want to be the best version of myself.

I intend to show her just how much they mean to me. Buying this house, which I'm hoping they'll help turn into a home, was the first big step in doing so.

Later that night, after we put Cadence to bed, Kenna and I are wrapping presents in the living room by the fireplace. I've just finished wrapping a book for Cadence when Kenna breaks the tense silence that's fallen upon us since we got back.

"Some nights are like tonight—harder, I mean. Especially when she's thrown off her schedule like she was this week," she explains. I can't gauge Kenna's emotions right now. I'm not sure if she's anxious, stressed, upset, or angry. Maybe all of the above. After we left my house to come back to Carson's, Cadence became inconsolable, and Kenna didn't want my help trying to soothe her.

"I understand not every day or night will be easy, Kenna. But I can't help but feel inadequate in those moments. How am I supposed to learn what will soothe her if you shut me out?" I question.

She pauses her wrapping and looks up at me. "How do I know you won't push us away again? When things get hard, or if one of us gets hurt, how do I know you won't just bail on Cadence?" Her eyes fill with unshed tears, making me curse myself for putting off this conversation.

Pushing aside the wrapping paper, I scooch closer to Kenna. "I understand where your concerns are coming from. I know I need to prove myself to you. But I promise you, I will never leave you or Cadence willingly ever again. I'm in this, McKenna."

Kenna's posture stiffens at my words. "Don't make promises you may not be able to keep, Griff," she whispers. "You can't leave us again if you get scared that we'll get hurt. What happens if something happens to me? Will you be there for Cadence, or will you get scared again that everyone you care about dies? You said a lot of awful things to me; whether you remember them or not, I do."

Closing my eyes, I try to take a calming breath to ease the emotions threatening to take over. When I open them again, Kenna is blurred from my watery eyes. I take another deep, shuddering breath before I say, "After almost two years of therapy, I've developed coping mechanisms. My therapist has taught me ways to work through and express my fears and concerns. Once I found out about Cadence, one of my first few calls was to my therapist. I still attend therapy sessions regularly, and it not only helps me be my best self but a better hockey player, father, and hopefully partner to you."

I pause before continuing, "I know the things I said and did to you were awful. I won't try to excuse my behavior. I'll never be able to express how sorry I am for pushing you away and for hurting you. I broke what we had because I was scared to lose you. In doing so, I not only lost the love of a lifetime, but I missed out on every step of your pregnancy and our daughter's first year and a half of her life."

Kenna reaches out, placing her hand in mine. "I have things I need to apologize for too, Griff. After seeing you in Boston, I was hesitant to reach out to you about Cadence. Even though I tried to contact you, in my heart I know I should've tried harder. Part of me knows I could've done more. But I was not only trying to protect Cadence but protect myself as well. I'll never be able to tell you how sorry I am for not trying harder. I robbed you of so many nights with her. I let the hurt I was feeling cloud my good sense."

"We both made mistakes in the past, but we can't keep rehashing them. We need to move on and move forward together, Kenna."

She just stares back at me, tears now streaming down her face.

"Sunshine, please don't. You were right to think I wasn't in the right place to bring a child into the world. I wasn't. Just know that I needed time to work on myself. While I hate that I missed so much, I wouldn't have been able to work on myself if things didn't work out the way they did."

Kenna just nods her head in response, hiccuping as her tears slowly stream down her cheeks.

"I know we haven't had a chance to talk about the future yet—but you're it, Kenna. You and Cadence are my future. I'm in this all the way. I've learned to be patient in the time we've spent apart. I understand that I need to prove myself to you."

"I just need some more time, Griff."

Squeezing her hand in mine, I reassure her, "We've got nothing but time, Sunshine. I'm not going anywhere."

One day at a time, I will prove myself to her by continuing to show up for them and support her. I meant what I said, I'm not going anywhere ever again. My world now revolves around my Sunshine and Little Ray.

It's my first Christmas morning with my girls. I stayed at Kenna's place last night since my new house isn't furnished yet. I asked Kenna if she would be willing to go furniture shopping with me tomorrow before I need to leave town the following day.

I didn't tell her this, but I want her to help pick out the furniture, so I know she likes what goes into what I hope will eventually be *our* home.

After our talk last night, we finished wrapping presents, watched a Christmas movie, and drank spiked hot chocolate. Even though Cadence is still far too young to catch us in the act, we still tiptoed around and acted as if she was going to come out of her room at any moment.

I'm just flipping the last batch of pancakes when I hear the door from the garage open and the house alarm beep. Carson, I realize, punches in the code, then heads to the kitchen.

"Merry Christmas, G. What are you making?" Carson asks.

"Merry Christmas, Carse. I'm making pancakes, scrambled eggs, and ground sausage. Kenna said Cadence loves all three of those, so I thought it was a good choice for the first Christmas I get to spend with her."

He nods at me but continues his stare into my eyes a few beats longer than I'm comfortable with.

"You're doing a good job with her—with them. You know, I feel partly responsible for how things went down. I was hurting too, seeing you like that, hearing what you said to Mack. I didn't handle it well. Obviously, punching you wasn't one of my finest moments."

He rubs the back of his neck and continues, "I've always taken on the role of a caretaker in our group. I guess I liked the idea of Mack, and eventually Cadence, needing me. I should've backed off and suggested Mack continue to reach out to you. To not give you the option of skirting your responsibilities. Looking back and knowing you, if you were in your right mind, you never would've abandoned them. I'm sorry, G. I feel like I got in the way."

His confession and apology are unexpected. I'm not quite sure what to make of it. What I do know is that if it weren't for Carson, Kenna wouldn't have had anyone to lean on when I broke us.

Turning off the burner, I plate the last of the pancakes.

Then, I clear the emotion clogging my throat and turn to Carson, looking him in the eyes. "Honestly, I should be thanking you, Carse. If it weren't for you, Kenna wouldn't have had anyone to lean on after Katie's death. I carelessly pushed her away, fooling myself into thinking I was doing what was best for her. Then, instead of trying to grieve in a healthy way, I coped by drowning myself in alcohol and prescription pills. You were there for her when I should've been along every step of the way. And while I'm jealous as hell that it wasn't me, I'm also thankful for each and every time you had her back."

"Shit. It's pretty early for these deep conversations. What do you say we hug it out and let the past stay in the past?" He gives me a watery-eyed grin.

I smile back at him, shaking my head at his theatrics, then bring him in for a real hug. I pat his back a few times, and we part when a throat clears from behind us.

"Care to share what has the two of you so emotional this morning? It's Christmas!" Kenna stands near the kitchen island, holding a grinning Cadence on her hip. My daughter's hair is wild, and she's still in her Christmas footie pajamas. Kenna's hair is pulled on the top of her head in a bun, and she's wearing a pair of pajamas that have the same Christmas print to match Cadence's. The two of them standing there together look like home. *My* home.

Instead of answering Kenna's question, I ask one of my own, "Are my girls hungry this morning?" I go to grab Cadence out of her arms.

She raises her eyebrow at my question, then shakes her head, a grin spreading over her face. "Are we ever not? What's on the menu?"

"All of Ray's favorites." I step aside so Kenna can see what's on the table behind me.

She smiles up at me and replies, "This looks delicious, Griff. Thank you. Did you just call her 'Ray'?"

I smirk back at her, "I did—it's my new nickname for her—she's my Little Ray of sunshine. She brightens up my life just like her mama."

Kenna's cheeks turn the most beautiful shade of scarlet. "I love it," she says before placing Cadence in her highchair.

After we finished breakfast, Kenna said it was time for Cadence to open her Christmas presents from Santa.

As our daughter opens her last present, looking more interested in the wrapping paper and the box the stuffed elephant came in, I walk over to the tree.

"There's a few more to open up," I say as I place a gift bag in front of Cadence and put the small box and two envelopes for Kenna and Carson in my hoodie pocket.

My Little Ray dives right into her present, throwing the tissue paper aside and pulling out a small blue and white jersey.

Kenna helps Cadence lift the jersey up, turning it around to show the ninety-one and DADDY across the back of a Colorado Summit jersey.

"Oh, this is so cute! It's actually perfect for what we got you for Christmas," Kenna says, becoming bashful and hiding her face behind Cadence.

I smile back at her, not knowing where she's going with this. "And what's that?"

Kenna pulls out her phone. Once she's swiped a few times, she turns her phone over for me to see.

On the screen is an airline confirmation for two flights from Minneapolis to Denver for New Year's Eve day, with the return flight coming back a week later.

"Sunshine, are you messing with me right now?" I question, not wanting to get my hopes up.

She shakes her head at me. "I thought since my season is over, and I'm on winter break from school, Cadence and I could come visit you for a week in Denver. I looked at your schedule, and your team has a stretch of home games, so I thought it'd be perfect timing for us to surprise you. Your dad even said he could make it out for a few days to meet Cadence."

I'm speechless. I don't even know what to say. This is the most thoughtful gift Kenna could've given me. The stress and sadness of not seeing Cadence have taken a toll on me.

Kenna's eyes widen at my silence. "Oh my gosh. This was so presumptuous of me. I was so caught up in surprising you, I didn't stop to think if you'd even want us to come. Griff, I can get a refund on the tickets."

"No," I say firmly, shaking my head. "No, that's not happening. I want you two to come. This means so much to me, Sunshine. I've never loved a surprise more than this one."

She still looks apprehensive. "Are you sure?"

I scoop the two of them into an awkward sitting hug, placing a kiss on each of their cheeks. "I'm already thinking of all the places I want to take the two of you. I've never been more sure of anything. This is the best Christmas present I've ever been given, Sunshine."

Kenna pulls her sleeves over her hands and then tries to hide her blush behind them. Knowing she doesn't like awkward moments, I steer the moment in a different direction.

"Alright, your turn." I hand the small wrapped jewelry box to Kenna.

She unwraps it and slowly opens the box to find a gold chain with Cadence's name and her aquamarine birthstone on each side of her name.

"How fitting that our daughter's birthstone matches the exact shade of her mama's eyes," I suggest.

Her breath hitches before she grabs the dainty chain from the box and turns around. "Will you help me clasp it?"

"Of course," I reply, letting my rough fingertips linger just a little longer than necessary.

Stepping back, I pull the two envelopes out of my pocket, handing one to Kenna and the other to Carse.

"What's this? You didn't have to get us anything," Kenna starts, but I send her a knowing look, and she smiles in resignation.

"Should we open them together?" Carse and Kenna ask at the same time, like true twins.

"Yeah," I reply.

They open the envelopes, and Kenna's eyes round so big I think they'll pop out of her head. "What? How? Are these for real?"

"G, are you serious? How the hell did you score floor tickets to Taylor Swift's sold-out Era's Tour?"

I don't attempt to hold back my cocky smirk. "I know people who know people. So, do you like them?"

"Like them? What's not to absolutely love? Tell me you got one for yourself, too!" Kenna squeals as she throws herself into my arms.

I nod my head to let her know I will also be joining them. "I, uh, actually got four tickets. Figured Katie could be there in spirit." I scratch the slight stubble covering my jaw.

Kenna pulls back, her eyes pooling with unshed tears. "She's always with us, but I love that you got her a ticket, Griffin."

"I'm going to have no voice for a month after this concert," Carse declares.

"I'm glad you love them, Sunshine. Does that date work for the two of you?" I ask, waiting for their reactions.

Carson looks down at the tickets again, then sheepishly says, "Uh, G, I don't know how to tell you this, but your people messed up. These tickets say the concert is in July in Milan. As in Milan, Italy."

"They didn't mess up. We're going to Italy for the concert."

Kenna stiffens, taking a step back and unwrapping her arms from around my waist.

"Griff, we can't just go to Italy. We have Cadence—"

Before she can continue to spiral, I cut her off, "I already asked your mom and Dakota if they could watch her while we're there for the two weeks."

"Two weeks? Griffin! That's crazy. You're insane. I haven't been away from her for more than two nights at a time. There's no way I'll be comfortable leaving her for that long."

"We can figure out the logistics and length of the vacation as it gets closer, Sunshine," I placate.

Little does she know that when it comes to her, I am completely insane. Probably delusional or certifiable. Because I'm crazy enough to believe that after everything we've been through, maybe we could still be each other's happy ending.

29

McKenna

December

I'm on my way to the airport now to come get my girls! Text me when you land.

We just landed! Excited to see you soon.

It's New Year's Eve, and I'm standing outside the airport in Colorado with a sleeping Cades on my shoulder. She was such a trooper on the flight to Denver. I timed it so it would be around her bedtime, but I had no idea if she would do okay as this was her first flight.

My mom suggested giving her a bottle at takeoff to help her ears adjust, and she fell asleep shortly after we were in the air.

I've got our luggage in her stroller, opting to hold her instead of strapping her in the stroller, and I've just walked to the curb when a red Jeep Wrangler pulls up in front of us.

Butterflies erupt in my stomach, and nostalgia hits at the sight of his Jeep.

Griff hops out, rounding the hood, and my god, does he look good. His brown hair peeks out beneath his black beanie. I love it when his hair gets a little longer during the season like this. He's wearing a black sweatshirt with a pair of . . . *are you kidding me?* He's wearing gray joggers that cling to his thick thighs, making the back of my neck sweat. He tops the look off with white sneakers.

Once he approaches us, Griff places a chaste peck on my cheek, then kisses Cadence's temple. God, I wish we could be those people who have a deep, passionate kiss at the airport.

"How did our girl do on her first flight?" Griff takes the luggage and stroller over to the trunk of his Jeep.

I follow behind him with Cadence. "She did great. She practically slept the whole flight, which made it easy on me."

He swings the back of the Jeep closed and then grabs our sleepy girl out of my arms. He squeezes her tight and whispers, "Good job, sweet girl. Thanks for going easy on your mama."

My stomach dips, and my chest constricts, just like it does every time he calls me that.

Griff smirks, knowing what he's doing to me. Placing his hand on the small of my back, he ushers me to the passenger door, opening it for me to get inside.

"I'll get her buckled, and then we can go to my place to get her settled for the night."

It doesn't go unnoticed that he got another car seat for Cadence and already installed it, so it's rear-facing.

I get buckled just as he opens the driver's door and gets situated. He turns to look over at me, my stomach swoops when I see his dimples pop. The same dimples he passed on to Cadence.

"I love that she has two of my favorite traits of yours: your brown eyes and your dimples, though she only has one on her left cheek."

Griff's answering wink makes me swoon.

"I don't know. The other day, when the two of you were FaceTiming me, I thought I saw a smaller dimple on her right cheek, though definitely not as pronounced. It was after you made her go into a giggle fit with her stuffed elephant."

I smile at the memory he's referring to. These past few months have been filled with daily FaceTime calls and countless text exchanges between the two of us. I've tried to keep it strictly platonic, centering solely around Cadence, but that doesn't stop Griff from asking me about my day and trying to get to know me better each time we talk.

"So, where are you taking us? I've actually never been to Colorado. The one tournament Carson had here, I had a volleyball tournament the same weekend in Florida."

"For tonight, we'll just head to my place and put Cadence to bed. After seeing your setup for her and doing her bedtime routine with you a few times, I tried to replicate as much of that as I could. I live right in downtown Denver in a two-bedroom apartment near the arena."

"I can't wait to see it," I tell him, and I really am excited to see what his place looks like.

We pull into an underground parking garage and park before Griff gets out, puts the luggage in Cadence's stroller, and then picks her up out of her car seat. She's miraculously still asleep somehow. I push the stroller, following Griff into an elevator, where he pushes the button for the twentieth floor.

I suck in a breath, instantly hit with a calming sense of warmth.

Griff notices and says, "I didn't get a chance to look at the place in person before I signed the lease. The first time I realized I was on the floor that was Katie's favorite number, it felt like a sign that everything would be okay."

Tears swell in my eyes. "I feel her around me all the time. She would be so proud of you, Griffin. I hope you know that. She was always telling me how proud of you she was and how much she looked up to you."

"I feel her with me, too. Like last season when I won the Calder trophy. Or the night I found out about Cadence. Memories of her drive me to push myself harder each day."

Griff opens the door to his apartment, and I'm not sure what I was thinking his place would look like, but it certainly wasn't this. It's much more spacious than I was anticipating, being that it is in the heart of the city.

Along one wall of the foyer, there's a bench with hooks hung above it for coats and purses. Against the other wall is a long entryway table with a round mirror hung above it. The furniture finish is a warm, natural wood, similar to what I've picked out for Cadence's room and my own at Carson's house.

Griff walks further into the apartment, and after slipping off my shoes and hanging my jacket and purse on the hooks, I park the stroller next to the entryway table. I walk through the open layout to the wall of floor-to-ceiling windows where Griff is holding Cadence.

"This view is breathtaking," I say in awe of the cityscape in front of us.

"It truly is," he agrees. I look over at him and am surprised to find him already staring at me intently.

Clearing the uncertainty from my throat, I ask, "Will you give me a tour?"

"Of course, Sunshine. Let's put Cadence in her crib first, though," he suggests as he leads us down to the end of the hallway.

"A crib? Griff, I hope you mean a pack and play," I start but am suddenly at a loss for words as I take in the room Griffin set up for Cadence.

In front of me is the most beautiful nursery. The walls are a crisp cream color, and the furniture has the same warm, natural wood tones as the entryway. The crib is centered along the back wall, which is windowless. The wall to the right of it has the same floor-to-ceiling windows; however, there are expensive-looking beige drapes falling from the ceiling to the floor. The same wide-plank wood flooring that runs throughout the rest of the apartment is in here as well, but there is a large, plush cream rug that takes up most of the floor space. There's also a large, white neon sign with Cadence's name written across it in a script font hung above her crib.

I'm still trying to take in the space when I catch Griff watching me from the corner of my eye. Griffin must take my silence as displeasure. He looks unsure of himself as he scratches the back of his neck with the hand not holding Cades.

"I just wanted to get a few things for when you two visit. I wasn't able to get as many books on her bookshelves yet, but I did get *Chicka Chicka Boom Boom* and about a dozen of her other favorites."

I hadn't even noticed the few rows of acrylic floating bookshelves hung along the wall behind me.

"I figured we could go shopping on my day off for some of the items I may have forgotten," he pauses. "Shit, Kenna. Say something, please," he pleads.

Why is it that this man always makes me lose any and all sense?

Shaking my head, I reply, "It's perfect—stunning."

"Really? Are you sure you like it? Do you think she'll like it?" he questions.

"She'll love everything in here. Griff, you didn't have to. When did you even have the time to do all of this?"

He moves to the left side of the room and places Cadence on a changing mat that sits on top of a dresser. Griff changes her into a clean diaper, then grabs an armless sleep sack out of one of the drawers for her to sleep in. It looks like just the one I packed for her from home.

Still waiting for him to answer, I take in more details of the room. He's got a little basket sitting atop the dresser that's filled with the same lotions, essential oils, and diaper rash balms I have in the diaper bag. He takes out an oil roller from one of them and rubs it along her feet before placing her in the sleep sack. Once he's got her zipped up, he places a kiss on her forehead and sits down in the glider in the corner of the room. Griff reaches out to the side table beside him, turns on the noise machine, and then connects his phone to a Bluetooth speaker that starts playing "You Are My Sunshine."

He's truly thought of every little detail. Tears well in my eyes as I watch him rock our daughter back to sleep while he softly sings our song to her. If you had told me a few months ago that I would be visiting Griff in Colorado with Cadence, watching him take on fatherhood in stride, I would have thought you were crazy.

But here I am, with a man I was once insanely in love with—quite possibly still might be in love with—and he's trying so damn hard to do right by us. I surprised him with this trip because I wanted to make an effort—to extend an olive branch in our agreement to try to leave the past behind us. But if I'm being honest with myself, I've built up walls around my heart and set boundaries for us to remain platonic to protect myself.

Protect myself from what, though? From a man who was once lost, broken, and destroyed, so he pushed me away and broke my heart. If I was in his shoes, can I honestly say I wouldn't have done the same? I loved Katie like a sister, but at the end of the day, she wasn't my sister; she was Griff's.

So now I have to choose. Do I let the fear of past mistakes repeating themselves consume me, allowing me to keep my walls up? Or do I finally let down my walls for this man who has suffered such devastating losses and then worked on himself to overcome his grief?

My heart has already made the choice for me. It's him. It's always been him.

Instead of grabbing a cup of coffee, though, I stop in my tracks when I turn the corner of the hallway. A shirtless, *tatted*, Griffin is sitting on the living room rug with Cadence between his legs as they wind up a Jack in the Box. The box pops open, springing the puppet out, and Cadence's answering giggle is music to my ears.

The next morning, Cadence does something she rarely ever does: she sleeps in. I roll over in Griffin's bed—yes, we slept in the same bed—because he absolutely refused to have either of us sleep on the couch. We haven't talked about us yet, so he kept a respectable distance between us at first, but when I asked him to hold me in his arms, he didn't protest.

Once I'm done brushing my teeth in Griffin's primary bathroom, I open his bedroom door and am instantly hit with the smell of coffee. *Come to Mama.*

Instead of grabbing a cup of coffee, though, I stop in my tracks when I turn the corner of the hallway. A shirtless, *tatted*, Griffin is sitting on the living room rug with Cadence between his legs as they wind up a Jack in the Box. The box pops open, springing the puppet out, and Cadence's answering giggle is music to my ears.

Griff catches me staring but doesn't call me out on it. Instead, he flashes me his dimples and says, "Good morning, Sunshine."

Cadence peeks up and squeals, "Mama!" Her matching dimple pops on her left cheek. Seeing the two of them together gives me literal heart eyes.

"Morning baby, how did my girl sleep?" I say to Cadence, bewildered by the sight of Griff, trying not to drool at his inked chest and shoulder.

"Remember when you used to call me 'baby?'" Griff pouts.

"I do." I chuckle.

"Well, now that you call Cadence 'baby,' what does that make me?"

"I was thinking now I'd just call you 'daddy.'" I didn't intentionally lower my voice, but it happened, and I'm not mad about it.

"Fuck—shit—oh god, I shouldn't be swearing," he places his hands over Cadence's ears. "What I meant to say was, I love the sound of that, Sunshine. A lot. Probably too much for you to say in public or when our daughter is awake."

I smile and shake my head at his slip of the tongue.

"Perhaps I'll take to calling you Hotshot again. You did win Rookie of the Year last season, after all." I give him a playful wink.

"You can call me anything you want. I made coffee and got some of that creamer you like in the fridge. There's also a newspaper with the Sunday crossword on the kitchen island."

That has me stopping in my tracks. How could he have possibly remembered? I used to love doing the crossword every Sunday when I would stay over at their house. Their dad used to save it for me.

"Griff, that was really thoughtful of you. I haven't done one since I've been in college."

"Oh, I'm sorry. I didn't realize," he pauses.

"No, it's okay, really. I told myself I wasn't going to let fear hold me back anymore."

"I'm here for you, Kenna. I know I still have to work to prove that to you, but I am."

"I know you are."

Nodding his head, he winds the Jack in the Box for Cadence again before he says, "I thought we could go get donuts at one of my favorite places down the street. Maybe we could bundle Cadence up and go for a little walk?"

"I'd love nothing more," I agree.

"I'll go get her ready," Griff tells me as he picks Cadence up off the ground. Before he brings her to her nursery, he stops over to where I'm seated at the kitchen island to place a kiss on my forehead.

Now that he's closer, I can see what the tattoos on his chest and shoulder are. "Griffin, what are these?"

"They're tattoos, Kenna."

"I can see that, but of what?"

He dips his left shoulder, where sunbeams radiate down his arm and onto his chest. Below the beams, he has a rose on his bicep. He moves his arm to show me the Roman numerals near his tricep.

"I got these my first week in Colorado so I could have my girls with me wherever I went. The rose is for my mom, the Roman numerals are Katie's birthday, and the sunbeams are for you, Sunshine. You were always with me."

"I love each one so much, Griff," I breathe as I trace my hands across the outlines, wanting to kiss each detail of them. "You've clearly been holding out on me."

"So you're a fan of tattoos, I take it?"

He must see my answer when he looks at me because he just gives me that panty-melting smirk-wink combination and heads off down the hall. I probably looked like the literal personification of the heart eyes emoji mixed with the drooling face emoji.

After we get Cadence ready, we walk to the donut store, holding hands while Griff pushes the stroller with one arm. I'm completely lost in my thoughts—struggling with the internal battle going on between my head and my heart, and Griff's taking notice.

I can't help but wonder if this is what our life would be like if I just opened my heart to this man. Would we go for family walks together? Would we spend our nights cooking dinner in the kitchen—singing, dancing, and laughing? Would we go through Cadence's bedtime routine together? Would we be there for each other to lean on on our hardest days? Would we spend every night wrapped up in one another for the rest of our lives, only to start each day the same way?

If so, it sounds like I'm holding myself back from the most beautiful life. My biggest fear in life is not taking risks. I'm done being scared he'll break my heart again. I need to tell him I'm ready to jump headfirst. Because what is this life if not risking it all for those you love?

I never stopped loving Griffin Turner, and it's about damn time he knows that.

Today has been one of the best days I've had in a long time.

Shortly after we got back from our walk to get donuts together, Griff's dad arrived in Colorado. Jack didn't bring his girlfriend, Bethany, this time. He said he didn't want to overwhelm Cadence with too many new faces at once, and I appreciated his thoughtfulness.

The moment Jack met Cadence, she had him wrapped around her perfect little finger. He cried, which made me start crying, which made Cadence laugh, which got us all laughing.

Cadence and Jack hit it off so well that he insisted he would babysit her while Griff took me to dinner. I was hesitant at first because I didn't know how Cades would do, and I didn't want to ruin what had been a great day, but Jack assured me he could feed her dinner and get her to sleep, though he joked that maybe he would stray from some of her bedtime routine just this once.

Griffin was able to get us reservations at an Italian restaurant a few blocks down from his place. He informed me it was cocktail attire, and when I told him I didn't pack anything to wear to a fancy restaurant, he gave me his black Amex and told me to buy "everything" I liked.

The town car Griff called is just pulling up to the restaurant, so he pulls his hand from mine to get out of the car. I instantly miss the warmth and the feel of his large hand eclipsing mine.

In typical Griffin Turner form, he rounds the back of the car and opens the door for me. He looks downright delectable in his black button-down and gray dress slacks.

"Why, thank you, Hotshot."

"Always, Sunshine. Have I told you yet how amazing you look?" he asks.

"Only about a dozen times before we left your place," I remind him. The moment I saw the sleeveless, mid-length red dress with a square neckline, I knew Griffin would love it. He's always been a sucker for me in red.

"This dress is going to bring me to my knees," he whispers into my ear before placing his large hand on the small of my back, leading me into the restaurant. My skin heats and a shiver runs up my spine just thinking about how much I love what this man does to my body when he's on his knees.

We've just ordered a bottle of wine when Griff leans over and says, "I got you something," before handing me a blue gift bag stuffed with white tissue paper.

"Griff! You've spoiled me enough today. You didn't have to do this."

"Oh, I absolutely did need to. Besides, you know I love showering you with gifts."

Once upon a time, I did know that Griff loved showering me with gifts. It was his love language.

I open Griff's gift with shaky hands to find a cobalt blue and white Colorado Summits jersey with TURNER and a number ninety-one on the back. Not even trying to hide my smile, I tell him, "I love it, Griff. Thank you."

"You're welcome, Sunshine. I should be the one thanking you. Now, both of my girls will be at my game tomorrow night wearing my name on their backs."

Both butterflies and guilt swarm my stomach, battling for the upper hand.

Griff must sense my internal struggle. "Don't, McKenna. We were young, we made mistakes, but we're here right now," he says as he grabs my hand, rubbing reassuring circles over the turquoise ring he gave me. His face lights up at the sight of it.

"I've only ever taken it off for volleyball matches." I'm not even sure why I say it. Maybe to comfort him? Maybe to vaguely remind both him and me that it's always been him?

Whatever the reason, the moment is stolen from us when a fan recognizes Griff and approaches our table.

"No way, you're Griffin Turner. You're my favorite Summits player," the boy, who can't be much older than fourteen, exclaims.

Griff holds out his hand for the boy to shake. "I am, and who am I talking to?"

The boy looks like he's about to swallow his tongue as he replies, "Stinner. Brogan Stinner."

"Nice to meet you, Brogan. Do you play hockey as well? Here, let's get a picture together," Griff says as he stands from the table.

Brogan can't hold back a grin that takes up almost the entirety of his face. "I do. I also play center."

They take a few pictures together before Griff says, "It was great to meet you, Brogan. If you don't mind, we were just about to order dinner."

"Oh, right! Thank you so much, Mr. Turner. I hope you have a great night," Brogan practically squeals.

Once the boy is far enough from the table, I can't help but playfully taunt Griffin for his stardom.

"Is it like that everywhere you go?" I ask, genuinely curious to get to know this version of the man who stole my heart when we were only teenagers.

He just shrugs, trying to downplay the notoriety. I'm not sure if he's worried I'll get scared or if he's just being bashful.

"Hey," I start before pulling his hand back in mine, "I want to know all your truths, remember?"

"How could I ever forget, Sunshine?" he retorts as his face lights up with a devastating smile.

30

Griffin

JANUARY

The cool, crisp air fills my lungs as I make my way around our half of the ice for warm-ups. I don't even try to hide my smile when I spot my dad and Kenna holding Cadence against the glass by our bench.

Skating over to them, I wave animatedly at Cadence to get her to giggle and see if both of her dimples will pop. They do, and I feel like I've just won the Stanley Cup.

Seeing Kenna and Cadence with my number and name on their backs makes me feel invincible. I feel the need to play the best game of my career to be worthy of having them here cheering for me. I want to convince them that maybe my name shouldn't only be on their backs but should be *their* name as well someday.

As warm-ups finish up, I skate over to our bench and place my gloves against the glass where Cadence is banging on it. Kenna's eyes widen when she sees what is stitched on my gloves—the sun and cat I've had embroidered into every pair of gloves since Katie passed, and the newest addition, "Ray," is stitched on the glove.

Kenna presses her palm against the glass, and I mirror mine on the other side. I smile back at her radiant one. I swear I could look into her mesmerizing eyes for an eternity, and it'd never be enough. But that's not an option. The moment is broken when I hear my assistant coach hollering at me to get my ass off the ice so they can resurface it before the first period.

"Good luck, Daddy!" I hear Kenna shout, and Cadence joins in, "Go, Dada!"

They're the best motivation a man could have to play my ass off.

I'm headed to center ice for the first faceoff of the third period, and I'm feeling unstoppable. I've got two goals and an assist already. I don't typically care about scoring a hat trick, but tonight would be the first of my NHL career, and I'd love nothing more than for my girls to be here to witness it.

After winning the faceoff back to Jonesy, I circle through the neutral zone and catch a pass back from him. The moment I enter the offensive zone, I deke the defense and take my open shot. I shoot a low-side blocker for the third time tonight, and it pays off.

The goal horn blares before they play our goal song, and fans' hats are flooding the ice. My teammates attack me in a big hug at the boards.

"Atta boy, Rookie!" Jonesy shouts.

We skate to the bench and give the rest of our teammates fist bumps. The maintenance crew is still clearing hats from the ice, so I circle over to where my dad, Kenna, and Cadence are sitting.

I hold up my gloved hands and make a large heart in the air before pointing at them.

Kenna tries to hide her blush behind her hands while Cadence stands on my dad's lap and claps her hands together.

Once the hats are cleared, we head back to center ice. I win the face-off back to Jonesy again, but this time, as I circle through the neutral zone, I'm stopped short when Arizona's defenseman takes my legs out from under me.

My body is immediately flooded with blinding pain. My focus blurs, spots dotting my vision from the throbbing.

The athletic trainers come out to tend to me and ask me a series of questions.

"Alright, let's get you up, Turner," one of the trainers suggests. They help me to my feet, but I quickly realize I can't put any weight on my right leg without searing pain radiating from my knee.

Two of my teammates are quick to give me their shoulders to help me to our bench that leads down the tunnel to our locker room.

"Fuck!" I shout as they get me into the locker room to be evaluated by the team doctor.

The team doctor just left the hospital exam room after she read the MRI results and then broke the news that I tore my meniscus in my right knee. I'll need surgery as soon as the swelling goes down to repair it.

Thankfully, my dad was at the game tonight, and he was able to get in touch with an orthopedic surgeon he used to work with in Minnesota who specializes in complex knee surgeries. My dad assured me my meniscal tear wasn't considered complex, but he wanted me to have the best of the best.

I asked him if he could help me get Cadence and McKenna packed up so we could take a jet back to Minnesota right away in the morning, if not tonight.

My dad and Kenna were able to figure out the logistics to get us back to Minnesota the same night. I was scheduled for surgery three days later.

I've been awake from the anesthesia for about a half hour when Dr. Jason Stone walks into my recovery room.

"Good morning, Griffin. How are you feeling?" Dr. Stone asks.

"I feel like shit, if I'm being honest, doc," I croak.

"That's to be expected. These first couple of days will be the toughest pain-wise. Be sure to get some rest and stay on top of ice and compression. I was able to successfully repair your meniscus. Everything else in your knee looked great. You'll likely be out the next four to six months, Griffin. You'll be non-weight-bearing for the next six weeks. Be sure to wear your immobilizer and use your crutches. Do you have any questions for me right now?"

I shake my head, and once he leaves the room, I cover my face, trying to keep my cool.

The pain curls around my leg and spreads up to the base of my spine and down to my toes. I refused their prescription for opioids, not wanting to risk taking them. But the pain is fucking real, and the extra-strength Tylenol isn't cutting it.

I'm taking a deep breath to complete my box breathing exercises my therapist went over with me when Kenna walks into my recovery room.

She takes one look at me and winces. "How bad is the pain, baby?"

Baby. God, I've missed having her call me that. Hearing her term of endearment alleviates some of the pain I'm feeling.

"It's rough, but nothing I can't handle now that you're here," I answer.

I see Kenna hesitate for only a moment before she musters the courage to approach the left side of my bed. She places my hand in hers, and the feel of her soft skin against mine brings another wave of reprieve from the pain.

"You know, there's one thing that would make me feel a lot better . . ." I start.

"Oh, yeah, and what's that?"

I scooch myself over as best as I can toward the right side of my bed. "Come snuggle me, Sunshine."

"G, I can't. What if I hurt you?"

"You won't. Besides, I think the anesthesia and nerve block haven't quite worn off yet."

"Fine, but you'll tell me right away if you're uncomfortable, right?"

"Of course," I reply, though I would rather tear off my own leg than tell her to get out of my arms.

Kenna places her purse on the chair next to the bed before climbing into the bed next to me. She snuggles up to me on her side, trying to take up less space. God, I love how considerate she is. How beautiful and smart and kind and athletic and thoughtful and selfless she is. I love everything about her—the good and the bad. Fuck, I just love *her*.

I can be myself, vulnerable even, with her in a way I haven't been comfortable doing since Katie died. I need to have her close. Not just now, but always.

"Move in with me, Kenna." I don't even ask, I just state it.

"What?" she asks incredulously.

"I want you and Cadence to move in with me."

"Griff, you're talking crazy. The pain must be getting to you. W-we can't. I mean, we're not even together." Kenna looks positively frazzled right now. She's so fucking cute when her brows furrow and her top lip quirks up just the slightest bit.

"It doesn't need to be a permanent change. Just while I'm here recovering, until I'm back in Colorado."

"I don't think I can do this. You make me feel so out of control, Griff," she whispers into my neck as she tries to hide from me.

"Look at me, Sunshine," I say as I grab her chin and meet her eyes. "We take this thing between us at your pace. You are in control. I promise not to push you. I just need the two of you close to me. Will you please consider staying at my house with me?" I look into her eyes, pleading she will say yes.

She sighs. "Okay, but only until you're through with recovery and back in Colorado."

Little does she know, she just signed up to stay with me for at least the next four months.

My Sunshine and my Little Ray are moving in with me. It's time to pull out the Turner charm and woo my girls so we can make this living arrangement a little more permanent.

31

McKenna

FEBRUARY

It's Valentine's Day, a holiday I've never really loved because I haven't been in a relationship on this day before. Cades and I have been staying at Griff's place in Minnesota for the past six weeks since he was injured. I told him we weren't moving in here permanently, that we were just staying until he was finished with recovery and back in Colorado.

What I didn't realize at the time was that his injury was season-ending, and Griff will be recovering and doing therapy through the offseason in Minnesota.

I've since amended our timeline to be until he's back on his feet, likely sometime around Cadence's second birthday at the end of March, which he insisted we now host her birthday party here instead of at Carson's as I had originally planned.

Griff hasn't pushed me regarding a relationship between us. He promised me we're going to take this at my pace, and he's honored that.

But . . . that hasn't kept me from sleeping in his bed each night. I can't help it! What if he needs his leg propped up in the middle of the night? Or for me to help him fill his bottle of water? It's just easier to be in the same room as him in case he needs me.

Yeah, that's the reason. It has nothing to do with how surreal it feels to wake up with his strong arms wrapped around you. Keep living in your delusional little bubble, McKenna.

We haven't done anything, though he does kiss me on the forehead before bed each night and pulls me into his chest, where I fall asleep. Needless to say, my restraint is hanging by a thread.

After a long stretch, I roll over to find an empty bed and Griff's crutches missing from beside his side of the bed. I quickly go to the bathroom, brush my teeth, wash my face, and throw my hair up in a messy bun before heading downstairs.

I get to the landing of the stairs, and the sight before me has me stopping in my tracks.

Holy. Shit.

There are two vases full of pink and red flowers on the kitchen island, balloons floating to the ceiling, and a shirtless Griffin is just placing a platter of crepes, fruit, and toppings next to the flowers.

"What's all this?" I ask, trying not to drool at the sight of him shirtless in the kitchen.

He wipes his hands on his gray sweatpants—which are slung so low on his hips I can see every delicious edge of his abs, the smattering of hair that disappears under his waistband, and the V of his adonis belt that makes me melt. Then he grabs his crutches and meets me at the bottom of the steps, where I'm still gawking.

Griff places a kiss on my forehead, then each of my cheeks. "Happy Valentine's Day, Sunshine."

His smile lights up his face, dimples on full display. My heart swells from the sincerity shining in his eyes, and I can't help but feel an overwhelming sense of belonging. These past few months since Griffin has come back into our lives have made me feel alive again.

"Happy V-Day, G." I take him in again now that he's closer and I'm spellbound by the intensity of my need for this man.

The trance I was in is broken when I hear a clang in the kitchen. He had me in such a stupor I didn't even see Cadence in her highchair.

"Good morning, baby," I coo to her.

"Mama! Look!" she points up at the balloons hanging from the ceiling next to her highchair. She's squirming around so excitedly I fear she'd fall out if she weren't strapped in.

"Oh my goodness, Cades, what are we going to do with your daddy? He's spoiled us silly this morning!"

Griff chuckles, probably laughing at the animated voice I use when talking to Cadence.

"I had to go all out for my girls on my very first Valentine's Day with the two of you."

I pull him in for a hug. Heat tugs low in my belly at the feel of his warm skin and toned muscles encasing me. His familiar scent is like my own personal drug—the pheromones making me feel like I'm an animal in heat.

"Well, thank you. We appreciate it, and you."

"No need to thank me, Sunshine." He places a quick kiss on the top of my head, and I can't help but long for his lips to land on mine.

"Now, let's get this little gremlin fed before our hangry Cadeygirl comes out."

We've just gotten Cadence to sleep when Griff asks, "Will you watch a movie with me, Valentine?"

I smirk at the new nickname.

GRAYCE RIAN

"That depends. Has your taste in movies changed for the better in our time apart?"

He covers his heart, feigning hurt at my subtle dig. "I'll have you know, I am not alone in my love for *The Lord of the Rings* trilogy."

We're walking down the steps that lead to the theater room in his basement. Thankfully, Griff no longer has to use crutches after the follow-up appointment he had today with his surgeon. He does have to continue to wear a large brace for the next several weeks to keep his knee stabilized, though.

"Oh, trust me, I know. But unless you want to put me right to sleep, we will skip over your *precious* and watch something with a little eye candy."

"Okay, now I'm really hurt," he says as he brings me in to tickle my sides.

"Stop! Please, oh my god, stop!" I laugh so hard I think I'll pass out.

"Not until you admit that I'm the only eye candy you need," he demands.

"Alright!" I gasp, "You're the only one I'll ever need."

He stops suddenly as my words sink in. It's not that I don't mean them in that way, I just haven't admitted my feelings out loud for him yet. I had planned on telling him how I felt in Colorado, but then he got hurt, and I've been so focused on trying to get him better and get us settled, and then school started again, that I haven't had the chance to tell him.

I turn to tell him, but his intense gaze on mine stops me, uncoiling something deep inside of me.

Longing.

In this moment, I'm more desperate for this man than I've ever been for anything in my life. Griff is still so in sync with me after all this time; it's like he can read my mind as he wraps his arms around my waist.

304

"I am, Sunshine. Don't doubt this. I'm the only one, and you're my one and only. It's always been you and me, Kenna. I'm yours, and you are *mine*. I think it's about time I remind you of that."

Griff grips my jaw, and then he finally brings his lips to mine in a kiss that stops time. It's slow at first, taking on an exploratory pace—we're getting reacquainted with one another.

The world stands still as we get lost in the kiss. He runs his hands through my hair and grips the strands. My skin feels like it's burning. The fire he ignites in me is all-consuming.

I'm so enraptured that I don't notice we've moved until the back of my knees connects with one of the theater sofas.

His calloused hands slide under my shirt, finding me braless. Griffin's touch sends heat racing through me. It's a heady feeling being worshiped by this man.

"I'm going to need you to keep quiet so you don't wake our daughter up. Can you do that for me, Sunshine?"

"Yes," I whisper.

"Good girl. Now, let me see your gorgeous body spread bare for me."

I hesitate for only a moment before he lifts my shirt off me and slides my sleep shorts down and tosses them across the room.

"Fuck, Kenna. You're so fucking perfect."

I bring one hand up, covering my breasts, and use the other to hide my stomach. "I look a lot different than the last time you saw me, Griff. I'm far from perfect."

"Don't."

"Don't what? I have stretch marks on my stomach, hips, and boobs now. The skin on my stomach is looser, no matter how much work I put in at the gym and on the court."

"Don't do that. Don't try to hide from me. Those changes are a result of the bravest thing you've ever done. Your body prospered while growing our beautiful daughter. Let me show you how appreciative I am for this body. Are you ready for me to kiss and worship every inch of your skin, McKenna?" he rasps.

I enthusiastically nod my head, not able to find my words.

Griff lays me back, placing soft kisses along my skin as he slides down my body and nestles himself between my legs.

When his fingers trace up the inside of my thighs, he groans, and the sound ricochets in my stomach, sending tingles straight to my core.

My eyes roll back, and a murmur of pleasure slips from my lips. Anticipation has my clit throbbing.

The first stroke of his tongue through my folds sends my hips flying from the sofa.

"Open your eyes, Sunshine. You need to see whose face you're going to come on." He licks me from my clit to the bottom of my slit.

Holy fuck. I have missed his dirty mouth so much.

Keeping eye contact with me, he flicks my clit vigorously with his tongue. It only takes a few moments for the pressure to build at the base of my spine. When he sinks two of his fingers inside my drenched pussy, I'm coming within seconds.

I waste no time convincing him I want more. "Strip for me, Hotshot."

He pulls his shirt over his head and, without missing a beat, yanks his pants and boxers down. His body is a work of art. My eyes trail down his chest, his abs, his mouth-watering cock, and stop when I notice something on his quad. Just above his left knee is a tattoo that looks fresh.

"What is that? Did you just get a new tattoo?"

"I did. Carson and I went to get them earlier this week. He seems to think I'm getting cabin fever. I got Cadence's birthday in Roman Numerals."

The way his quad muscles bulge under the tattoo makes it hotter than anything I've ever seen. I never thought I'd like a tattoo there, but knowing he has a piece of our daughter etched into his skin makes me absolutely feral.

"I love it, Griff."

"I'm hoping I'll have some more dates to ink on me soon," he smirks at me.

Griffin kneels down on the sofa, hovering above me. When he finally lays his gloriously sculpted body against mine, the warmth of his skin overtakes me.

His voice is husky as he says, "I can't promise I'll be gentle this first time, Sunshine. The past two years without you have been torturous. I need you hard and fast right this minute."

His breaths are labored, and his jaw ticks like he's fighting with his self-control.

I can't seem to be able to, but I need to quell this need—to quench my thirst for him.

I'm dickmatized—completely spellbound from the feel of his length grinding into me for the first time in too long.

"G, I need you to let go for me, baby. Show me that you're just as desperate to feel me as I am to feel you after all this time."

Griff groans, and I know that's exactly what he was hoping I'd say. He settles between my legs, his cock nudging my entrance.

"I don't have a condom. I haven't been with anyone since you. Let me fill you up, Sunshine. I honestly would love nothing more than to see you grow another one of my babies," he whispers in my ear.

Oh, fuck.

"You haven't been with anyone else, like at all?"

"I haven't looked at another woman since I pushed you away, McKenna."

Okay, I'll be circling back to that tidbit later. But right now, I need this man more than my next breath.

"I haven't been with anyone else either. But I have an IUD, Griff. We're good. For now," I pant.

"You may have one for now, Sunshine. But mark my words, I will put a ring on your finger. Soon. And we will be making more babies. Even sooner."

Before I can respond, Griff grips his cock and guides it inside me. When he's all the way in, filling me to the hilt, I can feel my second climax rushing to the surface. I haven't been this full in over two years, and the sensation alone is going to make me come undone.

Likely able to feel how close I am, he pistons his hips to meet mine, grinding his pelvis against my clit in a deliciously mind-numbing rhythm. It only takes a few more deep thrusts for my second orgasm to pull me under. Ecstasy floods my system. Griffin's cologne, mixed with his sexy musk that's all him, consumes me.

"Until then—less talking and more filling me up. Practice makes perfect," I sass.

His moans reverberate against my collarbone as I feel his cock pulse inside of me, filling me with his cum.

"Fuck, McKenna."

Griff reluctantly pulls out of me, grabbing my hand and leading us back upstairs to his bedroom to clean up.

I've barely hit the sheets before his erection presses against me. "How are you already hard?" I chuckle.

"I always want you," he answers.

"There's the insatiable man I know."

"We've got a lot of time apart to make up for, Sunshine."

And that he did. I had several more orgasms last night before I finally passed out. I've never been so gloriously sore from sex. But I've also never gone five rounds in one night.

My legs scream at me as I move to get out of bed. I groan loud enough for Griff to hear.

He shifts in bed and gives me a devilish smile. "Sore this morning, Sunshine?"

"Ugh, yes."

Griff sits up, and the sheet falls to his waist. Seeing the corded muscles of his back flex as he stretches turns me on so much I groan again.

"I'll run you a bath, Mama."

A few moments later, Griff returns from the ensuite with a bottle of massage oil.

"Let me give you a massage while the bath runs."

"Pinch me. I think I'm still dreaming."

He chuckles. "If I pinch your nipples, will you know this is real life?"

"Let's not start something I may not be able to finish. I'm pretty sore."

He turns me over and places a kiss along each vertebra of my spine before he pours some oil into his hands and begins to work my muscles.

I'm not sure how long he massaged my body—I must've dozed off, because when I wake back up, he's finishing kneading the arch of my left foot.

Griff grabs the book I've been reading from my nightstand and hands it to me before nodding toward the bathroom. "The bath is ready. Go read for a bit and relax. I'll go wake our Little Ray up for breakfast. Oh, and Sunshine, make sure to use the red tabs in your book for anything you want me to reference later." He waggles his eyebrows at me.

And just like that, Griff has turned my world upside down. Or maybe it's finally right-side up. Being with him again feels like finally coming home.

32

Griffin

MARCH

It's the morning of Cadence's second birthday party, and I'm just finishing setting up the balloon arch Kenna made for the entryway. Kenna chose to do a Born Two Be Wild theme, so we've got wildflowers and pictures of different wild animals all over the main floor.

I've just popped a balloon and curse under my breath in frustration when I hear Kenna ask, "Griffin, why did my brother just ask me if Cadence was going to wear his jersey or yours to the Wolverine games next season?"

Shit, I wanted to be the first to tell her. Good going, Carse.

With my back still to her, I try to make light of the situation. "Because in his heart of hearts, he knows the answer to that question. Without a doubt, Cadence will be wearing a Turner jersey all next season."

Kenna scoffs. "Well, of course, she can wear your jersey when you play against Carse, but I don't really understand why she can't wear Carson's jersey when she goes to his other games."

I slowly turn to face her. "If all goes well with my knee, I'm hoping every game Carson plays next season will be with me as his teammate, so she won't have any opportunities to wear his."

Kenna's forehead wrinkles in confusion—it's endearing, and I love it. "I'm sorry, did you just say as his teammate?"

I chuckle. "Yes, Sunshine. I'm back home in Minnesota for good."

"You're back for good?"

God, she's so cute when she repeats everything I've just said in a question back to me.

"Yes. The press release hasn't gone out yet, but I just met with Carlisle this morning. I'm officially a player for the Minnesota Wolverines."

"Griffin! What were you thinking? You can't just—just make life-changing decisions like this without consulting me. We have to think of Cades first, yes, but we also have dreams, ambitions and careers to consider. Colorado has always been your dream, Griff."

Taking a step forward, I move into her space. "Colorado *was* my dream. Cadence and you—the two of you—are my whole world. I've already missed so much of her life. I refuse to miss any more time than I need to. You know the travel schedule for the team is already crazy enough. It was agony those few weeks before my injury, only seeing her over FaceTime calls and short visits."

I lift her chin so she can look into my eyes. "Besides, I didn't have much of a choice except for trying to have Jared help me press Minnesota for the trade. Your brother and Bennett did most of the convincing on my behalf."

If it weren't for the newly appointed captain of the Wolverines, Bennett Wilson, I'm not sure Minnesota would've been convinced to finalize the trade. Bennett and I grew up together and played on many of the same teams from Squirts through high school. He's one of the top defensemen in the league, having been drafted and signed right out of high school.

Kenna sighs. "I refuse to let you give up your dreams for us, Griff. Colorado has been your dream team your entire life. I can't ask you to give that up for us—for her, I mean."

"I guess I haven't made myself clear yet, Kenna. My new dream team is you, Cadence, and I. And our mascot, Ranger. That's the only team I truly need, Sunshine. The hockey team I play for doesn't matter. My dream career is to play in the NHL, which I still get to do with the Wolverines. My heart is rooted in Minnesota with my girls."

She releases a breath, almost as if she's been holding it. There's a dreamy look in her eyes as she says, "Say it again."

"Say what?"

"Your girls," she says bashfully, trying to hide in my chest.

I chuckle at her shyness. "My girls," I rasp as I tip her chin up and bring her in for a slow kiss.

The moment is broken up when Carse asks, "Awe, aren't they sweet, Cadey Cat? Your mom and dad are finally figuring it out."

"Mama! Dada! Yay!" Cadence claps in excitement from where she sits on Carson's shoulders.

Kenna blushes from being caught, so naturally, I give her ass a light spank when she tries to wiggle from my arms. Her cheeks turn crimson. She pushes my chest away, shaking her head.

"Come here, baby. Let's go get you ready for your big party," Kenna says as she catches Cadence's dismount from Carson's hold.

When they've disappeared up the steps, Carson turns to me. "I'm happy to have you on the team, brother." He smacks my back and brings me in for a quick hug. When he pulls away, he adds, "But if you ever hurt them again, I'll make sure you never play another hockey game again. You won't even be able to play beer league if you fuck it up this time."

Carson's about as harmful as a dragonfly. Their dad, on the other hand, wouldn't hesitate to get away with my murder if I hurt them again.

I nod at Carson. "I will never do anything to intentionally hurt them again. You have my word, Carse."

He shakes my hand, his grip tighter than usual, as if he's trying to sell me on his tough guy act. "One more thing. I know you just figured it out with her, but don't make me wait too long to officially become your brother, yeah?"

The smile that takes over my face actually hurts my cheeks. "Is that you giving me your blessing, Carse?"

He smiles, scrubbing a hand over his scruff. "Yeah, I guess it is. Good luck getting my dad's blessing, though." He cackles.

I'll have to pull Theo and Liz aside later tonight. Probably best to wait until Theo has had a drink or two to soften him up a bit. Because I do plan on making Carson my brother, hopefully soon. If Kenna will have me, that is.

McKenna

We're in the Wolverines press room the day after Cadence's birthday party. The news of Griffin's trade broke yesterday, and things quickly turned to chaos. I'm standing at the back of the room as the media bombards Griff with questions about the trade news.

"Griffin, there are rumors swirling that you weren't even hurt in Colorado, that you decided to take a leave of absence due to a family matter. What do you have to say to those rumors?"

Griff's eyebrows shoot to his forehead in shock. "Well, Russ, I guess I'd show them the surgical scar on my knee."

The reporter continues, "So, are you saying there were no family matters that influenced your trade decision?"

Griff keeps his composure. "Look, you and I both know a guy on his rookie contract, no matter how good he is, doesn't get a seat at the table in these kinds of decisions. I am incredibly thankful to the Summits organization for giving me my start in the NHL. My coaches and teammates were incredible, as was the entire management staff. But I'm also honored and looking forward to playing for my hometown team. My focus right now is rehabbing my knee and getting back up to full speed for the start of next season."

Not willing to let it end there, the reporter presses, "What do you want to say to those who are worried that your focus has shifted since you found out you had a daughter in Minnesota?"

The room erupts in gasps and shouted questions aimed at Griff.

He lifts his arms at the podium to quiet the room.

"I keep my loved ones close to my chest. We'd like to provide as much privacy for our daughter as we can. That being said, my girlfriend is a badass on the volleyball court and has managed to not only raise our daughter but also maintain the highest grade point average on her team, as well as win a National Championship this year. So, to those who doubt my drive and focus, I'd say that I have the best example of how to raise our daughter, and succeed, sleeping beside me every night. If anything, I'll just try to absorb her tenacity through osmosis." He winks and walks away from the podium as if he didn't just metaphorically drop the mic with that closing statement.

My heart rate quickens, the sounds of the reporters fading to background noise as my brain repeats what he just said.

My girlfriend.

Did he just stake his claim by telling the entire world that we're together? Why does that make my chest tighten with longing and comfort instead of maddening frustration?

I mean, we are together. We're in a relationship. So technically, I *am* his girlfriend. But we've avoided making things public knowledge to avoid unnecessary media attention. Cadence's privacy has always been my number one concern.

There's also the fact that I haven't confessed the depth of my feelings to him yet. It's not that I don't think he reciprocates them. It's just that saying them out loud makes things so much more real. And I guess up until yesterday, that scared me because I wasn't sure what our future would look like. I was riddled with questions. Would we be able to make long-distance work this time? Should I try to transfer to a college in Colorado? Would he be able to re-sign with the Summits? Or would we be moving again once his rookie contract was up?

I walk over to where Griff is speaking to the team's head of PR.

"Can I borrow him for a minute?"

I don't wait for a response as I drag Griffin into a random office down the hall and shut the door behind me before turning on him. I walk toward him and push him back against the wall, resting my hands on his chest. His head is hung, like he's preparing for the lecture I'm about to unleash on him.

"I'm so sorry, Kenna. I didn't know they were going to ask about Cadence. Please don't be upset with me."

"This needs to stop. You keep making sacrifices on our behalf. It's like you're trying to make up for lost time. But you don't need to do that, Griff. Cadence loves and adores you. We both adore you. We both love you, too."

He quickly lifts his head, his deep brown eyes searching mine. Pleading for truth in what I just said.

315

"I love you, Griff. I never stopped loving you. And I never will. I've loved you through scraped knees, endless summers, through fireworks and loss, through distance and time apart, and I'll love you through the end of time."

He cuts me off from continuing with a blistering kiss. When he finally pulls his lips from mine, I'm trembling with need for the man that I've loved and adored for almost a decade.

Griff cups my face in his hands, holding me like I'm made of porcelain—right now, I feel as if I am.

"McKenna Marie, I haven't stopped loving you for a single moment since I so stupidly pushed you away. Hearing you say you love me, and our beautiful daughter loves me, heals me in ways nothing else ever could. Before you came back into my life with Cadence, I was going through the motions, unfeeling and completely void. But the moment you allowed me to be part of your lives, you shined your light onto my darkness and our world turned incandescent. I love you and Ray more than anything, Sunshine."

His words are like a balm to my aching heart. It's no longer broken because it was fixed almost two years ago when I first saw my baby girl open her eyes—her daddy's eyes.

But his words soothe my heart, making it feel whole again.

What we had, what we *were*—it was pure, untainted. It was smooth, not rough around the edges, riddled with heartache and loss. Our love can never go back to what it was. But this version of us—the one that's messy, polluted with heartbreak and hurt, is also filled with so much unwavering love, devotion, and dedication to make this work. What it was before was beautiful; it's the start of our story, a piece of us, but it's just that—the start. What it is now is more than I could've ever imagined for myself—it's raw, it's real, but it's not perfect because we had to work on ourselves apart in order for us to be stronger together.

33

McKenna

April

I 'm branching out of my typical athleisure style. I've got on my favorite pair of mom jeans; they've got a relaxed leg but are form-fitting across my waist and hips, making my ass look amazing, and I've got on a white bodysuit that tucks into my jeans. Dainty gold jewelry dangles from my ears and neck, and on my right pointer finger is the turquoise ring that Griff gave me.

Griffin said he was taking me, Cadence, and Ranger for a surprise mini staycation and to pack a bag for the weekend. In typical Griff fashion, he wouldn't give me any details beyond the fact that I wouldn't need to pack much for Cades since we would have a lot of things for her where we're going.

I have my guess as to where we're going, and I'm pretty sure I guessed right as we continue heading north toward my family's cabin.

Turning down the volume of Paramore's "Still Into You," I look over at Griff and take him in. He is so effortlessly sexy in his Raybans, with his hand gripping the steering wheel. He's got on his heathered gray Patagonia zip-up and dark-fitted jeans that cling to his athletic thighs, highlighting the perfect bulge that I can't wait to get my hands on later. And of course, he tops the look off with a black backward hat with the Wolverines logo and the number ninety-one on it.

Is he trying to make me jump him right this second?

"Like what you see, Sunshine?"

I continue to gaze longingly at him, not even trying to hide my desire. "How could I not? You're like my own personal brand of temptation."

He bites down on his bottom lip, releasing it only to clench his clean-shaven jaw. "McKenna," he warns, damn near growling my name. My stomach flutters, and I feel heat pooling between my legs.

Griff catches me squirming in my seat from the corner of his eye and adjusts himself in his seat.

"That's right, Sunshine. Get nice and worked up for me. I have plans for you once our Little Ray goes to bed. Hopefully, you weren't planning to get any sleep tonight."

Oh, fuck. It's only half past ten. If he plans to edge me all day, I might literally pass out when I finally come later.

Griffin

Cadence is still napping, so Kenna and I are sitting on the back porch next to the fire I lit. We're snuggled up on the daybed that overlooks the lake, where the sun is beginning to lower in the sky.

I've never felt so at peace as I do at this very moment.

"We're back at the water, Sunshine. Just like you made me promise you we always would. I haven't missed a year—but I regret not having been back together in the past two years. I want that to change, I want us to come together every year for the rest of our lives. Move in with me for real, Kenna. Please?"

Kenna's breath hitches, and I can't get a good read at the look on her face. Instead of her being able to answer me, though, the monitor alerts us that Cadence has woken up from her nap.

"I've got her," I say and head down the hall to get my Little Ray. Hopefully, I can soak up some of her radiance to help settle my nerves. I'm going to need it.

After dinner, I buckle my girls into my Jeep and start our fifteen-minute trek north to the destination of my surprise.

When we pull up to West Pier Beach, Kenna asks, "Isn't it a bit dark and cold for a beach outing, Hotshot?"

"We're not here for the beach, Sunshine. Come on, I'll show you what I've got up my sleeve," I request as I open the back, grab out the two blankets I packed, and hide the other items in my pocket.

Thankfully, it's an unseasonably warm night for late April in Minnesota, so Kenna and I are fine in our long sleeves. But that doesn't stop me from bundling Cadence in her fleece winter bodysuit, hat, mittens, and boots to prevent her from getting cold.

Once we've bundled her up, I carry her in one arm and hold Kenna's hand with the other as we walk toward the beach.

People are starting to crowd the beach for the festival, so I steer us toward the large booth with tables of paper lanterns for people to purchase.

"We'll take one, please," I tell the attendant before handing her my cash. "Thank you."

I turn to find Kenna's puzzled expression staring back at me.

"What is this?" she questions.

"It's a lantern lighting festival. I thought we could light one in honor of Katie," I explain as I take a marker from my pocket. "Do you want to write something on the lantern before we light it?"

"I'd love to. Griff, this is amazing." She starts scribbling something on the lantern, but I don't see what it is because Cadence distracts me with her excitement.

We move down the beach a little ways away from the booth to try to give us more space. Some people have already started lighting their lanterns, and the night sky begins to glow shades of orange and amber.

"How do we do this?"

I take a lighter from my pocket and hand it to Kenna. "If you grab one side, I'll grab the other while you light the candle." She lights it, and once she does, the message she inscribed on the side becomes illuminated. Kenna wrote a part of the chorus from Taylor Swift's "Bigger Than The Whole Sky," followed by *Rest easy, sweet Katie Cat.*

Tears fill my eyes as I lift my arm and release the lantern as it floats into the sky.

"She was a Swiftie through and through—I thought she would appreciate it," Kenna says sheepishly.

"She would, Sunshine. I'm sure of it."

I put my arm around Kenna's shoulders and pull her in, snuggling Cadence against my chest on the other side.

"Look up there, Cadeygirl. Aren't the lanterns so pretty?"

Cadence grabs my cheeks and points up at the sky ablaze with lanterns. "So pwetty, Dada!"

She's getting wiggly in my arms. "Dada, down," Cadence says, so I stand her up on the stiff sand below our feet. We're far enough from the water that I feel comfortable letting her down.

I turn to Kenna and place my arms around her waist.

"What do you think, Sunshine?"

"I think this is the most amazing sight I've ever seen, Griff. Thank you for taking us. Seeing the sky lit up like this is magical. I love that we got to do this for Katie."

I place my hands under her jaw and bring her in for a chaste kiss. When I pull back, Kenna places her hands on top of mine and says, "Yes."

"Yes?" I question.

"Yes, we'll move in with you, Griff. Full time."

"Are you for real right now, McKenna?"

"I'm for real, and just in case you thought you were dreaming, I'll gladly pinch you," she chuckles and lightly pinches my hand.

I scoop Cadence up in my arms and bring Kenna in for another kiss, this time dragging it out and crossing into semi-inappropriate territory with our daughter in my arms. I pull back and rest my forehead against Kenna's.

"Forever?" I ask.

"And it still won't be long enough, G," she replies before grabbing Cadence from my arms.

This moment just feels too perfect to pass up the opportunity.

Taking her left hand in mine, I rub small circles over her ring finger. "Kenna, you are my Sunshine on my darkest days, lighting the path back to you, to our family. With you as my teammate, I know we can get through anything. I want to know all your truths as we grow older together. Forever and always."

Dropping down to one knee, I open the black velvet box I pulled from my pocket and hold it up to her.

"McKenna Marie, will you make me the luckiest man in this lifetime and marry me?"

I'm not expecting it as she lets go of my hand to drop down to her knees, with Cadence still in her arms, and wraps her free arm around me.

She nods her head into my neck, and relief spreads through me.

"Is that a yes, Sunshine?"

Still nodding her head, she pulls back, her aqua eyes staring into mine. "Yes, Griffin. A thousand times, yes!"

Not able to contain my happiness, I pull her in for a deep kiss, quickly getting caught up in the passion of this moment.

She breaks the kiss and rests her forehead against mine.

"Is this real life?" she asks.

"As real as it gets, my love." I take the ring out of the box and slide it onto her finger.

Kenna gasps as she takes in the ornate ring I had custom-made for her. The center is a two-carat oval diamond that is surrounded by a halo of sunburst diamonds, making it look like a sun. Fuck, she looks so good finally wearing my ring on her left hand. She looks like *mine*.

Kenna nuzzles Cadence against her cheek, unshed tears still glistening in her eyes. My entire world begins and ends with the two of them.

Our love can never go back to what it was—we've grown, changed, hardened, and re-formed into who we both are now. Our love has evolved through our heartache and loss. Now that we've found our way back to each other, I never want to go back to what it was—I love what it is now so much more. I know I'll love Kenna for the rest of my life. But I'm certain I won't love her the way I love her today, tomorrow, or years from now. I'll love her more and more with each breath I take for the rest of my life.

THE END

Epilogue

MCKENNA - JUNE

It's the twenty-first of June, and today is the day my childhood crush becomes my husband.

We decided on a short engagement and a small ceremony at my parent's cabin on Lake Mille Lacs. Only family and a few of each of our close teammates and friends were invited.

I know today is bittersweet for Griffin and me. We both mourn not having Katie and Catherine here today, but I can feel their presence, and I know Griff will, too, if he doesn't already.

I've just stepped into the dressing room of our suite with my mom to put my dress on.

"Here you go, honey," Mom says as she takes the dress off the hanger.

Untying my robe, I try to be as modest as I can by quickly stepping into my dress. But there's not really a way around my mom getting an eye full of my bare chest and the scraps of lace I have on for later tonight.

Once I've stepped into the dress, I slide my arms through the delicate straps of the dress, and my mom zips me in before working on the buttons with a crochet hook.

The white trumpet wedding dress has a square neckline in the front with a plunging back enclosed by buttons that run along the curve of my ass. I know Griffin will appreciate the way the dress clings to and highlights his favorite feature of mine. The dress is made of crepe fabric, making it timeless and chic.

After the buttons are hooked, my mom helps put my cathedral-length veil encrusted with tiny pearls into my hair. I decided to keep my hair pinned half up, curled into loose waves down my back.

My makeup is natural, yet I feel more glamorous than I ever have.

I spin around and face my mom, taking her hands in mine.

"Oh, hun, you look so beautiful. I can't believe this day has already come. I just wish Catherine were here to see her dream come true. She always said you and Griffin would end up together, and here we are!" my mom says as she brings me in for a hug.

"She's with us today, I can feel it. She and Katie are both here." Taking a few steadying breaths, I pull back and swipe my tear ducts before any can fall.

"You're right, they are," my mom says, bringing a small jewelry box from the pocket of her dress. "These were Catherine's. Jack asked me this morning if I would give these to you."

Inside the box is a pair of pearl drop earrings that match my veil perfectly. Tears flood my vision again, and the ache in my heart that comes with missing Katie pangs. These would have been hers to wear on her wedding day. I gasp. "They're stunning."

"Oh, I'm so sorry. I was also supposed to give you this." My mom hands me an envelope addressed: To my son's bride on the day of your wedding.

"What is this?" I question.

"I'm not sure. Jack gave it to me when he handed me the jewelry box."

Turning the envelope over, I open it assuming it is from Jack. My breath hitches as I realize I was wrong. The letter is written in Catherine's delicate handwriting.

To my dearest daughter-in-law on your wedding day,

I feel as if I know who you are as I'm writing this, or at least I hope I do.

Even though he's still young, I know my son will choose a wonderful woman to be by his side one day.

How lucky are you to have found the one in my sweetest boy? And how lucky is he to have found a forever teammate in you?

I know as I write this that I will not be there with you on this special day, but you best believe I will be there in spirit, watching over the two of you.

I am at peace knowing my son has found his future in you.

Here are my hopes for the two of you: I hope you dance in the kitchen every chance you get—from a young age, my boy has always loved to cook. I hope you can cheer each other on from near and far, no matter where life takes you. I hope you give my dearest husband, Jack, as many grandkids as possible—I know he will spoil them rotten, but he does it out of pure love. I hope you are able to grow old together—and learn to fall in love again over and over at each new stage of life. There will be hard times, heartbreak, and devastation, but you're stronger together. I hope you're tender with my son's loving heart, and I hope he is unwavering in his devotion to you. But most of all, I hope you can find peace in each other's arms like I have with Jack.

I may not know you, but I love you for loving my son. Today you will be surrounded by love, including mine. Happy wedding day, my sweet daughter-in-law.

Love always,

Catherine

My mother stands beside me, tears streaming down her cheeks, matching my own.

"Knock knock," the photographer says as she peeks inside the door. "Are you ready for the first look?"

Nodding my head, I say, "I think we need to touch up our makeup quick, but then we will be."

I bring my mom in for another embrace—I hold on to her longer than usual, needing her warmth to help me through this moment.

After touching up my makeup, I grab my bouquet and follow the photographer outside to the gardens where we've planned to do the first look.

He's standing there in his black tux with his back to me, holding Cadence in his arms, and I can't help but smile. Walking up to them, I tap him on the shoulder. Carson turns around and matches my smile as tears fill his eyes.

"Holy shit, Mack. Griff is going to die on the spot when he sees you walking down the aisle. And Dad is going to weep like a baby. Look at your mama, Cadey Cat!"

"Mama so pwetty!" Cadence exclaims.

"Thank you, baby! Look at you—you're so beautiful, baby girl!" I tell her as I take in her blonde hair pulled back with a pearl headband and the crepe dress embellished with pearls to match my own.

We pose for a few portraits together before Carson tells me it's time to meet my dad and walk down the aisle. I follow the two of them inside to where my dad is waiting for me.

Tears fill his eyes when he sees me. I loop my arm though my dad's and give it a gentle squeeze. He brings his other hand up to clasp mine. "I can't believe my little princess is getting married."

"I love you so much, Dad."

"I love you too, Princess. It's not too late if you've changed your mind, I'll grab the car and we're out of here," he teases; or at least I think he's teasing.

"Dad, you know I love Griff with all my heart. I'd never dream of running from him."

"And he better never dream of running from you again. I just about made him do a blood oath that he would never hurt you again before I gave him my blessing."

"Dad!"

"What? You're my only daughter, and Cadence is my only grand-child. I will protect the two of you for the rest of my life. Just because Griffin is vowing to protect you now too, doesn't change the fact that you were my little girl first."

"I'll always have loved you first. Now let's not make my groom wait any longer. I could hardly sleep last night in anticipation for today. Just don't let me fall, Dad."

"I wouldn't dream of it," he says as he takes a shuddering breath. We walk hand in hand out the glass sliding doors of the walkout basement that leads to the backyard.

An acoustic cover of "Can't Help Falling in Love" plays as we walk to the end of the aisle.

The moment my eyes meet Griffin's, an audible gasp leaves his lips before his face crumbles into a beautiful quivering mess.

"So when's the wedding?" Katie asks me.

"You're hopeless," I tease.

"Wrong. I'm actually full of hope. That's how I just know this is going to end up just like I've always envisioned. Kenna, in a beautiful white dress, walking down the aisle to my amazing big brother, who will be bawling like a damn baby."

Katie shakes her head and holds her hands up in surrender. "Alright, alright. I'll lay off for now. But promise me one thing." She looks over at me expectantly.

"That depends," I reply.

"Promise me I'll have the best seat in the place. I don't want to miss a single tear or snot bubble on Griff's face."

Griffin looks so devastatingly handsome in his black tux and crisp white dress shirt. His hair is cut shorter on the sides, and his face is clean-shaven. He's standing beside Carson, who's holding Cadence.

Once we've reached the end of the aisle, Griff still hasn't composed himself and I've got matching tears streaming down my cheeks.

"You're stunning, Sunshine. Can I kiss you yet?" he asks through hiccupping breaths.

Bennett, who's officiating our wedding, cuts in, "No, you cannot. I haven't told you to kiss the bride yet. That's at the end, remember?"

"It's our wedding, we can do whatever we want, right my love?" Griff asks as he holds his hand out to me.

I turn and give my dad the biggest squeeze and he kisses my forehead before shaking Griff's hand and bringing him in for an embrace.

Before I turn to face Griff, I place my bouquet on the chair sitting beside me with Katie's picture on it. I promised her she would have the best seat in the house, and I reserved my maid-of-honor spot for her.

I face my groom and want to pinch myself to be sure this is real. I'm holding hands at the end of an aisle with Griffin Turner, about to exchange vows to spend the rest of our lives together.

Bennett begins the ceremony, and before I know it, it's my turn to exchange our vows. I look into Griffin's eyes, which look more caramel than chocolate-brown in the summer sun.

"Griff, you told me once that you wanted all my truths." I pause to take a deep breath.

He nods in response, giving my left hand a squeeze of encouragement.

"Here are the truths I know in my heart today. I don't love you the same as I did when I told you my first, second, or third truths. And I won't love you the same way I do today as I will when I tell you my last. I will never get over your devastating dimples. I will never get over seeing you with our daughter."

"And our future babies," he interrupts. Causing laughter to ring out amongst the guests.

"I want to continue to be each other's biggest cheerleaders in every aspect of our lives. I have chosen the best lifelong teammate in you. There will be times when I'm sure you'll push my buttons, and I won't be able to put up with your antics. There will be hard times, but I know we can get through them together. We've weathered the hardest storms apart, but we've learned we're stronger together. I love you endlessly, Griffin Owen Turner. Forever is just the start, baby."

Griff's megawatt smile is electric when he hears the term of endearment again. Unable to help himself, he leans in for a kiss before Bennett gives him a stern look.

He straightens up and begins his vows. "McKenna Marie almost-Turner." I shake my head and chuckle at him. "To some, it may seem like we've jumped the gun—skipped a few important steps to get here today—but to those, I would say they don't know a thing about us. Elvis may have been on to something, because I couldn't help falling in love with you. I don't think I could've resisted even if I wanted to. From the first time I chased after you when we were only kids, to watching you walk down the aisle today, it's always been you, Sunshine. You're woven into my soul—my innermost being. Without you, I was a shell of a man. With you and Cadence, I am home. Each day is brighter. Each breath is easier to breathe. Each night with you in my arms is the best night's sleep. I love you today, I'll love you tomorrow, and I'll love you always."

Tears fill my eyes. I know today is just the start of our next chapter, and I can't wait to see what this life has in store for the three of us.

Extended Epilogue

GRIFFIN - FIVE YEARS LATER

I t feels like only a few days ago Kenna was waking me up, bouncing on our bed, cheering excitedly that the pregnancy test she took was finally positive.

We'd been trying for baby number two for about ten months prior to getting pregnant. Our struggle this time around was somewhat shocking, considering how Cadence was conceived. But after running tests, our doctor told us it was likely due to Kenna's endometriosis causing irregular cycles. We were a month away from our first attempt at IUI when Kenna took the positive test.

We're just walking into our twenty-week ultrasound. Kenna and I get to see our baby today, and there's not a chance in hell we're not finding out the gender.

I've never been so happy as I have been in the past five months. My caretaker gene has been fully activated, and I'm loving every second of it. Well, aside from watching Kenna get sick repeatedly every day. I guess I didn't realize before this pregnancy that morning sickness didn't happen strictly in the morning.

And then there's the horrible cravings. I'm talking horrendous. Carson tried to warn me when we told him we were pregnant, but I didn't think it'd be this bad.

"Have fun, G. Just wait until she asks you to make her over-easy eggs with pickle slices and hot sauce in the middle of the night," Carson says.

I scrunch my face in horror.

"Yeah." He scoffs. "It's even more disgusting than it sounds." He visibly shakes, and I don't blame him.

"My sweet Cadeygirl was subjected to that horrible food in the womb?" I ask incredulously.

"That might not even have been the worst of it. Honestly, a hangry and hormonal Mack is not one to be messed with."

Carson wasn't wrong—that wasn't the worst of it. The other day, Kenna was dead set on eating a tuna and peanut butter sandwich. I tried to stop the madness, but there was no reasoning with her.

A few minutes after Kenna has checked in, her name is called and we're escorted to an exam room with an ultrasound machine and TV on the wall.

After Cadence's complicated pregnancy and birth, Kenna wanted to stay with Dr. Bahati since she knew her background.

Dr. Bahati knocks before opening the door and asking, "How are we doing today, Mom and Dad?"

"We're doing good; excited to see our little one," Kenna replies.

"If you don't have any questions for me, let's get to it."

I do have questions. A lot of them, like usual, but I'll keep them to myself until after the ultrasound is done.

Kenna lifts her shirt and the doctor squeezes some gel onto her abdomen before the TV screen displays our baby's profile.

"Before we take a look at baby, I'm going to get a measurement of your cervix considering your history."

That raises my hackles. I've been on edge worrying about Kenna and preemptively trying to put her on bed rest. She wasn't having it, though she did agree to lighten her activity.

"McKenna, your cervix is looking great. As we've discussed, just because you've had a shortened cervix in the past, doesn't mean you'll have it each pregnancy."

I give Kenna a reassuring squeeze with my hand and place a chaste kiss on her forehead.

Tears of relief fill Kenna's eyes and mine as we stare at the screen. Before us, our baby is growing, kicking, and thriving.

"Did you want to find out the gender today?"

"Yes," I say just as Kenna answers, "No."

Kenna rolls her eyes at me. "Fine. Yes, we would like to find out if we're able to."

I bring my fist to my mouth, trying to muffle my chuckle. It doesn't work because Kenna lightly pinches my hand she's holding.

"Alright, let's see if baby wants to cooperate with us today," the doctor says, and she moves the transducer across Kenna's small bump.

It doesn't take the doc to tell me what is clear as day on the screen. We are Turners, after all.

We're having a boy. A son.

"Congratulations, you're having a boy," Dr. Bahati confirms. "I'm going to finish taking some measurements, and then I'll get pictures printed."

"Come here, Sunshine." I bend down and kiss her softly while our tears mend together on our cheeks.

When I pull away, I brush my thumb across her cheeks to wipe her tears. "A boy, can you believe it?"

Shaking her head, Kenna says, "I have no idea how to be a boy mom. What if I'm terrible at it?"

"McKenna, you are the best mom ever to Cadence. There hasn't been a single thing you haven't succeeded at in the past seven years of motherhood. You've managed to get your teaching degree while raising our daughter and playing D1 volleyball. Oh, and need I remind you that you're a badass gold medal Olympian? Our son is going to be the luckiest boy in the world to have you as his mama. Now quit thinking nonsensical thoughts, and let's look at how big our Rook is."

"Rook?" she questions.

"Yeah, he's the newest rookie on our little team."

Tears spill down Kenna's cheeks again. I quickly wipe them away and bring her in for another kiss, wishing I could deepen it.

She's never looked more irresistible than she does growing my baby. That's another thing I was pleasantly surprised to learn about pregnancy. Once the first-trimester exhaustion subsided and her morning sickness waned, McKenna became *very* horny. Like, jump me in the middle of the airport parking lot to have sex in the back of her car, horny.

I'm loving every minute of it. Not just the horniness, because, yeah, I'm a guy. But all of the little moments I missed the first time around. I love that I'm the one to rub her back, get her water, and hold her hair when she's sick. That I was the first person she ran to when the test was positive. That I've been here for each doctor's appointment—hearing the heartbeat, seeing the baby today—all of it. That I get to see her belly grow with our child. That I get to witness Cadence snuggle up to Kenna's stomach and tell stories to her little brother. That I get to give her foot rubs before bed each night. Hell, I even like it when she gets feisty with me—she's so sexy when she's mad.

"I'm the luckiest man in the world to live this little life of ours, Sunshine. I can't wait to add our son to our wild bunch. I can already tell he will be such a good big brother someday to his four little siblings."

My Sunshine's head snaps toward me. "Griffin. Owen. We've discussed this. We will be capping it at three. I've only just made it halfway through this pregnancy. Are you crazy?"

"About you? Always." I kiss her again before whispering in her ear, "It's all those damn mafia romances you've been reading lately. My breeding kink has been activated, and there's no stopping me."

She shakes her head and even in the darkened room, I can see the blush in her cheeks as I pull away. I can't wait to see where life takes us. I know for certain as long as McKenna is by my side, we're in for the adventure of a lifetime.

Acknowledgements

So many people have helped shape me into the writer I am today. First and foremost—I'd like to thank my dear readers. As a debut author, you're taking a risk in reading my book baby. I appreciate your support more than I could ever express.

Thank you to my supportive family—without whom, I would never have had the courage to put this book out there. To my husband, my high school sweetheart, thank you for loving me each day and being better than any fictional book boyfriend I could ever create. Your unyielding support means the world to me. Thank you for growing old with me as we continue to grow, learn, and evolve in our love. Also, it's not fair how you continue to get better-looking with age!

To our three children. You have changed me in inexplicable ways, all for the better. I will never be able to express how much and how fiercely I love the three of you. I hope this dream of mine coming true shows you that you can do anything you set your minds to!

To my fur baby: a childhood and family dog plays one of the biggest roles in a young person's life. Thank you for being the OG Goodest Boy!

To my mother, who has been an avid reader my entire life, thank you for filling our sunroom with shelves of books, for trips to the library, for reading to me and my children, and for being a constant in my life. I would quite literally not be here without you, but I would not be

335

the woman, mother, wife, sister, friend, or author I am without your guidance. I hope you can soon bring your dream of publication to fruition.

To my dad, who has been my biggest cheerleader, the best coach, and the world's best girl dad: the love I have for you is endless. You're the best father a girl could ask for and the best papa to my kids. I am who I am because you laid the groundwork, led by example, and gave me the courage and guidance to reach for the stars.

To my two beautiful, strong, and smart older sisters: you're both my idols. I've looked up to you my entire life, and how lucky am I to call you both my best friends? You both are my day ones—whether you liked it or not—and you'll be my chosen people for as long as I live.

To my aunt and godmother, who has always been a second mom to me: I love you with all my heart and would not be the same without you. Thank you for your guidance, unwavering support, and love throughout my life.

To my best childhood friends: a girl can't go through life without her best friends by her side. Though time and distance have separated us at times, my love for you has never waned.

I have to thank my amazing in-laws. One of the biggest bonuses to marrying my husband was gaining the large, loud, and loving family I married into. I know I am so lucky to declare my love and gratitude for them! An extra special shoutout to my mother-in-law and sister-in-law for being two women I look up to, love, and cherish immensely.

I would not be here today without the education and love of reading I developed at an early age, to my favorite childhood teachers who helped me along the way: Mrs. Lubow, Mrs. Greer, Mrs. Karno, and Deena, and my English and Creative Writing professors at university.

I would like to give the biggest thanks to my alpha reader Suz and my incredible editor Caitlin. Without your pep talks, support, and guidance, I would have stopped midway! Thank you for helping me navigate through the confusing and intimidating debut indie author process.

To my book designer, Madison Lee: wow, your creativity amazes me! You were such a joy to work with and your enthusiasm for this project had me so much more excited. I cannot wait to work on the rest of the covers in this series together!

To my betas: I couldn't have shaped this book into what it was without your input and feedback. A special thanks to Brittany, Sarah, and Jenah for agreeing to beta read in addition to my beta team.

To my newfound bookish besties—your support and friendship means the world to me. I especially want to thank Sam, Brittany, and Sariah.

Hannah—you're a newfound friend and were a beta, but you deserve your own acknowledgement all on your own! You helped me so much with the ARC team process. And your spreadsheet skills are unmatched!

I would also like to thank the indie authors who helped answer countless questions. Samantha, Ashley, T. Leigh, Ginsa, Ruth, Paisley and Giuliana—you're all amazingly talented writers!

Lastly, I'd also like to thank Lauren McBride for sharing her journey to falling in love with reading again—it caused me to pick up a book again after taking too long away from my fictitious escapes.

About The Author

Grayce Rian is a contemporary romance author living in Wisconsin. Her debut novel, *What It Was*, is the first standalone novel in the Off Ice series.

Grayce's stories perfectly combine spice, angst, and sweetness to make readers swoon. When she's not writing about your new, favorite book boyfriend, you can find her with her high school sweetheart, chauffeuring their three kids to every activity imaginable, or with her nose buried in a book.

Grayce fell in love with reading and writing at a young age and pursued the creative outlet as a minor in college. She contributes a lot of her creativity and passion for reading to her mother, and Grayce now shares the same love for fictional escapes with her children.

Printed by Amazon Italia Logistica S.r.l.
Torrazza Piemonte (TO), Italy

59939288R00199